HOT BLOOD XI

Fatal Attractions

HOT BLOOD XI

Fatal Attractions

EDITED BY JEFF GELB AND MICHAEL GARRETT

KENSINGTON BOOKS
http://www.kensingtonbooks.com

KENSINGTON BOOKS are published by

Kensington Publishing Corp.
850 Third Avenue
New York, NY 10022

Dedicated to super fan, super writer, and super friend
Rex Miller, who was the first superstar to agree
to write an original story for Hot Blood.

Acknowledgments

Joshua Bilmes, agent supreme!

Del and Sue at Dark Delicacies—when's the signing party?

John Scognamiglio at Kensington Publishing—
thanks for your belief!

Contents

Introduction

Nothing beats the excitement of a developing new relationship. Testing the boundaries, checking out what each other has to offer, exploring new realms of companionship—there can be thrills galore! Can anything possibly be better?

Hot Blood itself has entered a new relationship with Kensington Publishing, and with this new union comes an opportunity to create the best of the *Hot Blood* concept yet. The marriage of *Hot Blood* and Kensington is off to a spicy start, and this initial volume of *Hot Blood* under the Kensington label is one hot honeymoon to be remembered!

For those of you who are new to *Hot Blood*, it's the original anthology series that weds horror and eroticism for a heart-stopping orgasm of consummate terror! Here you'll find stories of supernatural seductions, in which creatures unimagined—and unimaginably terrifying—commingle with humans for eternal nights of bliss . . . and blasphemy! And here too are stories set in our all-too-real world, where a one-night stand can end up spawning life-threatening consequences. Where today's fantasies become tomorrow's nightmares. Where the ultimate act of intimacy becomes the supreme act of betrayal—or worse.

We're dedicated to making each successive volume of *Hot Blood* the best it can be and would like to know what *you* think. Drop us a line from the e-mail link at www.writing2sell.com/ hotblood.htm. Tell us which stories you've liked best and *least*. Is there an important area of sexuality we've not yet covered? Or is there perhaps a type of story we've overdone? We'd love to hear from you!

For now, however, these pages are hot, and getting *hotter!* Take something off and join us!

Jeff Gelb and Michael Garrett

Manhandled

by P.D. Cacek

He had the most beautiful hands she had ever seen—smooth and soft, and without any of the defects she'd come to associate with men . . . with the violence men could do to themselves and others. She'd seen men like that, men in bars or on the bus—their hands, rough and raw, clutching drinks or newspapers. The ragged white scars that crisscrossed knuckles mashed to pulp, evidence of battles won over women or touch football. Skin weathered to the texture of goat hide, hard and rough and permanently tanned. A *man's* hand, they'd laugh when they caught her staring. And then try to touch her.

Abby pushed the memory away—far, far away where it couldn't do any harm—and took his hand. His wonderful, perfect hand. No scars, no marks, not even a paper cut. No shadow of dirt beneath the trimmed and polished nails. No calluses marring the silken palms. He was a careful man, fastidious . . . no, that was too fussy a word and he would have laughed if she'd told him that. He was just—a good man who cared about himself as he would care about her.

She knew that simply by holding his hand.

It was a man's hands, and not his eyes or mind or whatever

physical attributes genetics had given him, that revealed his soul. Abby had learned that lesson the hard way.

Hands never changed . . . especially the hands of a good man. And he was a good man.

Abby squeezed his hand softly, to let him know she understood. And kept holding his hand even though a small shudder lifted the hair along her arm. His hand was so cool, so perfect. God, she never wanted to feel the touch of a man's hand against her body more than at that moment.

She needed to feel him, his hand on her flesh . . . those long, tapered fingers, the color of unblemished white marble, gliding over her skin like butterfly wings. So soft, they'd be so soft she'd barely feel them. A touch here, across her breasts to harden the nipples. A brush of fingertips there, lingering over the flat, barren plain of her belly. A caress, the stroke of palm on thigh. Legs spreading, hips tilting upward. Fingers parting the folds of her vulva. Slipping inside. Deeper. Deeper.

"Like this," she whispered and her breath barely disturbed the flames of the candles she'd lit for him. "I want you to do it like this."

Lifting his hand to her face, she gently curled all but his index finger back against his palm. She pressed her own index finger against it, smoothing out the gentle arch. *Here's the church, here's the steeple . . . open the door and see all the people.* It was a game she'd played when she was little . . . just a game, her hand against some boy's, fingers laced—making a church, making a steeple. Her father's finger had been hard, the angles stiff along the arthritic joints when he'd shake it at her. *You're a bad girl, Abby. A stupid, silly, bad little girl who's going to get into a lot of trouble if you aren't careful.*

But she hadn't gotten into trouble. Never, not once. Because she'd been very, very careful.

"Like this," Abby repeated and slowly ran her tongue down his finger—from knuckle to tip—wetting it all over before sucking it into her mouth. She could taste a hint of almond and rose hand cream, the faintest suggestion of disinfectant on the clean skin, but not enough to make her gag. She pulled him deeper inside her mouth, showing him by example what she wanted that finger to do.

When his fingertip brushed against her uvula she groaned deep in her throat.

"Did you say something, Abby?"

Abby stood up quickly, drying his finger off across the front of her smock before letting go of his hand. The dark blue material absorbed the moisture quickly, not leaving a trace for anyone to see as she turned.

Mr. Nessleman was standing in front of the double doors at the opposite end of the room, hands folded in front of him. He had ugly hands. Red and rough as a plowman's, aged and wrinkled and smudged with liver spots. Gnarled as the roots of a dead tree and just as dry. They were hideous.

Abby would never let those hands touch her, not in a million years, but she smiled at her employer and shrugged.

"I was just talking to myself, Mr. Nesselman," she said. "It's a bad habit, I know."

He nodded understandingly. "Well, that's not as bad as when you start answering yourself, believe me. So, is our Mr. Peck ready?"

Abby turned around as if she wasn't sure and frowned. There was a tiny mark on his right index finger just above the second knuckle . . . a shallow impression left by her crooked incisor. Damn her parents for not making her wear braces.

"Is there something wrong, Abby?" The note of concern in Mr. Nesselman's voice was a perfect counterbalance, she thought, to the soft strains of Vivaldi coming from the room's hidden speakers.

"Lint," she said and refolded his hands—his beautiful hands—left over right to hide the blemish, then brushed the sleeve, making sure there was no more than a half inch of cuff showing. More than that might be a distraction away from his hands and she couldn't let that happen. She squeezed his hand once more, apologizing for her overbite.

"Ah, lint and dust and fluorescent lighting," Mr. Nesselman complained, his hands straightening the knot of his tie when Abby turned around, "the nemeses of our business. But I know I never have to worry about that with you around, Abby. You are a true perfectionist and that is so rare these days."

She blushed more than she'd intended to. "Thank you, Mr. Nesselman."

"No, thank you. Oh! A candle just went out."

Abby was already reaching into the smock's front pocket for the small BIC lighter she always carried—just for these types of emergencies. A thin trail of gray smoke curled up from the third taper in the standing brass candelabra next to a floral display. It took only a second to relight the candle, less time than that for the mingled scent of carnations, chrysanthemums, and roses to overpower the smell of smoke and butane, but if a casual observer had walked in at that moment and seen Mr. Nesselman's near swoon, he might have thought she'd just disarmed a nuclear device.

"Oh, I hate it when things don't go smoothly," the older man said, his ugly, gnarled fingers pressed against his temples. Abby slipped the lighter back into her pocket and polished the edge of Mr. Peck's coffin with her sleeve. "Thank you, Abby, you saved the day. Now, I think we'd better get started before anything else happens. I'll let you know when you can come back and begin cleaning up."

Abby acknowledged the dismissal but didn't move. She could hear the voices in the anteroom beyond the doors—soft voices, muffled by grief. His friends. His family. And they'd see it . . . notice it . . . the horrible mark she'd left on his beautiful hand.

"He—he does look all right, doesn't he?" she asked, suddenly nervous.

Mr. Nesselman's ugly hand waved the question away.

"Abby, stop worrying. You did a wonderful job on Mr. Peck and I'm sure his friends and family will appreciate all your hard work. The putty filled in the bullet hole beautifully. If I didn't know what to look for I'd miss the indentation completely." He clicked his tongue. "Suicide. You'd think a successful lawyer would have had everything to live for."

"Yes, sir."

"All right then. It's time."

Mr. Nesselman turned and squared his bony shoulders before walking to the door and grasping the handles, pausing a minute longer to give Abby time to scurry away—back to her small workroom next to the crematorium.

Here's the church, here's the steeple . . . open the doors and see all the people.

Abby bit her own finger as she ran, hard enough to draw blood . . . but it still didn't make her feel any better.

"But other than that it really was a nice service," Abby said as she poured out the perfectly chilled wine into their glasses. "And I have to agree with Mr. Nesselman . . . I did a wonderful job."

She clinked her glass against his, giggling to try and shake him out of his mood. But it didn't work any better than her impromptu striptease had—he wasn't happy and it was all her fault. Abby leaned back in her chair and crossed one arm over her breasts, suddenly a little shy about being naked in front of him. She took a sip of wine for courage. It helped a little.

"I know, I shouldn't have said anything, but it's just . . . It's just that I wondered why anyone would want to disrupt a memorial service like that. I mean, she was drunk—no, don't you shake your finger at me and say she wasn't. I heard her all the way back in my office. That's the only reason I poked my head in."

She took a longer sip this time.

"I mean, I don't make it a habit of intruding on people's grief. I think saying good-bye is a personal matter and shouldn't be treated like some kind of spectacle. Which is why I'm still a little shocked by your reaction. I mean, it *was* a spectacle and I know I'm not the only one who thought that. The things she said . . . all those awful things."

Abby pouted, hoping it would make her otherwise plain face (she knew she was plain, plain as rain) look cute and innocent, childlike. That ploy always seemed to work in movies, but unfortunately this was real life. His mood never changed and his hand never so much as moved from the stem of his glass.

She drained her glass and set it down on the table. He hadn't touched his wine, not a drop, so she took it from him. His fingers closed then, but he was too late.

Abby finished the wine in one long swallow.

"Of course I know that none of what she said could be true. It couldn't be. Hands that beautiful could never belong to a man who liked to beat up women. Seriously, she had to be crazy. No . . . I mean it. She *had* to be crazy."

Abby started to reach for the wine bottle, then thought better of it and took his hand instead. Their little misunderstanding had gone on long enough.

"A man who beats women would never kill himself," she said softly. "Suicide's the act of a soul in despair, a soul too gentle for the rough world. You must have been in so much pain, but it's all right . . . because now it's time for joy."

She lifted his hand to her lips, cradling it against her palms as she kissed it from the tips of each finger to the severed wrist. It'd been a clean cut with very little fraying around the edge. The poultry shears had been a good investment and did a lot better job than the hacksaw her first lovers had been subjected to. Yes, it was good . . . but there were better things on the market, and the minute she could afford it she was going to have to special-order a pair of surgical-steel medical loppers with twelve-inch blades.

It would make things so much easier.

Abby felt his hand move down her throat to her breast and trembled when his fingers found her nipple and—"Oops!"

He slipped out of her grasp and landed in her lap—palm up, fingers curled slightly . . . his stump snuggled into the nest of her pubic hair.

"Don't be so impatient," she scolded him as she picked him up. Tried to pick him up.

He was slippery from the glycerin she'd soaked him in after they got home, almost too slippery to hold on to, and that was upsetting. Abby had hoped the preservative would work better than the others she'd tried. Formaldehyde and pure grain alcohol gave her a rash. Salt brine could turn the softest skin to leather. Camphor gave her a sinus headache. And she didn't even want to think about her failed experiments with dehydration.

Ugh.

Abby scooped him up in both her hands and ignored the slime trail he left on her thighs. A minor inconvenience, she thought, if the glycerin kept him as supple as her research promised.

If not, it'd be back to the old drawing board . . . and the on-line reference library.

"It's okay," she whispered, "this isn't my first time, so you don't have to be nervous. I should tell you, though, that none of my other affairs lasted very long and I do have to take full responsibility for that."

Abby chuckled at the comment she knew he would have made, if he'd been able to.

"Let's just say I was a little naive when it came to sustaining a relationship. You'll laugh, I know you will . . . but I really did think Tupperware would work. Everyone says it's supposed to lock freshness in, but believe me, it doesn't. That was my first affair and it ended . . . badly."

Abby hugged him because he didn't laugh at her. He understood. He wasn't the man that drunken bitch was shouting about.

"There," she told him as they stood up and walked, hand in hand, to the bedroom, "I told you the woman was crazy. You could never hurt anyone. Okay, that's the last time I'm going to mention her, I promise. And even if what she said was true, I don't care what you did or what you were before . . . because you're *mine* now."

The dozen candles she'd lit earlier that night, while she showered and he soaked in his warm glycerin bath, filled the room with a soft, flickering glow that concealed the shabbiness of the room. She'd wanted to move for years, to upgrade to a better place, a better life . . . but knew she probably never would. The one-bedroom walk-up just held too many memories.

Among other things.

Setting him down on the nearly new satin bedspread, Abby walked over to the floor-to-ceiling storage cabinet and slowly closed the shower curtain that she'd hung in front of it. She could just make out their rough outlines through the opaque plastic—safe and snug inside their sealed jars—but she knew they couldn't see her . . . or him. As disappointing as they'd been as lovers, Abby still cared about them, in her own way, and didn't want them to feel jealous.

At least not until she found the *perfect* lover. Then she'd see about moving . . . and saying good-bye. But until then—the search went on.

Smiling at him as she walked to the CD player on her dresser, Abby pressed the REPEAT ALL option and swayed gently to the first song. It was a beautiful love song, absolutely perfect even though she'd selected the album before going to work that morning. She didn't know what man would be coming home with her that night . . . only that a man would. A man always came home with her from work.

A man with beautiful hands.

"This piece reminds me of you," she said, gliding against the worn carpet on the balls of her feet because she'd read somewhere that men tended to prefer tall women. "Powerful and strong, but with a soft melody beneath. That's you, strong but willing to give a woman everything she needs. I'm right, aren't I? You're just like that. I could tell it from your hands."

He didn't say anything, but turned to face her when she got on the bed . . . ready to show her that she was right.

"Yes," Abby said, lying back on the spread. "Show me."

Closing her eyes, she let the music guide her hand as she guided his and . . .

"Damn!"

Abby opened her eyes and looked at him, plopped into the hollow between her breasts. He'd slipped again and didn't even seem upset by it.

"It's okay," she told him, but still made sure she had a firmer grip, "don't be nervous. Just relax and do what comes naturally. I know you're going to be a great lover. Look how strong your fingers are."

And his fingers were strong, she could feel the taut muscles beneath the skin, but he didn't know how to use them. They dragged across her flesh instead of caressing it and bumped listlessly against her nipples.

Abby sighed and closed her eyes. Maybe he didn't like it when women watched him. Some men were like that.

"All right, I'll keep my eyes closed, but go slower," Abby whispered to him above the music. "That's right, like that. Slow and easy and—ow! No, no, it's okay. One of your nails is just a little ragged. I didn't notice that before, but I'll file it down later.

Oh, yes, that's right. Oh, God, yes . . . yes, right there. Touch me right—shit!"

Abby couldn't keep her promise. She opened her eyes and glared at him through the dancing candle-shadows. He'd curled his middle finger back on itself just as it reached her clitoris, almost as if he was disgusted by the thought of touching her "down there." Although she still didn't believe anything she'd heard the drunken woman say, Abby was beginning to realize that he had a bit of a stubborn streak in him.

And that would never do.

Not if he intended to be her lover.

"One more chance," Abby warned him, "and you won't like what happens if you don't do what I want."

She looked over at the curtained-off shelves. "Believe me, you won't."

But he didn't believe her. Or he just didn't care.

Abby decided it was the latter when they started again. He just didn't care about anyone but himself. *Maybe the drunken woman had been right, after all.*

She'd felt more desire from a slab of steak.

His fingers fell across her cheek without passion and a nail scraped the inside of her bottom lip when she tried to pull him into her mouth. His hand perched on her breast, then circled each areola in turn with the tenderness a small boy would show a particularly loathsome bug. He tugged at her belly button and yanked a pubic hair out by the roots.

But she would have forgiven him all that, and more, putting his lack of enthusiasm down to nerves or bashfulness, if he hadn't balled his hand into a fist between her legs and refused her ultimate gift.

Again.

"Damn you!"

Abby picked him up from the bedspread and threw him

across the room. He hit the wall next to her closet door with a dull thud and left a mark as he slid to the floor.

"I warned you," she screamed at him as she scrambled off the bed and ran to her tiny dresser. The CD skipped when she yanked open the topmost drawer. "Didn't I warn you? But you thought you didn't have to listen, didn't you? God, maybe that woman was right after all. Maybe you are just a misogynistic bastard. You stink in bed. You don't know the first thing about making love—but I'm going to show you how it's done."

His beautiful hands had somehow managed to fool her about the type of man he really was, but Abby knew what to do. Cutting five lengths of the seven-gauge copper wire she kept for just such an emergency, she shoved a piece at a time through the cauterized flesh at his wrist and into each of his fingers and his thumb.

"You just didn't listen and now look what you're making me do. I was going to be gentle, but I can see now that gentleness would be wasted on you. And I bet you didn't even commit suicide—poor tormented soul, my ass. I bet that woman shot you. Yeah, that's probably what happened. Well, you came here under false pretense and now you're going to pay."

"There," she said, holding him up. "What do you think?"

For an answer, Abby curled his index finger and thumb into a circle. *Okay.*

"I think so, too. So let's see if you're ready to play."

Abby heard the wires creak as she folded down all but his middle finger and inserted it into her vagina. She was already wet, but the wires hadn't made him any more cooperative. A sadistic gynecologist would have been gentler.

"Fine!"

No longer caring what he thought or felt, Abby yanked him out of her and tossed him on the bed. He bounced off the headboard and came to rest on her pillows. Pointing directly at her.

"Since you don't know, I'm going to show you how to make love to a woman." Walking to the shower curtain, she ripped it open and felt tears burn against her lashes. "There's not a man here who isn't a better lover than you are and I'll prove it! Who wants to come to an orgy?"

Raised hands pressed against the insides of their jars—they all wanted her, *all* of them. She was the best they'd ever had, the best they could ever have hoped for, and they knew it. But whom to pick?

Abby wanted to be fair, but more than that she wanted *him* to see what he wouldn't ever get. He failed her twice, he wasn't going to get another chance.

She made her decision—more on aesthetic than essence.

Her eyes and sinuses may have burned, but her chosen lovers were still the most handsome. She wanted him to be jealous . . . and she couldn't very well do that with lovers that were either rotting away beneath piles of mothballs or looked like dried-up pieces of rawhide.

Besides, she didn't mind suffering a little just as long as his ego suffered a lot.

Breathing as little as possible, Abby gathered her lovers into her arms, four in all, and carried them to the bed. He looked so smug nestled on her pillow like some ancient potentate. Arrogant, conceited . . . superior to everyone and everything around him. His whole attitude screamed at her: *Is that the best you can do? Hell, I'm more man than any of them.*

Abby felt the anger rush up from her belly and into her neck. "Oh, is that what you think?"

Tossing the first four onto the bed, she ran back and grabbed four more. Her options were limited, but now it was a matter of quantity, not quality.

"You want to know what real men can do?" she asked the pompous newcomer as she crawled back into bed and positioned her lovers on her body. "Just watch and learn . . . and maybe, if you're very good, I'll let you join in. Maybe."

Two hands rested on her thighs, two more on her breasts—their wired digits anchoring them to her. One hand stroked her head, the other touched her lips. A faint scent of camphor floated in the dusky air as she parted her legs and gently inserted two talented fingers of an ex-concert pianist into her vagina. The last, a brittle young man who'd been her first (and only) experiment with smoke curing, held her hand and waited. Other women might find his touch repulsive, but Abby had grown to love his leathery touch against her clitoris. In small doses, of course. The almost sandpaper roughness made her come harder and faster than any other lovers, but it did leave her tender and bowlegged for weeks afterward.

Abby didn't care. Not now. Not tonight. Tonight was going to be extra special. To show *him* what real men could do.

"Do you see how they love me?" she asked, closing her eyes so she could concentrate on the feel of their hands on her. "They only want me to be happy. Me. They never think of themselves. I'm the most important thing in their lives and they know it. . . . They're here just to please me."

She groaned as her young lover's rough finger gently pushed through the damp curls covering her pubic mound.

"Yes. There . . . right there." Abby pushed his finger down against her clitoris and slowly began moving his hand back and forth. "God, it feels so good. Touch me. . . ."

Lifting her free hand to her breasts, she found the wire loops protruding from the severed wrists of her breast men and shivered as they began stroking her nipples.

"See?" Abby asked, rubbing her head against another's open hand. "Are you watching? Are you taking notes?" She giggled, knowing he wouldn't. "No, you're not . . . because you think you're too good, don't you? You think you're better than I am

... than any woman. But look at me ... I'm surrounded by men who adore me. I'm their reason for being. Without me they'd be nothing.

"Nothing," she repeated as she turned her head, nuzzling the hand next to her lips before she sucked a finger into her mouth. The shock of salt brine against her tongue startled, then excited her ... added to the climax that was already building inside her.

Almost there. Oh, God. Yes. Yes! Are you watching? Do you see how popular I am? How the men all love me? Now ... now ... do it now.

Her concert pianist slipped out when the first spasm rocketed through her.

"No," Abby moaned and reached for him. Too fast, she moved too fast without thinking.

Her smoky lover's nail lacerated the tip of her clitoris. Abby had never felt pain like that before in her life and prayed, in one long, agonizing howl, that she'd never feel it again.

Yellow and purple star-bursts exploded behind her clenched eyelids as her body wrenched itself into a fetal position. Her lovers were no help, they abandoned her ... leaving her to the pain, none of them even attempting to see if they could help ease it.

She whimpered and heard him chuckling above the soft music. Abby knew what he was thinking and that hurt almost more than her torn clitoris. He was laughing at her and her so-called lovers.

"Shut up!" Abby shouted at him. "Shut the fuck up!"

But he kept laughing and now she heard the others join in. They'd been lying to her all this time, pretending to love her just to get a little pussy.

"No! It's a lie! You love me!"

They just kept laughing.

"Stop it!"

Not this time, you bitch.

Abby turned just as he leaped from the pillow to her throat.

She could hear the wires in his fingers grate against bone as he pressed down on her windpipe. The glycerin was a mistake, he kept slipping out of her grasp.

Give it up, baby. This has been a long time coming, so just enjoy it.

Hands grabbed her arms and legs and pinned her, spread-eagled, to the bed. Fingers reeking of formaldehyde and rot tangled themselves into her hair and yanked her head back to the sweat-soiled pillow.

"What are you doing? Stop it! Stop—"

Salt filled her mouth again. And this time Abby gagged.

But I thought you liked sucking on my fingers. I thought it really turned you on.

She is turned on. She's dripping wet.

So, it is only a game. You want it like this, don't you, bitch?

Yeah, I knew it. You like it rough, but you don't want people to know it. Miss Prim and Proper.

Lying cunt.

Open her wide, boys.

Abby's silent scream almost shattered her inner ear as they entered her—hands spreading her . . . holding her open while they crammed inside . . . all of them . . . fingers pumping in and out, in and out, while she fought and screamed and arched her back . . . hips jerking toward the ceiling as she bucked . . . tried to buck them out of her.

Take it, bitch!

"God."

You know you want it.

"Oh, God."

You like it like this.

"Yes . . . oh, God. Yes!"

Abby grabbed them, all of them, and pushed them in deeper . . . deeper as they thrashed on the bed . . . until they thought it was safe.

They never saw it coming.

"*Bastards!*"

The first, dripping with grain alcohol and pussy juice, burst into blue-tinted flames when it struck the candles. The next one was much less impressive . . . it burned slowly, but added to the growing fire. All of them burned—some in spurts and sizzles, others with the sound of dry leaves caught in a wind storm.

Abby kept him for last. So he could see that she'd won and could hear her laughter while he was consumed by the inferno.

She was still laughing when the firemen arrived, although they thought it was just shock and hysterics. A logical mistake that she didn't try to correct. Abby had heard them talking to each other from where she sat, wrapped in a blanket and sipping cocoa as if she were sitting in front of a campfire. It was a miracle she got out alive, they whispered to each other. A miracle.

Okay, she thought.

"And now I have to start all over," she said, to hear her voice instead of theirs.

"That's the right attitude," somebody said and she looked up.

It was the fireman who'd pulled her naked from the burning building. Abby knew that even though she hadn't been able to see his face through the protective mask—hadn't been able to feel his touch through the thick gloves he'd worn. But she knew.

"How are you doing?"

She nodded and pulled the scratchy woolen blanket tighter around her shoulders.

"Better," she said. "I'm doing better."

"Great. Here . . . I brought you this. Thought it might help. I've had two cups of the stuff myself."

Their fingers touched briefly when she took the Styrofoam

cup of hot chocolate from him, but that was all. There was no surge of emotion, no soul-crushing hunger to pursue. Instead, she watched his tongue—autumn-red in the dwindling firelight—discover an overlooked speck of hot chocolate on his upper lip. And the sudden realization almost toppled her out of the back of the ambulance. *God, she'd been wrong after all.*

"Are you sure you're okay?" he asked, his wide smile opening like the petals of a rose.

Smiling, Abby licked her lips and nodded.

"I don't mean to be forward," she said, "but has anyone ever told you that you have a great mouth?"

Making the Jump

Bob Ingersoll

"So, what *is* your secret fantasy?"

Xavier St. John knew where he wanted to go and how to get there. As always, he had carefully manipulated the conversation so its progression from what seemed a tentative hello to his real goal seemed natural. So that *the* question seemed casual, not prying. As usual, the woman he asked—Brenda, this one's name was Brenda, wasn't it?—hesitated. He was, after all, someone she met in a bar only that night, not someone to share her *secret* with. But the question made her think about the fantasy and that was all St. John needed.

He never took no for an answer. Instead, he reached into her mind and, as her thoughts came to her . . .

An enemy agent tries to get information from her. An escaped prisoner takes her hostage. A masked intruder seizes her from her bubble bath. She is taken, stripped, then bound and gagged. Helpless. Unable to fight back so whatever follows, she is not responsible—cannot feel guilt.

. . . they also came to him.

St. John felt her thoughts. Then felt her drive them from her mind as quickly as they came. But not quickly enough. He knew. Her deepest, most-suppressed, most-secret fantasy—the one she wanted more than anything; the one she barely admitted even to herself. And now *he* knew it.

It was what St. John was after and, having found it, he made a subtle, unseen, unfelt push with his mind, nudging her to let it out.

"Bondage," she said.

"What?"

"I want to be tied up and gagged."

St. John smiled as she blurted the words out, as if she had to get them out now, before she changed her mind. Then he quickly replaced the smile with another expression, one he had practiced many times before. He blushed.

"Oh, God, I'm sorry," she said. "I didn't mean to embarrass you." She turned and started to get up from the bar stool. St. John reached out, took her arm, and gently turned her back to face him. The redness still covered his face.

"No, *you* didn't embarrass me, I embarrassed myself. It's just that I've . . . Well, *I've* always wanted to try bondage, too. I've just been too ashamed to admit it."

St. John looked at her and again pulled her thoughts into him. *This* was the crucial moment. He went in deeper, walking along her thoughts . . .

He must be weird.

. . . giving little pushes as he did . . .

But look at him. His face. It's so red. He's so embarrassed.

. . . making her see things the way he wanted her to see them . . .

He must be like me. Curious about something new, something a little dangerous. Curious, but uncomfortable, even ashamed to admit it.

His mind reached into hers and he Nudged her thoughts, made her notice he was not looking at her but beside her. Then he Nudged again, until she put one finger on his cheek and turned his head so that he looked directly at her and, in the anxious expression on his face, she found the courage to say:

"We could stop at the store to pick up a few things and then go back to my place."

She lay before him on the bed of her sparse apartment completely naked, white hemp rope tying her wrists and ankles to the bed frame and biting ever so slightly into her soft flesh, her panties balled up in her mouth while a wide piece of adhesive tape sealed her lips shut.

St. John looked down at the woman. She was not unattractive, but not what anyone would call beautiful. She was thirty-two and slightly overweight, fleshy. Her breasts were a little too large for her frame and had succumbed to the pull of gravity. Her mousy brown hair hung straight and limp. She was the type of woman St. John always sought out in the bars, shy and reserved with little, if any, experience in sex but with a repressed desire that burned within, a secret that screamed to be set free. St. John noticed her eyes dancing over the gag; ready; open, even excited.

He stood motionless, rolling his eyes up in his head until nothing but white criss-crossed by bright red veins showed in his sockets. He reached out toward Brenda with his mind as he had before. Then with *more* than his mind. He entered her with his consciousness, his self. He made the Jump.

His mind entered her mind, tracing her neurons, bridging her synapses, surfing her personal Internet until it burrowed through the neurons and devoured the synapses. Until her thoughts were his thoughts, her memories his memories, what she felt he felt. Until her self was *his* self.

She lay spread-eagled, naked, bound, and gagged, the fantasy finally hers.

She tried to move. The ropes held her down. She tried to talk. The gag sealed her mouth.

She was excited. She writhed on the bed, pulling on the ropes until she could feel them rub against her. She moaned in ecstasy but the gag swallowed her sounds. He could not hear her or know what she wanted. She looked at him over the gag, pleading at him with her eyes, "Now. Now. Please now!"

Even as he made the Jump and was her, St. John was also himself. He felt her wriggle against the ropes and also watched the naked woman squirm on the bed before him, her every excitement visible in the drops of sweat that formed on her soft, white flesh. He enjoyed watching her pull against the ropes, almost as if struggling to get out. It made her more than a passably attractive female he had found in a bar that night, more than some disillusioned lady-in-waiting watching the more attractive, self-assured players leave with someone on their arms, while she hoped someone would glance her way. It made her fetching.

To St. John, that was the beauty of Jumping, merging. Being two people. He was her, experiencing these pleasures of the flesh for the first time. But he was still him, aware of his own sensations and gratifications. He could—how did the commercial put it?—double his pleasure.

She was ready. Then St. John rolled his eyes back again and Jumped.

She watched him approach. She closed her fists so hard she felt her nails burrow into her palms. She wanted him on her—in her—as she had never wanted anyone—anything—in her life.

He lay next to her, at first not touching her. Then he extended his index finger and placed it on the rope binding her left wrist. He moved the lone finger slowly down her arm following its contours, ran it along her collarbone, then traced the curves of her right side, down the outside of her right leg and up the inside.

She closed her eyes. She could see nothing. Her only sensations were the feel of the ropes, the gag, and him.

He moved his finger over the thatch of her pubic hair and across her stomach until it reached her breasts. Slowly he drew it around the circle of her left breast. Then he cupped her left breast and stroked it gently.

She moaned in delight, screaming, "Yes! Yes! Yes!" over and over, although what escaped the gag were unintelligible mewlings. He kissed her breasts even as he moved his hand down to stroke her vagina. His mouth darted over her breasts while his soft lips kissed them and his tongue lapped at her nipples.

Her nipples hardened beneath his tongue, even as she felt herself moisten. She wanted to tell him now, but could not. She cursed the gag that earlier she had desired so much. But again, as if he knew, he moved on top of her and carefully put his penis in her.

With strong, rhythmic motions, he moved his penis up and down, in and out, even as he still kissed her breasts. She felt the thrusts, felt the kisses.

It was the moment she most desired.

Then she convulsed, shaking wildly, spasmodically, as wave after wave of pure sensual pleasure pounded her. Still convulsing, she felt the hot jet of him shoot into her.

After the last surge of combined orgasm rushed over him, St. John pulled out of the woman. Twice. He had expected it to be good—whenever he found a truly repressed lady and got her to release her fantasies, it always was. But he hadn't expected it to be *this* good. She had years of desires and longings—of *needs*—so long and so deeply buried that they exploded out of their prison. What she felt—the mounting excitement and pure sensual pleasure—he felt. It washed over him as completely as it did her, combining with his own excitement and pleasure, each building on the other, doubling it, redoubling it, and more. He had timed his orgasm to coincide with hers and when they came, it was with an erotic ferocity that seemed capable of ripping him in two.

It was the best ever, which made St. John smile. It meant what would come next would be all the more satisfying. Especially because, as he pulled out of the Jump, he caught in her mind a newly forming hope that she had finally found the special someone for her.

St. John walked to the bathroom to clean himself off. He could hear her muffled protests coming from the bedroom, "Umiemee," a sound he had heard often enough to know it meant "Untie me." He ignored it and turned on the shower. Her noises got louder, as she tried to be heard above the running water, but he simply entered the shower, so that he could not hear her at all. That was what he wanted now, a brief respite from her as the needles of hot water removed what was left of her from his body before it crusted over.

He continued to ignore her noises, when he got out of the shower, dried himself off, and came back into the bedroom to dress himself, even though those sounds came with greater insistence than before. He could tell from the sudden strength with which she pulled against the ropes and the intensity with which her noises tried to escape the gag, that she was starting to wonder what he was up to. Good. The longer that wonder lasted, the more it built—preying on her, raising her doubts and fears—the better what would follow would be.

St. John walked casually over to the woman. She raised her head up and stared at him, her eyes narrowing into angry slits. "Umiemeusumich!" St. John shook his head, a slight smile turning up the corners of his otherwise expressionless mouth. He reached down and twisted her right breast hard. She screamed in pain behind the gag.

"Untie you? But we're so far from finished, cunt. I mean, what have you always wanted, what have you fantasized about? Being helpless. Not just being tied up but being helpless, completely unable to keep things from happening to you? This little game wasn't enough to give you the real sensation of helplessness. No, you'll need quite a bit *more* to happen, before you feel true helplessness."

St. John didn't even need to make the Jump to know her terror. Her eyes—open so wide that white surrounded them on all sides—told him. He stared at those eyes, taking in everything they told him, as he approached her; still looking at them as she shook her head from side to side and screamed futilely behind the gag.

He sat on top of her and pulled the roll of tape out of his pocket. He pressed the free end of the roll to her right cheek and wrapped the tape around her head and neck several times, so that her entire head, from the nose to the chin, was covered.

He used the rope they'd purchased that evening and retied her slowly—arms behind her back and tied at the wrists and elbows, legs lashed together at the ankles and knees. He took his time, making sure each rope was pulled tight and knotted frequently, immobilizing her completely. He especially delighted in the ropes he tied around her arms and torso, which pinned her arms to her sides and squeezed her tits between them. They *had* to hurt.

When he finished, she started to thrash against the ropes, struggling to get free. But St. John knew he had tied the bitch too securely. She screamed, but the gag swallowed her cries into pitiful kitten mewlings that were barely audible.

He allowed her to struggle briefly, letting her get a feeling of how helpless she was. Then he took a bottle of chloroform from his pocket and soaked a cloth with it. He walked toward her even as she tried to crawl away from him, looking like a large white worm inching along the ground. He grabbed her, pulling her head up by her hair, and clamped the rag over her nose. She struggled, but couldn't escape. Didn't matter. Struggling made her breathe more deeply, letting the chloroform take effect even faster.

The chloroform wasn't necessary, but it made things easier. When she was out, he'd get one of the wheeled trash bins and take her down to his car in the garage. If anyone saw him, a simple Jump/Nudge would make them think they were looking at the building's super taking out the garbage. But the illusion would sell better if the garbage wasn't moaning and kicking.

And while she was unconscious, there were a few other preparations . . .

He'd learned something about the bitch while he was in her mind and he wanted to use it to the best of his abilities. He wanted to stop at some stores for a few *special* purchases paid for with the cash—always cash, no paper trail—he'd gotten her to withdraw from her ATM. It wouldn't be enough. Not for all the purchases he needed to make or the secluded cabin he wanted to rent. But the streets were full of people he could Nudge into doing a favor for him, then forget. And they all had ATM cards.

As the woman's eyes started to take on the glaze he knew meant she was about to lose consciousness, he said, "I gave you the fantasy, bitch. Now it's time for the reality."

She wakened and did not know where she was. It was dark and smelled vaguely of mold.

She wanted to move but could not. She could lift her head but could move nothing else. She looked down at herself. She was still naked and tied up. She lay on her back, her wrists bound behind her so that she was on top of them. There was a board beneath her. Ropes were wrapped around her and threaded through holes in the board, binding her tightly to it at her ankles, knees, waist, hips, and torso. She could not move. There was so much rope binding her, she did not believe she could ever get free.

She felt the pressure of the panties inside her mouth as they held her tongue down. She felt the tape wrapped around her head and neck. She screamed for help, but could barely hear the sound that emerged from her mouth.

She was completely a prisoner.

She knew that he was there somewhere. She moved her head around until she saw him.

He was on the other side of the room, sitting in a chair and watching her—looking at her. He did not speak. He only watched and smiled.

The smile terrified her. It was nothing like the innocent, blushing face he had last night. It was too broad, too satisfied. It was evil.

She panicked. She thrashed against the ropes, hoping that they would loosen. She screamed and shook her head from side to side, praying that would dislodge the gag.

The ropes stayed taut, the gag held firm. There was no escaping them. And she knew: now he would do things to her.

He came out of the Jump and walked over to her, standing over her, smiling down with the same smile he had felt her call "evil."

"Does it feel like you imagined it, bitch? Being tied up and helpless? I went to a lot of trouble for you. Made that board special myself. Drilled the holes and everything, just to give you what you always wanted.

"So, do you feel truly helpless yet?

"You may think you do. But no. I have something else for you, something that *will* make you understand exactly what *truly* helpless is."

He went back to the chair and grasped a plastic trash bag lying on the floor behind it. Something inside it moved. He ripped the bag open even as he made the Jump into her one last time.

"I learned about more than just the bondage," he said, shaking the bag so its contents spilled to the floor. "I learned about *everything!*"

Then he was in her again, feeling what she felt even as she recognized what crawled out of the bag.

Spiders!

Dozens of large, black, hairy spiders—huge and ugly— crawled onto the floor. As they started skittering toward her, she knew he did know about everything.

Everything!

Even the arachnophobia.

The spiders moved. Crept toward her. She wanted to stop them, wanted to get up and run. She couldn't. Couldn't move. Couldn't scream for help. Couldn't do anything except watch as the spiders moved slowly, but definitely, toward her.

They came. Closer. Ever closer. Spiders. Never stopping. Inescapable. And ever, ever closer.

Three feet. Two feet. One. She wanted to close her eyes. To look away, but could not. She saw him behind the spiders. She looked at him, hoping maybe he would stop them. He stood over her stroking his penis.

She watched.

They came.

First one, then another and another touched her. Then almost all of them were on her, crawling over her. Dozens of spiders, huge, black, hairy, all over her, covering her, and she could do nothing about it.

She broke, sobbed uncontrollably, hysterically behind the gag. She knew she never, ever ever wanted to be tied up again. Never wanted to pretend or fantasize. Never even wanted to think of it. Not. Ever. Again.

He watched her and felt the terror and helplessness building up inside her as the tarantulas skittered over her naked, bound body. He watched and he masturbated. Hard, rhythmic but careful strokes. Making sure that he held off the orgasm until one final, special moment. Then, when she broke, when her bondage dreams—her secretmost fantasy—was taken from her forever, he allowed himself to climax onto her face.

The second orgasm, the moment he most desired, was every

bit as satisfying as the first had been. More. Bringing these stupid cows to their first real climax, as they finally satisfied their dreams, was good. Bringing himself to climax as he ripped the fantasies away from the women and left a hole in them they could never fill was better.

It was the moment he lived for.

He turned and walked away, pausing only at the door to say, "I'll be going now, bitch. The cabin's rented for a week, so you won't be bothered. Don't worry, you should be able to wriggle free. Eventually. Maybe a day or two. Till then, have fun. And try not to move too much. If you upset your friends they might bite. Again."

Before he left, he looked at her one last time. He didn't need to make the Jump to know what she was thinking, he had seen her expression many times on many others and recognized it: a tortured look that screamed, "Why?"

"Because I *can.*"

He shut the cabin door, leaving her bound and gagged within and screaming as the spiders explored her body. Judging from how she looked, he figured it would take all of the two days, probably more, before she managed to free herself from the ropes. An anonymous call to the police on the third day would be best. He didn't want her dying, after all. What was the point of taking something wonderful from her if she went and died? No, she had to live knowing that she could never get back what she had lost.

By the third day, her panic would have dulled most of her memories of him. And if any stayed, he had, as he always did, taken one last precaution; the same one he had used earlier that night; on those bar patrons not so busy with their own hunting that they noticed him, on the bartender, and the store clerks. He had given them and the woman one final Nudge that left two "memories"; his name was Ray Chong and he was Asian.

He walked toward his car, taking care not to whistle or

make any noise, so that he could listen to her muffled screams as he walked away. He did so slowly, until he couldn't hear them anymore.

During the next months, St. John looked for another like her, another Brenda. Yes, her name *was* Brenda, he remembered now. One should always remember the best. He had been to many bars scouting, had many encounters, made many Jumps.

Some were easy and obvious, such as forcing one bitch to drink her "Golden Shower." Others were physical, such as the "Poconos honeymoon" Jacuzzi that produced third-degree burns. And what he did to the cunt who wanted him to dress up like a woman, too, was truly creative. But none were as satisfying as Brenda had been.

No one else suppressed her fantasy as thoroughly as Brenda had, so that when it was finally released, it shot forth like a Saturn rocket. No other surrendered her fantasy as hard or was as devastated, as emptied, by its loss as Brenda had been. With no one else had he shared the extremes of ecstasy and agony that he got from Brenda. That was what he wanted now—the *only* thing he wanted now—another Brenda.

He moved beyond bars, hoping Laundromats or the public library might give him the more repressed quarry he sought. Both had proved to be infertile hunting grounds. Now he just wandered, going anywhere that the type of woman he was looking for might be, without any confidence that he'd find one.

He was in a Denny's, and St. John almost didn't give her a second glance, when she came in. She was built. There was no other word for it, an hourglass figure on which the sands of time had not yet begun its work. Someone with a body like hers could not possibly offer St. John the repression he craved.

Still, there was something about her, something that drew St. John's attention back to her. He didn't know what it was at first, but after some study, he realized she did nothing to complement herself, to play off her obvious assets. Her hair hung down limp, without style. She wore a loose-fitting print dress. She had no makeup on her face. Just a plain and unadorned look.

St. John smiled thinking about her potential. A woman who was looking for a one-nighter and who had a body like hers would wear tighter clothes, a Wonder bra, and makeup that heightened her features. She did not. She may have had the body of a Miss America, but she dressed and acted like a woman who was hopelessly trapped in the confessionals. Properly handled maybe she could be every bit as satisfying as Brenda.

The first step was to establish eye contact, so that he could make the Jump. He sat at the counter two stools away and ordered a hamburger. When it came, he casually asked her for the catsup. She reached over with the bottle and, as she looked at him, he Jumped.

He didn't stay long. Her fantasy was easy to find. It was not suppressed at all but there, plain and evident and on every level of her mind. Her fantasy was a fifties sitcom; all that she wanted out of life was a husband, two children, and a life no more complicated than that of Donna Reed or June Cleaver.

Finding sexual urges was another matter. She seemed to have none, or had them so deeply buried inside that they would never be released for anyone but her husband, as if she would ever have one. But that wouldn't be a problem for St. John. Another Jump coupled with a gentle Nudge and St. John would have her believing he was her husband. Then another Nudge or two until she realized that she wanted a nooner. That's all it would take. He never took no for an answer.

The prospect had St. John excited. To awaken the sexuality of this woman, for whom a man and woman could only be in the bedroom together if they were on separate beds, both were fully clothed and with one foot on the floor at all times, was a challenge. The promise of something unimaginable. To shatter the fantasies of this woman, destroy her dream of perfect marital bliss, was as exciting. He didn't know *what* he would do to her yet—that would come with time and a little probing—but the devastation she'd feel would be even more complete than Brenda's. As would the orgasm he'd enjoy while doing it to her. Today he would be a little hard on the beaver.

Tingling, almost salivating at the prospect, St. John made the Jump.

She looked up from her sandwich and saw her husband. She smiled at him thinking again how lucky she was to find the perfect husband in these troubled times. For some reason she thought of their bedroom, of going there with her husband. But that was impossible. Now, in the middle of the day? It just wasn't done. *She put it out of her mind.*

St. John frowned. For a moment he had her mind where he wanted, in the bedroom they shared with their twin beds only three feet apart. But she rejected the idea so quickly those beds might as well have been on opposite sides of the Grand Canyon. He went in deeper into her mind, looking, probing, and found nothing.

The woman did not have a repressed sex drive, she had *none.* Absolutely no sexual appetites to awaken at all. Nothing to stimulate or excite or reshape in his desired image. Nothing.

St. John realized it was hopeless, he would never be able to do anything with this woman. He came out of the Jump.

And found himself still inside her mind. He tried to Jump out again and failed. He tried again and failed again. And again. And again. And again, again, again, again, again, again . . .

Somehow she held him, so that he could not leave. He tried. He ran down her neurons frantically, pounded on her synapses hoping to smash them open, to shatter them. If he shattered her at the same time, he didn't care. He had to get out *now.*

He couldn't. Instead he felt her self swarming over his self, burrowing through his neurons, devouring his synapses; making his thoughts her thoughts.

Then *her* thoughts became his thoughts.

Bastard! Did you think you were the only one? That there weren't more who could do what you do? No others who could, what do you call it, Jump? Only do it better.

I've been looking for you for months, you son of a bitch! Ever since my sister killed herself because of the way you left her. Oh, you tried to cover your tracks, but you left traces that people like us could find. It wasn't hard to track you down. All it really required was patience.

Been waiting to find you, so that I could Nudge you and draw you to me. You didn't even think it strange that you gave a second glance to a woman who doesn't fit your normal victim profile? But, no, I suppose you wouldn't, *you're so secure that you're in charge.*

Now the waiting is over. This is the moment that I do to you what you've done to others. You see, I Jumped you. I know your secret fear. I made it my fantasy. And your nightmare.

Your prison!

He tried again to pull himself out of her but found, instead, that his only thoughts were the ones she pushed into him.

He didn't finish his hamburger; his appetite was gone. His wife, with her perm and print cocktail dress and costume pearls, smiled at him and said that it was just as well. It would leave more room for the meat loaf she was making that night. She promised it would be the perfect meat loaf.

Much like their life. The perfect life. Perfect husband. Perfect children. Perfect house. It could not get any better.

He put his arm around her to kiss her and ignite her passion. She removed it gently, reminding him that what he wanted was out of the question. They already had their children. Sex was just not something they did anymore.

Not ever.

She smiled. She was still in the Jump. She could feel him inside her, trapped in the fantasy she'd put him in. She could feel him pounding on the walls of that fantasy but unable to get out of it. He was where she wanted him to be, locked in the nightmare. She didn't need him in her any longer. It was time to throw him out.

She felt what he felt as she pushed him through her, then out of her. She was with him, as he felt both himself and her fantasy being expelled, sloughed away the way a snake discarded its unwanted dead skin. She went with him as he found himself returning to his own mind. Back in his head, but still in the bedroom. Then, as he watched, steel bars—eight inches thick and *part* of the walls—covered the door and windows.

He was back in his head but, somehow, trapped in her fantasy.

She felt him begging her to let him out. He wouldn't do it anymore. He'd go back and help all the people whose lives he had ruined. He'd do whatever she wanted. Only *please* let him out.

She left her one-word answer behind, making sure first that it would echo off the walls of his prison and bounce back to him again and again and again. "No. No. No. No. No . . ." Forever.

He screamed.

And she smiled.

It was the moment she most desired.

She locked him and her fantasy deep inside him; then she came out of the Jump leaving him trapped inside himself. She walked casually out of the restaurant, leaving him behind, stopping at the door only briefly to look back and make sure her one-word answer to his pleas for release still echoed in him. It did. That he was still screaming simply made things even better.

He didn't stop screaming. Not even as she walked out the door and the others in the restaurant rushed to him to see what was wrong. He was still screaming when the paramedics came. He did not respond to any external stimuli. Not even after the ER doctors failed in their every attempt to stop him. Not even after the psychiatrists wrapped him in the straitjacket and locked the door to the padded cell behind them.

He screamed. And screamed. And screamed. But he didn't hear himself screaming. He heard only the one lone thought she had left inside him to echo there forever. And he knew, with the last little crumb that remained of his sanity, he knew one thing. One horrible thing.

He would *always* take no for an answer.

Not a Meat Puppet, a Magic Puppet

Thea Hutcheson

The bar was hot and jangly. Not Tina's kind of place but that was the point. Running her fingers through her short hair, she turned to the bar and ordered a beer. Sipping a house ale, she checked out the crowd. Why had she come in here? There'd definitely been something—a scent maybe, she wasn't sure.

Face it, Tina, you turned in because you're so desperate you'd look under any rock, in any hole to find what you had with Dustin. Fucking cops. She sipped the beer, resisting the white-hot anger, slicking it back the way she slicked her hair back, automatically, the way she'd never let anyone ever take her master or that magic from her again.

Which brought her back to her current loose ends, scanning the smoky interior. There was a powerfully built man, a bear daddy, at the end of the bar. They were attracted to her tiny figure, her fine bones. And she was drawn to the power they represented with the same bad results every time.

I am not a meat puppet, she thought. *I'm a magical puppet, which, handled with finesse, becomes an instrument of many means.* Men like Bear Daddy would hurt you because they could.

Dustin hurt you because the pain got you through to the white-hot magic of his touch. She looked away from the man's smile.

Her eyes were drawn to a pocket of murk across the dance floor, near the far wall. She stared, sipping the beer and fancying it gave her superhero vision. It worked, because she now saw a person there. The figure was facing her, left ankle casually resting on right knee, bottle poised on the crossed knee.

Still unable to tell if it was a man or a woman, she toasted the darkness. The bottle returned it. Some time later the bartender came up behind her and said, "There's a beer heading over there if you want to join it."

She turned to him and he cocked his head to the murkiness across the way. He waited, ready to smile encouragement or shrug agreement. As she turned back to the murkiness, it took her a moment to see that the bottle was still lifted at an inviting angle.

"Hmph." This was different. It was a move worthy of Dustin, who held control in one hand and latex in the other. She finished her beer and made her way across the dance floor, her hips and arms swaying to the heavy beat. Each step made the tension flow off of her like water. This was it, or it wasn't. This was the stalk, the appraisal, go or no go.

When she reached the edge of murk, Tina slipped into it like a snake, head up, questing, body sinuous as she flowed up to the table and examined her host. He remained seated but she could tell he was lean and tight like her, not much taller, not five and a half feet, surely. There was a solid presence to him, though, and a whiff of . . . She wasn't sure but got a solid memory of Dustin smiling wickedly as he rolled the Trojan over the new goddess dildo. How she'd prayed that night.

This man's face was calculating; he could be cruel, no doubt, but there was a vulnerability about the mouth. He could be hurt terribly, but one wouldn't want to, couldn't bear to. She resisted the urge to fill the gap with some witless observation.

He continued to study her and she posed for him, carefully neutral, receptive.

Finally he spoke. "Beautifully made. How fortunate, I'd almost finished my beer." He uncrossed his leg and used it to nudge a chair out for her.

She pulled herself together, managing to let herself down into the chair gracefully. The very idea that she might meet someone like Dustin, the magic maestro, made her wanton. Flaunting a little made this man's eyes get big with—surprise, glee? He could be surprised. That was good to know.

When she smiled at him, he gave her a smile right back—from his eyes too, and it had an inquisitiveness that nudged, just nudged for now.

He didn't offer his name and she was going to ask when he spoke. "Music is good," he said.

She considered the statement. This music wasn't her first choice. It sported a heavy bass beat and the melody was savagely sexual, which made it more blatant and less sophisticated than she liked.

"Makes the body clamor, doesn't it?" he added, watching her.

"That's one way to say it." He gestured at the beer. She picked it up. This was pricier than she'd bought herself. She nodded to him and took a swig.

"Mmm," she said, smiling at him. "Thanks, this is good."

He continued to examine her. Putting the beer on the table, she settled back in the chair to let him. The flush that spread across her face and her breasts swelled the hungry little mouth between her legs each time she thought about what he might be thinking.

"Open your shirt one button."

The pleasure of that took her a moment to remember to breathe. He took that for hesitation.

"Why not? You enjoy me watching you."

Another blush slid across her face and a spasm of pleasure pierced her.

"You see? Don't deny it. If you enjoy it, wouldn't you want to encourage it? I want to see, you want me to see, what's the problem?" He smiled. He knew the problem. Just like Dustin knew the problems he posed. She wanted to be bad for him just as she had for Dustin. He gestured with his bottle for her to pick up hers.

"Drink up and we'll see what other mutual things we want."

She tipped the bottle at him and downed it. He'd recrossed his legs and his package made a solid bulge against the pale blue of his jeans. Tina took advantage of the view as she had with Dustin, who had known she liked it and affected the pose to enjoy her reaction.

When she settled back languidly, the man across the table nodded. "Now, where were we?" He pretended to think and she caught her smile before it broke.

"Yes, the button. Unbutton it now, please. I really would like to see."

She exhaled breathier than she meant and her hand went up to the button. She struggled for a moment, long nails catching the button before it obliged.

"Arrange it for me. You know what I want to see."

She shivered, remembering Dustin admiring the first latex fuck-me dress he'd bought her. Taking the edges of her blouse, she unfolded them gracefully, exposing her cleavage.

He nodded in appreciation. "Very nice. Let me see more." And when she didn't move he looked puzzled and said, "Another button, please."

She looked over her shoulder toward the bar. "No one will see us here," he said. His voice was a tenor, lilting and sly under the persuasion, and she believed him. "This is just a little show, a hint, the first taste."

A frisson of pleasure took her then and he followed it up

with, "We'll go somewhere else before I ask for anything really overt."

A smile broke then, she couldn't help it. He was just like Dustin, knowing exactly the right tack, the perfect comment to make her melt or beg or whatever he was looking for. *Just get through the pain, that little bit of pain, whatever it is, and you'll be dancing to that magic.*

Nodding as if she'd just told him something important, he smiled back. She was hot and her breath was short. Settling back she slowly undid the button. Her nails cooperated this time and the two sides fell away artfully. She looked up at him inquiringly.

"Good. Now slide your skirt up your legs, so I can see."

The music shifted to something languid and she played to it, inching the skirt up her thigh. There wasn't much room for this so she began to squirm to the music, giving him little look-sees. He nodded and she spread her legs as she pulled her skirt up and she was unveiled. He seemed disappointed.

Did he expect her not to wear panties? Well, she'd remember that. She ran a finger down the front and pulled the thong aside at the cusp of her pussy, where her clit was peering coyly from between her lips.

He peered closely as if he'd never seen one before. Was he a queer? This was different. She was glad she'd only recently waxed and sported a thin, closely cut runway of hair that ended at the top of her lips. That should give him a good look. She brushed a nail lightly across the head of her clit. It peeked out more earnestly and she smiled as his eyes widened.

His fingers were long and slim as they reached out. They paused and she held her breath, suffused with a memory of Dustin cradling her gently as he frigged her with rubber-gloved fingers.

This man's fingers were practical and objective, which countered the eager look in his eyes as he examined her. He made a small noise of surprise when her juice slicked his fingers. They stared at each other steadily, frankly.

"Oh," and, "Uhh," she moaned from farther back in her throat.

"Perhaps it's time to go." He kept his fingers exploring; he was very perceptive. At first she thought he meant he would go and she moaned, "No," before she realized he must surely mean her too.

"No?" He stared at her quizzically. "You aren't enjoying yourself?"

"Yes—I thought you were leaving."

He smiled. "You don't want me to leave?"

"No, sir, please, stay. Please keep doing that."

"You like it when I do this? You like it even though we're in a public place and you could be discovered at any time?"

When he put it like that she was aghast, but his finger was electric on her clit, sliding around and around on her thick juices. She was going to come. He seemed oblivious or maybe waiting to see what would happen. She let it wash over her, betrayed only by the shudders and the low "Hunh, hunh" that she couldn't keep inside.

He watched, amazed and then concerned, as she climaxed.

"Don't you think we should go?"

"I'll go anywhere if you keep making me come like that." She saw that he hadn't realized what had happened. Was he a virgin or a queer? Or both?

"Yes, I think it's time to go." He stood and she followed when he led her through an unobtrusive doorway beyond their table. They went down a short corridor, through a foyer, and into another set of corridors lined with occasional doors until they reached one that looked just like all the rest.

They entered a room that contained a bland, naturally themed living room set. Without windows, it was disconcerting. Did he live here? She realized she was now lost in a warren with a man whose name she didn't even know, and who had fingers of absolute joy.

"Hey, my name's Tina."

He turned to her and regarded her and her hand solemnly for a moment. Then he hastily stuck out his hand. "Russ."

They shook hands and he gestured to the couch.

"Where were we?" he asked.

Tina sank onto the couch and began to unbutton her blouse again. She could no longer hear the music from the bar. "Any tunes in this joint?"

Russ stared blankly at her for a moment and then shook his head. "There's been no need."

No need? "That's okay." She arranged the blouse halves artistically, hoping he'd lean over and investigate. He stayed where he was, watching as she hitched the skirt up and spread her legs. She pulled the panties aside and stared at him, daring him to come over and take a closer look at her pussy.

He obliged, going down on his knees. She felt a tremor of pleasure. "Mmm," she said to encourage him. His fingers traced the outlines of that hungry mouth.

She thrust forward to catch his fingers and sighed as they slid all the way in. She moaned and rode them. He explored the inside of her pussy with the same thoroughness her clit had enjoyed. He moaned as his other hand stroked her thighs and ass and gave them sharp little pinches.

It was incredible. She felt like she ought to give him some pleasure for all that he'd given her.

"Do you want me to suck your dick?"

He stared at her with a look of fascination or fear. He must be a queer, she thought.

"No." He paused and then, having made some decision, said, "That's not what I'm into. It's people's sex drives, the rituals, the acts, the little understandings that take place in order to facilitate mating. I'd rather do them to you."

Tina shook her head, smiling. "So you're a pervert. It takes all kinds."

He stared at her for a moment and then cocked his head, laughing. "You're right. What's your perversion?"

She considered. "My tastes are eclectic and depend upon my partner, whatever he or she wants."

"You engage in sexual acts with women too? This is fortunate. I'll want to see."

Tina would want him to see her with some little slut or, hell, in the arms of some big, tough dyke who would redden her ass as soon as look at it.

She smiled. Maybe he was one of those geeks who're so dysfunctional they know nothing except the videos they see.

"What do you want to do? What's in your toy bag?" she asked.

"A toy bag? Shades of my ancestor, Haro Chon, first here among us." He got a faraway look as the toy bag notion caught him by the scruff and took him places he'd never imagined.

Just then a wailing siren split the air. Tina clapped her hands over her ears. Russ said against her ears, "Get dressed, you've got to get out of here. I've got to go to work."

What did he do that a siren made him leap like that? And what was this place? She buttoned up her blouse as he took her hand and hurried her down the corridors. His hand was a little clammy and slick, like a come-slimed rubber glove. He finally stopped in front of a door.

"Tina, I've enjoyed meeting you. Come to the bar again— earlier if you can. They don't let me out for long."

"I will," she said like she could've said something else.

He opened the door and Tina looked out on a street a block away from the bar entrance. She touched him on the hand and her fingers slid across his until their tips touched. They stared at each other, amazed by the effect. Then they broke and he was pulling the door closed.

The siren faded as the door sealed and she practically skipped home. When she got there, there was an offer of a production assistant job that would help her on up the post-Dustin career ladder from rotten to survivable.

In the shower the next morning, she found tiny red pinpricks on her ass and thighs. They didn't hurt, but when she ran her fingertips across them, they tingled and she gasped, catching a flashback of Russ's hand on her, thorough, eager.

The photographer liked her and offered her more work the next day. As soon as she got home, she put on her favorite black leather have-me dress and the matching fuck-me pumps, slung her toy bag over her shoulder, and took off for the bar.

A different bartender served her a beer at the bar. She looked around for Russ and after she finished her beer, asked the man, "Have you seen Russ?"

"Who?"

"Russ, short, only a few more inches taller than me, brown wavy hair, hazel eyes?"

He shook his head.

"Well, then I'll have another beer." He gave it to her. When she turned back from the bar, Bear Daddy was there. He was even better looking up close. He smelled military. That was good and bad. Military knew how to hurt, so playing pushed boundaries. But if things went bad, military was ruthless.

"You won't see him tonight," Daddy said. "He's already been here."

"Who?" She played dumb.

"The man you went away with the other night." How much had he seen?

"Mm." She drank her beer, decided to leave. "Thanks, good night," she told Daddy. As she rounded the corner, he caught up to her.

He was easily six feet and over two hundred pounds. No fat, just a big man. The kind she loved to make her beg for more.

Then she remembered Meat Puppet, who always came later. No magic there. The only thing on the other side of that pain was the hospital.

"I've got to talk to you," Bear Daddy said, his hand out to slow her down.

"No." She looked down at his hand and up at his face. He dropped his hand and looked at her more closely.

"All right then, but let me tell you he isn't what he seems. We can't get close to them. We tried the night you were with him, but they're good. The government won't listen either. Maybe they know."

Not military, militia then. That was worse; they were all crazy.

"What does the government know? And what is he?"

"Maybe Russian. They might still be that good. Doubtful it's Iraqis, but who knows what they've got in those tunnels under the desert?"

Daddy kept staring at her but she couldn't think of anything except for Russ's fingers in her cunt and the way lightning shot through it when he suggested further opportunities for exploration. Finally she shook her head and began walking. He didn't follow.

By the time she was off work the next day, she was sure it'd be too late. She showered, changed, grabbed her toy bag, and rushed for the bar. When she arrived, the original bartender smiled at her and held up a beer, which he tilted toward that same patch of murk. She looked toward it and barely caught the raised bottle gleaming dully in the darkness.

Tina's heart lurched in her chest as she picked up her bag and made her way across the dance floor. When she reached the center, she was wet with the thought of what Russ could do with the toy bag.

There was also Bear Daddy's accusation. Was Russ a play on Russian? Was she a fool consorting with the enemy?

She shook her head and slid into the pool of dimness where

he waited, smiling. She answered it, telling herself Russian or enemy, she was glad he was pleased to see her.

"Good timing. I had almost finished my beer. What do we have here?" He gestured to the bag.

"Toys." Tina smiled at Russ.

"Toys?" He stared, finally standing as he realized the meaning of her smile.

"Well, then, let's go . . . play." He made like it was a really clever joke.

They exited through the unobtrusive door. When they reached the foyer, Russ looked back and Tina followed suit. Bear Daddy was closing on them.

A door opened off the foyer and another man stepped out, pointing a weapon at Bear Daddy. Daddy stood still. Russ nodded.

"I thought it might be you but only gave it a low-level probability. My compliments." He nodded at Bear Daddy, who nodded back. It was all very civil but Tina knew Russ was holding the strings of the man pointing the weapon, the situation, and possibly this warren. And she was his.

"Take him," Russ said. The man with the weapon gestured to Bear Daddy, who turned as if to go and then feinted, kicking the weapon out of the man's hands and slashing with a knife.

The man screamed high, like a woman, and a huge splurt of purple and green goo covered the man's waist and ran down to the floor. Tina at first wondered what the man had been carrying under his coat and then realized from the way the orange parts flopped wildly from his belly that there was nothing human in the man-shaped skin.

Was that what Russ was? And what about those tingly little pinpricks? Her pussy swelled as she remembered acquiring them.

"Oh, my God, what are you?" said Bear Daddy, shocked beyond any thought of Russian or Iraqi.

Tina stared at Russ, thinking, *He's much more perverted*

than I thought. Then she realized that Bear Daddy was advancing on Russ.

Daddy smiled wickedly and Tina remembered he was militia. And this wasn't much different than when the allergic reaction to the pepper spray closed up Dustin's trachea and he suffocated, jittering uselessly after another jolt from the cop's stick.

The familiar white-hot anger rose at the memory and she realized she didn't have to slick it back this time. It felt good to pick up the gun and point it at Bear Daddy, whispering, "No one will ever take my master or that magic from me again."

It was time to finish negotiating with Russ. She fired the gun. Daddy jerked, and when he landed, he contrived to look at her. Blood flowed out of his chest at a good clip.

"Jesus God, Tina, I'm your kind."

"But you don't wear a latex suit and you don't pull my strings the way he does."

Russ looked at her with pleased surprise. That told her she'd surpassed his first-round expectations. What would he offer in return? She shivered at the smell of latex thick in the air, and the memory of Russ's fingers manipulating her, coupled with the revealed knowledge that they were latex-clad, almost made her come or faint or weep with pleasure.

Bear Daddy lay on the floor, bleeding. He was probably going to bleed to death. Maybe she should shoot him again. Did it hurt to bleed to death?

"They're invading us, Tina," Daddy gasped. "What do you suppose they want?"

Russ smiled benevolently at Bear Daddy and Tina by turns. "Actually we want to manage things. That's what we do. All over the galaxy. We manage resources. We're really good at it too. Ask anybody."

Russ wanted to pull my strings; he calls it managing, Tina thought, smiling a little in spite of herself. She didn't care what he called it; the results were the same.

"How'd you find us?" Bear Daddy stared at her when he asked the question.

"Your signals," Russ said. "You're very loud. But the data would've just been another channel on our satellite dish if we hadn't discovered the worm hole. That makes the whole thing feasible."

"Who's Haro Chon?" Tina asked.

Russ looked at her, confused. "Ah, the other night. Haro Chon is my relative, one of the original team sent to explore Earth twenty years ago. He met a dominatrix and that meeting mapped the human management process."

Tina thought about those little pinpricks on her ass and thighs. "And the little marks?"

He paused, looking at her somewhat regretfully, she thought. "We're taught to taste our toys and you were so delightfully turned on. I never knew human desire was such a heady cocktail. It was just the tiniest sip, not even a swallow."

She never considered the tasting-with-his-fingers part, because the thought of him tasting his toys cut a straight path to her cunt. *Little prickles of pain will take you to the magic of the master's hands. There are worse kinds of pain to get through.* Control and latex in one hand. This was better than Dustin's control in one hand and latex in the other.

She understood all the Dustin memories then. She gestured to the dead alien and said, "Your latex suit has driven me crazy since the beginning."

"You smell my camouflage?" He considered, looking to her quizzically. "It does share some properties with latex. You have a good nose." She'd surprised him again.

"It's why I came into the bar." And it was true, it had been the scent of latex laid over the hot, throbbing music that had drawn her in.

He eyed her and the bag. "Do you need more? Are you ready?"

"Traitor bitch whore, go ahead and kill me," Bear Daddy said weakly. "It doesn't matter what happens to me. I'm wired. The world knows the truth now."

What would she lose by that truth, really? A long line of Bear Daddies waiting to hurt her? A career she cared nothing for? The rest of her life leaking out like Bear Daddy's blood? So she obliged Daddy and Russ in one fell swoop.

Russ stared at the dead Daddy. "You would choose me, shoot him, knowing that everyone would see, knowing that you betrayed your people?"

"I'll do anything if you just manage me the way you say you can."

He considered and then nodded. "It doesn't matter, your secret is safe; the building's transmissions are monitored constantly. I accept your generous offer and I will not forget the price you would have paid for it."

She nodded. They were done negotiating and she was a better deal than he'd realized. And she believed that he had the power to make his word a thing of value. There was just one thing left to ask.

"What happened to the dominatrix?"

"She and Haro Chon have a lucrative high-end business in the diet industry."

"He's tasting his toys too?"

"He enjoys his work. Virginia enjoys his finer points." She caught the emphasis on points. Were those what made little marks that took you to heaven?

"We're well trained," he continued. "In theory, anyway. It's all just videos until you've done it. I've never had a field job here."

A virgin perv! She could discover the extent of his training and give him field experience while he learned to play her like the delicate instrument she was.

And, if they were all as accommodating as Russ, how bad could it be, being managed by them? Like he said, "Ask anyone." Just ask Tina, she'd tell them, it's just that little bit of pain to get through and you're the magic puppet dancing to the magic of the master's touch.

"Ready?" he asked.

She didn't have to nod. He picked up the toy bag and took her down the corridor to his rooms where she would glory in his latex self as he pulled all of her strings. Oh, yes, there was just one more thing. There was a need now and she'd show him better music. Some Mozart for starters, yes, some Strauss. Now there was music to dance by.

Separate Vacations

Edo van Belkom

It had been her husband's idea for them to take separate vacations, but she hadn't needed any convincing. It was just the opportunity she'd been looking for to get her life back on track. She could go somewhere warm, spend a couple of weeks lounging around in a bathing suit, and if she was lucky, a few nights in the arms of some dark stranger.

She'd been on the lookout for just such a man for days, but all the ones out on the beach were old, fat, and wrinkled, just like their wives. She'd also spent plenty of time in the local bars, but without any luck.

Until now . . .

From across the beachside bar, a tall, olive-skinned man was studying her closely while she stirred her cocktail. When she first noticed him staring, she'd looked away, doing her best to avoid his gaze. But every time she glanced back in his direction, she found he was still staring at her, his eyes unwavering and just a little bit seductive.

After looking away several times she decided to take the plunge. She turned toward him and returned his stare, feeling her body starting to get warm the very moment she made eye contact.

He was young, early thirties at the most, and drop-dead handsome. His hair was thick and black, and trimmed short and neat. He was clean shaven, and although he looked like the type who would have a chest full of dark curly hair, he had none. Whether his hairless chest was nature's idea or he just preferred it that way didn't matter to her. His bare, tanned skin was tight and muscular, and . . .

He was still staring at her.

She gave him a smile.

He waved at her.

Her smile widened.

And then he got up to join her at her table.

She liked that he wore a Speedo. Of course he had the body for it. Her husband wore boxers and gym shorts without exception, and usually stained ones at that.

"Hello," he said, taking her hand and giving it a gentle kiss.

She found herself inhaling a gasp, then said, "Hi."

"My name's Marco. Marco Andruzzi."

My God, his name even sounded sexy. "Jane," she said. "Jane Levitt."

"A pleasure to meet you, Jane." He was still holding on to her hand as he sat down in the chair across the table from her. "I have been looking for you for days."

"Well," she said, playfully, "here I am."

"Yes, here you are. And now that I have found you, I will not let you out of my sight."

She knew he was just flirting, but it felt good to be the object of a man's attention for a change. Her husband didn't care what she did or where she went, and he certainly never said the kinds of things that this man was saying.

It was as if he knew exactly what she wanted to hear.

"You'll have to let me go sometime," she said, deciding to continue playing along. "There's only one bed in my room."

He looked deep into her eyes with a penetrating gaze that

seemed to reach down and touch the yearning in her soul. "Perfect!" he said. "We will be so close through the night, we will need only one bed."

Her knees suddenly went weak.

This man was being so bold, so forward with her, she wondered how long it would be before he reached out and took her in his arms and kissed her full on the lips.

She hoped not too long.

"So you don't mind sleeping on the floor, then?" she said, giving him a coy little smile.

He laughed at that, which was also different. Her husband never laughed at her jokes. He was always too worried about his dinner not being ready on time, or the money she was spending. Well, she wouldn't have that problem to deal with when her vacation was over. When she returned home things were going to be different. She was planning on starting a whole new life for herself, a life in which men found her attractive and funny, and *wanted* to spend as much time with her as they could.

Just like Marco, here.

"I've rented a fishing boat for this afternoon," he said. "It would be a shame to spend the time all alone when I could be in the company of a woman like you." He paused a moment, rubbing her hand between his. "Please, join me."

She was aware of her chest rising and falling with every breath she took. This was all so sudden. She was alone at the resort, and here was a strange man asking her to go out on a boat with him to who knew where. They'd be alone the whole time, and their playful flirting might turn into something more . . .

"All right," she said. "It sounds like fun."

"Wonderful," he said, getting up from his chair. "I will meet you on the dock at two."

"I'll be there."

"I know you will," he said, leaning over and kissing her full on the lips.

She resisted for a second, then returned his kiss with a hunger and urgency that surprised her.

"I'll see you at two."

She opened her mouth to respond, but was unable to say a word.

She agonized over what to wear for hours before deciding that nothing she had with her would be right for the occasion. After the romance and eroticism of this morning's meeting, all her swimsuits suddenly seemed so . . . plain Jane.

She visited the resort's gift shop and took a look at what they had for sale in her size. There were a few shimmering tank suits, but they were all too much like what she already had. In the end she decided on a periwinkle-blue two-piece with a push-up top and a high-waist bottom that she knew showed off a little too much of her chest and legs; but that, after all, was the whole point.

He was waiting for her at two.

"Wow!" he said, as she walked the length of the dock toward him.

"What?"

"You look fantastic."

"You mean this?" she said, stopping to look at the suit. "It's nothing."

"I know."

"So you like it?"

"I love it."

She let out a sigh. Even the way he said *love* thrilled her. His voice and mannerisms were so full of life, so full of passion that she couldn't wait to find out how sensuous and amorous he could be as a lover.

"Let me help you onto the boat."

She gave him her beach bag, then waited for him to take her

hand so she could step more easily onto the boat. But instead of her hand, he put both his hands around her waist and lifted her off the dock and into the boat. When he put her down they were just inches apart. At that moment, kissing him seemed like the most natural thing in the world to do.

And so she did, pressing her lips against his and snaking her tongue deep into his mouth. His hands began to roam her flesh, and the press of his hardened body against hers sent a series of tingling waves coursing through her body.

She never wanted the kiss to end, but of course it had to at some point. It left her dizzy and wanting more.

"Instead of fishing," he said, "how would you like me to take you to a tiny island where we can have the sun and the ocean all to ourselves for the entire afternoon?"

She stared into his slate-gray eyes and said, "Take me there!"

The island was a fifty-by-one-hundred-yard patch of clean white sand a little more than a mile offshore. To the south she could just make out the rise of the beachfront hotels on the horizon, but in every other direction there was nothing but blue clear skies and clear blue water.

"Here we are," he said, dropping the boat's anchor over the side and making sure all was secure.

"It's beautiful."

"And secluded."

She looked around again and couldn't find a boat anywhere. There wasn't even a single sail flying between their position and the shore.

And that frightened her.

This man had brought her here and now she was helpless and at his mercy. What if he left her out here alone? Surely the tide would eventually come in and the island would disappear under the waves. What would she do then?

"Shall we go for a swim?" he said.

"What?" She was still thinking the worst.

He dove off the bow of the boat into the water.

But then again, maybe all he wanted to do was spend time with her. Just because her husband didn't enjoy doing that sort of thing didn't mean other men wouldn't.

She watched him swim toward the island. When he was in shallow enough water he rolled over onto his back and lay in the surf, letting the water run over his legs and abs.

She so much wanted to be there, lying in the surf next to him.

She dove into the water and joined him on the beach.

They lay side by side for some time and her mind began thinking about how things would be different without her husband in her life anymore. It would be easier, for one thing, peaceful for another. And there would be lots of sex too, as much as she wanted, when she wanted, with as many different men as she wanted.

Starting now . . .

She looked over at him soaking up the sun next to her and without hesitation, put her hand on his leg. She stroked the inner thigh for a moment or two, then ran her hand up over his Speedo—

Unless she was mistaken, he'd been thinking the very same thing.

He rolled onto his side, took her firmly in his arms . . .

And they made love on the beach until the tide rolled in.

The island was almost gone by the time they were back on the boat. The sky was still clear and the sun was warm on their skin. He'd already taken off his Speedo and was lying back on one of the seats, working on his already impressive all-over tan.

During her entire stay at the resort, she'd never spent so much time in the sun and was worried about burning. She searched her bag for some lotion, and realized she'd put so much thought into her new bikini she'd forgotten all about the parts that wouldn't be covered up. Marco's beach bag was there at the back of the boat next to hers, and considering the tan he had, she figured there had to be some sort of lotion inside.

"Do you have any suntan oil in your bag, or maybe some sunscreen?"

"No!" he said quickly, jumping out of his chair.

"What is it?" she asked, wondering why he'd gotten so edgy since he'd been so laid-back up until now. . . .

"At least, I do not think so," he said, taking his bag from her. "Let me check."

She watched him search the inside of the bag.

"Ah, there is some in here." He held up a small brown plastic bottle with an orange top. "Can I put some on you?"

She couldn't resist his smile. "Of course you can."

He started shaking his head.

"What is it?"

"Your bikini."

"Oh." She reached behind her, undid the clasp on her back, and slipped the bikini top off her shoulders.

"Very nice," he said. "But you want the sun to caress you all over."

She slid her thumbs under the waistband of her bottom and slowly pulled it down over her thighs.

"Magnificent," he said, squeezing some lotion onto his hands.

She lay down on one of the seats.

He spread the lotion evenly over every inch of her body.

They spent their first night in bed making sweet, sweet love, and they never left the room for the next three days. True to his word, Marco had never let her out of his sight.

And she'd loved every moment of it.

But on the last morning at the resort before she had to leave, she sat up in bed and asked him a question that had been haunting her ever since they'd met in the beachside bar. "Why me?"

"What do you mean?" There was a nervous sort of smile on his face. It seemed unnatural. Wrong, somehow.

"Well, out of all the younger and more beautiful women on the beach and in the bars, why me? Why did you choose me?"

"But you are beautiful."

"Oh, you're just being kind."

"No, I am not." There was a cold, steely edge to his voice. "Your husband said you were a beautiful woman, and he was right."

"My husband?"

"I do not understand why he would want to get rid of you, but it is not my place to ask."

"Get rid of me?"

He pulled a gun out of his beach bag . . .

And things began to make sense about how he'd been looking for her, how he'd never let her out of his sight, and how he'd not wanted her to look inside his bag.

The gun was a deep black, and long, like there was an extra part connected to the end of the barrel.

"He paid me a lot of money to find you, and to kill you."

She believed it, and to tell the truth she wasn't all that surprised. "But you can't kill me . . ." She hated the pleading whine that had taken over her voice, but she couldn't help it. "You can't . . . not after what we did, after what we shared together."

He shrugged. "Sorry, but it is what I do for a living."

"I can pay you more. Double whatever he's paid you."

Marco shook his head. "One client at a time. First come, first served."

She opened her mouth to scream, but the gun in his hand popped twice and she felt something slam into her chest. It took the air from her throat, and the words out of her mouth.

He came closer, and put one knee on the bed. "For what it is worth," he said, "I enjoyed our time together. You were one of the best I have ever had."

She smiled weakly at that, even though she was now struggling to catch her breath.

He leaned over and put the end of the gun under and slightly behind her right ear.

Her last thought was the hope that the woman she'd hired to kill her husband had been as consummate a professional as Marco had been.

And then he pulled the trigger.

One to Die For

Michael Garrett

The spotlight's glare exaggerated each minor flaw of her otherwise perfect complexion, but she was so beautiful that few blemishes actually existed. I stared into her gorgeous blue eyes, my naked body smothering hers, her beauty so stunning that I was almost breathless. She appeared to be in her early to mid-twenties, just a few inches shorter than my own six-foot height, with shoulder-length brown hair and a body that defied criticism. Even shadowed by my own stark silhouette, she was one of the most naturally sensual women I'd ever laid eyes on and I was expected to fuck her in every way imaginable. I could be the envy of every heterosexual male on the planet, yet it was all wrong.

Terribly wrong.

The brightness of the lights blinded me, but this was far more than a mere pornographic video session. Above the abrasive sound of the encircling cameramen's shoes scratching against the floor, an occasional cough or sneeze echoed from a distance behind the floodlights, sometimes accompanied by an even louder than usual *ooooooh* or *aaaaaaah*. A select group of wealthy voyeurs had paid top dollar for a live sex show.

She trembled beneath me, but not from passion, not from the

promise of orgasm, but from fear for her life. I braced my hands against the mattress at both sides of her and lifted my weight. Tears flowed and I watched her chest rise and fall with every breath, her nipples stiff, but not from arousal. A steady cool draft blew across us, probably to keep her nipples perky and erect, my Viagra-spiked erection unaffected by the cold. The frightened girl's eye makeup streaked down her temples and I tried to be gentle, but orders from the intrusive cameramen directed our every move.

I lay against her again, my chest flattening her ample breasts. "Get to it," hissed the closest cameraman. My chemically enhanced dick prodded between her legs. She closed her eyes and wrapped her arms around me, trying to feign acceptance, but her trembling body spoke the truth.

"Open your eyes, bitch," one of the cameramen hissed.

She refused. Perhaps she was praying.

"Fuck her!" someone in the audience yelled.

"*Open your fucking eyes,*" the same cameraman commanded again.

Still she balked, and defiantly removed her arms from around me and laid them straight at her sides.

"This is bullshit!" someone in the audience yelled.

One of the cameramen leaned over us. "*If you don't give these people what they paid for,*" he hissed, "*you'll both be stiffer than road kill!*"

She opened her lovely eyes again and we locked stares. I tried to gaze deeply within her. Heckling from the audience grew louder and the pressure to perform increased. I hoped she realized we were in the same predicament. I had no idea what she'd been told. She looked so helpless, so vulnerable . . .

I prayed she understood.

* * *

Only a few days earlier the brisk morning air had chilled my forehead, my beard shielding my face at least partially from the cold.

Sunrise jogs had always been my favorites. My suburban neighborhood offered several diverse routes and I was on one of the best that Sunday, through a new subdivision under development along the river. Several homes were under construction, but none completed, and the unimproved street I trotted along dead-ended so I never worried about dodging traffic or avoiding aggressive dogs. No one lived there yet. In this relatively deserted area so early in the morning I occasionally spotted two or three deer grazing alongside the river or a family of foxes scampering into the brush. This area was a parallel universe for me, a peaceful, sleepy world seemingly hundreds of miles from the rigors of civilization, yet coexisting only minutes from the downtown business district.

As I ran that day, my mind also raced. Running helps me deal with the frustrations of life. I was maintaining a steady gait, not yet breaking a sweat, when an approaching late-model minivan caught my attention. Someone was obviously lost. The van slowed upon approach, and the driver's window glided down. Probably someone in need of directions—a courtesy we southerners are always more than happy to provide. I slowed my pace, catching my breath. From a distance, the driver appeared to be an unattractive woman. But as the van scratched to a stop on the gravel-based road directly beside me I realized the van wasn't driven by a woman at all, but a light-skinned, long-haired man probably in his mid-twenties.

"You live around here, man?" he called out to me.

He showed no respect for my graying, receding hair. I probably appeared older than I really was, but I expected at least superficial courtesy. Not a *Hello, how are you today?* Not even a *Sir, do you mind giving me directions?* Nope, just a vacant stare as his shifty eyes scanned the area and he asked his nosey-assed question—*you live around here . . . man?* Something was wrong with this picture. I didn't like the guy's looks, didn't care for his demeanor, and I suddenly grew fearful of my isolation. Not another human being was in sight, and my vulnerability mushroomed when the passenger door on the driver's side of the van began to slide open.

A rush of fear convinced me I was in danger. I pivoted and ran as fast as I could, bolting down a rather steep embankment in hope that a trail along the river's edge might allow me to escape. Briars snagged my sweatshirt and bit into my bare palms as I ran through offending brush. A pair of footsteps slapped the ground loudly behind me and then a gunshot rang out. I froze, literally feeling a bullet whiz past my ear. Nearby trees fluttered with squawking birds flying away as a voice behind me rang out, "I didn't aim that time, buddy. Next time, I *will.*"

My heart thumped harder than I've ever felt it before. What could anyone want with *me?* I was just a middle-management public relations manager with a middle-class home, a working wife, and two kids. I wasn't born with a silver spoon in my mouth and certainly wasn't important enough for my employer to pay a ransom, so what could these guys possibly have in mind?

I pivoted slowly. The guy with the gun coming straight at me appeared to be in his late thirties, somewhat heavyset and balding, huffing to catch his breath. Nothing about him appeared unusual except for the handgun daring me to run again. "Up to the van," he commanded with a nod toward the road above the embankment where the van now sat idling.

A thought suddenly occurred to me as I raised both hands above my head before being commanded to do so. "Hey," I said, gasping for air, "you guys've got the wrong man. I don't know who the hell you're looking for, but it couldn't possibly be me."

The gunman said nothing, just motioned with the gun up the

embankment toward the awaiting van. I prayed another car would pass and possibly frighten the thugs away, but no such luck. Like I said, this was an undeveloped neighborhood. No newspaper deliveries. No early walking of dogs. Nothing but myself and these gangsters who obviously had me confused for someone else. The driver stared blankly at me through the van's open window as I made my case a second time. "Come on," I said, "you're obviously looking for someone else. You're making a big mistake."

The driver smiled a wicked grin and snarled, "Let's see some ID."

My heart stopped. I was dressed in my running sweats and less than a half mile from home. I never carried identification when I ran in my own neighborhood. "Come on, guys," I said. "I don't have any fucking ID on me. But my name is Steve Foresta and there can't possibly be any business you guys could have with me."

The gunman sidled up close and jabbed me in the ribs with his gun. "*Foresta*, huh?" he said with a laugh, then glanced back up at the driver. "That's as good a name as any, ain't it, Meck?"

Meck, the driver, spat out the window and practically groaned. "Just shut the fuck up, Carl. Get him inside and let's get the hell out of here."

My heart sank. Either I *was* the guy they were looking for, or I'd been chosen at random and it didn't matter who the hell they grabbed. My mind began to spin. This wasn't supposed to happen to guys like me. I stepped slowly toward the open door of the van, my own words of wisdom flashing through my mind in microseconds, the strict warning I'd previously given my wife should she ever find herself in a similar situation. *Never let a man force you into a car. Once you're alone with him, you're as good as dead.* Now was the time to practice what I preached. I shoved the gunman aside and fled.

Luck wasn't on my side, however. My feet slid in the loose

gravel, sending me tumbling down the embankment again, this time banging myself against rocks and prickly plants. I hurt like hell, but not for long. As I was shoved inside the van, a rag soaked with something, probably chloroform, was pressed against my face and I fell instantly unconscious.

Disjointed moments of grogginess faded in and out of my mind. Muffled voices sounded faintly as if from a distance, but nothing made sense. I had no idea how long I'd been drugged, but when I finally began to regain my senses, I felt nauseated, probably from extended exposure to the stuff that kept me under.

As a greater sense of awareness crept over me I realized I was blindfolded and strapped to an uncomfortable straight-back chair. My hands were tied behind me and I felt dizzy, but there was no danger of falling to the floor because I was bound so tightly to the chair. The voices surrounding me converged into only one as the chloroform wore away and I became more sensitive to my immediate environment.

Fear swept over me like a wave of electricity. Total darkness engulfed me because of the blindfold. I was completely subdued with no idea where I was, who had control of me, or why the hell they snatched me or what they planned to do with me. How could this be happening to me? Finally a pair of footsteps approached and my blindfold was removed. I blinked furiously, my eyes watering from the sudden onrush of light.

I was inside an elaborately furnished office, sitting before a massive oak desk. Richly paneled walls displayed trophy heads of deer and elk and a large mahogany table with plushly cushioned chairs filled one end of the long room. Flowing crimson draperies hung from tapestried cornices along a row of windows, but my attention was quickly drawn to a man settling into an executive chair behind the desk. He was heavyset, middle-aged with thinning salt-and-pepper hair and silver-framed glasses. His fake smile grated my nerves; he was like a car salesman exuding an overdose of false courtesy. Numerous questions came to mind, but my captor spoke first.

"Ah, Mr. Foresta, it's a pleasure having you here with us," he said with a wicked grin. "Please forgive me for not introducing myself, but under the circumstances, I'm sure you understand."

I wrestled with the bonds at my wrists. "Can't you cut me loose? My arms are killing me."

He laughed. On retrospect I suppose it was rather stupid to expect compassion from a man who'd obviously orchestrated what had happened to me so far. "I'm not one to make careless mistakes, sir. I'm sure you'd like nothing better than to tighten your hands around my neck, and I'm in no mood for even the slightest scuffle until my bodyguards burst through the door."

I exhaled in deep disgust and stared at him blankly. "I run a highly lucrative business here, Mr. Foresta," he explained. "My clientele are wealthy, influential individuals—pillars of the community, many of whom I'm quite certain attend weekly church services. They lead secret lives, however, in that they indulge in somewhat unusual practices of a sexual nature. My clients pay a hefty fee and are quite demanding. They are unforgiving individuals you'd not likely wish to turn against you."

"So, what the hell does that have to do with me?"

"Well, first let me say, Mr. Foresta, that extensive precautions are taken to protect the identities of my clientele. They are fully aware of the illegal nature of the activities they witness and wear ski masks so as not to be recognized by each other. They have received the strongest assurance they will be in no danger of exposure."

I slowly shook my head. "I'm so fucking confused" was all I could think of to say. "You still haven't answered my question—what the hell does all of this have to do with *me?*"

"You're in precisely the state of mind in which I wish you to remain, Mr. Foresta. Your confusion provides a higher level of security for us all. For instance, do you have any idea where you are? You've been rendered unconscious for two full days, sir, and transported far from your home. There is not the slightest chance that you will be recognized or that you may identify anyone you might encounter while you're here."

"But what the hell do you want from *me?* I'm just an average guy. How could I possibly fit into whatever the hell you're doing?"

"Well, sir, it's quite simple. You'll be a star performer in our next show."

"What . . . show?"

"Let me explain. A young woman has also been abducted . . . Oh, that's such a harsh term. Let's just say that a beautiful young woman has also been *escorted* here far from her own home as well. The two of you will meet under our spotlights on stage, and as the crude saying goes, *fuck each other's brains out* before a live audience."

I was stunned. I'd been imagining the brutality that could be in store for me, yet this guy only wanted me to fuck! It sounded too good to be true. But why would anyone pay to watch a middle-aged guy have sex?

"Underground sex shows abound for those who have enough money and connections, Mr. Foresta," he continued. "However, I offer a decidedly different concept, something a bit more—how should I say?—high stakes. Two people who have never laid eyes on each other make a valiant effort to sexually satisfy each other under extremely stressful conditions. You see, your audience will vote on which of you gives the most authentic, enthusiastic performance. The loser . . . well, there's no kinder way to explain it—the loser is executed. The winner is transported unconsciously back to his or her original location and released."

Ice water shot through my veins. For some reason the term *little deaths* drifted through my mind. I'd heard orgasms described that way. I didn't like how close to reality the term now applied to me. "But this is impossible!" I managed to say. "In the first place, a man can't perform on demand, especially under such pressure! And even so, you expect me to commit rape and adultery at the same time? That can't happen. It *won't* happen."

"Ah, Mr. Foresta, you underestimate the miracles of modern medicine. As you well know, common drugs are available to assist your state of arousal, and I assure you, your partner will have more than enough incentive to stimulate you to perform."

"But my wife—"

"Your *wife* is irrelevant, Mr. Foresta. It's your *life* that should be of utmost concern to you at this time. If you wish to actually see your wife again, you would be wise to give supreme pleasure to the partner I've selected for you."

I slowly shook my head, trying to absorb it all. If I went through with this and actually gave my partner the fuck of a lifetime, I could in effect be killing her as well. Some *little* death. A big, fucking *permanent* death was at stake.

"Your other issues have been raised before as well, Mr. Foresta, and are subject to debate. Will your act meet the legal definition of rape? Your partner will not submit to you of her own free will, but then again you'll not be performing of your own volition either. You'll be acting under duress. So if the act should be considered rape, then who is the rapist—you or I?"

I couldn't answer. What did it really matter?

"And as for adultery—well, under the circumstances, could it truly meet that definition when self-preservation, not sex, is your primary motive?"

He smiled briefly and laughed. "It's only semantics, Mr. Foresta, and meaningless to discuss. You *will* pleasure the young lady and she *will* actively participate."

As my head cleared more from the drugs, I began to evaluate the situation more clearly. "You say one of us will live. How do you know the survivor won't find a way to bring you down?"

"You forget, sir, that we know where you live. If you value the lives of your immediate family, you'll create a believable excuse for your absence over these past few days and take our little secret to your eventual grave."

Would they actually take such a risk? I highly doubted it.

"Actually, Mr. Foresta, you have two choices," he said with a sigh. "To save your partner's life, you simply offer a lackluster performance of your own and allow her to ravage you in the process. You will, of course, sacrifice your own life as a result, but what a way to go! As the saying goes, she is truly *one to die for.*"

I sat openmouthed, wondering how the poor girl was being prepared for this.

"If instead you prefer to see your own wife and children again, you must simply outperform your partner."

A wicked silence allowed me to absorb the two choices.

"*That* is what my clientele prefer most," he finally continued, "when both parties give the performance of their lives. On two rare occasions the audience requested an encore performance to make a final decision. In one of those instances an unprecedented mandate demanded release of *both* parties. Mind you, that has happened only once and is indeed a long shot, but it is possible."

A knock sounded at the door and two men were permitted to enter. Cigarette smoke clouded the room as the team who'd kidnapped me stepped inside. Occasionally the gentle sobs of a woman from a nearby room drifted within earshot as the two stood before me in stark contrast to their boss. They were hoodlums, typical toughs, while their boss, the obvious brains of the operation, appeared highly educated and polished.

The asshole who vigorously puffed at a cigarette was the heavier and older of the two, the one who'd shot at me. He blew smoke in my face and I coughed spastically. The boss glanced at his watch and said, "Meck, get the girl ready. We mustn't be late."

Meck, the skinny long-haired creep, nodded and left the room, leaving the door slightly ajar. I wasn't sure if it was accidental or deliberate so I could hear my female partner's terror.

The smoker sneered at me and I noticed a scar above his left eye. "We got a real hot one for you, buddy. You're one lucky asshole," he said to me, then added, "Well, lucky only to a *point . . .*"

"Shut up, Carl," the boss scolded. The tone of his voice was decidedly different this time, exhibiting a momentary loss of composure. "If you don't get Mr. Foresta ready in time, you'll be just as dead as he may be."

The woman's sobs next door grew considerably more fearful. "Shut the fuck up," I heard Meck warn her. She didn't stop crying, but instead sobbed more softly.

Carl snapped his head in the direction of the woman's voice, then faced his boss. "How come *Meck* always gets to prep the bitches?"

The boss gave no response, but stared at Carl intensely. I took a deep breath and slowly shook my head. The woman next door mumbled, "Please, don't. Don't hurt me."

The boss then stood, stepped to the partially open door, and yelled, "Give her the fucking tranquilizer!"

Carl glared at me without another word. The reality of my own impending death became a stronger possibility.

"Listen, bitch," I heard Meck snarl in the next room. "You better practice saying shit like *fuck me, Steve! Fuck me harder!*" I imagined him directly in the poor girl's face. "Fuck me in the ass, Steve," he continued. "Say it, bitch! *Say it!*"

She didn't, but then I heard a hard slap and she muttered softly, "F-f-fuck me, S-S-Steve . . ."

"Where?" Meck growled impatiently.

She must've taken a long deep breath before finally gasping, "In the . . . *ass.*"

I never dreamed those words from such a sexy voice could send cold shivers down my spine. I wrestled harder with the bonds at my wrists, trying desperately to free myself so I could at least try to do something. It was hopeless, though. My arms were held impossibly tight.

Suddenly a different male voice sounded from down the hall loud enough for us all to hear. "Ten minutes. Don't be late."

Ten minutes till show time.

Carl's voice now sported a tone of heightened urgency. "I'll give you something to calm you down, too, old boy. Just enough to relax you so you won't have so much on your mind and can take care of business."

I couldn't allow my judgment to be hampered. I'd need a clear head to find a way out of this. "Now, take this fucking pill," Carl said. He jammed a small tablet between my lips and held a glass of water to my mouth. I took a sip and swallowed, but held the pill beneath my tongue. Fortunately it was small and easy to hide, but I had to get rid of it before it dissolved.

My heart pounded as I felt the tiny pill slowly melt beneath my tongue. Thank God, I hadn't trimmed my beard lately and the ends of my mustache drooped around the corners of my mouth. Slowly I worked the dissolving tablet to the edge of my mouth and pushed it with the tip of my tongue out and into the brisk hairs of my mustache, but by the time I managed to place it there, little of it remained. As soon as no one was looking, I nudged the remainder of the pill out of my mustache with my tongue and it fell into my lap. Despite my heroics, the drug would affect me, but to what degree I had no idea.

"Carl!" the boss growled. "Did you remember the Viagra?"

"Meck was supposed to give it to him," Carl answered.

The boss slammed his fist hard against the surface of his desk. "You fool! Viagra needs an hour to become effective."

Carl's voice now had a weary edge to it, probably realizing he'd fucked up one time too many. "I'll give him two," he said. "Maybe that'll help."

The boss exhaled deeply in disgust. "See that you do. Our guest here has an empty stomach. Perhaps that will help the drug take effect more quickly."

Carl jammed two blue pills between my lips along with the glass of water again. This time I swallowed, hoping the Viagra wouldn't cloud my thinking. I had to stay focused or the girl and I might never get out of this alive.

Carl stepped behind me and I felt my hands and feet freed. I stood slowly, feeling somewhat dizzy and disoriented. I was ordered at gunpoint to remove my clothes and was handed a blue bathrobe.

The show was about to begin.

I watched from stage left as the curtains opened. Blinding spotlights shielded the audience, and the auditorium seemed about the size of a small comedy club, a haze of cigarette smoke drifting toward its ceiling. A crude sound system crackled as the boss's voice introduced the program:

"Ladies and gentlemen, tonight's performance is about to begin. As is our custom, armed guards secure the entire premises to ensure your complete safety and confidentiality. Please relax and enjoy tonight's event as we once again present to you complete strangers who have never performed outside the privacy of their own bedrooms engaging in sex under extreme pressure. At the conclusion of tonight's performance, please drop your ballot for tonight's winning performer into the gray box at the rear of the auditorium. Thank you for your attendance, and enjoy the show."

I watched my partner across the stage. She stood in a pink bathrobe at gunpoint beside Meck, her legs shaking violently;

she was a bundle of nerves. The public address system sounded again:

"Ladies and gentlemen, meet Lori."

She took a few steps forward, then stopped momentarily, wobbling in an apparent state of dizziness. Meck finally stepped into view and escorted her robotlike to center stage where she faced the audience. Meck hurriedly left the stage and Lori stared silently across the auditorium. As if on cue she dropped the robe to her feet, the glare of the spotlights casting a milky-white glow over her nude pale skin. A cameraman stationed in the audience captured her every move from the front, while another backstage recorded her image from behind.

Lori was beautiful, almost angelic in appearance, but her pretty face couldn't hide her fear. She still visibly shook; hopefully the drug would kick in and make the rest of the ordeal easier for her.

She gave the audience several seconds to absorb a full frontal view, stumbled slightly, then cupped her breasts in both hands, kneading them sensually. She'd obviously been trained to the letter. She arched her back, thrust her hips forward, and spread her vaginal lips for all to see. The audience responded with explosive applause, hoots, and cheers. She then pivoted with her back to the audience, bent over and almost lost her balance before finally spreading her ass cheeks. More applause and cheers erupted; then someone in the back of the audience yelled, "I'll pay top dollar for a piece of that after the show."

I slowly shook my head. She was like a prime piece of chattel at a white slave auction.

A spotlight then illuminated a slowly rotating king-size bed behind her on a slightly raised platform. She gently stepped barefoot to the bed, crawled to its center, and positioned herself flat on her back. Now it was my turn, but I hadn't been instructed to give such a blatant display. My heart pounded as I heard my own brief introduction:

"And now, ladies and gentlemen, please welcome Lori's partner for the evening, Steve."

I walked to center stage focusing on Meck's wicked grin offstage as he taunted me with his gun. I faced the audience and dropped my robe as I'd been told. For only a split second I felt self-conscious. There was only light, scattered applause, a couple of groans, and some smart-ass guy yelled, "Hey, from the size of that dick, I'd say we all deserve a discount for tonight's show!" Most of the audience laughed.

My heart pounded harder. There seemed to be no way out—guns appeared to be everywhere—and I felt my own mental state begin to wane. I pivoted to join Lori on the bed, a growing dizziness of my own impeding me.

The auditorium cameraman rushed past me to join his colleague onstage as I approached Lori. I couldn't think straight; for some strange reason I worried about my appearance. I hadn't showered the morning I was snatched, having planned to do so upon my return home, so I knew I must look a fright. My scraggly beard and unwashed hair must have been terribly unsightly to this poor woman, but then in a fleeting moment of cognizance it dawned on me that my immediate mission was not to impress her, but to save her life as well as my own.

Easing across the mattress on my knees, I carefully positioned myself over her, and that's when Lori defiantly laid both arms straight at her sides. That's when the audience became unruly and one of the cameramen hissed, *"If you don't give these people what they paid for, you'll both be stiffer than road kill!"*

I admired her picture-perfect face again and considered what a charge it would be if circumstances were different, but even as I watched her closely, her eyes glazed over with a dazed expression, an eerie calmness settling over her as the drug took deeper effect. I leaned over her, compassionately stroked her hair, gently kissed her lips, then nuzzled my face against her ear and whispered, "Don't worry. I . . . ." I wanted to assure her that I'd think of a way out of this, but couldn't force the words. My tongue felt like cotton.

I took several deep breaths, trying to keep my mind clear, when Lori suddenly thrust her arms around me again and gave me the most passionate kiss of a lifetime. I was shocked at first, momentarily taken aback, but must honestly admit I enjoyed it. As the bed slowly rotated, the level of lighting varied. At times it was like coupling in a blinding snowstorm. My back sweated from the heat of the spotlight but Lori's shielded skin remained cool and soft beneath me.

She finally broke the kiss and softly hissed, "I have . . . an eighteen-month-old son. This is for him . . . not *you.*"

"No talking!" one of the cameramen yelled.

Another agreed, and apparently to remedy the situation, ordered us to assume the sixty-nine position. I lay on my back and she awkwardly crawled atop me, straddled me on her knees facing away, then bent over between my legs, thrusting her beautiful ass in my face. I stared at her sweet sex in my face and lust grew deep inside me, overpowering my determination to remain focused.

Lori obviously knew what she had to do to stay alive. She practically swallowed my dick whole and the audience response grew louder and more enthusiastic. Considering she was in a drug-induced state and acting under extreme duress, she was doing a magnificent job taking me in deeper and deeper and releasing me slowly, providing an indescribable sensation with obviously no desire whatsoever of receiving pleasure of her own. Her movement was mechanical and strictly business, but my own sex drive was so strong that despite my semidrugged state and the threat to my life, I was completely overcome by her performance. Lori knew exactly what she was doing, and was doing it very, very well. With her sex easily within tongue's reach, I couldn't help myself.

I nudged her legs farther apart and reached between them,

wrapping my arms around her outer thighs so I could grasp both ass cheeks and pull them apart. I buried my face between them, lapping and tonguing her in every way I knew how to reciprocate the intense pleasure she was delivering. Her pubic hair brushed against my lower lip as my whole face was engulfed by her sex. I managed to maintain my senses enough to stop regularly for deep breaths, somehow remembering in the back of my mind that something far more important was at stake. As my end of the bed rotated into view, the audience showed appreciation of my performance with scattered applause.

Despite flickering moments of guilt and faint awareness of my danger, I was caught up in the moment of raw sex with a virtual goddess. Even the idea of an audience became a momentary turn-on. I buried my face deeper between the cheeks of her ass, licking and nibbling her genitalia enough to drive a normal woman over the edge of orgasm, but when it dawned on me that Lori wasn't even wet, my sensibilities finally kicked in. This wasn't sex; it was an artificially induced performance strictly for the audience's pleasure, neither Lori's nor mine. Visions of my widowed-to-be wife drifted in and out of my consciousness, my fatherless kids, and I even imagined who might take custody of Lori's young son. Perhaps the boy's father was abusive; so many lives were about to be terribly disrupted if I couldn't find a way out. Within moments of exploding into Lori's mouth, my erection began to wane; my senses returned to me.

Our captors had filled us with bullshit. Neither Lori nor I would be allowed to leave this place alive. The powerful people in attendance could lose lifelong fortunes and reputations were they to be connected with such illegal activity. They'd paid premium prices for this perverse form of entertainment, and included in the cost of admission came an unwritten guarantee of complete anonymity. Whether the attendees endorsed it or not, Lori and I were both expendable, as apparently had been many others before us.

My own advice to my wife flashed back into my mind: *never let a man force you into a car. Once you're alone with him, you're as good as dead.* Then the big boss's reference to the audience echoed in my mind: *they are unforgiving individuals you'd not likely wish to turn against you.* At the moment, Lori and I weren't alone with our abductors. An audience was here with us—*unforgiving* witnesses—and I had to turn *them* against the perpetrators.

An idea occurred to me. I pushed Lori's ass away, but she resisted, determined to revive my erection to save herself. Finally I overpowered her and she slid to the bottom of the mattress into a fetal position. Two guns cocked to firing position nearby and a terse command sounded, "Do as you're told or *die!*"

I faked a smile and motioned the gunmen away. "Back off," I managed to say. "We're gonna give these people what they came here for."

I took Lori's hand and helped her stand on unsteady legs, then guided her to the front edge of the stage. Positioning her to face the audience, I stood close behind her and slid my dick between the cheeks of her ass to regain an erection. Despite the severity of the situation, it worked, thanks to the Viagra. I nudged her legs apart with my knees and entered her from behind, the audience responding with enthusiastic appreciation. She wobbled lightly on her feet, but standing seemed to help her regain her senses. I reached around and grabbed her breasts, pleasing the audience immensely, but more importantly steadying her on her feet. The applause grew louder and louder, with shrill whistles and catcalls.

I nuzzled against Lori's neck and whispered, "We can get out of this alive if you do as I say." I had no way of knowing if she understood, and was still a bit groggy myself as I attempted to keep a steady rhythm between her legs. "Lori, if you understand me, reach behind yourself and grab my hips."

Nothing. She stood there like a zombie. I was about to give

up when slowly, almost mechanically, she maneuvered her arms behind herself and obeyed.

Still I grinded her and it was feeling fantastic—so good in fact that my mind still wandered between my life and my dick. I hoped I wouldn't come before I could explain to Lori what to do. Still nuzzled against her neck, my face buried in her hair, I explained, "We're standing between the guns and the audience. They can't shoot without hitting one of the big shots." I continued to pump steadily. "If you understand, grab me harder."

This time she reacted swiftly and grasped the loose skin of my hips, pulling me against her as I pounded her harder. Lori was precariously hanging ten over the edge of the stage as I banged her from behind.

"At the count of three," I whispered, "jump off and run for the exit." The crowd was practically hysterical with excitement, clapping in rhythm to the thrusts of my dick. The place was going wild. "Get ready," I whispered. "One . . . two . . . *three!*"

We leaped together and tumbled to the floor. I scrambled to my feet, helped Lori stand, and we ran clumsily down a center aisle.

The boss stepped from behind the curtains onstage and yelled, "Stop them!" Following a moment of disbelief, the audience converged on us. Like a scene from a horror movie, throngs of ski-masked predators attacked us. Arms and hands groped from all directions to subdue us until our captors could take us away. Meck and Carl were frantically squeezing their way through the crowd toward us, their guns drawn but pointed to the ceiling.

"If you let them take us, you're all accessories to murder," I screamed. Some of the hands loosened their grip; others grasped even tighter.

Carl raised his head above the crowd and yelled, "They know that already, asshole, so shut the fuck up."

A few audience members surrounding us drew guns of their own and shoved them in our faces. "But what you don't know," I said, addressing the crowd again, "is how close to being busted these scumbags are. And when *they* go down, you *all* go down with them," I bluffed.

The audience quieted somewhat. "Your kidnapper buddies have made a critical mistake," I continued. "Ask them to show you my driver's license. They don't even know who they grabbed."

Gasps erupted from across the room. I'd clearly struck a nerve. Someone yelled, "Show us his ID, Anderton. You'd better have some damn good answers."

Anderton motioned for the audience to remain calm. "Please, ladies and gentlemen, don't listen to this man. He's—"

"Show us the fucking ID!" another audience member yelled. "I want *proof* that you know who you're fucking with."

A thin man standing closest to me held my arm with one hand and thrust a handgun in my face with the other. Somehow I managed to grind my heel into the toe of his shoe and as he loosened his grip on my arm, I wrestled the gun from him, an errant gunshot firing into a nearby wall before I gained complete control. A couple of women screamed and the crowd backed away, but I managed to grab one of the ladies as a hostage and held the rest of them at bay with the gun. "Let her go!" I ordered those who held Lori.

I pointed the gun at the thin man who wore a trench coat. "Give her your coat!" I commanded. Nervously, he surrendered the expensive garment. Lori wrapped herself inside it and stumbled to my side.

I placed the barrel of the handgun at my hostage's temple, shielding myself behind her; she trembled at my grasp. "Everybody, drop your guns!" I yelled. Some were slow to respond and I cocked the hammer. "If I shoot anyone here, cops will be crawling all over the place. It'll make the headlines." The remaining weapons went to the floor.

Anderton backed away. Motioning toward the nearest pistol on the carpet, I told Lori, "Grab that one to take with us." She did, and kept it trained on our hostage as I hustled a long coat from another audience member. Hiding my own nudity seemed to render a boost of confidence.

Adrenaline coursed through my veins. I held my hostage tighter, surveyed the crowd of onlookers, and felt a surge of anger grow within. "Off with the fucking masks!" I yelled. My heart thumped rapidly as I sensed the horror in everyone's minds. "*Now!*" I growled.

Slowly the ski masks peeled away. Shock registered in the eyes of those who embarrassingly recognized each other. It felt great to strike back. Lori nudged against me. "Let's get out of here," she said. "Please?"

I nodded, still holding tight to my hostage. Anderton's voice sounded above the murmuring crowd as cool and collected as ever. "You'll not get far, I assure you."

I glared at him and then at Lori. "Would you like to give him a good, hard kick in the nuts before we get out of here?"

Tears streamed down her cheeks as she slowly shook her head. "I just want to see my son as soon as possible," she sobbed.

I imagined forcing the smart-ass instigator to strip down in front of his angry clientele, commanding him to bend over and spread his ass cheeks. In my mind I inserted the barrel of my pistol into his asshole and pulled the trigger. It would've been only fitting.

My hostage shuddered within my grasp and a stream of urine ran down her leg, puddling on the floor at her feet. She was obviously terrified, but was our only ticket out of there and I was still pretty fucking scared myself.

I ordered Anderton to call off his guards in the parking lot, and once the way seemed clear, Lori and I backed our way outside shielding ourselves with our hostage. At her car, I put the hostage behind the steering wheel, told Lori to stay in the floorboard of the backseat to avoid possible gunfire, and kept the gun trained on the terrified woman's face.

I marched our hostage into a nearby police station at gunpoint without considering how the cops would react to an armed man on the premises. After manhandling and frisking me, they finally listened seriously to what Lori and I had to say. Following intense questioning they helped us get back to our families and then managed to arrest Meck and Carl a few weeks later. Anderton remains on the loose. I have no idea if any of the high-powered attendees faced charges. I suppose, as the old saying goes, money talks and they bought themselves out of any legal problems.

I convinced my wife not to attend the trials of the two thugs to spare her from graphic courtroom testimony of my onstage performance, but Lori's husband was there both times staring a hole through me as both the prosecuting and defense attorneys demanded explicit details. Have you ever been forced to describe the precise movements of a sexual encounter to your partner's spouse? I watched his face grow red, noticed his knuckles turn white as he gripped the bench seat's end armrest tighter and tighter in the courtroom while I spoke. I feared retaliation from him as much as from Anderton.

My guess, however, is that I'm far from Anderton's mind. He's probably relocated elsewhere, taken greater care hiring a new team of abductors, and has likely incorporated new stage practices to prevent another disruption of his operation.

Sometimes still when I lie awake at night and can't go back to sleep, I envision Lori's beautiful ass bouncing against my face and remember how great my dick felt inside her. Take away the fear factor and it had been every man's fantasy come true.

A man's sex drive is one of the most mysterious, unpredictable forces of nature. Men have risked everything for sex, including their lives. I now have a far better understanding of our former president. Yes, a dick can definitely subject its owner to danger. You see, I'm back to my old routine again and my Sunday morning jogs carry me back through that same undeveloped neighborhood. A couple of houses have been completed now, but nobody's moved in yet; it's still about as deserted as ever. Occasionally, though, I'll hear the engine of an approaching automobile as my feet scratch against the gravel-based road, and to this day when I do, despite my near-death experience with Lori, my heart begins to race.

But not from fear, my friend.

Graveyard Shift

Max Allan Collins and Matthew V. Clemens

Bobby Lamont loved women.

And women loved Bobby Lamont. So often, it seemed, his flowing black locks, high cheekbones, and lanky frame reminded them of magician David Copperfield, which in this town was a real plus. Bobby's job—room service waiter at the Beachcomber Hotel and Casino, off the Vegas strip—afforded him plenty of opportunity to chase (and on occasion catch) skirts.

Twenty-seven, bright but something of an underachiever, Bobby did even better when the entertainer he so closely resembled played one of the hotels on the strip—in fact, right now Copperfield and Lamont were in the midst of a two-week engagement.

Take the night before last, for example. Halfway through his shift, a middle-aged schoolteacher—with a plain face that lip gloss helped, and a bony but limber body—had practically attacked him when he had shown up with her late dinner of a chicken breast, small salad, and carafe of white wine. There had been a few minutes of flirting, almost no foreplay, and a quick jump right there on her bed. She had even tossed in a twenty-dollar tip.

He would have bet a week's salary that (a) she hadn't been laid for a year, and (b) her demeanor back home (somewhere out East) would resume its typical propriety . . . and those around her, male coworkers especially, would write her off as a spinster, never guessing the urgency and passion underneath. Of course, none of them had the kind of education Bobby Lamont had attained here in Vegas.

Right now Bobby carried lobster and champagne on a tray in front of him. Only a single order, he noted. That might be a good sign. He hoped he was on his way to the room of a single female tourist, another "spinster" or maybe a housewife having a fling, and not some middle-aged salesman treating himself on the company expense account.

Room 1232 would be at the far end of the hall on the left. The doors to each room were inset within tiny alcoves giving the hallway an abandoned look. Moving down the hall, Lamont heard a long, low moan . . . and several possibilities raced through his mind.

Always an alarmist, blessed (or cursed) with a vivid imagination, Bobby instantly knew that someone was being mugged . . . and he was walking into the middle of it.

His mind jumped ahead one step on the danger scale as a simple mugging escalated to a stabbing, then a leap as he envisioned blundering into a shooting. Though he had never even heard of a crime being committed on the Beachcomber premises, he spent hours of each shift envisioning the different things that could go wrong, with so many people and so much money floating around under one roof.

Now with these murders hitting Vegas—the media full of the three corpses over as many weeks—he was particularly skittish. The cops were keeping a lid on the case, and the exact circumstances of the deaths had not been revealed—other than some strange speculation in the press that the bodies . . . found discarded, one along a roadside, another in a restaurant parking lot, another on the UNLV campus . . . had somehow been "butchered."

Scuttlebutt around the hotel—among waiters, cocktail waitresses, bartenders, who heard everything, after all—had it that the victims were not so much butchered as drained . . . blood at the scene being scarce, the corpses—Bobby shuddered at the thought—white. Yet the other most persistent rumor was that the cops were looking for an animal of some kind.

Even as he considered that discretion might well be the better part of valor, and that maybe he should retreat as far as the elevator anyway, his feet—urged on by a curiosity as strong as his concern—moved him forward, past room 1210. Another moan—that same long, low sound of a wounded animal—summoned him, on his right.

Edging forward, ready now to throw the tray of food at a possible assailant, Lamont sneaked a peek into the doorway alcove. Standing there, back to the hall, completely oblivious of Lamont, a bald man in an off-the-rack black suit was grinding his loins into those of a brittlely attractive bottle blonde, an "escort" Bobby recognized as a regular at the hotel.

The hooker, her blue miniskirt riding up around her stomach, locked eyes with the waiter, and shared the tired smile of people working the graveyard shift. He nodded and the blonde rolled her eyes and shrugged her eyebrows in a-girl's-gotta-do-what-a-girl's-gotta-do fashion, just before Bobby slid on past the alcove, giving the couple their privacy.

Now, as he moved away, he was able to discern, not the moan of a wounded animal, but the fraudulent wail of a pro going through the motions for the sake of her client.

Bobby wished his imagination wouldn't play these games on him. He didn't know if it was the lateness of the hour and how the hotel was normally quiet at this time, or whether he was tired or bored or what. All he knew was, whenever he heard a strange sound, his mind seemed to immediately conjure up the worst possible scenario. In truth, he had been overreacting this way since he'd been a four-year-old afraid of the dark.

And having a murderer at large in Sin City only fired that four-year-old's imagination of his. . . .

Reaching the door to 1232, Bobby shifted the tray up onto his shoulder, using one hand to balance the edge as he knocked.

The door opened immediately and the room-service waiter found himself facing a pudgy, vaguely attractive blonde with formidable breasts obvious under a baby-blue see-through nightie that ended where her thighs began, an eager smile on her puffy Angelina Jolie lips. Heredity or collagen? Bobby wondered.

"Hi," she said, the word more an exhalation than actual speech. Somehow she had managed to slur the one-syllable word, despite its lack of a hard consonant.

"Room service."

"You can put it right over there," she said, her voice doing a funny breathy thing—Marilyn Monroe still exerting her hold on the culture—as she pointed to the round table across the room.

She was a little drunk—at least—and was perhaps thirty-five years old, a fairly hefty version of a woman who had been a knockout ten years ago.

Bobby thought, What the hell, and turned on his biggest smile as he strode in with the food. Truth be told, none of Bobby's conquests were dream-girl escapees from *Penthouse Forum*—at least, not until they were transformed in his memory, and in the raunchy anecdotes he so loved to spin to fellow employees.

When a woman greeted him in her nightie, Bobby could cut to the chase. "Surely a lovely lady like yourself can't be in Vegas all alone?"

Her grin turned upside down. "Freddie just left me here. Flat."

Not hardly, Bobby thought. "Your husband?"

"Boyfriend. We got here this afternoon—from Cleveland."

He nodded as if that would have been his assumption.

"And ever since we checked in," she continued, "he's been down in that casino. Makes a girl feel . . . unwanted."

Getting into the game, Bobby said, "Beautiful woman like you, that doesn't seem right. It's . . . it's criminal."

The smile returned. "You're sweet."

"You're from Cleveland."

"Yes. It's not as dull as you might think."

Right, Bobby thought. *That's why you're in Vegas parading in your nightie in front of a waiter.* He moved toward her, the check in one hand, a ballpoint pen in the other. "Expensive dinner like this, that's one way of getting back at him."

"I guess. But he can afford it."

Bobby pressed the pen into her hand, let his touch linger an extra second or two. "He's an idiot," Bobby said, shaking his head.

"Well . . ."

"Only an idiot would leave a fine woman like you up here all alone. I sure wouldn't." She filled in the tip line, signed the check, and beamed at him. "You're so sweet—what's your name?"

"Bobby."

She handed him the check—a crappy five-dollar tip written in! and then the pen, her hand wrapping around his. "That's a nice name. I'm Emily."

"Nice to meet you, Emily. That's a pretty name."

In Cleveland.

Still grasping his hand, she pulled it toward her, letting it brush against one of her breasts. "Have you got time for a drink, Bobby? There's plenty of champagne."

Reflexively, he glanced toward the door. "What about your boyfriend?"

Emily waved off this concern. "Freddie came up about an hour ago, got some money out of my purse, and left again. I don't look for him till morning."

"A guy with money, and he's into your purse?"

"He can be a real horse's ass."

"Sounds like it." Turning back to her, Bobby considered his options. She wasn't stunning by any stretch of the imagination, but she certainly was willing, and if her boyfriend was going to gamble away the night, maybe Bobby could afford to take a little risk himself. "How about a quick one?" he said, finally.

She frowned.

"Drink, I mean," he said.

The smile returned, and she lifted the bottle, took a long swig—as if the champagne were a Coke—then pulled the bottle away, the bubbly sloshing over her breasts and down her stomach. Giggling, she squeaked, "Oops."

The soaked nightie clung to her breasts and, being chivalrous by nature, Bobby stepped forward and buried his face in her champagne-soaked bosom, as if trying to suck the cloth dry.

The nightie peeled off, and those breasts were wonderful, boundless, generously tipped, and she fell to her knees, unzipped him, and swallowed all seven inches of him, a magician's trick even David Copperfield might envy. He stopped her before he climaxed, caught his breath, and led the plump flower to the bed and climbed aboard the lushly curvaceous woman and buried his face between those Mansfield breasts and the seven inches deep within her . . . wet for him but tight . . .

The whole encounter took less than ten minutes and almost before he knew it, they had finished in bed and drifted to the shower, which he found himself sharing with Cleveland's answer to nightshift boredom. Both of them were soaked, her nightie wadded in a ball on the bathroom floor.

His interest stirring, he was wondering just how to accommodate a zaftig lass like this one within the confines of the cubicle when he heard a voice beyond the bathroom, rising over the drill of the shower. "Baby! . . . Daddy's home!"

Daddy's home?

"Oops," she said.

"Oops?" Bobby said.

"That's Freddie," she explained, the sexiness gone from her voice, the slurry drunkenness, too, a finger moving to her puffy lips.

Oh, shit, Bobby thought. This was all he needed—the boyfriend. And if this guy was bigger than his girlfriend, that would make him a whole lot bigger than Bobby. "Oh, shit," he said, aloud this time.

Emily shushed him, then turning toward the door, said, "Be just a minute, hon! I'm in the shower!"

A mumbled, I'll-be-waitin' response came from the other side of the bathroom door and Bobby Lamont jumped out of the cubicle and grabbed a towel, got it around him.

"My clothes are in the other room," he whispered to his shower mate, as he remembered kicking them off in his haste to mount his latest conquest. Now they lay in a black heap, in the middle of the floor, waiting for the boyfriend to find them.

Piling out of the cubicle as well, wrapping a towel around her ample figure, Emily pushed in front of Bobby, standing between him and the door. "I'll distract him—you sneak out."

Bobby looked at her in stunned disbelief. "Sneak out?" She nodded and turned toward the door.

Making the sign of the cross, Bobby prepared to die.

Emily dropped the towel and opened the door a few inches. The harsh bathroom lighting did not do wonders for her. "Baby?" she whispered.

From behind her, Bobby couldn't see a thing, but she didn't seem to be generating any response. She crept into the darkened room (better lighting conditions), Bobby hanging back, waiting for the boyfriend to respond . . .

Nothing.

The waiter waited, straining to hear, then—after two minutes that seemed hours—moved into the doorway. That was when he heard the foghorn bellowing of Freddie snoring.

With Emily coaxing him on, Bobby grabbed up his clothes, careful to find every last scrap; then he slipped into the hall, still buck naked.

Closing the door to room 1232 behind him, jaybird Bobby had survived. Now he had to get into his clothes before somebody spotted him, and he lost his job. Hustling down the hall, pulling on undies, socks, shirt, and pants as he went, he left zaftig Emily and her drunken boyfriend to their own pleasures.

Breathing hard, he punched the button on the elevator and finished buttoning up. All the waiters had been complaining because they had to use the lobby elevators, but the maintenance company hadn't repaired the service elevator yet, so they waited their turns like everybody else.

When Bobby Lamont got back down to the kitchen, he found fellow waiter Dan Rivers sitting at a stainless steel table, listlessly folding silverware into rolled napkins for the upcoming breakfast rush.

Nodding for Bobby to take a seat across the table, Rivers asked, with hopeful lechery, "Gettin' any tonight?"

Bobby knew that the older, paunchier Rivers lived vicariously through his exploits. With a sly grin, he said, "Just did this blonde up on twelve."

Rivers licked his lips. "You nailed her?"

Bobby nodded, telling Rivers a story that left the encounter pretty much intact, removing years and pounds from his conquest, and ignoring only the interruption by the drunken boyfriend. "And then there was what she did with the champagne."

"Yeah?" Rivers asked, eyes saucering, his fingers working even faster now bundling up the silverware.

"Lamont," a voice growled.

Bobby turned to see Mike Devlin, the third-shift cook and kitchen supervisor. "Sir?"

"Got an order," Devlin said, jerking a thumb toward the food-prep area. "Get a move on—see if you can get it there before fungus grows on it."

"I'm on my way." He checked his watch—5:12. Either someone was having a very late dinner or a hell of an early breakfast.

Rivers turned his face up expectantly. "What about the champagne?"

Bobby grinned at the older man. "It'll keep till I get back, Danny—it'll keep."

Sullenly, Rivers started folding the silverware much more slowly, his touch turned limp.

Following Devlin to food prep, Lamont saw the tray in question on a counter, picked up the ticket, tried to decipher Devlin's sloppy handwriting.

"Room 815, scrambled eggs, bacon, toast, coffee," he read, then put the finishing touches on the tray: carnation in a vase, salt and pepper shakers, cream and sugar for the coffee, and finally a napkin wrapped around silverware. Hoisting the tray, Bobby headed out of the kitchen.

He pushed the UP button and stood there with the tray in both hands. Upstairs he'd transfer it to one hand and carry it in on his shoulder. It looked a little fancier and usually helped elicit a larger tip than just lugging a tray up there and dropping it on a table.

Preying on lonely women wasn't Bobby's only perk. Occasionally one of the high rollers would drop him a fifty or a hundred, just for bringing up a plate of eggs. Maybe he was a glorified busboy, but this job really did have some decent dividends.

The elevator seemed to take forever. Even though there were three cars, none of them had been on the first floor. One on six, one on nine, and the third one was all the way up on seventeen.

As he waited for one of the two lower ones to arrive, Bobby's mind wandered back to plump Emily.

That one had been too close—way too close. He almost wished he could really tell Rivers about this one, husband and all. A lot of the stories he told Dan were bullshit, from exaggerations to outright whoppers. But he knew the poor guy loved to hear these yarns, and he'd convinced Rivers he was getting some at least twice, if not three times, a night. And though he did do well, Bobby of course didn't do that well. Tonight's French farce was a story Rivers would have eaten up with a spoon; but if management ever found out, Bobby Lamont would be history.

Finally, the elevator dinged, doors slid open, and Bobby stepped inside with the tray. He vowed to be more careful from now on, not to push the envelope. That drunken guy had been as big as a house and if the guy had figured out what he'd stumbled into, slender Bobby would have wound up on the receiving end of a big fat ass-whooping. He pushed the button for the eighth floor and the elevator ascended, the aroma of bacon and eggs filling the car, reminding him how hungry he was.

Stepping out of the elevator, hefting the tray onto his shoulder, Bobby wondered what he would do if this delivery presented him an opportunity as inviting as Emily. . . .

Moving down the hall, lost in his thoughts, Bobby walked past the correct door and had to double back. He knocked, received no answer, then knocked again. The door jerked open so fast that the waiter lurched back, nearly dropping the tray.

"What do you want?" asked an angry bald man. He was wearing only boxer shorts.

Was this the same guy who'd been in the hallway with the hooker? Bobby wondered.

"Roo . . . room service."

"I didn't order goddamn room service," the bald man said through his teeth.

Bobby checked the ticket again and realized he'd misread

Devlin's chicken scratches. Eight-fifteen had really been eight-thirteen. "I'm sorry, sir." He held out the check for the man to see how easy it was to make the mistake, but the door slammed in his face.

Clearly this was not Bobby Lamont's day. Backtracking even farther, he knocked more timidly on the door to room 813.

The door opened and Bobby stood looking up at a giant of a man, at least a foot taller and nearly a foot wider than himself, dressed in a white T-shirt and tan slacks and dark socks.

"About damned time," the giant said, standing to one side, nodding Bobby inside.

"Sorry, sir," the waiter said automatically, as he moved past the guy's suit coat hanging in the open closet.

Bushy dark hair and one wide eyebrow gave the man a Cro-Magnon look. The guy's crisp white shirt and red-and-blue-patterned tie hung over a chair near the table he pointed to. "Yeah, yeah, just hurry it up. Put it there."

Bobby set the tray on the small round table, picked up the check, and turned to hand the bill to the big man. The waiter took two steps back toward the door before he finally noticed the pistol on the nightstand.

Stopping short, Bobby stood transfixed by the black automatic, its barrel pointing haphazardly toward him.

The big man's gaze followed Lamont's and he didn't seem to miss a beat.

"Don't worry about it—I'm FBI."

Tearing his eyes away from the gun, Bobby looked at the man and knew immediately the guy was lying.

But he said, "Fine. Fine."

Stepping forward, pushing the bill into the guy's massive paw, Bobby decided he didn't really care if the guy was lying or not—he just wanted the hell out.

The giant signed the check, at least Bobby thought he did,

and then the guy handed it back and held up a twenty in front of Bobby's face.

"Next time you'll be faster, right?"

Bobby nodded numbly, his mouth dry except for the metallic taste of fear.

"And I'm working undercover, so you didn't see a gun in this room, right?"

"What gun?"

Pressing the bill into Bobby's hand, the guy said, "Good," and eased Bobby through the open door, shutting it behind him, almost a slam.

Could he really be FBI? Investigating those murders, maybe? But murder wasn't a federal matter, usually . . . was it?

Bobby Lamont was nearly back to the kitchen before he drew what felt like a halfway normal breath. From now on, he was going to keep his head down. This was definitely not his night; and if he could just stay out of Devlin's way until 7:00, he could call it a day. It was already past 5:30, less than an hour and a half to go.

Devlin's voice assaulted him from behind. "Where you been?"

Bobby spun to face the supervisor. "Uh . . . upstairs. With that last order."

"Where the hell do you disappear to, anyway?" Devlin asked, but it wasn't exactly a question. "Orders are pilin' up. Grab one and get the goddamn lead out."

"I'm due for a break—I was gonna grab a smoke."

Devlin shook his head. "You want a break? Show a little hustle. Grab an order and if you see Rivers upstairs, tell him to get his ass back down here."

At least the tray had been prepped, Bobby thought, picking up the ticket and reading it twice, making sure Devlin's scratchings were legible.

"Four-twenty," he said aloud as he hefted the tray and ambled out of the kitchen.

The elevator deposited him on the fourth floor and Bobby decided that even if he had to hide somewhere after this one, it would be his last run of the night. Too much weirdness. He'd even lost his appetite. The food he carried now almost made him want to hurl. Who the hell ordered spaghetti drenched in meat sauce and Parmesan cheese at 5:30 in the morning?

Four-twenty would be ten doors down on the left side. The door opened and the woman standing there, in a red silk dressing gown, might have walked out of one of Bobby's tales of sexual conquest. This was no skinny schoolteacher turned by *Penthouse* letter B.S. into a goddess, no plump housewife transformed by baloney into Jenna Jameson . . . this was a goddess. This was Jenna Jameson, or, no—who was that other porn star? Tera something?

"You brought my food," she said, almost comically grateful. Her voice had a musical lilt.

She was on the tall side, five-eight easy, and her skin had a golden tan that wasn't entirely the sun—her brunette hair tumbled to her shoulders, her dark eyes had a vaguely Asian cast, her heart-shaped face and apple cheeks mixed something strangely wholesome into a mix of ethnic types that was absolutely dazzling.

"Yes" was all Bobby could manage.

"Please," she said, opening the door wider. Her smile teased her lips . . . no need for collagen, here. Those breasts, whose tips poked at the silk, might have had some help, though. . . .

The door closed behind him and she gestured to the table, saying, "Set it there, would you?"

He did.

When he turned, she was right there—like a jump cut in a movie . . . as if she had materialized from across the room. Her eyes danced.

"You . . . This isn't a practical joke, is it?" she asked.

"Huh? What? No . . ."

"Are you David Copperfield?"

He grinned, laughed a little. "No, I get that all the time."

Her eyes tightened. "This isn't some *Candid Camera* thing, is it?"

"No . . . it's just room service."

The pretty eyes widened again. "What's your name?"

"Bobby. Bobby Lamont."

"I'm Cynthia. Do you like girls, Bobby? I bet you meet a lot of pretty girls working in Vegas."

"Some . . . not as pretty as you, though."

She undid the robe and it slid down her curves and puddled at her feet.

No . . . no help for those breasts. Perfectly natural . . . she needed no embellishment. This time, Bobby's story would need no embellishment, either, to blow his coworker away. Dear *Penthouse* . . .

"Thank you, Bobby," she said, moving even closer, slipping an arm around his waist, drawing him gently closer.

"For what?"

She giggled. "For bringing my supper, silly," she said, and she kissed him.

Bobby was drunk with that kiss, smiling to himself, eyes half-lidded, already mentally composing his tale of conquest, and when she nuzzled his neck, it just felt good. He didn't see the animal-like teeth, extended razor-sharp canines, draw back to give him their generous tips.

Nude in Magenta

Debra Gray De Noux and O'Neil De Noux

Through the viewfinder of his Nikon, James Steele watches his wife sit in her red miniskirt on the finely trimmed lawn of Jackson Square. Her skirt is so short, her white panties are plainly visible. James focuses on her semisheer underwear and takes a picture. He feels an immediate rush, his wife sitting this way in public.

With her short brown hair, striking blue eyes, and model's face, Helen looks stunning on this bright Saturday morning. She's never looked prettier, especially with only a hint of makeup and that brown lipstick, which draws out her creamy complexion. She still looks much younger than thirty-two, although that's what her Louisiana driver's license says.

James takes another picture, then sits next to Helen to reload his Nikon. He catches a whiff of her light perfume again, which increases his turn-on. The calliope of a steamboat starts up, its shrill notes bouncing off the roofs of the French Quarter. James looks toward the seawall protecting New Orleans from the Mississippi and sees the steamboat's funnels over the top of the concrete wall, recalling the view before the wall was built, back when it was all wharves along here.

"Someone's out on the balcony," Helen says, turning James's

attention to the Pontalba House Apartments across narrow St. Peter Street from the square. A man stands leaning against the railing of the intricate, wrought-iron balcony running the length of the block-long, redbrick Pontalba House.

"I think it's him," Helen says quickly, "and he has *binoculars.*"

Helen raises her right knee, revealing even more of her panties, as James moves in front of her to take another picture. Beneath the brilliant sunlight, James can see his wife's dark pubic hair through her panties. He feels his heartbeat rising.

Helen leans back on her hands and raises her face to the sun, eyes closed. James moves to her side to give the man with the binoculars an unobstructed view up her skirt.

Three minutes later, as James snaps yet another photo, he spots their quarry hurrying through the iron gates of the square. Carrying his own camera, the Honorable Frederick Newman, associate justice of the Louisiana Supreme Court, heads straight for them. Helen raises both knees high, revealing the panty-covered lobes of her ass for James to photograph. Moving to his wife's side, James spots Newman pull up his camera to take a hurried picture up Helen's skirt.

In his mid-sixties, Judge Newman is a thin man, a good five inches shorter than James Steele's six-foot linebacker frame. Newman has intense green eyes, a hawkish nose, and sandy hair showing only a hint of gray around the temples. Like James, Newman wears a sport shirt and jeans.

James's sport shirt, worn out, covers his 9mm Beretta, tucked into his beltline at the small of his back.

"Hope you don't mind if I take your picture." Newman flashes a warm smile at Helen. Turning to James, he adds, "I'm a professional photographer and she looks so pretty. Hope you don't mind."

"No problem," James says as Helen sits cross-legged, like an Indian, the entire front of her panties exposed. Strands of her silky pubic hair stick out the sides of her skimpy underwear.

James focuses and snaps a photo as Newman does the same. Helen leans back on her hands again.

Two men pass behind James and he sees them ogling his wife. A mischievous glint comes to Helen's eyes as she smiles at her husband, her face flushed. She's getting turned on.

Helen stands and pushes down her skirt.

"Let's go to the Moonwalk," she says, taking James's hand.

"Mind if I tag along?" Newman smiles again.

Helen smiles back and Newman sticks out his hand, introducing himself as Fred Newman. Helen takes his hand as James introduces them.

"Such a gorgeous day for pictures," Newman adds as the three cross Decatur Street and move up the steps to the top of the concrete seawall. Over his shoulder, James notices a young man checking out Helen's rear as they climb the steps.

He's probably getting a good view, James thinks and feels a rush again. They cross the streetcar tracks to the wooden moonwalk atop a smaller levee next to the river. A warm breeze, smelling of coffee from one of the nearby wharves, tousles Helen's hair, and lifts her skirt momentarily. Moving to an open bench, Helen sits. Even with her knees together, James can see her underwear. He and Newman snap a photo and Helen goes into model mode, moving her feet up to the bench, showing off more of her panties.

James feels his heart pounding in his chest as several men move closer to watch. Helen drops one leg off the bench to show her crotch to the peering eyes. Smiling broadly, she playfully toys with the buttons on her blouse, unfastening the first two to reveal most of her cleavage. James and Newman both take pictures.

Suddenly, Helen stands and buttons her blouse. James turns to see a cop slowly approaching. Thankfully, he's looking at a passing ship on the river. James takes his wife's hand and leads her back up the moonwalk.

"James, Helen," Newman calls out as he follows, "would y'all like to go up to my place for some wine? I live in the Pontalba House."

"The Pontalba House, huh?" Helen smiles again. "Never been in there." For an instant she remembers watching the workers build the old apartment house, laying the red bricks, hoisting the pieces of the lacework balcony.

"It's the oldest apartment house in North America," Newman adds.

"What kind of wine?" Helen's flirting now. James squeezes her hand and she squeezes back, smiling even wider.

"I have a wine room."

Once a small closet, Newman's wine room is at the end of the long hall just inside his second-story apartment. He pulls out a bottle of French cabernet and motions them into the wide living room with its French doors opening to the balcony overlooking Jackson Square.

Pulling out the bottle's cork, he lets it breathe while he shows off the living room, neatly decorated with a mix of antique love seats, a modern sofa, an oriental screen, mahogany tables, oil paintings on two walls, the third with floor-to-ceiling bookshelves of leather-bound books. James catches a scent of lemon polish in the immaculately clean room.

"Delicious," Helen says, sipping the wine.

"The light in here is nearly golden," James says. Helen takes the hint and sits on the sofa, posing for the men. She kicks off her sandals and pulls her feet up on the sofa. Lying back, she spreads her feet apart for the photographers.

James feels a growing hard-on and is forced to adjust it. He sees Helen catch him, winking as she does. Newman lets out a long breath as Helen pulls her skirt up to show her dark mat of hair plainly visible now through her sheer underpants.

"You are truly beautiful," Newman gushes as he moves in for a closer picture.

Finishing her wine, Helen poses in different positions, always showing her panties, her face getting more flushed as James and Newman hover around her, snapping pictures.

Refilling her wineglass, Newman asks, "Why don't you finish unbuttoning your blouse?"

Helen takes the glass from him and sips it, her eyes lingering on his as she shakes her head. Stepping to one of the mahogany tables, Helen poses next to it, lifting the back of her skirt to show her ass. Away from the golden light of the French doors, James turns on his strobe unit as Helen continues moving around, posing for the men.

Returning to the sofa, she glances at her watch, then looks expectantly at James.

"Well," James says, "guess we're running out of poses." He tugs up his jeans, feeling the reassuring weight of his Beretta.

Newman quickly refills Helen's glass and hands it to her with a gleam in his eye. "Y'all want to see something truly exquisite?"

"Sure." Helen takes another drink of wine.

Newman leads them back into the hall to the far end where a pinkish red daybed sits beneath a large mirror.

"Nice." Helen shrugs, her heart suddenly pounding. She masks it with a calm question, "What's exquisite about this?"

"I'll show you mine if you show me yours." A smirk crosses Newman's face as he reaches to the side of the mirror and pushes something. Hidden lights illuminate the mirror and James hears a whirring sound. Slowly the mirror moves downward behind the daybed to reveal a painting in a gold frame. James keeps his face from reacting to the color of the painting as shades of magenta are revealed by the slowly descending mirror. He sees Helen's face is also expressionless.

The face in the portrait comes into view. James feels the hairs stand on the back of his neck as he stares at the long-missing

Degas, the *Nude in Magenta*. It has been so long since he's seen the portrait and that familiar face and even more familiar body captured by the master. The critics who call Degas's work *icy objectivity* are certainly wrong with this painting.

In tones of pinkish magenta, the nude woman reclines on a magenta daybed, much like the daybed lying beneath the picture here in Newman's hallway. She lies on her back, her legs extended, and looks longingly to her right as if her lover stands there, just off the painting. Typical Degas, James thinks, as if he's peeking at this woman, instead of her posing for him.

"It's . . . magnificent," Helen says, stepping closer to the portrait. Her face softens as she relives the pleasant memory of when she had lain on the daybed and the intense look on Degas's face as he painted her during that long, steamy summer of 1872 when he lived in that wonderful mansion on Esplanade Avenue with his mother's family.

Degas was a shy man but a keen observer of people. Helen remembers him taking her home, not by cab, but by streetcar. "I love to ride the streetcar," he told her. "I can look at people. We were created to look at each other, weren't we?"

This is the Degas she remembers, the great insecure man whose paintings were sometimes painted as if the subject did not know he was there, as if they were not posing, as if he were looking through a keyhole.

James stares at the portrait. The hairstyle is different but Helen's face hasn't changed. Her lipstick is darker today.

"Truly magnificent," James says.

"She's not so bad herself," Newman answers as he leers at Helen's backside. James smiles.

As if mesmerized by the texture of its strokes, Helen unbuttons her blouse and tosses it aside. She unzips her skirt and drops it behind her, then climbs out of her panties to stand with her back to the men. James takes a picture of Newman taking a picture of his wife's naked rear.

Newman moves frantically, snapping pictures, as Helen whispers to herself, "Oh, Degas. You always liked me best when I was naked." A vision of the great artist peeking at her from behind his canvas. Such a determined little man, he showed much more imagination in his art than in bed.

Running her fingers through her hair, Helen turns and faces them, her face nearly glowing with the big turn-on, being naked like this again. Both cameras bathe her with white strobe light as the men focus and photograph her.

Reclining on the daybed, Helen assumes the same position as the magenta nude. Her breasts more full than the woman in the portrait and her skin more tanned now. Back then a woman's body was rarely exposed to the sun. Helen looks to her right, directly at James as he carefully focuses and takes a picture. Her nipples are erect, her pink aureoles so inviting.

Both men hurriedly reload their cameras and take another picture of Helen posed as the woman in the portrait before she starts moving around on the daybed. Opening her arms and legs, she lies spread-eagle for them, then curls on her side, then rolls on her belly. Kneeling on the daybed, Helen poses, then climbs off to pose on the carpet.

James hears his own heavy breathing as he moves behind Newman to take a quick picture of the *Nude in Magenta* without Helen in the frame. He takes another to be sure he has it, then returns to photographing his nude wife.

Helen crawls away from the daybed, then rolls on her back as Newman stands between her legs. He snaps a picture and James snaps one as Helen inserts a finger into her pussy. Her hips rise to her fingering as the men photograph her.

Helen rolls on her belly, rises on all fours, and continues crawling away.

James turns around, carefully focusing on the Degas, and squeezes off another picture. Suddenly, Helen scoops up her clothes, stands, and begins dressing.

Newman looks at James, then back at Helen as she zips up her skirt and puts on her blouse.

"How about some more wine?"

"We have to go." Helen's voice is deeper, filled with passion.

"Whatever for?"

Helen reaches for James and pulls him close for a long French kiss.

"We have to go!" Helen is nearly breathless as she steps into the living room for her sandals. Passing Newman on their way out, she adds, "We have to go home and take care of this. This *turn-on.*"

"Y'all can do it here." Newman waves to his sofa, camera still in hand.

Helen turns back to Newman and brushes her lips across his.

"See ya around," she says as she leads her husband out.

Bounding down the ancient stairs, James tells her, "That was so damn hot!"

"You're telling *me?*" Helen fans her blouse and exhales loudly.

Driving straight home, James rubs Helen's breasts and fingers the wet lips of her hot pussy. Helen sighs and grinds her hips to his fingering. He keeps her high and hot until they get home.

They fuck on their sofa. Frantically at first, then in long, penetrating, loving strokes. Helen comes quickly, as usual, bucking against James, pulling the orgasm from him. He gushes in her and lies atop her for long moments.

Then slowly, they start a second round, the way Helen likes her seconds, very softly. He moves his mouth down to her breasts to nibble each pointy nipple, to run his teeth across them, to suck them. He kisses his way down to her navel, rolling his tongue into it, then kisses his way down to her bush and around to the softness of her upper thighs. He can smell the scents of their sex, her pussy juices mixed with his semen. He flicks his tongue across her clit and she shivers and starts grinding her hips again.

"You like that, little girl?" He rubs her clit with his thumb, slipping his middle finger deep inside. She shudders and pumps her hips to his fingering.

"He took pictures of you fingering yourself," he reminds her, and she gasps. He reminds her how yet another man has seen her naked, how she caused yet another stranger's erection to throb in his pants. Then he reminds her of the other spectators and how they gaped at her.

Helen pulls him up and inside and they go for long seconds, her face enraptured in pleasure, James working hard, and it's magnificent.

As always, once she's properly stimulated.

They fuck again, later that evening, after returning from their favorite one-hour developing center. The young man behind the counter grins mischievously as the pictures come out of his developing machine, starting Helen's juices flowing again, causing James's dick to stir and harden.

The following Saturday morning, Helen presses the buzzer below Judge Frederick Newman's apartment.

"Yes?" Newman's voice echoes through the intercom.

"It's Helen."

"Oh! Come on up."

The door buzzes and James pulls it open for his wife, two uniformed New Orleans police officers, a crime scene investigator, and Detective Nelson Dante, a huge man with mahogany skin, a shade darker than the fine tables in the apartment upstairs.

As the column of people moves up the narrow stairs, James watches Helen lead the way in her extra-short, denim minidress, so short the full rear of her pink panties are exposed to the men behind her.

Detective Dante, pulling legal papers from his coat pocket, moves next to Helen as she taps on Newman's door. James can't see Newman's face when he opens it, but watches Dante hold up the legal papers.

"Police! We have a search warrant for this residence." Dante moves straight into the apartment, followed by one of the uniformed officers and the crime scene man. James and Helen go in after them, leaving the second uniformed officer to guard the door.

Dante moves down the hall to the mirror. Newman, standing in a T-shirt and shorts in the doorway of his living room, stares owl-eyed at James as the couple passes. He couldn't look more innocent.

"The button or whatever is on the left side of the mirror," Helen explains as she and James arrives behind Dante. It takes the big detective less than a minute to find the switch and James hears the motor hum as the mirror descends.

Dante lets out a long whistle as the Degas is revealed.

Footsteps behind James turns him around to see a bespectacled man carrying a small silver case approaching. The man's gaze is locked on the portrait. He nods and says, in a thickly Italian accent, "I think so."

Dante waves everyone out of the new arrival's way.

"This man's the curator of the museum in Florence, Italy," Dante tells Newman. "This painting was stolen from there thirty years ago."

Newman doesn't react.

As the curator pulls an electronic magnifying glass from his case, Dante asks James and Helen to accompany him into the living room.

"I'd like to see that warrant," Newman says through gritted teeth.

Dante hands him the legal papers.

"What judge signed this?" Newman flips through the papers.

"You're instructed to remain in the living room," Dante tells Newman. "Officer Jones will stay with you." Stepping back into the hall, Dante adds, "We got an ad-hoc judge to sign the warrant. Barely knew who you were."

Jones, in his crisp N.O.P.D. uniform, grins at Newman and points to the sofa. "Make yourself at home, Your Honor."

Newman's shoulders sink and he steps back and plops on his sofa.

Helen sits in the love seat facing the sofa and crosses her legs. A small triangle of her panties can still be seen and James sees Jones looking. James sits next to his wife.

When Newman turns their way, Helen crosses her legs like a man, knees spread to give the judge an open view.

"What kind of cops are you?" Newman snarls.

"Cops? We're not cops." James shoots the judge a cold smile.

"We're private investigators," Helen adds quickly as she pulls the sides of her miniskirt up to show even more. Jones smiles in appreciation.

James points toward the hall. "The museum hired us. They didn't want to go through N.O.P.D. with you being a supreme court justice and all."

"Good idea," Jones agrees, folding his large arms as he stares between Helen's legs.

"The museum sent in a plumber and an electrician earlier," James explains, "but they couldn't find anything."

Newman closes his eyes and leans back.

"It took us a while to find your weakness," Helen says.

Newman's eyes open.

"Everyone has a weakness." Helen shrugs.

"What weakness?"

James cuts in. "That's where your ex-wife came in. You should never have hidden so many assets from her in your divorce."

Newman is suddenly pale.

Helen uncrosses her legs. "Your wife told us you're a voyeur."

James points to the hall again. "They'll be searching for the Mozart original score you picked up on the black market in Vienna. Your wife was more than helpful."

Newman's face reddens and he growls at Helen, "I still have those pictures of you, little lady."

"Good." Helen raises her right knee and plays with the side of her panties, revealing most of her pubic hair to Newman and the smiling Officer Jones.

"Don't feel so bad," Helen purrs. "We're your perfect foils. I'm an exhibitionist and my husband's a voyeur."

James looks at her with admiration.

They've come a long way since stumbling across each other in Hyde Park on that bright spring morning, the first day of April, 1700, both spotting that fancy-pants pickpocket at the same moment. Catching him red-handed and returning Lord Bristol's gold watch was a thrill, but not as thrilling as looking into Helen's eyes for the first time. She was a governess back then, he a common copper, a constable on patrol.

Over the years, they've had so many adventures, have been able to right so many wrongs graduating from pickpocketed gold watches to tracking down the burglars who lifted Queen Victoria's emerald necklace to recovering the legendary crown of Alexander the Great. And now a long-lost Degas to go along with the van Gogh recovered in Vienna and the Renoir they pilfered from that old lecherous general in Buenos Aires two months ago.

He took in a deep breath. Doing what they do, for as long as they have, hasn't been hard at all. The hard part was finding each other.

Well, James thinks, *it's time we got back to Kashmir to pick up the trail of the lost jewels of Amthor. It'll be so nice seeing them around Helen's neck again.*

Switchblade

Christa Faust

I'll never forget the night I finally hooked the Razor.

It was happy hour at the Hi-Hat Lounge, complete with the usual downwardly mobile clientele. Has-beens and never-beens rubbing elbows with slumming film students and shopworn strippers stopping in for a shot or three before their shift at Jumbo's. And the Razor.

Johnny "the Razor" Reyes. The gloss of his slicked black hair mirrored the gloss of his spit-shined shoes. Lit only by the sultry glow of his unfiltered cigarette, his face was a car crash of harsh angles under acne-scarred skin the color of skim milk. Maybe Asian, maybe Hispanic, roughened by a kind of Caucasian brutality in the profile. His mouth was wry, his eyes dark as 3:00 A.M. He dressed in various shades of shadow, always in a jacket and fastidiously knotted tie, and when he reached for his glass or brought his cigarette to his lips, his cuff would slide back over his thick wrist to reveal cryptic flashes of crude indigo tattoos. He came in at 11:45 every night, sat at the same table (invariably empty even when only moments before it had been filled with clueless trendettes), had the same drink (a single tequila shot), and sat and chain-smoked, never saying a word to anyone. Exactly thirty minutes later he would leave and it was as if the whole joint would let out its breath at once. Most people were glad to see him go. Not me. I guess you can tell that I was in love with him.

You see, my whole life over the past three months had been leading up to that moment in that shitty bar with some kind of oleaginous retro-lounge number oozing from the jukebox and a shot of Jack in my shaking hand for courage. It's hard to believe it was only three months since it felt more like forever. I can't remember the first time I saw him. It seemed he was always there, like the sound of traffic or the moon peeking out between the buildings. It wasn't until that night me and Nanette had stopped in to meet this guy she was trying to set me up with that the Razor became real to me.

She was sitting there with her legs crossed and her little skirt riding up so high I could see her stocking tops and telling me about this guy and what a great master he is and for some reason, my eyes were drawn to that little patch of darker dark, that certain table in the corner, and he was there looking right back at me. He looked casually away and it was almost as if I had imagined it except that my pussy had gone all hot and liquid against the bar stool. Nanette saw me looking and pinched me, pulling me close enough to whisper in my ear.

"You don't want that action."

"Why not?" I asked, still feeling aftershocks in my belly and thighs.

She looked at me as if I'd lost my mind.

"That's Johnny the Razor," she said as if that explained everything.

"Who?"

"Listen." She grabbed my chin as I tried to look back at him again. "Don't look, just listen."

Her voice dropped even lower, barely audible above the jukebox and the chatter.

"He's a collector for a local shark. Been in and out of jail. They say he's a real hard case. Sleeps with a straight razor." She licked her lips. "They say he cuts girls. Not play cuts . . . hospital cuts."

I could feel her breath on my ear and shivered. *They say he cuts girls.* The scars across my thighs and breasts started pulsing in time to the miniature heartbeat between my legs. That's when I knew I had to have him.

I excused myself and in the dim stench of the toilet I couldn't seem to shove enough fingers into my pussy. I was starving for him, for the burning intimacy of blade and flesh and the dark electricity of his gaze. It was as if every lurid fantasy, every adolescent hunger that consumed me as I flirted with kitchen knives and stolen Exacto blades had coalesced into this one man. As if every frenzied, stolen afternoon of exquisite pain running over my skin like quicksilver and fear of discovery like gasoline on the fire were all some elaborate spell to conjure up this demon, this angel.

My night with Nanette's friend was a resounding failure. His name was Shane and he was nice enough, if a little Renfair-ish around the edges, but as I lay trussed and splayed in his hinky little dungeon I couldn't get Johnny the Razor out of my mind. Shane had agreed to use my scalpel, but his hands shook and his cuts were as tentative as a reluctant suicide. The itchy, superficial pain was nothing but fuel for my burning frustration. I let him fuck me anyway, just to be done with it, and in the gray dawn outside my apartment I pressed my cheek to the building's cool brick skin and swore the next man that touched me would be the Razor.

I had rehearsed a thousand times but I felt as if my heart would rupture in my chest each time he raised his cigarette to his lips. When the song ended and something slow and smoky came on to replace it, I downed my shot and made my way to his table.

He looked up at me as soon as I stood, the gravity of that hot black gaze making each step like falling, inevitable. Around me, everyone averted their eyes like death-row prisoners turning away as one of the damned took the long and final walk. When I was close enough to touch him, I stopped, awkward and silent, teeth sinking into the inside of my cheek until the words spilled out like blood.

"Is it true?" I asked, heady taste of pennies on my tongue.

He took a last drag from the nub of his cigarette and crushed it into the tin ashtray beside his empty shot glass.

"Don't ask what you already know," he said.

He stood then, so close to me that I could feel his breath on my lips. His gaze laid me open like a knife sliding between the shells of an oyster, twisting. My heart clenched, veins racing with adrenaline, and I squeezed my eyes shut, unable to withstand the tension for a second longer. I was sure he was going to do something, kiss me, bite me, slit my throat, but when I was able to open my eyes again he was gone.

Crushing humiliation drenched me like cold pig's blood. I could feel my cheeks burning as I took a shaky step forward and collapsed into his chair. For a long minute I could do nothing but rest my forehead against the table and wish a trapdoor would open in the beer-sticky floor and swallow me up. Eventually I turned my head to see his empty shot glass inches from my nose. I reached out and tilted it toward me, tongue against the cold rim, questing for the flavor of his mouth beneath the ghost of tequila. When I set the glass back up again, I saw that I had left behind a pinkish film of blood and spit.

In full stalker mode now, I waited for him in my shitty Cutlass parked across the street from the Hi-Hat. Inside that stuffy prison I found my fingers creeping like independent creatures under the elastic of my panties. My scalpel was burning a hole in my pocket, but I wanted to save myself for him. It had been nearly two whole months since I'd cut myself.

When he appeared from around the corner, I nearly gasped out loud, heart triple-timing in my chest. He slid inside the bar and I got ready for the longest thirty minutes of my life.

Seconds ticked by with infuriating nonchalance. The radio spewed some kind of impotent white-boy rap full of suburban angst and bleeped-out cusswords. The dark doorway gaped, taking on sinister, Lovecraftian proportions, and every time it opened to spit out a staggering slacker or stripper or a million other useless, faceless extras my gut would twist and my nails would dig deeper crescents into the burgundy Naugahyde cover on the steering wheel. And when my heart finally slowed to under a thousand beats a second I swore I was gonna give up, go home, stop this crazy shit, and I was just about to when there he was and I hadn't even seen the door open.

He stood there on the sidewalk with a cigarette burning between his thumb and forefinger looking up at the dark gray sky like a man checking for rain. His sharp black gaze scanned the empty block and swept over me with only the slightest pause. He brought the cigarette to his lips again and I swear I saw a curl of humor there in the corner of his mouth. Then he threw the butt to the ground and strolled away at an almost mockingly slow and leisurely pace.

I scrambled gracelessly out of the car, keys jittering noisily in my numb fingers, waiting for a ponderous SUV to slide by before crossing the street and setting off after him.

He walked for what seemed like miles and miles, much farther than any self-respecting Angeleno ever would. My legs ached and I huffed like a Pekingese but refused to give up following him turn after seemingly arbitrary turn, deeper and deeper into a dark and upscale residential neighborhood I'd never even driven through before. Finally he paused in front of a sprawling, Spanish-style home with his back to me, scenting the wind like an animal. I held my breath and tried to will myself to shrink and melt into the leafy shadows. When I looked again he was on the porch and the door was opening just a crack, just enough to slice his face in half with a bright knife of light. What happened next was almost too fast to register. Like a trapdoor spider in reverse he had slammed the door wide, grabbed the person on the other side, and shut it behind him, disappearing as if he had never been.

I waited several minutes in a state of weirdly dead and heavy near-paralysis, one hand pressed too hard against the rough bark of a palm tree. I was sure that he knew I had followed him, that he was leading me, reeling me in as surely as if there had been a barbed hook through my cheek. He could have seen me a hundred times but he chose not to, showing me his narrow back the entire way. Now something bad was going down inside that quiet, tasteful house and I couldn't walk away, I couldn't. Instead I found myself creeping up to the porch, slipping around to the side where a low, half-open window tempted me with the promise of some kind of answer.

Inside I saw high-tech toys and expensive bachelor furniture, all trendy angles and leather. Framed monster movie one-sheets and hundred-dollar comic books, details that spoke of too much money and no feminine interference. There was a pale and terrified guy in flawless *GQ* casual sitting in, scratch that, duct-taped to a chunky high-end leather desk chair. I couldn't see the Razor but the guy obviously could because he was blubbering a mile a minute about some advance that was virtually guaranteed by the end of the week, no later, it was just a matter of lawyers at this point but before the end of the month for sure.

Then I saw the Razor too. He stepped into my window's movie screen with his head tilted slightly like he was really listening to what the guy was saying, genuinely considering the possibility of returning some other time, next week or the end of the month for sure, when his hands flashed out one and then the other with blinding Jackie Chan speed. The guy *mmphed* loudly behind the duct tape that now covered his mouth. As I watched, wide red replacement mouths opened across each cheek. When he realized he'd been cut, the guy started to go completely ape shit, wrenching himself as hard as he could back and forth in the inch of space his bonds allowed him, snot bubbling from his nose and mingling with blood across the dull silver tape stifling his howls. I was so entranced by this spectacle that I lost sight of the Razor for a moment and it wasn't until I saw the guy go still, his eyes suddenly Animé-huge, that I thought to look again. When I followed his gaze back to the source I saw something that made me go all molten inside, full of some kind of mad ecstatic fear and desire and a million other nameless things. The Razor was undressing, blood-dappled blade still held delicately in one hand.

Peeling his clothing away he slowly revealed pale flesh, like the flesh of the moon exposed by a waning eclipse. His body was weirdly proportioned, tattooed arms too long, shoulders too narrow, torso lanky and curiously muscled. He seemed to have far too many ribs. His flesh was hairless, clean-shaven around his uncircumcised cock. The deep V of his hipbones seemed as elongated and dangerous as the jaw of a crocodile. I felt as if I would asphyxiate beneath the weight of my desire for him.

I could not take my eyes off him as he moved forward like a cautious spider, razor switching from hand to hand. The guy in the chair seemed mesmerized, short-circuited, unable to do anything but stare like a rabbit in the shadow of the raptor's claws. The Razor leaned in and whispered to him, caressing the guy's bleeding cheek with the back of his knuckles, the gleaming blade inches from his wide glassy eye. Whatever he had said to the guy had set him off again, thrashing and crying, and the Razor did nothing, just watched him flail with the mild interest of a shopper perusing some holiday display in a department store window. He touched the blade to the guy's lips and his whole body tensed up, face screwed up like a child waiting for an injection. This tableau held for a few moments and the guy opened one eye, body held rigid for a handful more seconds, until he let out his breath in a thick whoosh through his gummed-up nostrils. Before he could suck in another breath to start his muffled pleading again, the Razor cut his throat.

The guy arched his back so violently that he finally managed to knock the chair over backward, painting the expensive posters and the ceiling and the Razor's white flesh with bright, arterial spray. My breath caught and I found myself thinking of a time when I had gone in too deep at one end of a long cut and inadvertently struck an artery in my thigh, just a tiny bit, but the force from the hypodermic-thin stream of blood had been enough to spatter the mirror nearly six feet away. It was then that I had learned to sink my own sutures. For years after that, I still found myself fingering the luscious veins in my arms, my legs, my neck, and thinking about that day.

The Razor stood, transfixed as I was, watching as the panic in the guy's huge eyes started to dull, death filling them like frost obscuring the view through a window.

Then the Razor was gone.

It seemed impossible to move, impossible to take my eyes from the blood, so much blood puddled and coagulating into a nauseating moldy-jam texture on the hardwood floor. I could hear the creak-thump of a cantankerous shower turning on somewhere in the house. I wanted to go, to get away and never look back, but I just couldn't seem to make my body obey my screaming brain. My gaze returned again and again to the gaping wound beneath the dead man's tipped-back chin. The lips of the cut were lush with still-slick blood, seductive and inviting as an open pussy. I felt an overwhelming urge to slip inside and kneel beside him, to run the ball of my thumb along the wet length of that lurid gash. Or my tongue.

After an eternity I was finally able to turn my head and bunch my muscles up in preparation for the backward step that would take me out of the flower bed and away from this insanity, but instead I backed directly into the Razor. I hadn't even heard the shower turn off but here he was, suit sleek and unrumpled as always as if he had only just stepped out of the bar.

But his palms and the hair at the nape of his neck were still slightly damp and there was a rich citrusy smell of overpriced shampoo and exotic soap laid over the more profound scent of him, the ghost of cigarettes and salt and a strangely meaty smell spiced with something like smashed metal and fresh white paper. There was only the tiniest flecks of dark dried blood around his mouth and in the crow's-feet at the edges of his black black eyes.

"What do you want, hungry girl?" he asked and his voice was barely more than a breath but it seemed plane-crash loud inside my whirling head. The blade was out now and pressed beneath my ear, clean like him but like him still vibrant with the memory of blood. I was afraid that if he pressed even the slightest bit harder I would explode, shatter, erupt, or simply die.

"I want . . . I want . . ." I managed to gasp.

"I want you to give me one good reason not to kill you."

I could not speak. He didn't seem particularly angry and there was still a kind of subtle humor around his eyes, but I didn't doubt for a second that he would kill me in a heartbeat without the slightest thought. I bit deeply into my lower lip as he grabbed the front of my cheap man's shirt. One of the buttons popped loose and clicked to the poured-concrete path with a noise as huge and terrifying as the sound of a cocked hammer of a gun inches from your face. The night air slipped down the open front of my shirt and teased my sweaty skin, hardening my nipples and rippling my flesh with goose bumps. The Razor's gaze flicked down into the deep V of skin exposed by the traitorous button, and he blinked, eyebrows bunched together, lips slightly parted. He paused, looked up to my face and down again, and then tore my shirt the rest of the way open. I flinched and held my breath for a handful of heartbeats, but he did nothing, only stared and stared until I realized it was not my unremarkable tits he was looking at. It was my scars.

I've lived with them so long, watching them grow and twist like kudzu across my skin, an endlessly infected work in progress that was as much a part of me as the blue of my eyes or the boyish angles of my awkward body. But in that moment I saw them with fresh eyes, his eyes, and there was this eternity where I waited for the inevitable disgust, condemnation, and pity. If *he* thought they were ugly, if he turned away from me with the old hurtful words on his lips, words like *freak* and *crazy bitch*, I knew that I would wither and crumble into the well-kept flower bed like the crushed husk of a long-dead insect.

He didn't. He didn't take me in his arms and kiss me and tell me I was beautiful either. He just looked at me for a very long time, gaze flitting from my scars to my face and back again. He ran a callused fingertip along a particularly thick one that snaked down the left side of my belly and under the waistband of my Dickies. I shivered, almost nauseated with desire. Then he did something so unexpected that I could do nothing but stand there stupidly like some understudy with no time to rehearse.

"You drive," he said.

He pulled a single car key on a chunky plastic tag from his pocket and tossed it to me. It bounced off my naked sternum and fell into the lavender. I dropped to my knees, scrambling to retrieve it while he turned and walked away as if he did not care if I followed or not.

Of course I followed.

He led me to an unremarkable compact car parked across the street and stood by the passenger door, shaking a cigarette from a soft pack of some brand I'd never heard of and sliding it between his lips. He lit up while I fumbled with the key.

Inside the car was clean and devoid of personal touches. It smelled like industrial disinfectant. I sat behind the wheel and stared hopelessly at the unfamiliar controls until the Razor tapped impatiently on the window. I started a little and then stretched ungracefully across the seat to flick the lock for him. My baroque fantasies of seducing my demon lover had never included anything this . . . *ordinary.*

When he was in, seat belt fastened and cigarette held out the rolled-down window for my benefit, I suppose, I finally spoke.

"Where are we going?" I asked.

"Left," he said, taking a drag from his cigarette and exhaling through the side of his mouth, toward the window. "There at the end of this street."

So I drove. He gave directions in a lazy near-whisper, left, right, turn here, at the light up ahead, and smoked one cigarette after another. I felt a weird kind of electric numbness settle over me, kind of like what I imagine soldiers must feel when the first skirmish is over and they wait to see what will happen next, waiting and waiting with a strange jittery boredom that could be shattered at any moment by gunfire.

He directed me to turn into the gate of some kind of planned community with a ridiculous name like Sunswept Estates or Tanglewood Terrace. He produced a key card from a sealed white envelope and pressed it into my sweating hand. I used it to open the ponderous white gate and pulled inside.

Every house along the too-wide and too-perfect streets was identical and soulless, as devoid of personality as the car. The only variation was in the pale sherbet shades of paint and the number of cars that could be housed in the garages. It looked like an artificial environment for humans created by aliens who had seen human dwellings on TV.

"Here," he said as we pulled up to a peach house halfway down a street named after a tree. He popped the glove box and used a garage door opener he found inside to let us in to an empty two-car garage.

I twisted the key, cutting the ignition, and sat like a lump of clay staring at the wall in front of me. The engine ticked quietly and the Razor ground his latest cigarette into the ashtray and pushed the door open, unfolding his lanky body as the garage door ratcheted shut behind us. My shirt was still open. My heart suddenly started beating too fast again, jolting my sluggish body into action. I pocketed the key and climbed out, breathless.

"C'mon," he said and I trailed him into the house, following him as if I had been doing it my entire life.

There was no furniture. The thickly carpeted rooms seemed to swallow all sound. He led me up some padded stairs and down a dim hallway to a room with floor-to-ceiling vertical blinds at one end and pale pink walls and nothing else.

He turned to me and said, "Now, show me." He cocked his head like he had when he was listening to that guy, that *dead* guy, begging for more time. "Show me everything."

I undressed, heart still kicking like a caught frog in my chest.

Again I felt time folding in on itself while I stood, dying inside and waiting to see what was going to come next. Then his arm was snaking around my waist and he bent to put his mouth to my left breast, reptile-cool tongue sliding, not over my nipple, but around the curving knot of scar beneath, and I swear that was the singlemost erotic act I have ever experienced. I could no longer stand and he lowered me to the ugly, brand-new carpet, his long bony thigh pressing between my legs. His smell was stronger now, aggressively asserting itself through the polite veneer of the rich guy's grooming products, like the shape of his stiffening cock through the expensive fabric of his trousers. He took his mouth from my scars and looked into my face, eyes unreadable. I started to shiver uncontrollably.

He produced the blade again from an inner pocket and flicked it open an inch from my lips. The shivering stopped and I felt suddenly intensely focused. I looked up into the shadowed pits of his eyes and kissed the blade.

The sensation as I slid the vulnerable meat of my lower lip across the razor's edge was vicious and exquisite. There was no blood yet, just a sweet taste of rawness and metal, and I did not pull away, allowing the blade to rest in its intimacy with my flesh for a heartbeat, then two and three. His breath quickened and he slid the blade deeper into my lip for a fragment of a second, then out.

Now there was blood and he was kissing me, agony and unbearable desire sizzling through me as he took my wounded lower lip between his teeth. His chilly tongue was warming now against mine. The familiar taste of my own blood and the curious unnatural flavor of his mouth melded together in the alchemical furnace of our kiss to form some brutal aphrodisiac so powerful I could barely breathe. My pussy was as hot and wet as an open wound.

He broke the kiss then but his eyes remained closed for an endless second. When he opened them, they were filled with hunger. He sat up, straddling me, and put his long spidery hand palm down in the center of my chest. With the other hand he brought the blade down until it rested, barely touching, against my right breast.

My lip throbbed in time with my heart and the pulse between my legs. The spot where the blade lay against me seemed hypersensitive, an unremarkable inch of skin a handsbreadth beneath my collarbone suddenly transformed into the focal point of every nerve in my body. I have never wanted anything in my life as badly as I wanted that first cut.

Teasing, he flicked the blade over my skin in tight little C shapes, barely penetrating the first layer of my skin. The spiky little jolts of pain had me gasping with frustration and he smiled in the dark, teeth too white between lips still smeared with my blood. Just when I felt I would fly into a thousand jagged pieces he really cut me, a deep curving spiral around my breast. The pain was like a slowly acceding note swelling in volume as the pitch slid higher and higher until it reached an ecstatic crescendo as the blade neatly bifurcated my aching nipple. I felt as if I were screaming but I couldn't seem to hear any sound but his low and rapid breath. But when he followed the blade with his tongue, probing deep inside the fresh cut, spreading it open, I finally did scream, only for a second before his long, nicotine-stinking fingers wrapped around my face, reducing my scream to a comical squeak. He took my nipple into his mouth and I howled against his palm. The pain was huge now, completely obliterating everything.

Then he stopped.

It took me a second to realize what had happened. The pain was so bright, glittering through my body, that I couldn't see. The bed carpet was soaked with blood beneath me. I shook my head and forced my eyes to focus on his dark shape. Something was happening, *eclipse,* my mind whispered, and I understood then that he was undressing. I thought at that point that he was going to kill me after all and found that I wasn't the least bit un-happy or frightened. Only . . . hungry. Every vein in my body seemed erect, pulsing with desire. But again he did something that took me completely by surprise. Something so unexpected that for a moment I was utterly incapable of comprehending what was happening at all.

Naked he knelt beside me, holding the blade out to me.

"Now you," he said.

"Umm . . ." I swallowed, stupid with lust and the scent of my own blood. "You mean? . . ."

"You know what I mean," he said, pressing the hot handle of the razor into my shaking hand, his eyes so full of heat, all pre-tence of nonchalance obliterated by desire.

Holding his razor in my hand, I once again felt that strange sense of sudden crystalline focus and I realized how badly I wanted this. I had never in my entire love affair with cutting even considered the possibility of cutting someone else, and yet here was this incredible, unfathomable man offering his flesh, his blood to me. More than anything it was his desire, the aching hunger that mirrored my own, that drove me to that first exquisite cut.

I brought the blade down against his long thigh and pushed him back till he was prone on the sodden carpet. The blade slid into his flesh with such delicious ease, opening a deep diagonal gash across his taut white skin. I pressed my hungry lips to the warm lips of the wound, ravenous for the taste of him, and he gasped, hips twitching. I had never tasted any blood but my own and the rich, unmistakable *otherness* of it made me nauseated with desire. His hard cock was inches from my face and I gripped it in my blood-sticky fist, drawing a low stifled sound out of him as I slid back the foreskin and pressed the warm blade to the tender spot where it joined to the exposed head. I made a quick series of tiny slits along that meaty connection and his body shuddered, a transparent tear of pre-cum oozing out to mingle with the trickle of blood running down the underside of his cock and between my fingers.

That sharp sense of hyperawareness made every tiny detail seem momentous as I made neat quarter-inch cuts around the crown of his cock head until it seemed jeweled with shivering garnets and I couldn't help but take it into my mouth, savoring the raw coppery flavor before sucking the length of it deep into my throat.

He pulled back and then thrust in again and a third time before grunting between his teeth and pulling me off, rolling me onto my back, and in an instant he was inside me, fucking me, hungry mouth sucking my split lip until it bled again, and I felt blood trickling down my neck, my thighs, between my breasts, and the smell and taste of it smothered the world, destroying everything. Pain ensnared me like barbed wire, coiling around me, inescapable and unrelenting. The sharp angle of his pubic bone ground into my swollen clit with every thrust and I felt the hooks of orgasm sinking into me, drawing me down inexorably into ecstatic oblivion. It hit me and I bit down on the mingled meat of our lips and tongues, no longer capable of distinguishing his flesh from my flesh, his blood from my blood. As a second, stronger wave drenched me in viscous sensation, he pulled out and my aborted whimper of disappointment turned to a half-swallowed gasp as he slid his blood-slick cock into my ass. He took my split nipple into his mouth and the idling pain there screamed into bright and brutal life, flash-fusing to the razor-edge pleasure suffusing my tortured flesh, and I came again and again until I could no longer distinguish peaks from valleys, pain from pleasure. My body became music, howling through the hollow rooms of this empty house in a single endless note as the core of who I thought I was melted away to exquisite nothingness. I felt his cock clench inside me and he came shuddering, teeth sinking into the flesh of my shoulder, and a jagged sound ripped loose from me that felt like the end of the world.

I have no idea how long I lay there, blood pooling around me on the scratchy carpet and the soft trickle of his nicotine-scented breath warming the hollow of my throat while his cock softened inside me. I only know that eventually he pulled out in a hot gush of blood and semen and took me in his arms, helping me to my feet and into the adjoining bathroom where I sat dazed on the furry pink toilet seat lid while he ran hot water in the pristine bathtub. He lifted me into the tub and washed me with such gentle tenderness that I continuously drifted into near-sleep until his soapy fingers would slide over a fresh cut and the sharp zing of pain would snap me back into awareness. Finally he lifted me, wrapped in a thick flowered towel, and carried me down the stairs into some other part of the house where a bare mattress wrapped in plastic leaned against one freshly painted wall. Pulling a cartoony red and blue comforter from a plastic shopping bag, he laid me down and wrapped the blanket around me, sliding in beside me. I think he put his arms around me because I remember leaning my head against the scant meat of his chest, but then I was asleep, the sound of his breath chasing me into my dreams.

I was totally unsurprised to wake up alone. I had harbored no illusions of happily ever after, and in the weak morning light I sat up and rubbed my sticky eyes, wincing as my skin stretched and the delicate new scab would not. I hadn't even begun to think of him or whether or not I would ever see him again when my groggy fingers brushed something hard and cold in the bed beside me. A box, unmarked and constructed of plain, unstained wood. I poked it, studying it with knitted eyebrows. Nothing to do but open it.

Was I surprised by what I found? Not really. I knew the Razor would change my life but I didn't know how profound, how fundamental that epiphany would be.

In the box was a white envelope. The envelope contained a sheet of paper with a typewritten name and address, a photo of a squirrelly young man with red hair and small, suspicious eyes behind expensive glasses, and a pair of keys, one a house key and one a rental car key. It also contained a smaller envelope full of hundred-dollar bills. But all these things were just garnish for the other object in the box, the *true* object of my desire. The razor itself. I removed it and opened it with one hand. I swore I could still smell his blood in the hinge of the blade. It felt warm in my hand. I knew then that I would never see my demon lover again, if he had ever really existed in the first place. I brought the blade to my lips and closed my eyes, knowing it didn't matter anyway because me and the razor were going to live happily ever after after all.

Night of the Giving Head

Jeff Gelb

Night twenty-seven

"Let me in," she begged through the locked door of his apartment. "Let me in and I'll fuck you till you're raw."

That was Onika, Craig Stafford thought. The beautiful Onika, his apartment neighbor and, until less than a week ago, his confidant and lifeline.

"Don't listen to her!" And that was Sherri. "Let me in and I'll let you watch me fuck my snake!"

Sherri, Craig sighed. She lived three floors down in the San Diego apartment building. He'd first met her in the elevator, and then at local punk clubs, where she'd smiled at him as they danced, the silver stud piercing her tongue gleaming in the neon lights. He'd never had the chance to see where else she'd been pierced but he had his ideas.

"Screw those bitches," snarled a third female voice from outside his bolted door. Craig didn't have to gaze through the peephole to recognize the raspy-throated voice of Amanda, who didn't actually live in the building, but was visiting her brother, who was just down the hall from Craig. Amanda was small-breasted but had a J-Lo bubble butt to die for. "I've seen you staring at my ass, Craig. Let me in and you can fuck it, you can ram it in until I scream for mercy!"

Craig sighed and rested his head against the door as the scratching and pounding started, just as it had every night for nearly the past week. Finally he dared to look through the peephole and shuddered as he saw the distorted images of three beautiful women he would have been thrilled to have sex with just weeks earlier. Now, he wouldn't touch them if his life depended on it. Which it did.

Day one

Craig was exhausted as he rode the crowded bus to his stop. Another day behind the counter at Bookstop, San Diego's largest independent bookstore, another day of stupid customers with their stupid complaints. But at least it'd been a slower-than-usual day, now that the Christmas season was over. It had given him time to read a wild article in the free local entertainment newspaper about a new drug that was all the rage in Tijuana and now, spreading north to San Diego and elsewhere in the state. No one knew where it had been brewed originally; some suggested it was a government experiment in mind control, but it had quickly crossed the border and made the rounds of the California raves, after-hours clubs, and discos. Someone had dubbed it Free Love, because it made everyone horny as hell and took away any conscience he or she might have possessed. The drug had already ruined relationships and marriages, and was well on its way to creating a mass epidemic of abuse in less than a week. Craig shook his head and laughed as an attractive young woman approached his register. He nodded toward the paper. "Have you read this?" he asked as he totaled her order. "Unbelievable!"

She smiled and, with a lascivious wink, said, "Believe this!" Right there, in front of the whole store and Craig, she raised her blouse to show off her perky breasts and erect nipples. She handed him two bills, some change, and a small yellow pill. He looked at her quizzically. "From the very first batch," she said with obvious pride. "Take it and meet me behind the store on your break."

He managed to gasp, "But that's not for another hour. . . ."

"I'll wait." She laughed as she exited the store.

He examined the pill as if it could tell him something. But it had no marks or imprints—it was just an anonymous tiny disc. He shrugged. What the hell? He'd taken his share of drugs in his time, and he downed the pill with some soda. He found to his astonishment that he was so horny in twenty minutes that he took his break early, found the attractive customer awaiting him as promised in the dirty back alley, and fucked her standing up against the store's smelly garbage bins. Afterward he'd tried to apologize, but she'd just laughed. As she pulled up her tight jeans, he could see his juices still running down her leg. In an instant she'd rounded a corner and he could hear her laughter blowing by him in the breeze. What the fuck had come over him? he thought. He'd never done anything like that in his life—and without any protection, no less. Hadn't even thought of it! Ever since he'd taken the Free Love pill, all he could think about was getting off. Normally he'd never have the guts to attempt to entice a customer into sex, let alone in public! But with Free Love coursing through his veins, he couldn't have stopped himself from fucking that customer if a cop, a priest, and his mother had been watching. What the fuck! What a drug!

But he was scared. Free Love had played hell with his mind the rest of that day. Not only was Craig not normally so cavalier sexually, he wasn't even comfortable asking a girl to kiss him at the end of a date. Now, with the drug still sending palpable pulses through his veins, he wasn't sure who he was sexually anymore. At the store the rest of that day, he'd had an impossible time concentrating. Instead, he was eyeballing every customer, from youngest to oldest, male to female, as potential sex partners. He'd left work early, closing his eyes on the bus ride so he wouldn't ogle the people sitting next to him, and rushed back to his apartment. Now he was fantasizing about the perfect stranger he'd fucked, the guy on the elevator in his building, and he was beginning to look at his cat funny. He beat off till he reached a wild orgasm, took a long hot shower, beat off again, and finally collapsed on his bed and fell into a sleep full of shockingly erotic dreams.

Night twenty-eight

Craig woke up to a pounding in his head. As he shook off sleep, he realized it was just the nightly knocking at his door. He looked at the clock. It was 11:00 P.M. Of course. They always came by around 11:00 P.M. The scientists had found something in Free Love that was time-released, and one of the times it hit hardest was just before midnight. No one knew for certain why. Maybe the bastards who'd designed it had thought people's inhibitions were already loose at that time of night, from booze, other drugs, or just exhaustion from their long days of work. Craig sighed, got out of bed, and walked to the door.

"Quit your banging, Onika," he yelled through the bolted door without even gazing through the peephole. It was always Onika first, damn her! Then Sherri. Then . . .

"Onika's dead," came the voice from the other side of the door. Craig blinked and looked through the peephole. It was Sherri, her mouth covered in blood.

"Oh, Lord," Craig moaned, his stomach doing somersaults. He retreated from the door, ran to the kitchen, and threw up in the sink. When he was done, he ran the disposal, and grabbed the longest cutting knife he owned.

"I fucked her," Sherri shouted through the door. "Fucked her and killed her while she was coming. And, Craig?" She paused for effect. "She loved it!"

Craig put his hands to his ears. "Get lost, Sherri."

"And after she was dead, I cut her up and fed her to Big Tom." Big Tom was her boa constrictor, whose cage, she'd once told him, took up her entire living room.

"Aw, c'mon, Craig. Be a sport. You're the only one left in the whole building who isn't . . . like me. Maybe in the whole city. I need you, Craig!"

He still felt queasy. Onika was dead. He blew a long breath out of his mouth. "Where's Amanda?"

"I killed her, too," came the breathy response.

"Oh, shit," Craig whispered, and stuffed cotton in his ears so he wouldn't hear her incessant taunts and pounding. He took two sleeping pills and finally fell into a restless sleep. In his dreams, he saw Onika's head being engulfed by the boa's huge maw. His own screams awakened him.

Day two

Craig woke up feeling almost normal again, and was relieved to find that, on his bus ride, he wasn't abnormally attracted to the overweight driver or any of the occupants seated around him. At work, he listened to the radio as he totaled orders, still avoiding direct eye contact with anyone even remotely attractive, female or male. The news on all the stations was all about Free Love, and how it was the biggest thing since LSD. The newscasters said its reputation was spreading beyond California at the speed of light. In fact, a near-panicking Congress was going to vote later that day about making it illegal.

"You tried it yet?" the young man in front of his register whispered to him as he caught the newscast and tried to hand Craig the now-familiar yellow pill. Craig pulled his hand away and the pill dropped on the counter. The young man quickly picked it up and popped it in his mouth. "I'm on my third dose today," he confided in Craig. "God, I wanna fuck!" His shout made Craig blink, and customers throughout the store looked up from their books and magazines. Some scowled but most smiled, and three people, two men and one woman, came up to the customer and took his hands, all but dragging him out the door to some sexual tryst, Craig imagined. What the *fuck* was really going on here?

Day seven

The news reports were now on all the TV channels as well. Government officials were postulating that Free Love was actually a product of overseas terrorist cells intent on quite literally fucking civilization. Craig thought it was as reasonable an explanation as any he'd heard. The government had ruled Free Love illegal and its ownership a federal offense, but that hadn't stopped the rush of customers across the country from somehow finding it. Now people were afraid to step out of their houses for fear of being propositioned or, worse, finding themselves incapable of saying no.

Just that morning, while shopping, Craig had been propositioned none too secretly by the grocery store checker and bag boy, and when he'd reported them to a cop in the parking lot, the cop had winked and asked Craig if he wanted in on a four-way. Craig had run for his bus stop and luckily the cop had not followed. On the bus, an innocent-looking Hispanic couple had offered him their sweet-looking daughter, seated one row ahead of them. Craig had taken an early stop and run the rest of the way back to his apartment.

Day sixteen

He decided not to go to work anymore. Hell, barely anyone was still working. The President had declared a national state of emergency, a sunset curfew, and the National Guard was patrolling the streets. But that was about as effective as an umbrella in a hurricane, since most of the Guard had also fallen prey to Free Love, deserting their posts faster than they could be replaced.

Craig only ventured out of his apartment to buy essentials, and each trip outside had become more dangerous. Roving bands of Free Love addicts had taken to kidnapping fresh victims, popping pills in their mouths, and then just waiting fifteen minutes until they became willing participants in mad orgies.

Craig was carrying a bag of groceries into the elevator when Onika had approached him. He had taken to carrying a baseball bat for protection, and when he saw Onika, he raised it for a moment. "Don't even think about it. . . ."

"Relax," she said, touching his arm. "I'm still . . . normal."

"Wow, thank heavens," he said as the elevator rose to their floor. "How'd you escape?"

"I stopped going to work a week ago," she said. "Isn't it all just terrible?"

"Well, I guess if you love sex . . ." he offered weakly, immediately regretting it as she backed into a corner of the elevator. "Hey, don't misunderstand. I'm not one of them either."

She relaxed a bit as the elevator doors opened. They both peered down the corridor and he raised his baseball bat, but no one was in sight. They ran to his apartment, which was two doors down from the elevator. He quickly unlocked his door. "You . . . want to come in and—just talk?"

She hesitated. He handed her the bat. "Here," he said. "Clobber me if I make a move." She laughed and followed him inside.

He put away his groceries as she looked around his studio apartment, which was impeccably clean. "You sure you're a guy?" she teased. They both laughed and it helped to break the tension. "Tea or coffee?" he asked.

She shook her head. "I can't stay long. It's gonna be dark

soon." She sat on his well-worn couch and he sat at the opposite end. "Isn't it awful?" she moaned. "I think it's the end of the world."

He nodded. "I wish I could disagree. But it's impossible to go anywhere, do anything."

She leaned toward him and he couldn't help but notice her inviting cleavage through her V-necked T-shirt. But this was definitely not the time for those sorts of thoughts. "It's so good to talk with someone," she enthused. "I called my folks in up-state New York and they say it's even worse up there. I mean, people are hunting in mobs and killing each other when they find a . . . 'Virgin.'"

Craig nodded. He'd heard the term used for someone who'd not been infected by the Free Love virus. He didn't want to admit that he was not a Virgin himself.

He still wondered why he hadn't become addicted to Free Love. He remembered the customer proudly proclaiming it as a "first batch." Craig could only assume that it was a faulty batch, made before the addictive nature of the drug had been purified or upgraded or whatever they called it. He asked Onika, "Have you thought of moving out? Maybe to the mountains or some-place?"

She nodded. "Sure. But you know—the chances of getting out of the city safe . . ." She trailed off, not having to complete the sentence. They'd both seen the reports on TV about the armed groups of sex maniacs who were overpowering the Na-tional Guard and other troops who were attempting ineffectu-ally to protect the populace.

"And besides," he said, "where would we go? Now they say this Free Love thing is all over the world. It's spread faster than anyone thought possible." He shook his head in resignation.

"It all seems so hopeless," she said, looking into his eyes. "Why haven't you just . . . you know, given in?"

He shook his head. "I don't really know. I mean, at first it was certainly . . . inviting." He blushed as he said it, but figured there was no longer any sense in playing games with anyone. "But it all got out of control so quickly . . . Still, sometimes it seems like it might just be easier to give in, as you say."

She was quiet for a moment, as if something had changed between them. Then she rose to her feet and moved toward the door. "I . . . I'd better get back to my place. Thanks for talking."

He unlocked the door so she could leave. He wanted her to stay; he craved companionship and he'd always found her sexy. But this was just not the time to push. And besides, he didn't even know how. "I . . . hope we can talk again," he managed.

"We will," she promised and touched his cheek for a moment before leaving. He watched as she ran down the hall to her apartment, and then she waved at him, smiling as she unlocked her door and went in. He rubbed the spot she'd touched on his cheek as he reset the bolts on his door.

Day twenty

Craig turned on the TV. There wasn't really anything else to do. Daily, there were fewer channels available, but he'd found one newscaster he found attractive, and fortunately, her station was still on the air.

"Jane Adler for Channel Five News," she said breathlessly. "The government is now reporting that the Free Love drug mutates in a deadly way in its users' bloodstreams. In twenty to thirty days, its presence encourages users to kill without mercy or reason."

Craig gasped at this new, astonishing turn of events. *As if things weren't bad enough already.* Jane Adler brushed her well-coiffed bangs away from her eyes as she regarded the camera. "There seems to be no hope that this drug can be stopped."

Day twenty-two

As he did each day now, he awakened with his heart thumping madly, victimized by some half-forgotten nightmare. He got up groggily, wishing the real world were just one of those nightmares he could awaken from as easily. He turned on the TV to the sight of Jane Adler, her blouse torn, a sheer pink bra showing. She didn't seem to care as she gasped, "Someone please help me! I've locked myself in the studio but they're using fire axes. I don't know how much longer I've got. Please, if you can hear me, and if you're still a Virgin, please come to the studio and save me!"

Before he could even consider leaving his apartment—though what he could do to help he had no idea—Craig's attention was riveted to the screen as he saw the panicked newscaster glance away from the camera, and a loud crash could be heard offscreen. He watched as she was pulled out of view by both male and female hands. He turned off the TV so he wouldn't be haunted by her screams all day.

Night twenty-three

Craig's phone rang. He ran to pick it up. Phone service had been intermittent these past few days. What was left of the media had reported that it was impossible to get anyone to repair anything anymore, and that no one should expect to have any phone service in the next few days. Electrical power was sure to be the next to go. "Hello?"

"Craig?"

"Onika! Are you okay?"

"I'm . . . I'm fine, but I'm lonely and . . . I'm scared, Craig. I can't get any TV reception anymore, and I don't even own a radio. What's going on . . . out there?"

Craig took the phone to his windowsill. It was pitch-dark

out, the streetlights having failed two nights ago. It was impossible to tell what was going on outside anymore, but occasionally, if he kept his window open, he could hear screams—or were they moans of ecstasy?

"Do you want me to come down and see you?"

"No," she quickly responded, a hint of panic in her voice. No one trusted anyone anymore, he thought. How could they? "Just talk to me. It's comforting to . . . to hear your voice."

He nodded. He felt the same about her. In fact, in the past few nights he'd fantasized a lot about Onika, about running away with her to some island where they'd be safe. . . .

"Craig?"

"Sorry. Well, you're right—the cable's gone dead. And I can only get one radio station anymore, and even then, sometimes all I get is the sound of the DJ—um—screwing someone in the studio. But now they're saying the Free Love pills may be some sort of alien invasion. I don't know—it's all so fucking nuts."

"Oh, Craig," she sniffled. "Are we the last two sane people left alive?"

He had no answer for that.

Night twenty-four

He waited for her to call him again, willing the phone to ring, to connect him with Onika. But sunset came with no call. He picked up the phone but there was no dial tone. That was it, then: His last connection to normalcy was gone, and along with it, any fantasies of seeing Onika again.

Night twenty-five

The banging on the door began around 11:00 P.M. Craig jumped up from his couch, heart racing. "Onika?"

He ran to the door, checking the peephole, and he grinned widely. "Onika!"

He unbolted the door and threw it open wide, but the face on the other side was not Onika's, but Sherri's. "Fuck me, Craig! Fuck me first and then I'll let you have Onika."

Then Sherri was pushed out of the way by Amanda, the sister of a neighbor, who was equally attractive. "No, me! I'm a better fuck than both of them put together. Let me suck your cock and I'll prove it!"

He slammed the door shut before they could grab him, and shouted, "Onika! What are you doing? Are you—one of them?" There was no answer. He looked through the peephole. They were gone . . . until the next night. And the next.

Day twenty-nine

Craig decided he'd kill Sherri. He couldn't live with himself if he didn't avenge Onika's death. Onika, he realized, had been his lifeline—his only ray of hope against this endless darkness. And if he failed and died in the attempt, at least it would be a hero's death. Sherri was bound to start killing others—perhaps already had. And anyway, just waiting in his apartment for his food supplies and water to run out made no sense to him any longer.

He spent hours sharpening his largest kitchen knife, and then waited by the door.

Night twenty-nine

He watched through his peephole for Sherri's familiar shape. And then he saw her, right on time, shambling down the hall, naked, ribs showing, stomach distended. She was clearly starving. And then she was at his door. She started her nightly sales pitch. "Craig, I need you. I promise I'll fuck you—"

Craig yanked open the door, which he'd unbolted hours earlier, and thrust the knife deep into her protruding belly, an easy target. She gasped and pulled away from him, and the knife retracted, bringing bloody gore along with its blade. She fell to the floor, screaming. "You . . . you fucker!"

He stood over her, panting, and she stared at him with glassy eyes. "Fuck me," she groaned. "Please . . . fuck me before I die. . . ." And then her eyes closed.

Craig started crying, the knife falling onto her breasts, bouncing off and hitting the bloodstained carpet. Suddenly Sherri's eyes opened and she grabbed the knife, pushing it into Craig's meaty calf. "Shit!" he screamed as he kicked the knife out of Sherri's hands and fell to his knees. Sherri grabbed his calf and dug her fingers into the open wound as he screamed in pain. She pulled out her fingers and licked them and then her eyes closed, and her head hit the carpet with a dull thud.

Craig groaned as he heard a door open down the hall. He struggled into a sitting position against a wall but was unable to get up. He hyperventilated as he watched the door opening to Onika's apartment! What the hell?

And then Onika was running down the hall to his side. "Are you—oh, my God," she gasped as she saw his wound.

Craig was certain he was hallucinating. "Sherri said . . . she had fed you to her snake. . . ." And then he blacked out.

Night thirty

He awoke with a start, not recognizing his surroundings. He rose to his elbows up in a bed that was unfamiliar. He tried to jump up but his left leg was killing him. Then he remembered the events leading up to his blackout, and saw Onika at the door to what was obviously her bedroom. She was holding two steaming mugs.

He smiled weakly at her. "How long was I out?"

"Almost twenty-four hours," she said as she handed him a mug. "It's chicken soup." She smiled. "Mom always said it would cure what ailed me. I think the whole world needs to be drowned in chicken soup."

He grabbed it thankfully as he realized how hungry he was. She sat next to him on the bed and started sobbing quietly. He put down the mug and ran his fingers through her hair. "It's okay," he lied. What had happened to "no games"? Nothing would ever be okay again, he thought.

She wiped away her tears and smiled weakly at him. "No, it's not, but thanks for saying so."

"I thought you were . . . one of them. And then I thought you were dead."

"I know, I know." She took hold of one of his hands. Her touch was electrifying. He felt himself becoming aroused from her touch alone. It had been so long, and he was so happy she was alive.

"I faked being one of them to try and get out of here," she explained. "And it almost worked. I came with them to your door to try and make a rush for the elevator, and I almost made it a couple of times. But somehow, ultimately, they knew . . . they seem to sense who is a Virgin and who isn't. And they almost did catch me, but I was able to fight them off until I got back to my room. I tried to call you but the phones were dead."

"I know," he said. Inside, he was counting his blessings. She was still a Virgin . . . like him. Well, almost like him, he admitted to himself. He laughed.

"What?"

"Sherri—she said she fed you to her snake!"

"Oh. Well—that was Amanda, actually."

"Oh, shit. I'm . . . sorry." But actually he wasn't; he was so elated that Onika was alive that he didn't care if Amanda had been chopped up into snake supper.

He looked down at his leg, dressed in torn white sheets. She followed his gaze. "I did the best I could." She shrugged. "Does it hurt?"

"Only when I breathe." He laughed weakly. It was true, too. His calf muscle felt as if Sherri had kneaded it like bread dough. Still, he had to admit that seeing Onika was so invigorating, it almost balanced the pain he was feeling. In fact, he looked at an embarrassing tent in the sheets between them. He placed his hands over his erection in a lame attempt to hide it from her.

She blushed at him and placed a hand over his, squeezing his hands and applying pressure, through his hands, on his own erection. He gasped.

"The last Virgins left alive," she breathed softly in his ear, and kissed him. He kissed her back, hungrily. It felt so good to feel her lips on his, his dream come to life.

Gently she pulled away and took off her blouse. Slowly she grabbed at his pants and pulled them down, until his engorged penis escaped from his underwear.

"Mmm." She nodded approvingly.

"Are you sure—" he started to ask, and then she placed a finger over his mouth as she lowered her mouth to its target.

"Oh, Lord." Craig sucked in his breath. It was the first sex he'd had with another person since that damned bookstore customer had given him the drug. But this was so much better than that experience, because he'd fallen in love with Onika.

He put his hands on her soft blond hair and guided her head up and down, up and down. He felt a familiar pulsing, starting in his engorged penis and traveling throughout his body with the speed of blood through veins.

"The last Virgins left alive," he repeated.

She stopped for a moment. "What?"

"Nothing, don't stop."

She smiled and went back to work on him as he watched the top of her head bobbing, almost as if she was agreeing with her own statement that he'd repeated.

Only they weren't the last Virgins left alive, he thought. She might be, but he wasn't. He stroked her hair, her face, as she continued to play with him. She was talented beyond his wildest dreams.

No, there was only one Virgin in the apartment, and it was not him, he realized with a sinking heart. That single dose of Free Love he'd taken about a month ago—it had lain dormant in his system, he now realized, mutating in its own time frame, now awakening because they were having sex. His hands reached past her cheeks to her neck and he stroked it as she stroked him, moaning in her own private ecstasy.

He could so easily crush her windpipe now, and God, how he wanted to. He wanted to kill her as much as he wanted to love her. And just as he made his decision, he felt her teeth bite into his penis. Hard. Harder. Drawing blood. And harder still.

He screamed as his hands pressed into her neck. She bit harder and he screamed louder and pressed harder until he felt something crack in her neck. She gasped for air, half his penis still in her mouth. She spat him out and he watched his own body part roll off the bed and onto the carpet.

They both stared at each other's dying eyes for a second before saying simultaneously:

"I'm so sorry."

Cry of the Loogaroo

John Edward Ames

"Feature this: A dark, dank, fetid, wildly overgrown place dominated by alligators and snakes, by tall tupelo trees marching on stilts that, on closer inspection, turn out to be exposed roots. Imagine a dripping, insect-humming monotony of sound that's eerily akin to the uneventful stillness of a mausoleum. This is a place where death is lazy, primitive, and anonymous, and thus vastly more terrifying in its pitilessness."

I gave a little fluming snort as I switched off Libby Mumford's microcassette recorder.

"Fetid?" I repeated, watching Captain Breaux. "The hell's that mean?"

He shrugged one beefy shoulder. "I look like a dictionary? I think it means stinky. This chick's got a nice voice."

"Nice everything. In fact, she's a certified traffic hazard. Most of these award-winning female journalist types look like constipated librarians. Not Libby. She was a model before she got into photojournalism. Here, check her out."

I opened a folder on my knee and handed him a color glossy of Libby Mumford; she was running along a beach somewhere, damn near butt naked in a yellow bikini thong.

Breaux, who normally has all the elan of a deep coma, loosed a sharp whistle.

"She's a tidy little bit of frippit, all right," he allowed, visibly impressed.

Libby was a blue-chip *chica* all the way, pampered and sleek and boob-enhanced. Breaux took in the shoulder-length platinum hair, eyes the soft blue of forget-me-nots, skin tanned to the exact shade of sunlit honey.

"Yeah, boy," he added, handing it back to me. "That's something to wrap your leg around. Where'd you say she's from?"

"Houston."

"What, she's with one of the crap sheets there?"

"Nah, she's freelance. But not a scoop merchant, just fluff and feature stuff. Specializes in travel pieces and photo features for the Sunday supplements. Also writes hot romance novels under the name Deanna Chambers. But when she disappeared last week, she was working on a series for *Eros* magazine called 'Hot and Haunted America'—which her editor described as—"

I glanced down at the notes on my flip-back pad.

"—'a showcase for some of America's most colorful and steamy regional bogey legends.'"

Breaux, negligently sprawled on a swivel chair behind a messy pecan-veneer desk, raised one hand like a traffic cop to stop me. He was a huge and sloppy rag bag of a man with a lopsided mouth and big pouches like bruises under his eyes.

"Yeah, well, let me guess: Our hot little infobabe caught wind of the scuttlebutt about Shrieking Swamp, uh? Figured being diddled by an 'invisible sex fiend' might be more of a rush than the politically correct coffee-shop weenies who usually *schtupp* her?"

"Somehow I doubt she went there to get laid," I assured him from a deadpan. "But yeah, she knew about the stories, her editor confirmed that."

"He the one reported her missing?"

I nodded. "After she failed to check in by phone."

He pointed at the microrecorder. "How'd you get that?"

"Search and Rescue turned it in. It's all they found."

"Play some more."

I switched it on. Her throaty contralto voice again filled Breaux's cubbyhole office on the second floor of the New Orleans French Quarter Precinct Building.

The recordings were obviously made at intervals as time passed and her location varied. For a few minutes there was more of the same tour-guide stuff; just verbal notes of her physical impressions, ideas she obviously intended to help her when she wrote her article later.

"Vast Honey Island Swamp has formed around the mouth of the Pearl River where it empties into the Gulf of Mexico along the Louisiana-Mississippi border. Since the earliest days of settlement in the Deep South, this remote area has played host to French, Spaniards, Creoles, Acadians, various Indian tribes, pirates, runaway slaves, criminals, and deserters from countless armies.

"Where I'm standing right now, however, is actually the one-thousand-acre 'inner circle' of Honey Island, a taboo place known to locals as Shrieking Swamp. It is this area, so the well-established legend goes, that's haunted by a mythical demon known as the *loup-garou,* or 'loogaroo' to locals, a distinctly American variation of the European werewolf."

Breaux raised a hand, and I switched the recorder off again.

"'Well-established legend' my sweet ass," he repeated, his tone mocking the words. "It's pure horseshit being shoveled by a bunch of redneck chawbacons. Did you say this dizzy broad went in there alone?"

"She hired a local Cajun guide who took her into Honey Island. But he refused to go into Shrieking Swamp, so she made him wait while she took the boat in alone. He claims she never returned."

"You've put him under the light?"

I nodded. "He's got no priors, and we can't poke any holes in his story. He also volunteered for and passed a polygraph."

"Mm . . . well, the way this chick looks, *some*body fucked her and killed her, you can make book on it. That or the silly little twat fell into some quicksand. Either way, by now she's fermenting in a gator hole, end of story."

It never took Breaux long to get into his hard-ass riff. He was a gruff old coot, notorious for his impatience when subordinates failed to produce, and he could be a pigheaded son of a bitch when his hems were flaring—as I suspected they were now judging from the way he fidgeted in his chair. Made me wonder how many solvable investigations he had closed down just because his asshole was on fire.

"That's pretty much what I thought, too," I assured him. "But there's more on the tape; you need to hear it."

I thumbed the microcassette back on.

"In the case of Shrieking Swamp, however, the loogaroo tale has taken an . . . interesting deviation from the usual reports of violent killer attacks. For this loogaroo does not kill or injure— reportedly, it sexually ravishes its victims. It is an invisible, supernatural sex fiend, and according to its supposed victims, it is either male or female depending on the gender of the person attacked. In fact, I talked to a husband and wife who were attacked simultaneously, only a few feet apart, and each one reported the attacker as 'of the opposite sex.'"

"Screw this," Breaux interrupted again. "Why do I need to hear this shit? It's the same old doo-dah we been hearing for years now. You a cop or one of the fuckin' squirrels?"

"You need to hear some more," I insisted.

"And *you* need some serious couch time, Savoy."

But he piped down when I turned the recording back on.

"I could no longer avoid this story once it became a persistent rumor. Oh, it never makes the airwaves or establishment print media, not even locally in Louisiana or Mississippi. But it's creating a growing fascination on the Internet. Yesterday I interviewed a Tulane University graduate student in anthropology who claims to have been 'ravished' by the sex demon of Shrieking Swamp. She has developed an interesting theory that the 'loogaroo' angle developed back in the earlier days because attack victims were too scandalized to openly report the sexual nature of their bizarre experiences. Some cover story was needed to explain torn clothing, scratch marks, and bites left by the—"

"Shut that fucking drivel off," Breaux growled.

"It's coming up," I insisted. "Just listen."

"—and I've also interviewed folks who live near Shrieking Swamp, for no one actually lives *in* it. And most of them concur: The eerie sounds emanating from the swamp seem much more like gasps than shrieks; howls of ecstasy, not terror. And as another attack victim admitted to me: 'Once you've had it, you may well wander back in for more. I have and so have others who—'"

Breaux heaved himself out of the chair, nearly three hundred pounds of pissed-off precinct captain angling around his desk and bearing down on me like the Apocalypse.

"Savoy, you *and* this broad are so full of shit your feet are sliding. I said turn that fucking thing—"

A sharp gasp sliced into his threat, and Breaux froze like a hound on point, staring at the microcassette recorder.

"What? Oh, good heart of *God!* What's happening to me?"

Her voice had suddenly grown a few octaves sharper. Her breathing, barely audible to this point, became rushed and heavy panting.

"I don't understa—oh! *Oh!* What's—wha-wha-what's—*oh!* Oh, my God, oh, *oh!* That—oh, Christ, yes, *yess,* that, *that!* Jesus God, *yes!*"

There was a sudden rush of frenzied noises: clothes being

ripped, undergrowth rustling as if she were thrashing around, groans and moans and sharp little yipping cries even a Vestal Virgin would know were sex noises. And a steady, rapidly increasing noise like dozens of cats hungrily lapping milk.

Her voice was hardly recognizable as human now, escalating to a shrieking pitch that seemed as much pain as pleasure.

"Yes, yes, *yes* . . . ahh, ahh, *ahh* . . . do that, do it, do it, faster . . . lick me, *lick* me, I . . . oh, I'm going to . . . oh, Jesus, I'm going tooo exx-*plode!*"

And she did, a banshee cry welling up so loud that, even on the tiny speaker, it seemed to fill the office.

The recorder went silent, and I thumbed it off again, watching Breaux.

He looked shell-shocked. I watched him return to his chair and slack into it, scrubbing his face with his hands as if trying to wake up. For a minute he refused to even look at me, studying his office as if seeing it for the first time. His eyes went first to the framed prints of Louisiana shore birds lining one wall, then to the old print sampler he'd swiped from a now defunct Basin Street brothel: IT TAKES A HEAP O' LOVIN' TO MAKE A HOME A HOUSE.

"She could've faked this, Cap," I finally remarked. "Publicity, whatever. If she did, she's one hell of a porno actress."

Breaux mopped his glistening face with a handkerchief.

"The best," he conceded. "Christ, I got a Viagra hard-on just listening to her."

He looked at me, and I could tell he didn't think she faked any of it.

"It's like the way you never confuse TV voices with real people talking," he told me. "There's just this difference you can always tell. Same with fake sex noises versus real. Neal, am I fucking bonkers here, or did Miss Libby get her little muff licked eight beats to the bar?"

"There's one last recording before the tape goes silent."

I flicked the recorder on again and fast-forwarded past some empty tape.

"Though few of us can name it, we all search for something transcendent, something that takes us out of ourselves. Sex, when it works right, is the ultimate no-mindedness. For me it has never worked right. Until now. Until this place. Until . . . you. Now I have sloughed my old self as surely as a snake sloughs its old skin."

I turned the recorder off, watching Breaux closely.

"Very weird," I volunteered.

"I know *that's* real," he agreed. "Shit! I'm fed up to *here* with that freakin' swamp. At least a dozen people have disappeared there over the past ten years. And each time, the department takes it in the shorts."

"French Emma's curse," I said, mainly just to piss him off. And I succeeded. I watched a vein over his left temple swell until it looked like a hyperventilating worm.

"You sorry-ass dip shit," he growled at me. "Since you think it's so funny, Sergeant Savoy, I want your ass in that swamp tomorrow. You know that area, check it out good. And keep this fucking recording under wraps. I shit thee not—if the media bozos get hold of this, I'll have your guts for garters."

"French Emma's curse" is part of the tourist-oriented local mythology in southeastern Louisiana. French Emma Johnson was rumored to be an avid practitioner of obeah, sometimes called Cajun voodoo, a hybrid of African and southern American black magic. She was also the most notorious "landlady" in Storyville, the infamous yet legal New Orleans tenderloin that thrived, adjacent to the French Quarter, between 1898 and 1917, when the U.S. Navy razed it as a public-health menace to the military.

Emma's "sporting house" was the first to be leveled. Not only did she lose a fortune in this raid, she became the whipping girl for the bluenosed crusaders. She was literally run out of town after her head was shaved to shame her. Forced to flee penniless into Honey Island Swamp, she reportedly laid a strange curse on her tormentors: "Long after my bones rot in this swamp, the siren's song will endure like an angel with savage weapons."

Of course the hoodoo angle was a crock, and I never met one local who seriously believed it. But there was no denying that Shrieking Swamp, the remote heart of Honey Island, had become a black hole into which people simply vanished forever, prompting the rubes to make up the "cry of the loogaroo" crap. There was never even a hint of any crime, and because the area was a virtual sinkhole of quicksand pockets, it was natural for the authorities to assume accidental deaths with no hope of recovering bodies.

But Libby Mumford's bizarre tape recording suggested it might not be that simple.

Her strange final message to the world, complete with sounds of orgasmic overdrive, had lit a fire under me to solve this long-standing mystery. Ever since I was a kid I had hunted and fished along Honey Island's meandering bayous, so I had no trouble guiding a borrowed pirogue deep into the dark, tangled swamp. A pirogue's shallow draw and flat bottom allow it to float in only inches of water, and there's no current to fight in a swamp, only mud banks and submerged tree roots.

The sun, only rarely visible through the dense overgrowth, nonetheless seemed to remain stuck high in the sky as if pegged there, radiating a merciless furnace heat. Thick humidity clung to my skin like wet cloth. Eerie fingers of sunlight poked through the thick canopy of trees, and I became almost hypnotized by the power-line hum of insects, the only sound besides my paddle slicing through the dark, still water.

"Libby! Libby Mumford!" I called over and over into a megaphone.

But my words simply disappeared like stones into a well, and after a while I gave up calling her name—each time I disturbed that breathing stillness, I felt as if I were shouting swear words in church.

Uneventful hours ticked by until at last I was following the final bayou that snaked through Shrinking Swamp on its eastern edge. I decided to paddle through the next dogleg bend, then head back to my car for the hour-long drive back to New Orleans. I was halfway through the bend when I heard it—a keening, ululating noise I couldn't even find the vocabulary to describe.

You really *can* be "shocked to the marrow," just as surely as your blood really can carbonate with fear as mine did at that moment. The noise did not seem human or animal, but hell-spawned and demonic, and yet it literally and instantly aroused me, my erection so hard that it throbbed painfully against my restraining jeans.

The pirouge glided through the bend, and I spotted Libby Mumford.

She was lying on her back along the muddy bank of the bayou, completely naked, both shapely legs raised into the air and spread wide as she writhed and wiggled like a *mambo* who'd been mounted by the *loa.* The honey-colored skin was splotched with dried mud, the platinum hair tangled with leaves and twigs.

"That!" she cried out in a voice distorted by intense lust. "*That,* oh yes, *do* that! Do me deeper, harder, oh, yes, your big cock is tamping my shit! Yes, like *that!*"

Her taut round ass began flexing and releasing like a blowfish, her pelvis thrusting up rapidly from the ground, and her nipples were swollen so stiff they looked like little chocolate thumbs. She was so amped up with passion that every breath included a slight groan. Clearly she was enjoying the fuck of her life.

Or *thought* she was. Because in fact she was all alone on that muddy bank.

I was witnessing some kind of insanity. Yet, all I could feel was my own demanding lust. My cock throbbed as if there were a tourniquet around it, and I could hear my pulse surf-crashing in my ears.

"Like *that!*" she howled, thrashing like a gut-hooked fish. "That's it! Yes, yes, *yes,* I'm going to—oh, Christ, I'm gonna—*anhh!*"

In my time I've watched a few babes get their rocks off, and if I'm lying, I'm dying—Libby climaxed just then, a shuddering, screaming orgasm that left her gasping, spent, and weak.

Don't get me wrong. The objective cop in me knew damn well that even a PERK—a physical-evidence recovery kit—would've turned up no signs in her vagina of actual sexual intercourse. Yet, "real" it was. Beyond the swamp's fungoid stink of rot and decay, I could detect another odor staining the air: the faint bleach smell of spent semen.

"Libby!" I called out, starting to paddle toward the bank.

She sat up quickly, and I received another jolt when she looked in my direction: Her lips were visibly swollen, as if from passionate kissing.

Her glassy-eyed glance touched me and slid away. She scrambled to her feet and turned to flee into the swamp.

"Libby, wait! I'm a cop! Damn it, stop!"

For a moment she obeyed, but when she looked at me again her eyes were mutinous.

"I don't need any cops!" she flung back at me. "Just leave me alone! *Don't* take this away from me, please don't!"

"Take what away? The hell you talking about?"

I had stood up to leap ashore. She pointed toward my crotch. I didn't have to glance down to know there was a huge furrow along my left thigh, the outline of my raging blue-veiner.

"That! You felt it, too, didn't you? Come back if you want the best sex of your life!"

"Wait! You can't survive in this—"

But it was no use. She had already disappeared like a frightened rabbit.

"What, I gotta pop you on your snot locker just to get a freakin' report out of you, Neal?"

Breaux stared at me across his bomb-rubbled desk, that lopsided mouth of his twisted into an impatient scowl.

I opened my mouth to reply, but the words snagged in my throat like half-chewed bread.

"Well, Jesus Katy Christ!" Breaux exploded. "You *did* search the swamp this weekend?"

I nodded.

"As much of it as I could," I qualified. "But it'd be easier to bite your own teeth than for one man to search that entire swamp."

Breaux's eyes puckered with suspicion.

"That dog won't hunt, Sergeant. What are you holding back?"

Again I opened my mouth to report, but I felt like a snake trying to get started on loose sand. Since Saturday I hadn't been able to shake the retinal afterimage of Libby's gorgeous body thrashing around like a downed power line. *Come back if you want the best sex of your life.*

"All right, I get it," he assayed next, changing tactics. "You didn't find out jack shit, did you?"

Holding back was one thing. But in twenty years of being a cop, I'd never lied to a superior yet.

"I saw Libby," I finally told him.

Breaux's eyes bulged out like wet white marbles.

"You saw her *alive?*"

I nodded, thinking: Oh, she was sure-God alive, all right. More alive, probably, than any other woman on Planet Earth.

"Did you talk to her?"

"Sure. She told me to leave her alone. Then she ran off."

"And you let her?"

I shrugged. "How could I stop her? Honey Island is public land, after all, and she's broken no laws I know of."

I watched him turn the problem back and forth for a while, studying all the facets and angles.

"I s'poze you're right," he finally acceded. "It ain't none of our picnic if some pert skirt decides to play Jane in the jungle. So what do we do now, sit and play a harp? This chick's got family looking for her."

I said nothing for perhaps thirty seconds, hearing Libby's urgent voice in my auditory memory: *You felt it too, didn't you?*

Since Saturday I'd been trying to convince myself I had only gotten aroused at the sight of her in sexual ecstasy. But it was more than that, different somehow. As if I had wandered onto the periphery of an area of electrically charged particles. And as if, had I gone any closer to her, *I* might have been "mounted," too.

"I think I should go back," I finally replied. "Try to find her and talk her into resurfacing. Hell, how can she survive there?"

Breaux approved this with a nod, shrewd eyes studying me like a bug under a magnifying glass.

"You do that. Just one more question: Has this got anything to do with that porno soundtrack she left behind? Or the last comment we heard on her tape recorder? All that doo-dah about how fucking is the 'ultimate no-mindedness?'"

I shook my head. "Hell if I know."

"Who's the 'you' she's talking to?" he added, eyes piercing me like a pair of bullets.

"Nobody I know," I answered truthfully.

He watched me a few seconds longer, trying to read the unspoken subtext but drawing a blank.

"You bolted to that chair?" he finally growled. "Get the hell outta here, and don't come back without Libby."

The next day, when I made my return trip to Shrieking Swamp, one part of me intended to carry out Breaux's order. Libby, I told myself repeatedly, needed help. Sure, she had begged me not to "take this away from me." But heroin addicts felt the same loyalty toward their sickness, too.

Another part of me, however, rejected this supposedly noble impulse of mine. Piss on the humanitarian schmaltz about "helping"—she had invited me back for the best sex of my life, and naturally I assumed she meant with her.

And *with* her is how it turned out. As in "in the presence of."

I returned to the very same spot where I had last seen her. For hours I waited, slapping at bugs, until the waning sun was replaced by a moon bright enough to make shadows.

I could hear the nocturnal predators coming to life, slithering and splashing all around me, and still no sign of Libby. Bored and dejected, I started to drag the pirogue back into the water, intending to return to my car.

"You came back," a voice behind me said softly.

I whirled around. Libby stood there in the buttery moonlight, wearing a muddy and torn *brisa del mar* dress. Her platinum hair gleamed like quicksilver.

"Yeah, but I'm not sure why," I admitted.

"You're about to find out why," she assured me, starting to unbutton her dress.

She let it fall in a puddle at her feet, naked now, and the sight of those huge, high-thrusting tits on such a slim girl sent blood surging into my cock.

"You get naked, too," she ordered me, and I didn't require any further persuading to peel off my clothes. I expected the mosquitoes to eat me alive, but oddly, there was no longer an insect in our vicinity.

"Not too close," she told me when I started toward her.

"But I've been thinking about you since Saturday."

"About *me?*" Her laughter was softly melodic. "You still don't understand. But you will. Oh, you *will.* Be patient."

A few minutes passed in a strange, communal silence. She hadn't even asked my name, and yet, I felt as if we were already close—closer, even, than lovers.

"You're here," she said abruptly, joy sparking her tone, and it was clear she wasn't talking to me this time.

Soon I heard urgent sucking noises and watched in slack-jawed astonishment as both her nipples stiffened in the moon-light. Whimpering, she sank to her knees, her breathing suddenly ragged and hoarse.

I was on the verge of stepping closer to take her right there in the muck. But invisible hands seemed to grip my shoulders and propel me down onto the ground. My first reaction was abject fear, but that quickly passed as the incredible pleasure took over.

Moist heat flowed over my erection, the unmistakable feel of a hungry mouth pleasuring me. An invisible tongue swirled all around my swollen glans, invisible teeth raked along my length with just enough pain to hurt so nice. A hot, tingling pressure began to build between my asshole and my balls, and it felt like every nerve ending in my prick had been raised to the fifth power as a pleasure receptor.

Whoever or whatever was sucking me into a spastic frenzy never did take any recognizable form. Yet, the "substance" was all there: a feminine odor like honeysuckle and lilacs, even the tickle of long, silky hair brushing my belly while this . . . de-monic nymph teased me to the brink of explosive release.

"*Lick* my cunt!" Libby screamed from only a few feet away. "Faster, *faster,* yes, like *that,* you fucking stud!"

I managed a quick glance in her direction. Her legs were raised, drawn back to expose her sex, and the wet slapping sounds of a good tongue-lashing were unmistakable. Her pleasure-glazed eyes met mine in that eldritch moon wash, and watching each other had a powerful booster effect on our lust.

Her sharp cry of orgasmic release was followed almost immediately by my own. Both of us came so violently that we went limp and comatose afterward, floating on a sea of dazed bliss.

But that supernatural blow job was only the beginning of my initiation into the erotic addiction that had already claimed Libby. I came to with my erection back in full force. A tight velvet glove seemed to slip over it, I felt invisible vaginal walls parting, and for hours Shrieking Swamp lived up to its name as Libby and I were both fucked with savage sweetness while the moon crept toward its zenith.

It's been several months since that night, and I haven't left the swamp except for brief trips to a little Cajun grocery store near the mouth of the Pearl River. I live with Libby in an old shack built on stilts, somebody's long-abandoned fishing camp. It's primitive: a rusted hand pump for water, no toilet, and when it rains the place leaks like a perforated bladder.

Search parties have come through a few times, and we hid in a giant deadfall until they left. Neither one of us ever wants to leave our invisible lover.

It's weird, but neither of us wants to fuck each other, either. Oh, sure, we've bonded, all right, grown inseparable. We even sleep together naked in the shack's old leather-webbing bed. And we love watching each other in the throes of carnal abandon. But Libby was right when she claimed that "normal sex" pales in comparison to what we now have.

But all is far from bliss. We bought a battery-powered radio. Late one night, when it was too hot to sleep, we were listening to some stump-screaming evangelist: "My friends, the devil is sailing on a sinking ship, and the place where he reigns is called Doomed Domains."

After that we tossed the radio out. It was a reminder that we ourselves are doomed—doomed and damned. For neither of us doubts that whatever holds us in thrall is demonic. We simply aren't strong enough to resist it. We have willingly immersed ourselves in the destructive element.

There's shame—and fear. When lust becomes your drug, you must constantly up the dose. Each night the sex becomes more savage, more physically punishing. What will our ravenous libidos demand by this time next year—if we even live that long?

The darkness within us all is deep, and for some it makes demands like a stomach that must be fed. I only know one thing for sure about Shrieking Swamp: Whatever lurks there lusts there, and now it lusts within the two of us.

Wrench

Sephera Giron

"Turn it, tweak it, torque it . . . and if it still don't fit, force it!" he said, hazel eyes twinkling.

Laura nodded and stared under the hood of her car.

"Riiight," she sighed.

The labyrinth of wire and metal might as well have been a maze to the Minotaur as far as she was concerned. All she knew was that one minute, she was flying along the highway and the next, thick clouds of smoke were billowing from under the hood of her car. She looked over at the mechanic, who was shaking his head.

"It's those damn caps, and those fittings there. They just don't make 'em right," he said, reaching over with a cloth to fiddle with something.

She didn't look where he was pointing; instead she looked at his face. He was young. Late twenties? Early thirties? Strong jawed, wide, soulful eyes, dark hair. How she loved dark hair. . . .

"So . . . how long do you think this will take?" she asked, glancing at his name tag. "Darren?"

Darren leaned farther into the car and Laura studied him. Nice lean body, nice tight ass . . . a fine specimen indeed. She rubbed her neck, tracing beads of sweat.

Darren turned to look at her and caught her studying him. She blushed as he grinned and stood up.

"Can you leave it here for a couple of hours?" he asked.

"Do I have a choice?" Laura said.

Darren shrugged. "There's always a choice."

"Is there somewhere I can get a coffee and a bite to eat?" she asked, staring along the highway strip. A truck roared by, kicking up dust and pebbles. How the hell did she end up in this nowhere place anyway?

"There's a little restaurant down a ways. Take you about ten minutes to walk."

"Thanks," she said. "I'll be back in a couple of hours then."

"Sure."

Laura walked toward the little restaurant. Damn car. Damnable car troubles. She would lose precious time.

Time.

But what was time, really?

She wasn't going anywhere she *had* to be. She was running away, running to, just running. All she had was a suitcase, a wad of cash, and the urge to just jet. Start again. Reinvent herself.

Reinvent herself indeed. She laughed cynically.

She thought about the mechanic. Darren. She wondered how he saw himself, how he saw *her*.

She knew what he saw when he looked at her. The same all of them saw.

A forty-year-old woman who might once have been called voluptuous but with anorexia in vogue was now just plain fat. No one wanted hips and thighs anymore. Large breasts and a stomach just weren't cool. It was hard enough to grow up with a body that rebelled against fashion, but it was even harder to grow old in one.

Those eyes . . . those big beautiful eyes . . . he had those weird eyes that changed . . . brown . . . green . . .

Laura shook her head. She wouldn't think about it. A handsome young man like that wouldn't think twice about someone like her. She was a joke. A lonely old divorcee who wasn't allowed to feel, to dream, to *desire.*

How easy it was for a man to go out and find a new woman and remarry, while she raised a child by herself. Now that child was a man out in the world and she had nothing.

So she ran. Just threw a few things in a suitcase and took off. She didn't know where she was going. She just knew she couldn't stay in that city any longer or she would go mad.

There was nothing to fill the hole, even chocolate didn't do the trick anymore.

There was just a vast echo reverberating around inside her. A hole searching for that missing piece. She had had everything, a child, a job, an uneventful yet not traumatic life, but still, she needed that final piece to the puzzle.

It had nothing to do with self-esteem, self-love, all that shit that the psychology gurus prattled on about. It had to do with being human, being animal, needing a mate, needing to be needed . . . to be desired. The primal urge to love and lust and touch and suck and fuck. To experience sensation.

As an animal, it was her *right* to have what everyone else had.

It was almost as if men could sense her loneliness. Some would circle in like sharks, feeding her lines, inciting her loins, taking her home only to never call again. Most just veered away. After all, she was middle-aged. Plain. Average job. Average kid.

And she wore glasses. . . .

Men don't make passes at girls who wear glasses.

It wasn't her fault that contacts irritated her eyes and she refused to have laser surgery. She didn't want anyone touching her eyes.

He had those large expressive eyes you could drown in.

Laura put her hand on her heart. It thumped wildly.

Maybe this time would be different. Maybe this time someone

would see past the outside, would want to know what was inside. Maybe want to take a chance.

Other people took chances. They met and just took that giant leap of "what the hell, let's see what happens" and whirl-winded around until they were twisted around each other or blown apart.

That's what she needed. A heady whirlwind adventure.

So she had set off on the road, running from, running to . . . just running.

As Laura sat in the restaurant, sipping coffee and reading the newspaper, the door whooshed open and an oddly dressed old woman wandered in.

"Hey, Maria!" one of the waitresses called out. "You gonna read my fortune today?"

Maria laughed.

"I told you yesterday, a new man is coming. . . ." Maria smiled, her wizened face lighting up.

"But he ain't here yet!" the waitress said. "I'm not getting any younger!"

Maria raised her hand and nodded.

"He's coming, he's coming . . . not to worry."

Maria sat down in a booth at the very back of the restaurant and started to unpack her bag. The waitress refilled Laura's coffee cup.

"Is that the neighborhood psychic?" Laura asked.

"That's Maria. She comes in a couple of times a week to read tarots and sell spells. She's pretty cheap and very accurate."

"Hmmm . . . I've never been to a psychic," Laura said.

"You should try it, it's fun."

The waitress wandered off and Laura watched Maria finish setting up her table. She didn't know if she even believed in psychics but it would be a while before the car was ready. Laura walked over to the booth.

"Sit, sit . . . let Maria help you," the old woman said, waving to the seat across from her.

"I've never—"

"No worries . . . there's a first time for everything." Maria squinted her eyes and stared at Laura's face. "You are so lonely. You want to find a man but aren't having much luck."

"You got that right," Laura said.

"I have a great little spell kit. Guaranteed success."

"What do I do?"

"All the instructions are inside. It's very simple and very powerful." Maria dangled a pouch before Laura's eyes.

A chill crept up Laura's back.

"With a little help, you can have anything you desire."

"Even love?"

"Even love, but . . . " Maria leaned over and touched Laura's hand, "I'm not responsible for whatever happens."

"Of course," said Laura as she dug through her purse.

"I really appreciate all the work," Laura said to Darren as she paid her bill. The station was quiet except for a distant radio playing a Tool song about pieces fitting.

Laura slipped off her glasses and wiped them with a tissue. She cocked her head, looking up at Darren with beetle-black eyes.

"Can I buy you a coffee or a snack or something?" Laura asked, her heart pounding into her throat. How did the words fall out of her mouth like that? She swallowed, willing herself not to blush. His eyes were green now as the sun shone on him.

"Well, I am due for a break . . . Yeah, I could use some joe, thanks."

Laura put her glasses back on.

"Should we go over to that place?" she asked.

"It's the closest unless you want to go back toward town, but I'm sure you're anxious to get back on the road again."

They walked until they reached a pickup truck.

"I'll drive us over. It's faster. Hotter than a son of a bitch today."

Laura watched him eat. How she loved to watch young men eat. Especially hardworking ones that were so thin. Somehow the burger and fries and salad mysteriously and efficiently disappeared. She stared at his hands—no wedding band. They were worker's hands. Strong hands that moved with purpose and direction.

"Just tooling across the country then, are you?" he asked her, disturbing her from her thoughts. She wondered if she looked like a vulture watching him so closely, like a voyeur watching Internet porn, only she was just watching a handsome young man chew and swallow.

"Yes, just wandering, I guess. I just feel like I want to break free, maybe be a little wild." She raised an eyebrow at him, but she knew from experience that unless a man had his beer goggles on there would be no response.

"Just quit your job and took off," he said, nodding. "Yep, I've done that a couple times myself."

"What brought you here?"

He shrugged. "Not sure really . . . Like I said, I've been a bit of a wanderer myself. You know how it is. Job goes sour. Love goes sour . . . you move on. I was driving through here and on an impulse stopped to see if they needed a mechanic. Shit, yes, they did, so here I am."

"Lucky."

"Eh, maybe, maybe not. Maybe I should have kept going."

"Hey, you could tag along with me. Road trip!" Laura joked. Darren laughed.

"Yeah, well, not today." He looked at his watch. "I'd better get back."

Several candles flickered around the little hotel room. When the last one was lit, Laura slipped off her nightgown. She caught a glimpse of her naked self in the mirror and quickly looked away. She didn't want to remember how old she looked. How her body was marred with stretch marks and scars. The outside was what others saw. The outside was what repelled *them* from anything more than a night or two of companionship. It didn't matter if she was smart or stupid or what she did for a living. They could put up with her for a night, maybe two, get it up, get off, then run like hell.

Of course, she had friends much like herself. Some even larger and older, who managed to find companions, new husbands. Somehow they got past the "standards."

But then again, they didn't have the same taste as she . . . the same *craving*. . . .

Those weird green brown eyes, that cute little ass, lean, lithe body, so young, just a boy, barely thirty, dark hair, dark hair . . .

She had her own set of standards. Standards that were utterly ridiculous for someone her age and her type.

But she knew how she felt on the inside, where her flesh stretched over and under bones and organs. Her nerves quivered and her senses sang as they waited expectantly. She knew that if she could find just the right one, she could make the pieces fit. Fill that burning hole.

On the dresser, a black cloth was laid out and on it, a goblet of water, a few stones, a little silver-handled knife, and a necklace. Laura picked up the necklace and put it on. It was a silver heart with a pentagram inside that had been in the spell kit Maria had sold her. She picked up the knife and stared at it. Putting it down, she took the little scroll of paper that had the directions and the spell on it. She muttered a few words, a prayer, and drew the knife lightly across her wrist. Blood bubbled up from the wound. She smiled. She held her bleeding wrist over a candle.

"Darren, you will hear my cry.

"Wherever it is in dreams you lie.

"Darren, you will welcome me.

"And so fulfill our destiny."

A few drops of blood fell into the candle and sizzled. A waft of smoke spiraled up. Laura hummed and dipped her finger into the blood on her wrist. She wiped the blood along her cheeks, and dabbing as she went, drew a pentagram on her chest while muttering the spell.

When she was finished she lay back on the bed. She thought about all the men who had used her, who had lied to her, who had broken her heart.

Then she thought of other men. The waiter in Baltimore, the variety store clerk in Providence, the dark-haired actor in Vermont. Thinking about them spread a delicious sensation through her and she shuddered, her nipples tingling.

She closed her eyes and traced her body with her hands, her full, heavy breasts, her stomach, her groin. She was warm and wet as she thought about Darren.

She imagined being with him. Feeling his strong hands stroking her flesh, his lean hard body pressed against hers. How soft his lips would be. His eyes, large and doelike, watching her watching him.

She writhed and cried and chanted. Fingers pulled at her hair, her breasts, smearing more blood along her body till the bed was spattered with it. The candle flames grew taller and flickered feverishly as if mimicking the woman rolling along the bed.

A vague fog hung in the air from candle smoke and incense.

Suddenly, she lay very still and then, she felt it. Just as the spell said it would . . . her spirit lifted from her body.

One minute, she was staring at her human form on the bed, then next, she flashed somehow, and was hovering over sleeping Darren. She was frozen with trepidation for a moment, trying to figure out if she was dreaming this or was she really here?

She lowered herself to the floor and drank him in by the light of the moon shining through the window. A low growl came from the darkness, and she realized there was a dog lying on the bed with him.

Sleeping, Darren was even more beautiful. Laura sighed as she reached over to touch his face. The dog leaped up and barked. Laura pulled her hand away as Darren opened his eyes.

"Hey . . ." he said, sitting up and looking around the room. The dog stared and growled.

"What's wrong, Max?" he asked. Darren clicked on the lamp by the bed. He blinked, then shook his head.

Laura felt herself being pulled back and in a wink, was gone.

Laura sat in a corner of the restaurant, sipping on a coffee and nibbling on toast. She was trying to read the paper, but she kept looking up, hoping she wouldn't miss him. She fingered the amulet around her neck.

The door opened and she looked up again. Darren surveyed the room, then walked over to her.

"Hey, what are you doing here? I thought you beat feet."

"I decided to stay the night. Get a fresh start. . . . Care to join me?"

"Why not?" Darren was looking at her in an odd manner and she smiled slyly. He slid into the booth across from her. He ordered coffee, eggs, and toast.

"Car running all right?" he asked.

"As near as I can tell. . . . I haven't gone too far yet." She smiled.

She watched him sip his coffee. His eyes were clouded. "What are you thinking about?" she asked.

"I had the weirdest dream last night," he said.

"What happened?"

"I don't really remember, but it was odd. . . ." He shook his head.

"Yeah, I sometimes have dreams that cling to me all day long," Laura said. "Wonder why that is."

Darren shrugged. "Our subconscious playing tricks with us, I guess."

He sipped his coffee.

"So . . . you're just wandering across this great land of ours?" he said.

"Yep."

"Gonna write down your adventures when you're done?"

"Hadn't thought about it," Laura said. "It could be something the grandchildren could check out, I guess."

"You have kids?"

"Just one. He's all grown up now. Doesn't need his mommy anymore."

"I doubt that. All boys need their moms."

"What about you? Any kids?"

"Nope. No kids, no wife. Just me and my dog against the world."

"Enjoy it while you can," Laura said. "Responsibility comes soon enough."

"So they say. . . . Still . . . would be nice to settle down . . . would be nice to have someone to come home to. . . ."

"I hear you."

* * *

A week went by.

Laura spent her nights casting the spell and her days watching Darren.

Every morning she waited for him in the coffee shop and every morning they had breakfast. She was biding her time, getting to know him. He stopped being startled when he saw her there, and even seemed to like having company in the morning.

Today would be different.

Today was the seventh day of the spell.

Laura watched Darren from her car as he closed up the shop. As he locked the front door, she climbed out and walked over to him. As he turned, he jumped when he saw her standing there.

"What are you doing here?" he asked.

"I think you know," she said, rubbing her neck. She wore a tight red shirt that accentuated her cleavage and had taken extra care with her makeup. He looked her over and continued to walk.

"No, I don't know."

"Darren . . . you have been dreaming about me . . ." she whispered huskily.

"Uh . . . no." he said as he double-checked the front door.

"I think you have," she said insistently.

Darren swallowed. "What do you want?" he asked.

"I want . . . I want you to come over to my motel, have a drink with me."

"I'm not sure that's a good idea," he said.

"Oh? Do you have plans?" she asked, her eyes narrowing.

"Uh, no. I don't have plans. I just don't think it's a good idea."

"I think it's a great idea. We can order in some food and have a nice relaxing dinner."

"I don't think so. Besides, I'm all grungy from the day. . . . I need a shower."

"That's okay. You can have one at my place. I don't mind," Laura said, fingering her necklace and piercing him with coal-black eyes.

"I don't know if I would feel comfortable. . . ."

"Hey, I'm an adult . . . I won't look." She smiled.

"It's not that. . . ."

"Then what is it? Would you like to go home alone or would you like to spend some time having a nice meal?"

Darren sighed.

"It *is* tiring going home alone every night."

"So, it's settled then."

Darren sat in one of the little wooden chairs at the tiny table while Laura set the Chinese food out on the dresser. He wore her white cotton bathrobe, his hair damp from the shower.

She tried not to stare at him. At the way the thin robe accentuated his long lean lines far more than his coveralls ever did. There was something so delicious about a man in a woman's bathrobe that it made her insides quiver. Especially this particular man.

He looked nervous, giving him a childlike innocence that stirred her blood. She scooped some food onto his paper plate.

"Thank you."

She lit several candles and some incense and then she sat down across from him. Darren looked down at his food and back up at Laura, who was still staring at him.

"Is everything all right?" she asked. Darren nodded and started to eat.

"Yes," he said softly, looking back down at his plate. He ate quickly and efficiently, while Laura picked at her rice. She watched his hands, stared at the dark chest hair curling out from his bathrobe that had fallen open slightly.

"If you could have one wish in the world, what would it be?" Laura asked as he cleaned his plate.

"To wish for more wishes, of course!" Darren laughed.

She smiled. "And after that?"

"Money. Lots of it. Maybe . . . oh, ten million!" he said. "What about you?"

"To have dinner with a handsome man and to have him make love to me afterward," she said, slipping out of her chair. Before Darren could speak, she had her mouth on his. At first he resisted, but her kisses were hot and hungry. Her persistence and size overwhelmed his loneliness.

She led him to the bed, pulling his robe open, licking his chest while he nuzzled her neck.

Candle flames flickered higher as their passion soared. Incense smoke curled and hung like a fog in the air.

Hands roamed across warm damp flesh. Mouths pressed against lips and shoulders. He pulled off her blouse and then her bra, touching her breasts. He took her breast into his mouth, sucking on her nipple until it was stiff as she quivered beneath his touch. He pulled at her pants. She helped him unsnap them and she wriggled self-consciously out of them, pressing her nakedness against his before he could see her body. He kissed her again, full on the mouth, then down her neck, and back to her delicious cleavage, burying his face between her tits.

Laura reached for his cock, was thrilled to feel it hard and pulsing, and larger than she had dreamed it would be. Just touching him made her moan throatily. This beautiful man kissing and sucking her body thrilled her exquisitely; she was wet and hungry already. She guided him into her, gasping as he filled her. He was so big and so hard, she felt pinned for a moment; then she relaxed as he filled her. She looked at his face and into his eyes and a rush of orgasm flooded her before he even began to thrust.

She closed her eyes. Him. Darren. Inside her, just as she had been dreaming for the past week. Incense filled her nostrils and she was aware of the candles sizzling, of the flames flickering wildly.

"God, I love how you feel inside me . . ." she cried out, her mind exploding with a kaleidoscope of color.

He kissed her again, thrusting feverishly as she rode the wave of yet another orgasm.

His eyes, his face, that jaw, that body, that cute little ass is all here, is all mine, for the moment.

She wrapped her legs around him, pulling him in deeper, excruciatingly deep, and pain-pleasure soared through her.

You will be mine, you will be mine, you will be mine.

She sucked on his shoulder, her fingers clenching his ass.

You fit in me so perfectly, the pieces fit, the pieces fit.

The room was hot, the smoke growing thicker. Laura slipped a piece of thin nylon rope from under her pillow and wound it around Darren, who was oblivious of what she was doing. She ran her nails up and down his back, weaving another piece of rope across his back and along his arms. Darren moaned and lifted his head for a moment, but Laura kissed him lustily so he wouldn't see her take yet another piece of rope and wind it around him.

Darren, eyes shut, thrust one last time and cried out. Laura felt him release into her. Warm and throbbing. She pulled him against her tightly with her legs, her own body riding another wave of ecstasy, as her fingers fumbled with the knots of the rope.

They lay gasping for air. Darren lifted his torso up from her, their slick sweaty chests smacking as the suction was broken. Before he could slide himself out of her, she reached up for his face. He opened his eyes as she cupped his cheeks.

"Come away with me . . ." she whispered.

He looked at her, as if he was just realizing who he was with.

"You know I can't," he said.

"But why? You aren't happy here, we could have an adventure, discover the world, and each other."

"I'm sorry, I just don't see it," he sighed. He jerked his head away from her touch.

"I don't know what came over me . . . " he said, trying to pull out of her again. "I didn't plan for this at all. . . ."

"You *do* like me . . . don't you?" she asked, trying to lock him to her with her ankles clenched around his back.

"Of course I *like* you, but I'm not running away with you." He tried to unlock her legs with one hand. "I have to go. . . ."

"No!" Laura clutched the rope, pulling it; the slipknots tightened, binding him to her.

"What the . . ." he cried out, not only locked by her legs and hands but by the rope. Every movement he made reinforced the web.

His face filled with terror. Laura felt him inside her, his struggle against her tingling her already heightened sensation. Another ripple surged through her. She couldn't believe she was coming yet again. Every time she looked at his face now flush with panic, she was struck by his beauty and couldn't stop shuddering.

He screamed and flailed, impossibly tied to a woman who couldn't seem to stop coming.

Her lips covered his, melted into his, and his screams were silenced as her fingers busily wove more rope around his neck.

Laura jolted awake. The sun was shining. She sat up and looked around the room. With a sigh, she realized she had done it again. The love spell had made no difference.

In the end, it was still the same. He didn't love her. He had barely even wanted a one-night stand with her.

She had had to force him to be with her . . . always.

She shook her head. The memory of what had happened was still hazy but the result was real.

The bloodstained bed, the bits of flesh scattered around the room, strands of rope: mere reminders of what Darren had once been.

The waiter in Baltimore, the variety store clerk in Providence, the dark-haired actor in Vermont, and now the wrench in New York.

She had discarded the waiter, the clerk, and the actor a while ago. They just never felt "right." Close, but not right.

As she stood up, the knife fell from the bedsheets unnoticed. Her vagina was full. Darren had fit perfectly inside her. That part of him was still there.

She ran her hands along her blood-smeared breasts. She imagined his strong, forceful hands tweaking her nipples. She stepped over what was left of his body and went to the mirror and stared into it.

What was it he had said?

Turn it, tweak it, torque it . . . and if it still don't fit, force it.

With a smile she realized, that this time, the pieces did fit.

Moist Dreams

Stanley Wiater

This has to be at least the eleventh time it happens.

You don't understand why you are still afraid—by now you know for certain it is just a bad dream. Nothing more serious or profound. Already you've realized how this is one of those dreams where—even though you're asleep—your mind is conscious to the extent that you're fully aware the dream is occurring again.

This dream.

Now a specified number of increasingly troubling events will occur, and when you finally awaken, you can play back the entire experience almost as if you had it recorded on a VCR. Except for a few minor, really trivial, variations, it is always the same, from beginning to middle to end—

Then why are you trembling so violently as it starts once again?

Relax—it's nothing! Simply realize where you are: fast asleep in your king-size water bed, right next to the woman you love with all your heart. She is sleeping in the raw, as usual; naked except for the outrageously sexy red panties she'll wear to bed just to drive you over the edge. You both know it's a signal whenever your hands move down her voluptuous body, until the clingy silk panties somehow slide so slowly and smoothly down her long, tanned-to-perfection legs.

Remember? It's always been the unspoken signal: the match to ignite the flame.

The simple truth is, that area of your relationship is so wonderfully intense you sometimes worry if perhaps it should all be considered just a wet dream! Yet one coming true every morning when you finally awake—with such a devastatingly beautiful, openly sensual woman who has selected you alone as her mate.

An undeniably experienced lover who arouses the desires of nearly every man—and woman—who ogles her on the beach in her designer string bikini. Or follows her walking down the street, her full breasts bouncing freely beneath sheer white blouses or blindingly low-cut sweater dresses. The once hidden nipples so gloriously noticeable as they become aroused and erect coming into contact against her always skintight clothes. Or far better still, when they are tenderly caressed by your roaming hands or playful lips or mischievously fluttering eyelids . . .

Yes, oh, *yes*—there are the naughty, pleasant thoughts beginning again, right on schedule. So wicked and so, so *nice*. And now you can't help feeling the strength of your own hardness, and how your fingers are slinking down across her softly yielding form until the damp panties are pulled off and away like some petal plucked from a dew-heavy rose.

The water bed rocks gently at first in response to your passion. Meanwhile the mutual heat becomes steadily more intense, the flame burning brighter and longer between you. The battered water bed seems to purposely ebb and flow with every passionate twist and loving turn and thrust.

And then something—as it always does—something goes . . . terribly *wrong*.

Suddenly you can't concentrate any longer on what you're doing for pleasure; for no sane reason you start thinking again of the damn letter opener. The ornate, obviously handcrafted,

steel and gold and ivory letter opener that came in the mail last
month. A strange and anonymous gift that she repeatedly and
vehemently denies knowing anything about who sent it or why.
And yet she has already hidden the skull-handled blade somewhere in the house, presumably so that you won't ever be reminded to bring up the troubling subject. . . .

Once again, the details in this section of the lucid dream are
disturbingly vague, like something small yet brightly glistening
at the bottom of a pond, which may or may not be worth the
risk of going after alone.

You can't understand why anyone would send her such an
unusual—and perhaps even illegal—gift, one certainly more appropriate to your admittedly bizarre literary career. Yet you've
always been keenly aware of her multitude of amoral admirers,
and had mounting suspicions that one day she would at last suc-
cumb to someone far brighter, better recognized, and even more
darkly imaginative than yourself.

So you keep frantically striving to please her, plunging farther and harder and deeper with each and every stroke, making
this time infinitely better than all the others. Ensuring that it's
the very best of her life so she will never be tempted to seek the
affections and attentions of any other. The sweat drips from
your face as you swing your head back and forth between her
perfect breasts. While the song with no ending plays again in
your head. Your very private love song.

> *She is yours.*
> *She has always been yours.*
> *She must always remain yours.*
> *She is yours or no one's.*
> *She is yours.*

And then . . . then the truly bad part begins . . . as you realize that the mysterious letter opener—for which you've been

secretly searching and obsessing about for weeks—is in fact *here*. Right here beneath your rock-hard belly, horribly transformed from a natural instrument of devotion into an unyielding weapon of destruction. Which is plunging deeper and deeper into her as the cold liquid once imprisoned inside the bed's floatation system mixes with the fresh warm wetness spurting in thick cascades of black scarlet pain against your sweating, writhing body.

For perhaps the eleventh time in as many nights, every action is completely and impossibly reversed. Tumbling over and over and over again lost amongst moaning waves of a drenching, burning darkness. Caught in a bottomless, sucking whirlpool that is never going to stop until you are totally consumed within its hot vortex.

Of course, you've known all along this is going to happen.

And though its always-terrifying outcome never seems to change, you're still somewhat comforted by the knowledge that this part ends very soon, and how, eventually, this entire gruesome nightmare will be completely erased from memory. Maybe this time for good.

Yet, for some odd reason, the imagined pain seems much more tangible, somehow even more cruelly encompassing than ever before. Crazily, there actually appears to be a growing difficulty with breathing, as if the blood-splattered air is escaping from newly opened holes other than her slashed nose and shattered mouth. . . . You try, as desperately and futilely as always, to scream out a warning before it's all too late.

But for whom are you screaming?

Like a drowning skater desperately racing back toward the ice-locked surface, you smash again and again against the slowly crumbling barriers of eternal, merciless sleep until you know for certain you're finally awake once more. Totally and completely feet-back-on-the-ground *awake*.

And totally soaking wet.

You want to first cry out, like some ineptly molested school-girl, then laugh wildly from sheer relief. *But wait . . .* the warm, sticky wetness is not just sweat, and these shrill cries of anguish are not coming from your beloved, so jealously butchered moments ago in a lurid anxiety dream. While only for the next few fleeting seconds does the mirror of reality finally expose the true reflection of your projected innermost fears.

Even without opening your eyes, you realize she has found the custom-made letter opener you've been attempting to keep from her—the one that came with the unsigned yet highly provocative note from an ardent follower of your work. Not that it matters anymore how foolishly and insanely jealous she has always been of your occasional female admirers. Or how she could never be fully convinced that the often perverse way you treated women in your so-called "arrested adolescent porno" stories and screenplays had *nothing* to do with the way you all but worshipped them in real life.

For as the razor-sharp letter opener plunges repeatedly into your tearing eyes and shattered mouth, you can only assure yourself that this—*right now*—must be the ending to this very bad dream she claimed had been making her a nervous wreck for the past several weeks. Maybe the very one that you could no longer bother to listen to or even pretend to relate because it was way too far-fetched—even for you.

Funny how it all comes rushing back: an unusually vivid nightmare that becomes progressively worse with the replaying, even though you had previously always blacked out before the unexpected yet no doubt ultimately terminal climax. And which, except for some minor, almost trivial variations, seemed to parallel this very bad dream you now only dimly recall having had ten, eleven, no, more than a dozen, times bef—

Share My Strength

Yvonne Navarro

It's three o'clock on Tuesday afternoon and the funeral is over.

It is a spectacular day, unseasonably warm for November and much more suited to weddings, or birthdays, or even a spur-of-the-moment picnic. The sun is painfully bright, the breeze warm and full of birdsong and the far-off smell of burning leaves. It hasn't snowed yet, so the grass is still a lush green below trees laden with the colors of autumn. Reds, yellows, oranges, and browns, all the colors of life on the downswing of recycling itself. There is a line of sculpted, pine-type trees, tall and thin, stretching along one side of the narrow road; Erin doesn't know what they're called but she's always hated them because they remind her of skinny sentinels, more like the bars of a prison than trees. Leslie never cared for them either.

From where she's parked at the back of the line of cars, Erin sits quietly in her black Lincoln Navigator and watches the rest of the mourners as they climb into limousines with darkened windows, fancy family cars, lots of Cadillacs and BMWs; no doubt they are all on their way to the grandparents' big house in Barrington, the one Leslie hated because it always smelled like old lavender and mothballs. No one looks her way, no one comes to the window to offer a soothing word or a sympathetic glance. No, Leslie's family will draw comfort from each other, and Erin has never been welcome within that chaotic, privileged circle. Now they—the father, the mother, the siblings and grandparents and cousins and God only knows who else—will all rebuild the deception that Leslie tore down three years after she graduated from college, the lie that said she was a general heterosexual someday-I'll-give-you-grandchildren woman.

Through the window of the Lincoln, Erin can see the hole in the ground.

A blanket of pseudo-lawn tries unsuccessfully to hide it, but Erin knows that beneath the too-bright green, the grave gapes like a big brown mouth. It's cold, and big, and no longer empty. A few feet down inside it lies Leslie's body, an empty shell that was once her lover and best friend. Leslie would hate all this— the smell of freshly mown grass, the too-sweet twitter of a hundred birds, the nauseous scent of the funeral wreaths arranged around the grave like gossiping old ladies dressed in ribbon-festooned, gaudy print dresses. Leslie had always said that if anything happened to her, she wanted to be cremated, burned beyond the possibility of cold ground and decay. "Take my ashes out to Sedona and spread them down the side of Cathedral Rock," she'd said. "That's as close to a church as I ever want to be."

But Leslie's wishes had meant nothing in the hearts of her family, and her words had been worthless in their ears. On the morning after, Mom and Pop had swooped into the emergency room like parental vultures, taking charge, taking control, taking *Leslie.* But did it really matter? As far as Erin was concerned, she had already lost everything.

That was then, this is now. And now is where Erin is, parked in a cemetery in tree-choked suburban Lisle with the sun shining bright and warm through the windshield on an unseasonably warm November day. She has never felt so dark and alone in her life.

She stays until the last of the cars has gone, thinking she will get out and go sit by Leslie's grave, talk to her as if she were still there with her. Before she can do this, a groundskeeper drives across the manicured lawn on one of those little yellow machines. What is it called? A backhoe, that's it. The gears shift and the engine noise builds; then another groundskeeper strolls up and pulls away the piece of fake lawn. A moment later the bucket on the machine is swooping and scooping and dropping dirt onto the mahogany casket that contains everything that meant anything in the world to her, and Erin loses her courage and effectively runs.

She has nowhere to go but the café or home, and both are unthinkable. They are nothing but reminders of the picture-perfect life she shared with Leslie, the same life that disintegrated Saturday morning when she woke to find her mate dead of a brain aneurysm in bed beside her. Erin has slept on the couch ever since. Home is a three-bedroom bungalow in Elmhurst with a professionally outfitted bright yellow kitchen and brand-new Berber carpeting in the living room, a carefully decorated guest room in which no one has ever stayed and a messy office once shared by the two of them. It's a basement they never got around to finishing and a yard with grass that is always a little too long and a bedroom where a ghost lay waiting on the unchanged sheets of the king-size four-poster bed.

Erin can't go there. Not just yet.

The restaurant then, Erlie's Café. Not a very imaginative name but they'd liked the combination of their names and the double meaning—Erlie, early—and had sunk savings and brains and sweat into making it the success it was. The breakfast crowd was fast and demanding, the light lunch flocks more thoughtful and slow, prone to reading a book or working on a laptop while they lingered over homemade moussaka, bowls of chili thick with meat and onions, or Hungarian goulash soup with ground veal and sliced potatoes. Their afternoon clientele was usually women, some business-minded, others more creative and dreamy-eyed; most of them are lesbians like Erin and Leslie, and they know that Erlie's is a place they can relax and be themselves. That was one of the biggest reasons Erin and Leslie had opened the café to begin with—to offer a place of solitude and peace to women living alternate lifestyles.

The café has been closed since she and Leslie went home Friday afternoon at four. If she goes there, Erin will have to unlock it and step inside a place built by two and never meant to be run by one. No, not today—tomorrow she will do this, reopen the business and learn to do all the parts that Leslie had always taken care of, think about hiring someone to wait tables while Erin does the cooking. Erin doesn't want to, but she has no choice. Hadn't Leslie always told her that whatever didn't kill her would make her stronger?

Right now Erin wishes she could be weak enough to die.

But she doesn't. Instead she starts the Lincoln and drives out of the cemetery, as if she were leaving most of her soul behind. She gets on I-355 and heads north, numbly putting distance between her and the ground that has wrapped its soil fingers around Leslie's corpse. Instead of getting off at her exit, Erin decides to keep going for a while. She goes and goes and goes, and then there is a hotel off Route 53, a high-end Wyndham Suites where she once attended a culinary seminar. She remembers the lounge in it, recalls lots of glass and growing things, muted music. It will be a good place to stop for a drink to soothe her nerves and give her alcoholic courage to face the empty house.

The bar is just as Erin remembers it, almost like an oversize greenhouse but with smoke-tinted windows that block out the sunshine that, for today anyway, she has come to despise. She finds a table in the back, one shrouded in big-leafed philodendrons and by one of the windows where she can look out at the sky while she nurses her drink, a straight-up glass of mandarin-flavored Smirnoff's. The sky is a brilliant, painful blue even through the colored glass, and it is only at times like these, when someone she knows or especially someone she cares about has just died, that the sky . . . *expands* in her vision every time she looks at it. It seems to be suddenly endless, stretching as far as she can see in every direction as though it must grow to envelope the spirit that Mother Earth just rejected.

And it is only at times like these that Erin looks up at the sky and thinks about the concept of heaven, and God, and about where people's souls go when they die.

Leslie is up there somewhere.

"Damn you, Leslie," Erin whispers, still very careful to keep her voice inaudible. "Damn you for dying and leaving me here all alone."

"Good evening," a male voice says.

Erin glances up, feeling her professional face slide over her features, that mask of pleasantness that she uses day in and day out at the café. Leslie used to laugh at how Erin had honed it to perfection over the years, how she could make anyone seem as if they were the most interesting person in the universe no matter what was really going on inside her. "Hello," she says automatically.

"May I join you?" he asks. "I don't mean to be a bother, but I'm just in town for the evening. I had a wedding to attend this afternoon and I don't know anyone in the area."

Ironic, Erin thinks. *This stranger goes to a wedding where two people start their lives, while I go to a funeral as part of mine comes to an end.* "Please," she says, and nods at the empty spot across the table.

He settles across from her, draping himself onto the leather-backed chair with unconscious comfort. He is tall and athletic, slightly younger than Erin, with longish dark hair speckled with premature silver and eyes the color of a clear, green ocean.

Expensive suit and tasteful tie, and Erin can tell by the way he's moving that he's in good shape; the whole package seems very carefully put together and is what Leslie would have called *Men's Fitness in a GQ Box.*

"This is a nice area," he says after the waiter comes and he orders an extra-dry martini with two olives. "It's the first time I've been out here."

"Oh, really?" Erin says. "Where are you from?" She rotates her glass and gets a whiff of her own vodka's citrus. It reminds her of the orange crepes that Leslie would sometimes make her on the mornings that the café was closed.

"Oh, downtown. I'm sorry—I didn't mean to make it sound like I was some out-of-state salesman or something. I just meant I'd never been out in this part of the suburbs."

Erin's mouth turns up a bit. "Because of the traffic, sometimes it might as well *be* another state."

He nods. "I feel the same way about living downtown. Coming out here—it's almost refreshing. In spite of the traffic, there's so much space and air. Lower buildings and less concrete, more places for the sun to touch. My name is Trevor, by the way."

"Erin." She thinks about his comment for a moment but her thoughts invariably turn to the much-too-recent memory of a sun-soaked cemetery. "So you went to a wedding," she says. Anything to get her thoughts away from the way her lover lies quietly rotting in a grave thirty miles south. "Friends or relatives?"

He laughs and it is a nice sound that goes well with the rest of him, again that perfectly balanced package. "Neither. Business associates. I was asked to escort one of their female clients, someone they wanted treated particularly well." He looks to the side for a moment and there is a genuinely puzzled expression on his face. "I'm afraid she and I didn't quite hit it off and she declined to spend the rest of the evening with me."

"That's unfortunate," Erin says. It is a strange way of describing a failed date, but she doesn't care enough to think any more about it.

"I thought so." He takes a discreet sip from his martini. "And you? What did you spend today doing?"

Erin hesitates, not sure she wants to share this part of herself with a total stranger. "I went to a funeral," she finally says.

A shadow of sympathy passes over his handsome face. "I'm sorry. Someone close?"

"Very." Erin stares at her drink and wills herself not to cry, not to allow the slightest glint of moisture to seep from beneath her carefully maintained mask.

"I'm sorry," he says again, and he sounds very much like he means it. "It must have been difficult."

Erin doesn't answer—to say that it was seems somehow trite. There is nothing in this world, no word or gesture or emotion, that can describe the abyss that Leslie's death has opened inside her. She takes a long drink—nothing discreet about it—of her vodka and asks instead, "So what do you do? Most of the people I know who live downtown are lawyers or politicians."

Trevor chuckles. "No, thank you. I suppose you could call my career a form of public relations. That way I can be up front about my intentions without having to be oily."

Now it's Erin's turn to smile, although the gesture comes reluctantly, the pulling of a splinter from beneath the skin, the guilty enjoyment of its sting—*yes, you will find something funny again in the world no matter how much you resist.*

"And you?" he asks. "You seem very outgoing and confident—you must be familiar with dealing with strangers."

"Yes," Erin replies. "Every day." She goes on to tell him about the café, allowing, no, *willing* her passion for her work to take first place where before it had always been usurped by Leslie's electric presence. She talks of the way the business was started, finding herself carefully avoiding any mention of Leslie;

she can't forget, she will never forget, but for a few hours, maybe she can *forestall* the agony. It is only later, much later, that it will come back to her how skillfully Trevor kept the conversation turned away from himself and anything too personal, how he manipulated her into revealing everything—or at least what he *thought* was everything—while giving next to nothing in return.

But in the meantime, the talk is good, the company is better, and the vodka is the best they can buy, all good, solid emotional anesthesia; Erin is on her third martini and feeling tingly when decorum and common sense make her refuse another. The pain is there, ever present, but temporarily melting at the edges, like a frozen puddle in the noon-high sun of a late winter day. Somewhere along the line she realizes he has begun touching her; not much—a fingertip brush on her forearm, a squeeze on her elbow, the gentle brush of his hand across her shoulder. Perhaps it is the alcohol, perhaps it is his picture-perfect maleness . . . but more likely it is the loss that makes her respond, makes Erin lean toward him to take in his scent, to feel the heat that his body gives off, to see the play of his muscles beneath the expensive Pierre Cardin shirt that doesn't seem so much tailored for him as grown to fit his form. When he makes his move, he doesn't ask her to his room or anything so crude—

"Will you join me for dinner?"

Company, just for the duration of a meal, Erin thinks, will be a good thing, a *blessed* thing. A harmless thing, even, to spend another hour or so with this man, to let him place a temporary wall between her and the bleakness of her empty home and bed—for God's sake, she's eaten next to nothing since the awful morning she pressed her mouth against Leslie's death-cold lips in a clumsy and futile attempt at CPR.

"Yes," she says. "That would be great." The words, *her* words, echo a bit at the edges, as if she were standing on the edge of a great cliff and shouting her pain into a blackness that has no end. That, of course, is the alcohol; it gives her distance in sight, sound, and sensation, lets her step back and watch the ordeal that her life has become from the point of view of an onlooker. And really, when a woman is singled out to bear this much agony, how bad can that be?

There is a restaurant in the hotel, some four-star steak house with a name she doesn't catch. The food is excellent and Erin purposely orders a Sicilian dish called *quaglie alla melagrana*—quail with pomegranate—only because it is something she has never tasted before. She does not want to eat anything familiar tonight, she cannot bear to put anything in her mouth that will somehow find a way to tie itself to a memory of Leslie. Thanks to the alcohol and the food and the company, she has gone from drowning herself in despair to smothering herself with the unfamiliar, using it as a sort of soft, spongy trampoline onto which she can bounce each time she hits bottom . . . at least for the next few hours.

Erin knows she is going to sleep with Trevor long before the waiter shows them the dessert tray.

It is not so much that she wants him, but that she wants . . . *different.* She has desire, yes, but he is only the smallest part of that. Her lust has more to do with the need to smother memories both good and bad, to erase, even just for a few hours, the last ten years. Once upon a time she had been a heterosexual college girl; she had dreamed of marriage and babies and a career in business that would give her an office overlooking Michigan Avenue that came with a secretary and a six-figure salary. All she had left of those dreams today was the money, and God knows there was precious little comfort to be found in the successful business of the café and the half-million-dollar insurance policy Leslie left her. Could it be anything but therapeutic, a fleeting balm, to back-step in time and pretend that she is once again that carefree young woman?

She wonders if Trevor knows what she has decided and

thinks that he does, also knows in some distant and still brutally sober part of her mind that he's probably planned the entire escapade. He's too smooth at everything—the words, the moves, the way he reaches out and gives her comforting touches at all the right times, sending his sexual *I'm available* message but never going too far. Fifteen years ago she would have been infuriated, but tonight . . .

He is a man, as unfamiliar as the food she just ate, as foreign to her as the room into which she will step in a very short time. Tonight, he is just what Erin needs.

When the check comes, Trevor reaches for it. "I'll take care of this for now."

As he pays, Erin watches and thinks of when she and Leslie met. They had been friends first, both straight, and then just sort of naturally discovered each other. There had been nothing fast and furious about it, nothing dirty or perverted. It had been simply that they enjoyed each other's company and had spent more and more time together; the touching that had progressed between them had been nothing like Trevor's tonight, with his subtle undertones of desire. A helping hand, a friendly hug, more and more often, the passage of weeks and months until it was a year and both realized that their hearts and minds were one and, really, the only thing they *hadn't* yet shared with each other was their bodies. It had all been so smooth and instinctive and, *supposedly,* forever.

After he's paid, Trevor comes around and pulls out her chair. As Erin stands he brushes her cheek and meets her gaze; she sees the question there and she smiles as best she can. "Would you like to spend some time with me tonight?" he asks, very softly so that no one else can hear.

Erin finds his question oddly touching—most men, she believes, would simply assume, but it's as if he wants to make very sure that this is want she wants. "Yes," she answers. "I would." Her heart is beating rapidly, fueled by excitement, alcohol, and a guilt that she knows she will be able to brush away without too much effort. Before Leslie, Erin had had the requisite number of ill-fated relationships with men, and she had thought the pain of those failures was over with the melding of herself with Leslie. So wrong—where was the kindness in Leslie's leaving her behind, and alone, and floundering? Tonight then, she needs comfort, a contentment that only the kindness of a temporary stranger can provide. She and Leslie had been soul mates and mind mates; Leslie would have perfectly understood Erin's choices tonight.

Trevor's room is nice but nothing remarkable, a better-than-average hotel suite. He opens the little bar and Erin chooses a tiny bottle of Smirnoff's Vodka, cold and plain after her earlier citrus-scented martinis. He pours the liquor over ice and they sip; then he sets his drink on the table and takes her glass from her hand. Erin turns to face him and Trevor puts his hands on her shoulders carefully, as if he's testing her; he lowers his mouth to hers, more testing, and when he tastes her response he moves in like a hungry tiger.

Trevor is almost *too* perfect, the dream evening date. He seems to know just where to touch first, how hard or soft, where to lick and nibble and bite down just a bit harder. Everything about him screams maleness and sexual desire, but he isn't pushy; he undresses her slowly, as if he relishes the expanding sight of her skin as each button slides open, each piece of clothing slips off. She does the same to him, matching him piece for piece; when he unhooks her bra and frees her breasts, she gasps as his hands encircle each and his lips close firmly on her left nipple. The liquor has dulled her inhibitions and Erin arches against his mouth and throws her head back; in response, Trevor touches her for the first time through her clothes, slipping one hand beneath her skirt and stroking between her legs, fingers sliding exquisitely over the nylon-covered satin underwear there.

Her fingers dig into his back and he probes a bit harder, then propels her backward with his body. When the edge of the bed stops her movement, he keeps pushing until her knees bend and she goes down. He kneels in front of her but his one hand never leaves her breast, the fingers massaging and sending swirls of enjoyment all the way down her belly; the other reaches up and catches the waistband of her panty hose and underwear, tugs them down to her ankles.

Then his mouth is on her and Erin nearly screams at the heat and pleasure that razors through her nerves. His tongue moves and circles, and somewhere out of sight her shoes and the hose and underwear are gone; she is lying there with her skirt hiked up to her hips and Trevor's teeth and lips are on the center of her while she cries out as an orgasm ripples fiercely through her body. Her insides are still pulsing when she realizes he's freed himself and discreetly donned a condom. He slides up and into her, repositioning her on the bed as he does so.

The sensation of penetration is . . . *strange*. Fulfilling but uncomfortably invasive—in just over a decade Erin has forgotten what it feels like to have the warmth and mass of a man's flesh inside her. He rocks against her hips, delicious friction in all the right spots as he nuzzles her neck, her ears, her lips, and she comes again just before he does, perfect timing just like everything else.

Afterward Trevor seems inclined to stay joined with her on top of the bedspread, but he feels heavy and Erin gets antsy almost immediately; he picks up the body language and pulls out, rolling next to her and stroking her belly lightly. After a couple of minutes, he reaches over and hands Erin her drink, sipping his own and watching her. There is something unnerving in his gaze, but Erin can't put her finger on it; whatever it is disappears when he smiles. "Did I make you feel good?"

"Definitely." There doesn't seem to be any reason to elaborate, and she knows from his appraising expression that he is trying to determine if she wants to go again. Erin doesn't; to stay would mean more intimacy, this time on a more extended level. He will want her to give more than she has this first time, will likely want to feel her mouth on him, perhaps be more experimental. She can't give any more and has no wish to reexperience levels of male/female interaction she left behind years before. For her this sex has been good, mind-numbing and physically exhausting; she has had her release, and while it may not have been as extensive for him, she doesn't think he has anything to complain about.

"I need to leave," Erin says and sits up. "I'm sorry."

Trevor pulls back, but there is nothing hurt in his expression—rather, it seems oddly empty and accepting. "No need to apologize. I hope you enjoyed our time together as much as I did."

"Yes," she says honestly. "I did." He watches as she pulls on her blouse first, then her underwear, nylons, and high heels. Erin is not stupid enough to expect him to ask for her telephone number, would tell him no if he did. She is shrugging on her jacket, part of the black suit she bought to wear to Leslie's funeral and will never wear again, when Trevor drops his bomb.

"Then I guess it's time to settle up."

At first Erin thinks she's heard him incorrectly, although her mind can't provide what else it is that he might have said. "I'm sorry?"

Trevor swings his lean legs over the side of the bed and stands, pulling his slacks up in a single smooth motion. "I thought we were clear on this."

Erin stares at him, hands frozen on the lapels of her jacket. "Clear on *what?*"

The look he gives her is vaguely reproachful. "That my time isn't free. I have to make a living, you know. Just like you or anyone else."

"What?" she asks faintly. She feels like she needs to find

something behind her to hold on to, but she'll be damned if she will show that kind of weakness.

"I guess we have a misunderstanding here." Now he sounds slightly apologetic. "I was sure I laid it out without being too crass."

"Crass?" She suddenly wants to laugh, although what there is that's funny about this situation she simply can't fathom. "You don't think *this* is crass?"

Trevor shakes his head. "No. This is just business." He slides his hand into his pocket and pulls out a piece of paper—his charge slip for dinner. "The cost for dinner was seventy-five. That means the total comes to five hundred twenty-five dollars."

Erin stares at him, so surprised it actually goes *beyond* shock. "You're charging me for *dinner?*" Some vague part of her mind reminds her that in all this, she should, perhaps, be grateful that he didn't charge her for the vodka he took out of the room's minibar; perhaps he simply chalks that up to a business expense.

His eyes widen. "You didn't think *I* was going to pay for that, did you?"

Erin's jaw works, but for a moment nothing comes out. She feels very calm and very . . . detached. Cold inside, not as if this were happening to someone else, but as if it *couldn't* be happening, because simply too *much* has happened to her over these last few days. After all, how much was one person expected to bear? "I don't pay for sex," she says, ignoring the statement about the dinner tab. "Any more than I pay for dinner when a man asks me out." She picks up her purse and turns toward the door.

"You will this time."

Something about the tone of his voice makes her stop and glance back. He is still standing there, hands casually in his pockets as though they were having no more complicated a conversation than deciding where to meet for lunch; his eyes, however, hold that same odd light that she'd found so disconcerting a bit earlier. No, not disconcerting. *Threatening.*

"It's very simple," he continues. "I gave you all the appropriate clues. That you chose to disregard them was your doing, not mine. I think I've learned enough about you from our conversation this evening to make things quite awkward for you should you maintain your decision not to pay. The first thing I'll do when you walk out that door is call hotel security and tell them *you* came up to my room with me, we had sex; then *you* tried to extort money in return for your favors. This is a top-notch hotel and I know they won't view this favorably. They'll no doubt stop you before you exit the building, then detain you while they call the police." His eyes glitter in his handsome face. "Imagine your embarrassment, not only tonight but tomorrow when news of this reaches the local paper in Wooddale—as I'll make sure it does—and all your loyal restaurant customers read about what you've done." His smile is predatory. "You're really not a very good lesbian, you know."

The insult burns but Erin has no time to dwell on it. Had she told him that much about herself, about her lifestyle and her work? She can't recall—too much fog and liquor and pain, too much of a desire to escape—but she must have. He has not only a weapon but ammunition, and while Erin may have been a fool to put herself in this situation, she is not so stupid that she doesn't realize she is trapped. *She* is the outsider here, the lesbian caught with a stranger who could be the businessman or the lawyer from out of town. How clever he has been— she knows precious little about what he really does beyond prostitute himself and find diabolical ways to ensure that he gets his fee. The police and embarrassment will be bad enough, the exposure to her customers at the café worse . . . but the humiliation she will endure when Leslie's family finds out—and, because they live in Wooddale, they will—will be unspeakable.

"I don't have that kind of money with me," she says. Her

voice is hoarse, defeated. She already knows how he will respond, and he doesn't disappoint.

"Then I'll go with you while you get it." He walks over and picks up his shirt. "I assume you'll need to go to an ATM machine. I believe there's one in the lobby."

"You assume wrong," she says, taking a minute bit of pleasure at the look of irritation that passes over his face. "My bank is closed, and I can't withdraw that much cash in one day."

"Then you'll need to find another way to raise the money," Trevor says. His voice is flat, with an undercurrent of venom. "I don't extend credit, and I have no intention of not getting paid *tonight* without causing you severe repercussions."

His vicious tone of voice takes the joy away from her small victory, even though Erin knew it was coming to this. "If you want your money, you'll need to come back to the café with me. I'll have to get it from the safe."

"Fine. You're driving."

She says nothing, waiting as he shrugs on his suit jacket and fussily combs his hair. Still acting the gentleman, he holds open the door for her as they walk out of the room and then again at the elevator. The inside of the elevator is mirrored and Erin stares at herself during the ride down. She supposes she is pretty but then lots of women are; what had attracted Trevor to her to begin with? Had she given off some sort of *Use me—I'm vulnerable!* signal that only feral people like him could sense? At the last second, she smoothes the mussed reddish curls of her hair with her hand, not wanting to be noticed as they walk through the lobby.

The silent drive is long and, for her, awkward. Perhaps tonight is routine for Trevor, a move-in-and-victimize procedure that he's perfected. For Erin, however, it has been a day filled with horrors. After searching for the unfamiliar behind which to hide, now the only thing that is helping her hold it together is the familiar, a phrase running through her mind that Leslie used to repeat when things became difficult. . . .

"Whatever doesn't kill you makes you stronger."

Leslie had always been the one with strength and will when things got rough; she had a ferocity and creativity of spirit other people could only wish for. She had always insisted it didn't come from herself but from everyone, that in the worst of times, *"You take in the pain and then you dissipate it, take it in and give it back, share it with others so that they, too, can be stronger."* It sounded so simple, that sharing of feeling and heartbreak—in fact, it was exactly what people did at wakes and funerals. But how in God's name could Erin share tonight's insanity with anyone?

The café is dark when they arrive, of course, the sign notifying the customers of Leslie's passing like a blight on the clean window of the front door. The office is in the back, on the other side of the kitchen, and Erin is glad that in the dimness Trevor can't see the cheerful way the walls have been hand-painted, the lovingly chosen country-style bowls and pitchers that are arranged on the carved wooden shelves above the windows and booths, the hundreds of other meticulous details that went into this dream she had once shared with her dead lover. This is a sacred place and Trevor's presence here, his very existence, is almost blasphemous to Leslie's beautiful memory.

Erin doesn't speak as she leads him through the door marked EMPLOYEES ONLY without turning on the lights—she can maneuver in here with her eyes closed. When he stumbles against one of the metal racks in the nearly dark kitchen, she turns back and reaches out to steady him. In her hand is an exquisitely sharp Henckels carving knife.

It is over quickly, so much so that Trevor does not have the time or breath to cry out. She stares down at his still form, watching the blood spread below his body like a pool of oil against the gray and black tones of the kitchen's cold tile floor, and realizes that her decision to perform this deed came not from his deception or attempt to blackmail her. No, she did what she did because he used her and her own darkest hour for monetary gain—she can think of nothing more despicable. The problem had been in the lack of sharing—she had shared her body with him, and her grief, but Trevor had given nothing in return. He could have, *should* have, shared of himself, taken in her pain and helped dilute it. Instead, he had chosen to rob her of what little comfort she would have drawn from their encounter, then cause her more grief.

Leslie's credo runs through Erin's mind again, the way her beloved had dealt with pain. It is quite late, and the small strip mall outside had been quiet and dark; no one had seen Erin bring this man inside. In the cool shadows of the still-dark café, Erin kneels beside Trevor's body and lets her chef's training take control of her hand and the knife.

"Whatever doesn't kill you makes you stronger. You take in the pain and then you dissipate it, take it in and give it back, share it with others so that they, too, can be stronger."

The café, hers alone now, still serves its simple meals of homemade chili and Leslie's moussaka recipe, special breakfast casseroles of egg, café-made sausage, and potatoes.

And as Leslie had always tried to teach her, Erin would break down her pain and share it with others.

Epiphany

Graham Masterton

The instant she stepped out onto the sidewalk, the sky cracked open and thunder echoed all around the office buildings like a car bomb. A few large spots of rain started to patter onto the concrete, and so she ran to the corner of Forty-ninth Street and waved frantically for a taxi. She was wearing her new cream linen suit and her new Manolo Blahnik shoes and she had just had her hair cut at Vidal Sassoon.

Like a happy miracle, a taxi with a lighted FOR HIRE sign came jouncing down Lexington Avenue toward her, and she stepped out into the road with her arm still lifted. As she did so, however, a sandy-haired man in a loud green summer suit pushed right out in front of her and let out a piercing two-fingered whistle. The taxi pulled over and the man opened the door, just as the rain began to lash down in earnest.

"Excuse me!" Jessica screamed. *"Excuse me! That's my cab!"*

The man was half in and half out of the taxi door. He blinked at her as if he couldn't understand what she was talking about.

"This is *my* cab," Jessica repeated, possessively gripping the top of the door. The rain was clattering onto the taxi's yellow roof and soaking her shoulders.

"*Your* cab?" The man looked around in mock bewilderment. "I'm sorry. I don't see your name on it any place."

"It's mine because I hailed it first; the driver was slowing down for me."

"Listen, I think I was nearer to the cab than you were. What do you want me to say?"

Still she clung on to the door. "You asshole. You unmitigated *asshole!* You know this is my cab."

"Hey, lady, you getting in or what?" the taxi driver wanted to know.

"You saw me first, didn't you?" Jessica demanded. "You were stopping for me."

"I just want to get the hell out of here, all right?"

Jessica tried to seize the sandy man's shoulder but he twisted his arm away and slammed the door, breaking her middle fingernail. The taxi pulled out into the traffic and sped off down Lexington, leaving her standing in the middle of the road.

She tried to hail another taxi, and there were dozens of them, splashing across the intersection like shoals of bright yellow dolphins, but the rain was really hammering down now and every one of them was occupied. She had never hated anybody in her life, not really, but when she saw those smug, dry people sailing past in their taxis, she wished they would all have cardiac arrests over their lunch tables, or choke on a fish bone. Her linen jacket was almost transparent and her strappy little shoes were filled with water, and her hair was sticking to her forehead. There was another flicker of lightning, followed by a deafening thunderclap.

Miserable, furious, she retreated to the nearest doorway. Even here the rain bounced against her shins, and the temperature was beginning to drop, so that she started shivering. She turned around to see if she could find any shelter inside the building. It was a small private art gallery with heavy glass and stainless steel doors. She pushed her way inside and immediately found herself in a world that was hushed and warm, thickly carpeted, with bronze mirrors all around, and elegant arrangements of arum lilies in glass Japanese vases. The walls and the furnishings were pale and beige and restful.

She took off her shoes and wiped the insides with a Kleenex. Three hundred and eight dollars, and they were ruined.

Two young men were sitting talking at a creamy marble desk, both of them dressed in expensive suits, their shirts gleaming white and their hair glossed back. The taller one turned and stared in surprise at her bare feet. "*Ye-e-es?* May I help you?"

"I, er . . . I just came in to take a look around, if that's okay."

"Please do . . . you're more than welcome. My God, you poor thing, you're *soaked!* Listen—why don't you go to the rest room and dry yourself off? We have some lovely Turkish towels in there."

"Well, thank you, I appreciate it."

She went into the silent, expensively fitted rest room. The mirror was tinted a flattering pink, but she still looked as if the Coast Guard had just fished her out of the East River with a billhook. She opened her purse and tried to comb her hair, but her feathery brunette bob had been ruined, and all she could do was slick it straight back in a style that was strangely reflective of the two young men.

When she came back out the two young men were waiting for her, smiling. "Better?"

"Much, thanks."

The taller one opened a drawer in the desk and took out a thick shiny catalog. "Here . . . you'll probably want one of these. Seventy-nine fifty, I'm afraid."

"*How* much?"

"Oh, don't worry. It'll be worth *twice* that in six months' time."

She took the catalog and somehow she felt like a Dayak tribeswoman being handed a Manhattan telephone directory.

The young man smiled and said, "The prints are all for sale, too, starting at twenty-five."

He gave a little cough and added, "Thousand." Then, "Each."

Jessica looked down at the catalog. On the front cover there was a black-and-white photograph of a young Mexican man. He had gappy teeth, and he was smiling wide-eyed and mocking at the camera. About twenty feet behind him, on a wide verandah, a silver-haired white man in a light gray suit was looking over a garden of impossible lushness, crowded with orchids and ferns and amaryllis. The brochure was entitled *Queer Nation, the photography of Jamie Starck.*

Oh, my God, she thought. She had read about this exhibition only yesterday. Jamie Starck had been a protégé of the notorious homosexual photographer Robert Mapplethorpe, and this exhibition had been furiously and publicly condemned by Mayor Rudolph Guiliani. The mayor had tried to close it down, but there had been demonstrations in Gracie Square by hundreds of gay rights activists, and in the end the mayor had been forced to give way. Or at least to come up with the grudging acceptance that "graphic depictions of alternative lifestyles, in context, may not be wholly deleterious to the city's moral fabric."

"I, ah—I seem to have made a mistake," she said, trying to hand the catalog back.

"Of course you haven't," the young man replied. "Or, even if you *have,* how will you know unless you see for yourself?" He was handsome in an otherworldly way and perfectly groomed. His skin was exfoliated and honey-tanned, and his fingernails were lightly polished. His necktie was silk, an impressionistic splash of carmine and gold. His spectacles were fashionably lozenge-shaped, and immaculately clean. He wore a loose gold wristwatch by Jaeger-le-Coultre and a spicy and expensive cologne. Jessica could imagine that his underwear was Calvin Klein, blindingly white, without a single stain.

"I've come to the wrong gallery, that's all."

But the young man said, "Does it matter?" and took hold of her arm, and guided her toward the exhibits.

"Honestly," Jessica protested, "I only came in here to shelter from the rain. I really didn't—"

It was then that she saw the first photograph. It was black-and-white, as all of them were, taken on a high-intensity film that gave startling clarity to every single hair, every single goose bump, every single blemish. It was a picture of two young men—one black, one white, facing each other with their arms loosely linked over each other's shoulders. They were both slim, muscular, and almost laughably good looking. Both of them had fully erect penises, and their glans were touching each other, almost kissing each other. The photograph was labeled *Racial Accord.*

Jessica stood and stared at it for nearly ten seconds. Then she turned to the young man in the lozenge-shaped spectacles and looked in his face for an explanation.

"You're looking for a meaning," he said, as if he could read her mind.

She shook her head in confusion. "I never thought that—"

"I know. This exhibition strikes everybody the same way, men and women both. They come here with all kinds of pre-conceptions, 'I hate queers' or 'I'm straight but curious,' but they all walk out enlightened. Like Saul, you know, on the road to Damascus."

Jessica moved to the next photograph, and the young man followed her, although he kept his distance. The photograph depicted a naked Arab, kneeling in the desert, his cheek pressed against the hot sand as if he were listening for the sound of distant hoof beats. On the far horizon there were sand dunes, ribbed by the wind, and a cluster of palm trees. Close to the palm trees stood a white-bearded man wrapped in Bedouin black, holding the halter of a highly disinterested camel.

The Arab was pulling apart the cheeks of his bottom to expose his anus, in a gesture of extreme submission. His penis was erect and the glans was seasoned with grains of glittering sand. The title of the photograph was *Abid.*

"In Arabic, *abid* means 'slave,'" said the young man, although he still kept his distance.

"I, ah—I think I should go now," said Jessica.

"Well, that's up to you. But you'll never see anything like this again, ever. Jamie's dying of AIDS, and he's already lost eighty percent of his sight."

As if she were dreaming, Jessica moved to the next picture. It showed a very thin middle-aged man lying naked on a chaise lounge. His eyes were half closed as if he was dozing, and his hair was long and blond and wavy, like a woman's. On the elaborately tiled floor beneath him lay a borzoi dog, sulking, as borzois do. A young Moroccan man in a huge top-heavy silk turban was kneeling next to the chaise lounge. His turban was draped with strings of pearls and he wore large dangly earrings. The young man's lips were closed around the Englishman's penis, while one long-fingered hand was cupping his testicles. The young man wore an embroidered waistcoat, but he was naked from the waist down, and semen was dripping like strings of pearls down his thighs.

"What does it mean?" said Jessica. "Is it just perversion, or what?"

The man in the glasses gave her a strangely confidential smile. "Perhaps it means that people should be free to express themselves in whatever ways they wish, no matter how bizarre."

"Oh, yes? And perhaps it's nothing but hard-core porn, masquerading as art."

The man approached the photograph, and said, "You see it though, don't you? Each picture is a mystery but each picture is also an answer."

"So what's this picture an answer to? Some bony old faggot's prayer?"

The man laughed. "I like you . . . you're very direct. That's unusual."

"I think I should leave now," said Jessica. "I recognize the quality of this photography, and I guess it's arguably art. But if you really want to know, I find it embarrassing."

"All right. At least you're honest."

She gave him the catalog back. "Good luck, anyway."

On her way out, she caught sight of a photograph that she hadn't seen before, because the light had been shining on the glass, and obscured it. She stopped, even though she didn't really want to. The man in the glasses waited so close behind her that she could hear his measured breathing. *I'll bet that even the hairs in his nostrils are immaculately trimmed,* she thought.

The photograph had been taken on the landing of a grand marble staircase, with high leaded windows that let in a thin, restrained light. A young man of nineteen or twenty, naked except for thong sandals, was leaning languidly against a marble pillar. He looked Thai, or Cambodian, and his hair was fastened with chopsticks in a geishalike bun.

His skin shone with a silky, almost unearthly radiance. His nipples were like ripe sultanas. His penis was half erect, with a foreskin that looked as if it was just beginning to slide back, and his scrotum was the texture of crumpled silk. A single sparkling drop of liquid quivered on the end of his penis, like a diamond.

More than anything else, though, it was the expression on his face that caught Jessica's breath. He had high cheekbones and large, dark, unfocused eyes, as if he was drugged, or hypnotized. He was utterly exquisite.

"Ah," said the man in glasses. "All our women fall in love with Lo Duc Tho."

"That's his name? Lo Duc Tho? Who is he?"

"He was actually Vietnamese. Jamie found him in a grand house in Paris, next door to the apartment building where Marlene Dietrich used to live."

Jessica approached the picture and touched one finger lightly against the glass. Lo Duc Tho stared back at her enigmatically. *Each picture is an answer, but each picture is also a mystery.*

"What was he doing in Paris?" she asked.

"He was a toy. I think that's the best description. The house was owned by a very wealthy lady whose father had made a fortune in Vietnam when it was still owned by the French. After the battle of Dien Bien Phu in 1954, when the French were forced to give up all of their possessions in Indochina, her father came back to Paris—bringing not only his daughter but the orphaned son of one of his servants, a child of ten years old, and that was Lo Duc Tho.

"Lo Duc Tho was fed well and educated by private tutors and pampered in every way that you could think of. But in 1962, when he was eighteen, the father died suddenly of a stroke, and his daughter took over Lo Duc Tho's upbringing completely."

"You called him a toy."

"Exactly so. Lo Duc Tho was mademoiselle's plaything. After her father's death, she expected him to amuse her all day, playing the violin for her, singing for her, dancing for her. She also expected him to be nude at all times, except when they went out."

"Nude? Like, all day?"

The man leaned against the wall beside her and nodded. "She made him pose for her in all kinds of exotic positions and sit close to her so that she could fondle him whenever she felt like it."

"That's extraordinary. What did Lo Duc Tho think about it?"

"I don't have any idea. But he didn't appear to mind, because he never attempted to run away. He hardly ever spoke, and when he did he used to refer to himself in the third person, as if he were talking about somebody else."

"What a strange life."

"You don't have any idea. Mademoiselle used to invite her friends for afternoon tea, and Lo Duc Tho would be sprawled on a chaise lounge next to them, so that these thirtyish ladies could kiss him and caress him and even fellate him, if they wanted to. Jamie told me that madam's friends use to smear the boy's private parts with raspberry preserves so that they could lick it off."

"My God. Talk about decadent."

"I don't know. I've heard about worse in New York. Guinea pigs, being used in all kinds of inventive ways, things like that. And at least the French make very decent preserves."

"You're teasing me."

The man gave her the faintest of smiles. "Tell me now that you won't leave here feeling enlightened. Or *different*, at least."

"Well, I guess you're right. I will. Do you know what happened to Lo Duc Tho? He must be middle aged himself now."

"Mademoiselle became very ill and the house had to be sold. Jamie made some inquiries, but nobody found out where Lo Duc Tho disappeared to."

The man accompanied Jessica to the front door. It had stopped raining now and the sidewalks were blinding with reflected light.

"Thank you," she said. "It's been very interesting. Possibly obscene, but very interesting."

"The pleasure," he assured her, "is totally mine."

"So how was *your* day?" asked Michael, pouring himself another large glass of chardonnay.

"Unusual," she said.

"Oh, yes? Unusual in what way?"

"I did something I never imagined that I would ever do in a million years. I went to see that Queer Nation exhibition. Well, I didn't actually go out with the intention of seeing it, but I got caught in the rain and that's where I ended up."

Michael blinked at her. He was thirty-one, two years younger than she was, but his short-cropped iron-gray hair made him look much older. He had very pale blue eyes, the color of bleached denim, and a broad, Scandinavian-looking face. He was wearing a blue-and-white-striped English-tailored shirt and a pair of expensive fawn slacks, and no socks. His ankles were still tanned after two weeks' filming in Bermuda.

"And?" he said, at last. "What did you think of it? The exhibition?"

"I was . . . corrupted, I think."

"Seriously? You're serious?"

"It was strange. I don't know exactly what I felt. Some of the pictures were very beautiful and they were all technically brilliant. But there was something *poisoned* about them."

"Maybe you'll make a point of taking an umbrella next time." He checked his heavy steel wristwatch. "Jesus, look at the time. I have to call Bertrand in Vancouver."

"Can't you just finish your dinner?"

"Listen, I'm going to miss him if I do. He's flying to Montreal this evening and I have to talk to him about the Harrington account." He took his glass of wine and left his half-finished tagliatelle on the plate. He went across to the living area and sat on the large black leather chair next to the window, where the phone was. Jessica stayed at the table with its shiny black glass top and continued to eat and watched him while he talked. Outside the window she could see the sparkling lights of the Jersey shoreline, and two helicopters circling like fireflies.

Both Michael and she worked in advertising. He was a freelance director for TV commercials while she was a senior copywriter at Nedick Kuhl Friedman. They had lived together for eleven months now, renting between them this huge condominium overlooking the Hudson. They had furnished and decorated it in minimalist style, but very expensively. On the opposite wall, discreetly lit, hung a dot painting by Damien Hirst for which they had paid $78,000.

Michael said, "We could meet up in Cancun on the twenty-fifth. Yes, that's right. I need that very special light they have on the beach there. No, the Gulf Coast is no good at all. Far too harsh. What are you talking about, filters? If you want perfection you have to *start* with perfection."

Jessica wound her tagliatelle around her fork. She couldn't help thinking about Lo Duc Tho, and how he had wandered around naked all day. She could almost imagine him sitting in the large leather chair opposite her, his hair pinned up like a geisha's, one leg insouciantly slung over the armrest, his eyes as dark and blurry as a court portrait by Velasquez. He would be idly playing with his half-erect penis, rolling his foreskin backward and forward in a slow, dreamy rhythm.

"I need at least two lighting cameramen. Well, I'd prefer David Weill, but if you can't get him . . . Yes, I know all about budget, Jim. But you're talking false economy here."

Perhaps she would beckon Lo Duc Tho and he would rise from his chair and walk across to the table. He would lay one long-fingered arm on her shoulder, respectfully, as lightly as a hummingbird. She would beckon him again to stand even closer, so that she could see every vein beneath his ivory skin. His pubic hair was like shiny black silk, and pomaded, and combed, so that it stuck to his stomach in waves.

"I'm telling you, if we shoot it and it doesn't work, which it *won't*, the way you're describing it, then we'll have to shoot it over, and that's going to cost us more than double."

She took hold of Lo Duc Tho's penis and gently massaged it. It grew harder and harder, until the foreskin peeled right back and the glans swelled as dark as a damson plum. She gripped it even tighter, as tight as she possibly could, but when she looked up at Lo Duc Tho he did nothing but give her the most abstract of smiles, as if he were thinking about something else altogether.

Between finger and thumb, she lifted a strand of tagliatelle from her plate. She encircled the shaft of his penis, and tied the tagliatelle in a slippery little bow. Then she took another strand, and another, until his erection was decorated with eight or nine ribbons of pasta.

"Now for some sauce," she told him. She took a handful of garlic and tomato sauce out of the bowl and smeared it all over his scrotum and between the cheeks of his taut, rounded bottom. "You like that?" she asked him, gently rolling his testicles between her fingers. "Now you're a meal in yourself."

She leaned forward and licked his wrinkled, tomato-tasting skin. She nuzzled him and sucked him, sucking each testicle one after the other. "You're beautiful, aren't you?" she said. "You're absolutely gorgeous."

She took the swollen head of his penis into her mouth and slowly slid her hand up the shaft, so that one by the one the ribbons of tagliatelle slipped over his glans and into her mouth. When she had swallowed them she stuck out her tongue and probed the hole in his penis with it. As she did so, she rubbed him harder and harder. "Come on, you can give me my dessert now. Don't be shy."

It was then that she became aware that Michael had finished his phone call to Bertrand and was standing staring at her. Immediately, embarrassed, she sat up straight, and it was then that she realized that there was nobody there, no Lo Duc Tho, and that she had been smearing tomato and garlic sauce all over her chin and her cheeks and beating with her fist at nothing but thin air.

Michael slowly pulled his chair out and sat down, still staring at her. "What the hell are you doing?" he asked her, at last.

"I'm, ah—I seem to have made a bit of a mess."

"What is this? Some kind of attention-seeking stunt? Listen, I'm sorry I had to call Bertrand right in the middle of dinner, but for Christ's sake, look at you."

Jessica wiped her face with her napkin, and then stood up. "I was—I don't know. I was trying to eat it the Italian way."

"I've been to Italy six times and I never saw *anybody* eat like that. I never saw anybody eat like that *ever.* Maybe my sister's two-year-old kid."

"Well, I just wanted to relish it, that's all. Like really, really relish it."

With that, she threw down her napkin and walked stiffly to the bathroom. She stood in front of the mirror staring at herself. She still had tomato and garlic sauce in her hair, and the front of her cream cotton blouse was spattered all over, so that she looked as if somebody had hit her in the nose.

How could I have done that? she thought. *I was sure that I could see Lo Duc Tho. I was sure that I could actually* taste *him. God . . . maybe I'm working under too much pressure. Maybe I'm cracking up.*

She looked down at her hand, and slowly reproduced the rubbing motion she had used to stimulate Lo Duc Tho's penis. She could still feel his hardness. She could still feel his foreskin, as slippery and pliable as a wonton. She took a deep breath and then she unbuttoned her blouse, filled up the washbasin with cold water, and pushed it in to soak.

When they went to bed, they both read for half an hour. Then Michael abruptly slapped his book shut, put on his American Airlines sleep mask, and heaved himself sideways, with his sun-freckled back to her.

"Good night, then," said Jessica, but Michael didn't answer. He didn't like weirdness, or anything unpredictable (like his partner smearing her face with tomato and garlic sauce), and he was obviously making a point. One of the things that had first attracted her was his solidity, the feeling of security he had given her, but as time went by she was beginning to find it increasingly repressive, like living with a disapproving parent.

She had been reading Coleridge, an old dog-eared copy she had found in a cardboard box in the cellar. It wasn't easy to understand. Yet she felt that it was just like Lo Duc Tho's photograph, a mystery and an answer, both at the same time.

In his loneliness and his fixedness he yearns towards the journeying Moon, and the stars that still sojourn, yet still move onward; and everywhere the blue sky belongs to them, and is their appointed rest, and their native country, and their own natural homes, which they enter unannounced, as lords that are certainly expected and yet there is silent joy at their arrival.

She felt as if Lo Duc Tho had been waiting in the wings of her life ever since she had first felt sexual stirrings. Thinking back on her reaction this afternoon when she had first seen his picture, she realized now that what had stopped her in her tracks was *recognition.* Here was the man who would sit beside her under the journeying moon and the lordly stars, and offer his nakedness and his docile beauty so that she could discover the true meaning of pleasure.

She laid her book on the nightstand and switched off the light. In the darkness she could hear the plaintive mating call of a ferry crossing to the Jersey shore. Michael had started that persistent *pish, pish, pish,* which meant that he was already asleep.

She was very tired. Before she had been caught in the rain she had been working for more than five hours with her creative team, trying to develop a series of magazine advertisements for Moist-Your-Eyes antiwrinkle cream. Then—after she had briefly come home to change—she had gone down to Ray MacConnick's studio in the Village to supervise a three-and-a-half-hour photo shoot.

All the same, she found it difficult to sleep. She couldn't stop thinking about Lo Duc Tho, and the way in which he had seemed to materialize in front of her. She couldn't stop thinking about his strange, detached smile, and the feeling of his skin.

She turned over, and as she did so she felt fingers trailing gently down her back. "Not now, Michael," she murmured. But the fingers kept on tracing patterns around her shoulder blades and down her spine, and back again. The touch was so light that it made her skin tingle.

"Michael—" she said, but then she heard him grunt and stir and start that monotonous *pish, pish, pish*.

"Michael?" She propped herself up on one elbow, and looked around. Michael still had his back turned toward her, and he was deeply asleep.

She looked around the darkened bedroom, frowning. She even slapped the comforter, as if there could be somebody hiding underneath it. Nobody. She must have imagined those fingers, or maybe they were nothing more than the draft from the air-con unit.

Uneasily, she lay back down again. It was true that she had been working far too hard for the past three months, but she knew that if she could pull off a really successful campaign for Moist-Your-Eyes there was a vice presidency waiting for her, and $25,000 more salary. She didn't want to come to pieces, not now. Not when everything for which she had sacrificed so much time and so much effort was right within her grasp.

She tried to empty her mind, the way that she had been taught at her yoga class. Imagine your thoughts pouring out of your ear, and soaking into your pillow. Imagine blackness, infinite blackness. No sound, no sensation, just seamless darkness and total detachment. But then she felt the fingers again, delicately teasing her shoulders, and following the curve of her body so that she shivered as they reached her hips.

She turned onto her back. Immediately—without a sound—
Lo Duc Tho materialized out of the darkness and lightly
climbed astride her. She let out an *"ah!"* of shock, but he
pressed his fingertips against her lips. He sat gazing down at her,
his face barely visible in the gloom.

"You're not real," Jessica breathed. "There's nobody here
but me and Michael."

Lo Duc Tho leaned forward and kissed her lips, and she was
sure that she could taste lemon grass on his breath. As he kissed
her, he took hold of her right hand and guided it toward his
penis, so that she could feel it rising between her fingers. He
showed her how to roll it against her nipples, round and round,
and it gradually grew so hard that it felt as if it were carved out
of polished ivory. Her nipples stiffened in response.

Her breathing began to grow shallow. With her left hand she
reached between Lo Duc Tho's thighs and fondled his testicles,
tugging at the skin of his scrotum with her sharpened fingernails. She tugged harder and harder, but Lo Duc Tho didn't
utter a sound, although the head of his penis was slippery now,
and so were her nipples.

This was a kind of heaven . . . to have a beautiful and exotic
young man who didn't speak or argue or complain. A young
man with whom she could have any variety of sex she wanted,
whenever she wanted. She closed her eyes and already she could
feel a dark, compressed sensation between her legs. It was the
first stirring of an orgasm that she knew would be almost unbearable. She pressed his penis harder and harder against her
breasts, and kept up her rhythmical pulling at his scrotum.

He suddenly arched his back and ejaculated. Warm sperm
flipped against her cheek, and then anointed her neck, and then
her breasts. Lo Duc Tho sat utterly still for a moment, and then
he began to stroke her face and massage her breasts until the
sperm began to dry. She closed her eyes and she could smell him
and she felt as if she had never been so pampered in her life.

Then he disappeared. She didn't know how he did it, but he simply unraveled in the darkness like a knotted silk sheet, and he was gone. She sat up again, trying to see if he was hiding behind the armchair, or buried in the shadow of the armoire, but there was nobody there.

She couldn't have imagined him. She touched her breasts and she could still feel his sperm on her. She waited for a long time, almost five minutes, to see if he would reappear. She didn't call out.

At last, exhausted, she lay back and closed her eyes. Michael grunted and turned over again, and his arm dropped heavily across her.

"Got to call Henry," he mumbled.

During her lunch break the next day, Jessica went back to the gallery. The smart young man with the glasses was still there, but this time he was alone. Jessica went directly to the picture of Lo Duc Tho and stood staring at it, as if she expected it to talk to her.

"You're back, then?" said the man, circling around behind her. He was wearing a smart navy blazer and a very white shirt and his aftershave had strong notes of vetiver grass.

"I wanted to take another look, that's all. You were right. This exhibition is a revelation. The trouble is, I can't work out what it's a revelation *of*."

"I think you will, if you give yourself time."

"Tell me more about Lo Duc Tho."

"There's nothing more to tell. He was content to be used, that's all. Whatever Mademoiselle asked of him, he obliged. I suppose you and I find it difficult to imagine anybody being so docile. But there can be great spirituality in such docility. I think that Lo Duc Tho was closer to heaven than we can possibly imagine."

"You knew him yourself," said Jessica.

"Yes, I did."

"In fact . . . you're Jamie Starck, aren't you, and you're not dying of AIDS at all."

The man gave her a smile that was almost coy. "Well guessed. I tend not to advertise my identity. When they find out, some people react in a very negative way. Negative—I suppose that's a joke, for a photographer."

"I need to find out who Lo Duc Tho actually was."

Jamie Starck took off his glasses and looked at her seriously. "You *need* to?"

"Yes, whatever you know. Anything."

"You've seen him."

"No. But I imagined that I saw him."

"It counts for the same thing."

"Who is he? *What* is he?"

"I can't really explain."

"Is he a ghost? Is that it?" She didn't even know how she could bring herself to think such a thing, let alone suggest it out loud, on a bright summer day.

Jamie Starck shook his head. "I don't think that I believe in ghosts. But perhaps I believe in the overwhelming power of human desires—particularly sexual desires. Think about it— Sometimes we can almost bring ourselves to orgasm, can't we, just by thinking sexual thoughts? Lo Duc Tho is one of our desires, and that's what gives him such a grip on our imagination."

Jessica said, "You've seen him too, haven't you? I mean, after you took his picture? Did he come to your bed?"

Jamie Starck said nothing. Jessica hesitated for a moment, and then she said, "He's very alluring. I'm not sure what to do."

"No, it isn't easy, I'll admit. It's that mixture of absolute innocence and absolute corruption. Let me tell you . . . I walked into Mademoiselle's salon one afternoon when she and her friends were gathered for tea. Lo Duc Tho was sitting on the chaise lounge, wearing a girl's velvet hat, his cheeks rouged, his eyes made up with eye shadow, his lips painted with lipstick. His legs were wide apart and he was erect. An elegant woman in a Balenciaga suit was sitting beside him, a truly classic French beauty of a certain age, and she was slowly pushing her long pearl necklace into his anus, pearl by pearl, right up to the clasp, and then slowly pulling it out again, over and over, until he climaxed all over her skirt. She laughed with delight."

"Is he dead, do you think?" asked Jessica.

"I don't know. Probably. Even if he isn't, I wouldn't even know where to start looking for him."

That night Michael had to take three of his clients to Le Cirque, so Jessica spent the evening alone, washing her hair and giving herself a pedicure. At 11:00 P.M., Michael called to say that he was going to be very late, so not to wait up for him. She went to bed with the television switched on but the sound turned right down and tried to read, but she was too tired to make much sense of Coleridge.

And all should cry Beware! Beware! His flashing eyes, his floating hair! Weave a circle round him thrice, And close your eyes with holy dread, For he on honey-dew hath fed, And drunk the milk of Paradise!

Without realizing it, she fell asleep, and the book dropped out of her hand and onto the comforter. And it was only a few minutes afterward that a young long-fingered hand gently lifted the book away, and stroked her forehead and her hair, and kissed her cheek.

She opened her eyes. Lo Duc Tho had climbed onto the bed next to her, on all fours. His glossy black hair was hanging loose, so that he looked like a wild young animal. He was staring at her intently, his lips slightly parted, but he didn't speak. She could see between his thighs that his penis was already stiff, and that his testicles were as tight as two walnuts.

"What do you want?" she asked him, and her voice seemed unnecessarily loud. The light from the television gleamed on his naked back. "Are you alive? Or dead? Or am I going mad?"

He kissed her again, and then he drew down the comforter. She was wearing a pink sleep T, and he reached down with both hands and softly squeezed her breasts through the warm brushed cotton. She no longer felt frightened. She could see now that Lo Duc Tho was everything that Jamie Starck had described. He was everything that she had secretly desired, and never dared to tell anybody, come to life.

She sat up in bed, crossed her arms, and took off her T-shirt. She stroked Lo Duc Tho's cheeks and upper lip, and pushed the tips of her fingers into his mouth, so that he could kiss them and lick them and nip them with his perfect white teeth. Strongly but gently she pushed him onto his back, and then she sat astride him, as he had sat astride her. With both hands, she moved his penis up and down, quite forcefully, so that on her downward stroke his foreskin was stretched right back.

"Are you never going to talk to me?" she said. Lo Duc Tho gave her his abstract smile, but still didn't speak.

"I suppose that's the nature of fantasies," she told him. "They don't argue with you and they don't involve you in idle conversation."

She leaned forward so that her nipples touched his chest, and she swung her breasts from side to side. "I think we're going to have to decorate you a little," she said. "How about some silver rings through your nipples, and some tattoos? You'd look gorgeous with a few flowery tattoos."

She kissed him and ran her fingers deep into his clean shining hair. His skin was absolutely flawless, except for a tiny star-shaped scar on his right shoulder. "Touch me," she said, sitting up again; and he slid one hand beneath her thigh and stroked her clitoris with the tip of his middle finger, so lightly that it was almost like being licked. She was so aroused that his stroking made a wet clicking noise like somebody softly smacking their lips.

She raised her hips, and took hold of his penis in her hand, and positioned it between her thighs. Then she sank down on it, all the way down, until she could feel his scrotum squashed against the cheeks of her bottom, and she let out a long quavering moan of absolute pleasure. If this was nothing but a fantasy—if this was nothing but her own desire—it was a fantasy of unbelievable intensity, and she didn't care if she was going mad or not.

"Lo—Duc—Tho—" she breathed, again and again. "Lo—Duc—Tho—"

He felt so long and hard and slippery that he seemed to penetrate deeper into her body than any man who had ever made love to her before. She could almost believe that the head of his penis would nudge her heart.

"You're driving me out of my mind," she gasped. "You're killing me." They were both glistening with sweat and yet Lo Duc Tho still didn't appear to be exerting himself, or involved in what he was doing to her in any way. She rode up and down on his penis even more forcefully, *smack, smack, smack* against his thighs, and she caught him closing his eyes for a moment, as if at last he was beginning to feel something like the same pleasure that she was.

Exhausted, she lifted herself off him and rolled onto her back. Lo Duc Tho rose up next to her, as if he was going to climb on top of her, but she threaded her fingers into his hair and said, "You're *my* fantasy, remember? I want you to lick me." This time, *she* wanted an orgasm, too. This time she urgently needed one.

In silent obedience, Lo Duc Tho crawled down the bed and lay between her thighs. She watched him enthralled as his narrow tongue flickered on her clitoris, and he watched her back, never taking his eyes off her once. The feeling he gave her was so strong that she felt as if they were on a raft, on the ocean, at night, being washed out on an overwhelming swell.

Jessica had an orgasm that made her deaf and blind. It went on and on, until she couldn't tolerate any more back-breaking spasms, and she reached down to push Lo Duc Tho away from her.

Except that Lo Duc Tho wasn't there anymore. She was lying alone on the twisted sheets, with the silent television still flickering, and her book of Coleridge lying on the floor where she must have dropped it.

She couldn't move. She knew that she should have got up, but she couldn't. She lay staring at the ceiling and breathing like a marathon runner. She thought: *What's happening to me? I've never had sex like that before, ever. But maybe I haven't had it even now.*

She was still lying there when the bedroom door and Michael came in, tugging off his stripy silk necktie. "Hey, there! You still awake? Jesus—I thought those guys were going to go on drinking all night."

He came over to the bed and sat down beside her. "You look hot, are you okay?"

"I'm fine, I'm okay."

He reached out and touched her forehead. "Jesus, you're burning up. I'm not kidding you—you look like you're coming down with the flu. You should keep yourself warm, not lie here undressed like this."

She couldn't think what to say. She couldn't stop trembling and she was still short of breath.

"I'll call Dr. Biedermeyer first thing. And there's no way you're going into work tomorrow."

* * *

He came back with two glasses of milk. "How are you feeling now? I should have known something was wrong when you had that accident with the pasta sauce."

She was sitting up straight in bed in a black silk kimono, with her hair in a towel turban. "That was no accident, Michael."

"I don't get you. You didn't make all that mess on purpose?"

"Michael, there's something I have to tell you."

He took off his robe and climbed into bed next to her. "You're very stressed out, honey. I know that. That's why I'm going to call Dr. Biedermeyer. He can give you something to keep you together until this Moist-Your-Eyes account's all wrapped up. You know, maybe Prozac."

"I don't need Dr. Biedermeyer, Michael, and I don't need Prozac. I've been seeing somebody."

Michael had just taken a mouthful of milk but now he slowly put his hand to his throat as if she had told him that she had poisoned it. "You've been *seeing* somebody? Who?"

"It's not what it sounds like. I haven't been having an affair. I've been seeing somebody, like a hallucination. Here in the house."

"*What?*" he said, with a disbelieving laugh that was almost a bark. "I don't understand you. A hallucination? Like a mirage?"

"More like a ghost. Except that he doesn't walk through walls or anything like that. I can feel him. I can actually smell him."

"A *ghost?* For Christ's sake, Jessica. I thought you were the most pragmatic woman I ever met."

She was tempted for a second to tell him the truth, but then she decided that he wouldn't be able to take it. Apart from being very straitlaced about sex, he was also fiercely possessive. Even the thought of a *ghost* making love to her would upset him.

He took hold of her hands. "Listen, sweetheart. I still think this is definitely a stress thing. You know and I know that ghosts don't exist. What you're seeing, what you're feeling, it's all in your head. You remember Chet Lewis, who used to work with

Langton and Clarke? He got so overworked that he started believing that black dogs were chasing him down the street."

"Please, Michael. I don't want to see Dr. Biedermeyer and I don't want Prozac. This is nothing to do with stress. I guess the best way to describe it is that it's some kind of epiphany."

Michael looked completely baffled. "An epiphany? Like a *revelation*? The burning bush, something like that? Jesus, you *do* need a doctor."

"There's only one way I can explain it to you, and that's to show you. Meet me tomorrow at lunchtime on Forty-ninth and Lex."

"This is crazy, Jessica. This doesn't make any sense at all."

She leaned forward and kissed him on the lips. "Michael, I love you. When you see this for yourself, I promise you, you'll understand."

"I don't know . . . I'm supposed to be meeting Ron Shulman at twelve."

"Meet me at eleven-thirty then. Please."

He puffed out his cheeks. "Okay, if you insist. But I still think you need some help with this. Really."

It was raining again when she met him outside the gallery. He stepped out of a cab, paid the driver, and came over with his coat collar turned up. Then he saw the poster outside announcing *Queer Nation* and even before he said hello, he said *"Here?* This is where you had your epiphany? I can't go in here."

"Please, Michael, you must."

He looked around uneasily. "For Christ's sake. Supposing somebody sees me."

"It's a legitimate photography exhibition, Michael, and you're a professional photographer."

"I don't think so, sweetheart. This kind of thing really isn't my scene."

"I need you to understand, Michael. Please." She grasped his hand and led him through the door into the softly carpeted interior. Jamie Starck wasn't there today, but his young assistant was. He came over with a wonderfully hip-swaying hands-flapping walk and said, "Hel-*lo!*"

"Hi," said Michael, in the gruffest of voices, and held on to Jessica's hand as tightly as he could.

"Come for another peek?" the young assistant said. "You're in luck, we close tomorrow. Next week it's the Reuben French, the gray period. Very *dour,* Reuben French."

Jessica said, "My partner and I just want to take a quick— you know—"

"Professional interest," put in Michael. "I'm photographic director for J.D. Philips."

"Oh, I *am* impressed," the young assistant told him. "Do feel free, won't you? And if you need anything . . . " And here he gave Michael a long, lingering look ". . . you won't shy away from asking me, will you?"

"Yes," Michael told him. "I mean, no, we don't need anything."

As they walked into the gallery, Jessica said, "You're not coming down with a cold, are you?"

"No, why?"

"You were talking like *thurss,*" she said, mimicking his gruffness.

"I always talk like that."

"You mean you always talk like that when you think another man's taken a fancy to you."

They reached the photograph of the Arab boy bending over in the desert. Michael stopped and said, "Oh, my God."

"*Abid,*" Jessica explained. "That means slave."

Michael didn't say anything but slowly shook his head.

"Anyhow," said Jessica, "that wasn't what I brought you here to see."

She led him around the corner and there was the photograph of Lo Duc Tho. Michael looked at it for a moment and then turned his back on it.

"This?" he said, pointing his finger over his shoulder. "This faggot is your epiphany?"

"You don't see it?"

"I see a dirty picture, that's all."

Jessica approached the photograph and stared into Lo Duc Tho's unfocused eyes. "He was a plaything," she said. "He would allow women to do anything they wanted."

Michael turned back. "I can't see what you're trying to show me."

"He was naked all day, so that women could touch him and kiss him and pet him. Don't you understand? He was completely open, completely unthreatening, completely compliant. Men expect that in women, but sometimes women need that in men."

"I'm sorry, Jessica, I really don't get it."

"Look at him, Michael. Look at his face. Look at his eyes."

Michael looked at him, and then he shook his head. "You've lost me, sweetheart. You've completely and utterly lost me."

Michael took her to the Park Bistro on Park Avenue that evening, where she toyed with sautéed skate wing in vinegar sauce while he had a messy saddle of rabbit, and kept tearing off large lumps of bread and stuffing them into his mouth.

"They have the best bread here. They fly the flour in from France."

"I'm sorry about today," she said. "I guess you're right. I've been trying to take on too much."

"Don't even think about it," he told her, with his cheeks full like Chip'n'Dale's. "You ought to try some of this rabbit, it's out of this world."

* * *

That night she thought about Lo Duc Tho, but she was too tired to want him to visit her. All the same, she wondered what it would be like if she tattooed him all over—his back, his buttocks, his thighs, his face. She would cover him in large blue chrysanthemums, like the chrysanthemums on her silk scarf from Galeries Lafayette. She would decorate his nipples with gold rings, and his belly button with a gold stud. Then she would have a large gold ring pierced through his foreskin, so that she could lead him all the way around the apartment by a long silk cord.

In his sleep, Michael grunted, *"Won't."*

The following evening she had to stay late at the office to finish off the last of the Moist-Your-Eyes layouts. She didn't finish until way past one o'clock in the morning, and she was hyped up with too much coffee. She caught a cab home, and the seats were sticky and smelled of sick.

The apartment was in darkness when she let herself in, apart from the silent-movie flickering of the television under the bedroom door. She went into the kitchen and poured herself a large glass of Evian water. She could see herself reflected in the window, and she thought that she looked almost like a skull. White face, high cheekbones, dark rings under her eyes. She finished the water and rinsed the glass under the faucet.

She opened the bedroom door and at first she couldn't understand what she was looking at. Michael was crouched on the bed on all fours, and he didn't see her at first because his face was turned away from her. It was only when he slowly turned around and lifted up his head that she realized that he wasn't alone. There was a slight, mottled figure crouched beneath him.

In the stroboscopic light from the television, she saw that it was Lo Duc Tho, his long black hair hanging loose on the pillow, his thin elbows propping him up. He was decorated all over in chrysanthemum tattoos, and she saw the sparkle of nipple rings. Michael was hunched over him in the way that a stallion covers a mare.

"*Michael?*" Jessica whispered.

Michael sat up, withdrawing himself, his penis gleaming, one hand laid protectively flat on Lo Duc Tho's slender back. He said nothing at all, but simply stared at her, caught in the act, waiting for her to say something.

Jessica approached the bed.

"Michael?"

Lo Duc Tho turned his head toward her and smiled at her slyly, his face half covered by his hair, like a girl.

"I fell asleep," said Michael, in a parched voice. "I felt somebody touching me and I thought it was you."

"I never knew you—well, I never imagined you ever wanted *men.*"

"I didn't. I mean I don't." Michael's penis was sinking. Lo Duc Tho reached around and took hold of it, and started lasciviously to rub it. All the time he kept on smiling at Jessica in that secretive, superior way, as if he knew that she wouldn't do anything to stop him.

Michael said, "He's not a man, is he? He's just an illusion."

"If he's such an illusion, why is your cock going hard?"

"You were right. It's just like you said. It's an epiphany. It's like understanding what you want for the very first time."

Jessica stood beside the bed for the time it took her to breathe in and out, in and out, ten deep breaths. Then she unfastened the buttons of her thin-ribbed cardigan, and pulled it off. Neither Michael nor Lo Duc Tho said a word, but both of them watched her unblinkingly.

She unfastened her bra and dropped it on the floor. Last she stepped out of her pale silk La Perla panties. Michael held out his hand to her and she climbed onto the bed next to him. Sweat was sparkling in his sandy-colored chest hair.

"What are we doing?" Jessica whispered, kissing Michael's lips, kissing his nose, kissing his eyes. All the time Lo Duc Tho kept massaging Michael's penis, deliberately rubbing it against Jessica's thigh, so that she could feel its snail slime on her.

Michael said, "Maybe this is what we always wanted, both of us. Maybe this is what we always needed."

He pushed her back gently onto the pillow, and parted her thighs. Then he helped Lo Duc Tho to climb on top of her. With two fingertips he opened her lips and guided Lo Duc Tho inside her. She felt Lo Duc Tho's long smooth penis slide so deep that she couldn't help herself from quivering. Lo Duc Tho's hair trailed all over her face, and when she looked up she could see him staring at her, with that same distant but strangely self-satisfied smile.

It was then that Michael mounted Lo Duc Tho, and forced himself into him in one powerful thrust. Lo Duc Tho arched his back and uttered a single, high-pitched *"oh,"* as if he were practicing his pitch for an aria.

After that the three of them were silent, Lo Duc Tho pushing himself as far into Jessica's body as her imagination would allow, and then farther; and Michael gripping Lo Duc Tho's hips and rhythmically forcing him backward and downward. Jessica reached down between her legs and felt four slippery testicles jostling with each other, and it was then that she started quite unexpectedly to climax and couldn't stop.

She lay in the flickering light from the television for a long time afterward, staring at the ceiling. When she sat up, Lo Duc Tho had dematerialized, and there was only Michael lying there, already asleep. She started to reach out to touch him, but then she changed her mind. She began to wonder if she still loved him anymore.

The next day she finished work early. She had lunch with her old school friend Minnie at Dosanko noodle restaurant on Madison Avenue and then she went home. When she opened the front door she was surprised to hear music playing from the living room, one of Michael's favorites, *Samba Pa Ti.*

"I didn't know you were taking the day off," she called, kicking off her shoes. "I met Minnie for lunch. You could have joined us."

She walked into the living room. Michael was lying on the couch, naked except for his Argyle socks. Lo Duc Tho was kneeling on the carpet next to him, his skin still tattooed all over with chrysanthemum patterns. His shining black hair was draped all over Michael's lap and his head was bobbing up and down.

"Christ, Michael, what's going on?"

"What? You're going to start getting all censorious? You were the first one to conjure him up."

"I know. But I don't know what to say. I never knew you were gay."

Lo Duc Tho's head kept on bobbing and in the end Michael had to grab hold of his hair to stop him. Lo Duc Tho looked up, and turned around, and when he smiled at Jessica his lips were glistening.

Michael said, "It's not a question of being gay, is it? It's a question of finding yourself."

"Don't you understand?" Jessica retorted. "He isn't even real!"

"Then it doesn't matter, does it? Maybe you'd like to have sex with another woman, but if she wasn't real, that wouldn't make you a lesbian, would it?"

"I don't know. I can't handle this, Michael. I don't *want* to handle it."

"Lo Duc Tho gave you your revelation, didn't he? He gave you yours! Well, he gave me mine, too! He made me realize what I was and what I really wanted!"

"You want other men? Is that it?"

"For the first time in my life somebody allowed me to do what I've always wanted to do. Without any shame. Without any guilt. Without making me feel disgusted with myself."

"So where does that leave us?"

"Why should it affect us at all, except to make our relationship more exciting, and more honest?"

"You call it honest when I come home in the middle of the afternoon and find you with another man?"

"You said it yourself, he isn't real. We're imagining him, that's all."

Jessica knew this had to stop. Lo Duc Tho was still kneeling beside the couch, still fondling Michael's softening penis, and the expression on his face told her what she was already starting to suspect. His appearance wasn't a sexual epiphany at all. It was a revelation of something much darker than that. It was the beginning of a downward journey into sexual self-indulgence that could only end in acts so obscene that they could scarcely be imagined. It was the ground opening up, right beneath their feet.

"Jessica! Listen to me!" Michael demanded. But Jessica went through to the kitchen, opened the cutlery drawer, and took out the largest knife she could find. She returned to the living room, where Lo Duc Tho had risen to his feet and Michael was standing with his arms wrapped protectively around his narrow shoulders.

"Don't touch him, Jessica. You're not thinking straight. Put down the knife and we can talk this over like sensible adults."

Jessica approached them with the knife held out stiffly in

front of her. "This isn't something you can talk about, Michael. This is corruption, mine as well as yours."

"Jessica, put down the knife before somebody gets hurt."

She came closer. Lo Duc Tho was staring up at her with his dark, inexplicable eyes, his lips slightly parted. He was tattooed all over in the way that she had imagined he would be. His penis was half erect and there was a large gold ring through the end of it.

Michael held out his hand. "Come on, sweetheart, give me the knife, will you?"

Jessica put the knife behind her back. With her left hand she took hold of Lo Duc Tho's erection, slowly massaging it up and down. He grew harder and harder, until he was fully erect. Jessica looked at Michael and Michael looked at Jessica and there was caution in Michael's face but also expectation, as if he was waiting for her to say that everything was going to be all right, and that they could share Lo Duc Tho between them. After all, if he was nothing more than a fantasy, what difference did it make?

Jessica rolled the ball of her thumb around the head of Lo Duc Tho's penis and at the same time she stared into his eyes. She didn't say anything, but she wanted him to know that she understood what he really was.

"Can we—?" Michael began, and it was then that Jessica swung her arm around from behind her back and cut with a gristly crunch clean through Lo Duc Tho's penis.

Michael shouted, *"No!"* Like a curtain caught by the wind, Lo Duc Tho melted away in front of Jessica's eyes but suddenly the world was smothered in blood—the carpet, the couch, the cushions. There was blood all over Jessica's hands and blood all over her blouse and blood was spraying in her face.

"Oh, God! Oh, God!" Michael was screaming and clutching his hand between his thighs. Blood was spurting out from between his fingers and halfway up the wall.

Jessica stepped back. One step and then another. She looked at the knife in her hand and then she dropped it.

"Call the paramedics! For Christ's sake! Call the paramedics!"

Michael fell onto his knees, his forehead pressed against the floor. Blood was streaming down his thighs in dark red rivers. He started to sob, but all Jessica could do was stand and watch him.

"Call me the fucking paramedics, for Christ's sake, you witch!"

She didn't say anything, couldn't understand what was happening. Lo Duc Tho had vanished but after all he wasn't real and now she had proved it.

Michael collapsed onto his back. He stared up at her glassy-eyed, gasping. "Help me," he croaked. "Jessica, for Christ's sake, help me."

He slowly lifted his hands away from his thighs, and Jessica could see that all he had left was two crimson testicles and a two-inch stump, which was still pumping out blood. *"Jessica, help me!"*

But Jessica couldn't, or wouldn't. She turned away, and there on the arm of the couch she saw her chrysanthemum scarf from Galeries Lafayette, and the gold scarf-ring that went with it. She picked up the scarf and pressed it to her lips, and it was cool and silky and smelled just like Lo Duc Tho.

Two months later, a thirtyish woman wandered into the Wabash Gallery in Chicago. She stopped, looking bewildered. An immaculately dressed man rose from his desk and approached her. "Yes, can I help you?"

"I don't know. I think I must have come to the wrong gallery. I was looking for the Edward Hoppers."

"Last week, I'm afraid. But you're more than welcome to take a look around here."

She frowned at the poster. "Oh, no. I don't think this is quite me."

The man took hold of her sleeve and guided her along the soft-carpeted corridor. "How will you know, if you never even have a look?"

With a smile, he steered her toward her epiphany.

Pickman's Centerfold, Or: The Dunwich Ho

Nancy Holder

Your recorder on? Shit, everybody uses the same kind these days. Of course you have my permission. You're here, aren't you?

So.

It was not good, where I found Gilman. He was sitting in a sleaze pit in the Combat Zone in Boston, empty shot glasses lined up, more than a few good soldiers who had kept their powder wet; and he was there, mumbling something like "Donledaseemanayka," which I eventually learned was Drunkese for "Don't let her see me naked."

Gil has had some rough times in the Bureau. We all do, but he'd been shot in the line of the duty—hostage situation—and they'd made him ride a desk as if it were his fault. They talked about stress and psycho profiles and crap like that, but that was just TV talk. He'd fired his gun so he had to walk their walk. Million Mom March, yada yada; we had a Democrat running the country and you know how *they* are.

Anyway, Gil is my friend, and I didn't tell anybody he'd called me because I wanted to talk to him before our own guys did. He had gone awol during a surveillance assignment. For the moment, we had lost the bad guy as a result, and things were not looking good for Special Agent Gilman Innsmouth.

I sat down beside him at the bar; he saw me and burst into tears. He said, "Donledaseemanayka" about ten times, and then I ordered a shot because drunks open up to other drunks and he knew my history. The FBI is a tough gig, very short on the Dirty Harry, very heavy on sitting on your butt in an unheated car, watching for some mook to do what they all eventually do, which is get caught.

So, Gil was there in this total dive, and he was crazed or drunk on his ass or whatever, and I had one shot and waited for the sweet, hot backwash and the comforting green pastures down unto my soul. It came to pass; I don't care what they tell you in AA, this stuff is good to Daddy, and I calmly sat across from Gil in the booth and waited for him to stop with the In-nagaddadavida chant and give it up.

Gil's subject was a computer geek named Richard Upton Pickman, and Prickman—we were calling him—had made a specialty of designing web spreads for pros—hoochie mamas setting up their own Web sites, doing the live, wired spread-'em cams for the married guys who had ceased to get any at home. Weird thing was, the hot luscious babes who hired him to showcase their wanton teenage desire to suck it, lick it, whip it, baby, oh baby, oh baby all over Boston and the Northeast corridor were ending up dead in a very, very ugly way. As in, eviscerated, their tits and ass and everything up front where it counted scooped out and carted somewhere else. The tabs had dubbed them "the Hooker Mutilations" and not even the *Onion* touched that. It was just too damn horrifying. Hookers are people too, and we have a lot of those people in Boston, don't let nobody lie to you that we have "cleaned up" our city. It gets cold here.

Richard Upton Pickman was fantastic at what he did. A true

master of the pixel, a genius, a pro in his own right. If he was a hooker he wouldn't be a hooker anymore because he would be worth millions.

The Web sites he designed for the girls boggled the gonads. The boys couldn't help returning again and again, paying and paying and *paying* to stick around, to type with one hand, and do it till there were blisters. Who knows from angles or subliminal seduction or what, but the pix and the streaming live cam hypnotized them, drew them in, and would not let them go. Guys had blown paychecks, pension funds, great heapin' mortgage payments to stay connected, jacked in, so they could jack off on one of the nearly hundred Web sites designed by Pickman.

That was enough to draw our attention, but hey, free country and freedom of speech, ra ra, we are not the fuckin' CIA. Hell, here in Beantown we've got a local porno shop where the lady owner dresses up like a goddamn gift-wrapped package and tap-dances in the St. Patrick's Day parade. No skin off our noses, guys shooting their wads, literally, for stuff they would never get in real life.

As per above, the "Prickman Chicks" were dying very ugly deaths. They were dying so ugly we couldn't figure out what was killing them. Whatever was doing it seemed subhuman, or superhuman, and the guys were starting to call the killer "Wolfman" and "Leatherface" and beneath the macabre humor, we didn't like it.

I didn't look at the Web sites. I looked at other pictures of the girls. I looked at the pictures of them dead. I looked at them laid out frozen in the morgue. Other guys had Web site detail, and I have to say that I was spooked by how they couldn't seem to kick logging on once they had gotten a taste, so to speak. Your tax dollars at work.

Our main suspect re the killings was the Prickster himself, of course. But we couldn't figure out where he was. You know all that shit like in *The Matrix?* There's a lot of woo-woo stuff we can do, and it's usually pretty easy for us to get a warrant to do it. But even with all our resources and smarts and geniuses in wheelchairs, we couldn't locate Pickman. We figured he was in Boston because the majority—but not all—of his lady customers were in the metro area. We had agents watching computer parts stores and ISP storefronts and the university computer science departments—we practically lived in the dorms at MIT—but we couldn't get a bead on anybody. We couldn't find that face that leaps out at you when you're lucky. We couldn't catch the scent.

Then one of those guys who watches waaaay too much *X-Files* tipped us to a bunch of hatcheries—so they're called—tiny cubicles inside even smaller office lofts that are rented to guys who have no problem sitting in front of a computer twenty-four-seven or thereabouts in order to R-and-D their way to the Great American Dream. He knew about a hatchery close to the Cambridge campus of Ye Harvard, gave us some vague directions, and after that, we figured all we had to do was follow the pizza delivery trucks.

This particular Cambridge-locale hatchery had the standard locked front door Avec security buzzer you find in apartment and office buildings, and a list of buttons to summon the various renting inhabitants to open the entry for the pizza guy. And one was listed as RUP.

Search warrant: we burst in on nothing but a table, a chair, a lukewarm can of Diet Coke, and a half-eaten bag of stale Cheetos. Also, a phone jack and evidence that a laptop had sat on that table, but not today. We figured we were on to something, that he'd been tipped off or moved to a new phone jack or loved the wireless service at the airport or whatever.

That's when Gil drew duty to sit in an unmarked car and watch and wait. Now the thing is, everybody does it; it's not like a punishment or something. You'd be amazed how much of our work is pretty damn boring. The devil is in the details, and the details is how we usually make our busts.

It was not part of desk jockey purgatory, but Gil took it like that. He was royally pissed that it was the middle of friggin' winter and he was going to spend his shift in an unheated Toyota, but I reminded him that he was on the streets again, and that had to be a better thing than filing paperwork. I didn't cheer him up very much, but he told me I was the only guy in the Bureau he gave a rat's ass about, that he was the outsider and he knew that. That worried me but he got down to business, that being the business of sitting in a freezing cold car, watching pizzas come and go. So I didn't say anything to anybody, just kept my opinions about Gil's mental state to myself.

He did his job for about a week. He reported in like he was supposed to, he drank lots of coffee and peed in the cup like he was supposed to. He ate donuts.

Then he went missing. He had called in on a Tuesday morning at 3:33 A.M., saying something about being on to something, that he was tailing somebody, but after that the dispatcher couldn't really catch it. The recording was extremely garbled even with all our fancy-schmancy cleanup technology. He said, "I'm gonna stop the car and get out." Then he said, "Oh, holy shit! Fuck!" And then after a while—he panted or screamed into his hand or into someone's chest or something, and then he said something very weird. This is the closest I can come to imitating it: *"Iä! Iä! Cthulhu fhtagn! Ph'nglui mglw'nafh Cthulhu R'lyeh wgah-nagl-fhtagn!"*

Yeah, that's easy for me to say.

We all started making jokes about Welsh—how many Welshmen does it take to screw in a lightbulb, screw up a surveillance, but truth is, most of us spooks were spooked.

Because the Tuesday morning Gil acted out, another Pickman hooker got gutted. She was discovered about 5:00 A.M. six blocks from Gil's abandoned car. His door was open. Her body cavity was, too, and it was still steaming.

The deaths went on, and we kept missing the boat, and we

were all really fried. I should have alerted my superiors the minute I heard Gil's voice on my phone two weeks later, but I remembered him saying I was special or whatever the fuck he said, and maybe I wanted to be a hero, I dunno. So here I was, sitting in the scuzzy bar with the sticky floor with Gil hisownself, and he was weeping and pleading, "Don't let her see me naked" in the Welsh dialect Drunkese.

So I said, "Why not?"

For a while he cried a lot, until I ordered some more shots. I thought about calling for backup but he begged me not to "mix anybody else up in this," which made me think *Oh, gee, thanks, buddy, for mixing* me *up in it.*

It was late—almost 11:00 P.M.—when he finally said, "I need to tell you some things before we go." While he shifted in the booth and picked up a pile of books, I made sure the miniature tape recorder I had secreted in my pocket—I had *that* much sense—was still streaming recordable tape.

So *wham!* the books got put on the table front and center, and the first one had a picture of a really buffed-out Hannibal Lecter on the front and the title was *Tales of the Cthulhu Mythos.* I picked the next one up and the title was *At the Mountains of Madness,* with a corpse in a hooded robe on the cover.

I waited for Gil to explain. Was Pickman into this, was there a code in the books, what? Gil buried his face in his hands. I kept waiting—hey, he was pretty wasted by then, and if there was one thing we learned in the Bureau, it was how to wait—and finally he let his hands fall to the table and said, "It's all true."

I waited.

"The stories."

I lifted my eyebrows. "Okay." I waited some more.

"There really is a . . . really . . ." He burst into fresh tears.

I waited, and he managed to hoist himself to a standing position. He said, "Come with me."

I had on my holster and I had my cell phone. I had my tape recorder.

We left. It was freezing cold outside and I pulled my coat tight around myself. When I started heading for the parking lot, he shook his hand at me and headed on down the street. I followed. Right then, I thought about placing a call to the special agent in charge of my squad.

I wish to God I had.

Gil lurched on down the street, drawing looks from the very infrequent passersby we met. Crazed man walking; I kept his stride and gave myself enough berth to answer any attack we got with a good defense.

We stomped down streets jumbled with trash and dirty snow; the occasional open liquor store, the pawnshops, and the strip clubs. The Combat Zone had seen better days.

It began to snow, not the pretty kind but the wet, sloppy kind. I was turning to ice, and I was just about to tell Gil we were going to have to pack it in and go get him honest at HQ, when a truly awful smell wafted through the Boston winter odor of car exhaust, mud, and garbage. It was so bad I missed a step, and fell right on my ass on the slippery sidewalk. Gil looked down at me, and then raised his sights above and behind me.

"No," he whispered. "Oh, God, they're here."

I had never seen someone so completely and utterly terrified. I figured someone from the Bureau had shown after all, maybe tracked him down, but as I began to turn my head, Gil shrieked in Welsh, pulled out his .45, and slammed it over my head.

I went down, and I was out.

I thought I was going to be able to tell this story like it was no big deal. Eliot Blake, the big joker; show me a morgue glossy, I'll say something that makes everybody groan and say, "You're sick."

I *was* like that . . . oh, God, turn it off for a minute. Get the nurse, I'm overdue for my meds . . . sorry . . . Maybe I shouldn't have called you here. You're a kid looking to make a name for yourself; shit, you get this right, you'll get a Pulitzer.

Oh, God, I can't do it. I can't. Get the hell out of here!

Get me a fuckin' tranquilizer! Get me some help!

Nurse!

That's better. Thanks. Yeah, I want to keep going. I got to talk to someone. I know too much to keep it to myself.

I don't know how long I was out. I was nearly frozen when I came to. My head hurt so much that for a few minutes I couldn't focus on anything. I was in total darkness except for a computer screen, and I had been tied to a metal office chair by someone who knew his job.

My hands were numb; the duct tape and nylon cord had been cinched way too tight around my wrists. My feet were aching; they were wrapped halfway around the sides of the chair, probably to keep me from trying to use them to wheel myself the hell out of there.

My pockets were lighter. I figured he'd taken my gun, my phone, and my tape recorder. I think I was sorriest about the recorder. If I was gonna die, it'd be nice if someone got some evidence—bust the assholes who did it.

After a time, I could see the screen. Gil's face filled it, in extreme close-up. It was covered with blood and gore, and what looked like tears.

He murmured, "I'm going to end it. Now."

Since I could only hear him through the system speaker, I figured he wasn't in the same room with me. For all I knew he could be in friggin' Rhode Island. I couldn't ask him. A ball gag was in my mouth, the kind they use for S&M to keep the screams in. I remembered the morgue shots of the girls and panicked, started to hyperventilate through my nose, caught myself in time, and forced myself to slow down and stay conscious. That was the only way out I had at the moment, plus I wasn't insane and Gil obviously was.

Served me right, I know. I shouldn't have gone to see him alone. I should have alerted my boss. I replay it and I still don't know why I skipped all the instructions on the game box; Gil and I just weren't that close that I should have jeopardized everything for him.

But I did, and least of my worries now is my job. . . .

Fuck. Gimme another minute, okay? I wish to God they let me drink in here. . . . You can't fucking believe what I saw. Oh, Jesus. . . .

Sorry. If you're not using the voice-activation mechanism, I'm costing you in microcassettes. We have to pay for our own on the job, you know that? Our own business cards, too. *My tax dollars at work.*

What did they feed you downstairs in the cafeteria while I was out? All the food here is so freakin' starchy. State mental hospital, thought Reagan closed 'em all down. Me? I spent lunch in the rubber room. It's okay. They're just doing their jobs.

Back to it, kid. Just tape it. Hear me out. Then write it up. You'll be a hero.

Next thing I saw on the computer screen was a close-up of a drawing in a book of what looked to me like a big, enormous cock with tentacles and a beaked glans. I thought, *Oh, Jesus, he's the one for sure been cutting up the hookers. He's got some kind of psychosexual thing going.*

Gil slurred, "This's Cthulhu." Then he started crying.

Without another word, he backed away from the screen, giving me a view of the space behind him.

A naked, gagged girl lay spread-eagled on a canopy bed

covered and draped with black silk. Strange geometric shapes made of shiny black metals or gemstones hung from the edge of the silk canopy like heavy fringe. She was a truly awesome sight, with silicone tits of rounded perfection, big red nipples pointed directly toward the North Star. Her pussy had been shaved, and she looked fantastic. I figured, professional girl. Then I realized: one of Prickman's girls.

Oh, shit.

While I watched, Gil staggered back into frame wearing a black robe spangled with stars and moons. He was carrying a big book and he lifted it toward the camera so I could read the title. In horror-font letters, it read *Necromonicon.*

"I'm gonna send 'em away," he said. His face was chalk white. I have rarely seen anyone so afraid, and I've been a witness at criminal executions. "Him. Her, too."

That sounded bad. That sounded like he was planning to off the chick and maybe himself. I tried to speak around the gag, but I couldn't. I struggled to move the chair, maybe shove over the computer, make some noise in case someone could hear me and come save me. But I was helpless. I couldn't stop it. I couldn't fucking stop it!

"First . . ." Gil said. He staggered out of frame again. Sweat poured down my face even though I was so cold I couldn't stop shivering even though I was tied too tightly *to* shiver. Then he came back, half dragging a very beat-up-looking guy. And this guy was Richard Upton Pickman.

Pickman saw the girl. Then he took in Gil's robe. His eye line went to the book and he looked really shocked. He turned to Gil and hissed, "You've got the *Necromonicon.*"

"Yeah, and I'm calling them," Gil told him.

Pickman went ballistic "You set me up! You motherfucker! You fuckin' *pig!*" He swung at Gil, missed, and bolted away. "No!" he was screaming. "No!"

Gil launched at him and brought him down. He rammed his

fist into Pickman's face and bellowed at him, "You have the nerve, you jerk-off psycho? You have the fuckin' *nerve* to say that?" Gil spat in his face.

Then he hoisted Pickman toward the camera like a ventriloquist with a dummy and said, "Confess. On camera and I'll let you run before I call them."

"Oh, God. Oh, holy Jesus," Pickman babbled. "Please, please let me go."

"He was pimping for a fuckin' *alien*," Gil ground out, speaking to me through the camera. "There was something he did to the Web sites to beam 'em to outer space where this . . . this *monster asshole Jack the Ripper* would see the girls and get off, just like we do."

I didn't believe that for a moment. I knew Gil had lost his mind, and I worried for Pickman's safety.

Then the Prickman himself murmured, "It was okay. It worked. For years. He . . . he gave me things. Nobody got hurt."

"Yeah, till *she* found out," Gil replied, his voice a controlled fury. I knew that voice. It's when an agent has had all he can take. Gil was going to beat this guy to death unless something happened to change his mind. Which was coming apart while I looked at him.

Gil stared at me. "Cthulhu's wife. Jealous broad. She's the one gutted all the girls." He shook Pickman by the shoulders. "You knew she was here killing them and you didn't stop the transmissions to her mate, did you? You fucker, you didn't stop!" He swung his head at me. "This asshole started picking out guys for her! Like me!"

"No, I swear it." Pickman was freaking. "Oh, God, please, don't call them!"

"*You let her see me!*" Gil roared. "You beamed her a picture of me naked and she saw me!"

"Only just in case," Pickman blurted. "When I saw you in the car, watching my place, I thought you were someone who knew for sure. I thought you might kill me, and then I could never stop them. I've been trying to stop them. I *have*," he insisted, when Gil snorted.

The Prickman must have realized he'd better talk faster, because he did.

"When I realized what was happening, that she . . . that I had messed up, I wanted to stop doing it once and for all. But I had to be careful. The Old Ones have a lot of followers in Boston, and they keep track of everything. They can control your mind, make you say and do things. So I had to pretend, make them think I was still on their side. . . ."

"By sending them a picture of *me?*"

Pickman nodded wildly. "Yes, *yes!*"

"You fuckin' liar," Gil roared. "If you knew enough about me to find a naked picture of me, you knew I was in the fuckin' FBI!"

Yo, Gilman, chill, I thought desperately. *Prickman's got a conspiracy theory going here. Of course he believes the Feds are in on it. And where have you been naked lately, that he could obtain a pic of you?*

Pickman tried to grab the book out of Gil's hands. "I already tried to stop them. I said all the spells in there, I swear it. Don't call them. *It won't work!*"

Gil hit him again and again and again, dropping the book. "Fuck you. I read all that shit you read. I know whassup. The *Necromonicon* is the big kahuna. I've got the fuckin' book. I figured out the fuckin' code. And I'm going to fuckin' use it."

He gestured to the naked woman, who was unconscious. "I'm gonna let them have you two while I say the spell." He swung his head toward the camera. "It's gonna send 'em back to their hell dimension and put up a no-trespassing sign here on Earth forever."

Despite the fact that he was totally fucked, Pickman ground out, "Code? What code?"

I wanted like anything to say, *Gil, we studied this at Quantico. This is called a* folie a deux. *A shared delusion. You've bought into this madman's insane fantasy.*

But I couldn't do anything. All I could do was watch Pickman's frantic struggle to grab the book, while Gil stalked over to the naked girl and opened the book. He thumbed to a certain page, and began to read, and it sounded like more Welsh.

Oh, my God. Oh, my God, I can't tell you what I saw next. I have kept it together, I have been a good soldier and a reliable reporter and I have only broken down twice but I promise you, you do not want to know what happened next. You don't want to know. Don't want to know. Don't want to . . .

Gil didn't know what the fuck he was doing. He didn't know how to stop them. Have you ever seen the great god Cthulhu? Do you have any idea of His power and grandeur? *Iä! Iä! Cthulhu fhtagn! Ph'nglui mglw'nafh Cthulhu R'lyeh wgah-nagl-fhtagn!*

The room became stars and shadows out of colors out of time. They arrived together; I saw them; oh, great Cthulhu is the dread manhood of the stars, and his female is the yawning cave of all the Dark Ones; through their copulation with humans they shall bring back the days when the Old Ones walked the earth.

The girl on the bed was first. While She of Starfields watched, Cthulhu fucked the human; the enormous, cock-headed god slammed his long tentacles into that chick and ennobled her; and his wife grabbed Pickman and shredded off his clothes and most of his skin; she didn't know the difference. She didn't care. And her long, thick tendrils swooped around him and she engulfed him as all long to be engulfed by the Fuckers out of Space, into the black, gaping starry hole of herself where he was a piece of her, and of the Great Coming; she fucked him and tore him to pieces.

Then they—they . . . oh, God, Gil, with his code . . . it worked, nobody gave him credit in the Bureau for how smart he . . . there was nothing left of him by the time . . . how long since they rescued me? . . . sorry, I'm . . . I'm confused . . . I'm dreaming . . . did I say things that . . . hey, that's *my* tape recorder. How did you get my tape recorder? What is that tape you're putting in it?

Holy shit, that's Gil's voice. That's Gil calling them. My recorder got it after all!

Don't play it! It works! It'll call Them!

You *know?*

You know?

Who the fuck are you? Nurse! Help! For God's sake, stop him! No, not me, *him!* He's one of them! Turn that off or they're going to come here! He's *not* a reporter! Shut that fuckin' thing off! They'll come and the mate of the great god Cthulhu will rip us to pieces and—

—and—

Oh, my God.

Iä! Iä! Cthulhu fhtagn! Ph'nglui mglw'nafh Cthulhu R'lyeh wgah-nagl-fhtagn!

Cthulu, my love, my darling, my god!

There is a monstrous odour . . . senses transfigured . . . *Iä . . . ngai . . . ygg . . .*

Fucker of the Million Favored ones . . .

Phantasmagoric delirium . . .

Hurry, baby, oh, baby, baby, baby, I can't wait for you to eat me!

Saturnalia

David J. Schow

"So, uh, would you like me to drop my, uh, pants?" Colin was halfway out of his seat, belt already unbuckled above a growing erection, when his interviewer's wave sat him back down, unexposed.

"I don't need to see it," Valentina Sykes said, looking him straight in the eye. "You would not be here if I held any doubts about your ability to function. Mere function doesn't interest me. Performance is the key word here."

Valentina gave Colin Freehand—real name, Dex Wilson— the once-over for about the eighth time, scalp to shoes. *About now,* she thought, *he's concocting a mental porn loop in which he figures out how to make all the right sounds while he hammers a woman slightly older than his eldest grandma.* She had no doubt she could still teach him a thing or six; he was the eager puppy type, straining to prove how big, how long, how humpable, how easy to be hard. His stage name, Freehand, came from the gag about how he could pilot a car, among other things, without using his hands. His abs were ripped, his back marbled with superfluous show-off muscle, purest gym steak. The concerns of his life were his hyperthyroidal sports car (and how soon he could score a flashier one), his daily intake of hydrolyzed soy protein, and how long he could keep his name at the top of the treacherously mercurial adult film biz. Average burnout ceiling for a newcomer was eighteen months to two years—after that, the blur of double penetrations, condomless fucking and sucking, HIV scares, easy access to rock and dust and worse, plus the erosions of casual brutality and even more casual usury, generally caused new meat to run back to Iowa, blow out their brains, or decay into walking ghosts, background players in the flesh trade; no lines except the ones that vanished up their noses.

How simple it would be to make him grovel, thought Valentina. To beg for something he could never have when he was used to getting everything he wanted.

"That look you're directing toward me might have been flattering, forty years ago," said Valentina. "You're generally always on the make, aren't you?"

Colin shrugged. Seduction was coded into his RNA factor.

"I think you'd be surprised," she said. "But it's not to be. I didn't bring you here, after culling so many candidates, to give an old lady her jollies by slipping it in and pretending."

"You mean I don't get paid?"

She enjoyed the abrupt alarm in his tone. "You get paid."

"I mean, for you and all, it's kind of an honor, anyway."

"What are you talking about?" She wanted to see if he could form coherent thoughts into sentences, maybe even extrapolate.

"I saw all your movies you made in the fifties," he said, happy to chance onto a subject he could do at least partially on autopilot. "Marilyn Monroe was blowsy, a tart for the masses to idolize. You didn't do the squeaky little-girl voice or stick your thumb in your mouth or play that white-trash sexy schtick. You were beautiful, and you knew it, and you didn't have to advertise. I've always admired that."

She imagined him a few years younger, furiously whacking off to a black-and-white photo of her on the cover of *Photoplay.* If she wanted him to play with himself right now, in front of her, he'd probably do it. She was seventy-three years old and no one had taken her photograph for nearly a quarter of a century. She could completely unman him, this instant.

Instead she lowered her eyes and said quietly, "Thank you."

Colin was the one, all right; she had selected him well. Now she felt linked to him. Besides, she had always thought Norma Jean was a coddled little tramp, as well.

She handed Colin a photograph of a young woman who had, just the month before, been available to the nation, via newsstand, in a magazine for which she constituted a precedent-setting center spread.

"Do you think you could make love to her?"

Colin barely glanced. "Yeah, I could fu—" He caught Valentina's look and decided to mind his manners, and not cuss. "Yes."

"Tonight at eight, she's yours."

It took Colin a minute and a half to locate the copy of the overpriced men's mag in his bathroom stack. The monthly gatefold queens of this particular publication were notable for their apparent lack of personal history—they were photo-perfect, gorgeous to a fault, fantasy food for millions of male hetero underachievers . . . and they issued, seemingly, from the heartland of America without preamble, back story, or nasty personal habits. They listed their fatuous pastimes and favorite boring movies, all the false assurances of their attainability . . .

. . . to legions of substance-abusing ground-pounders who called themselves men, who bellowed *yee-hah* and wore their baseball caps backward, who depended on armpit funk (or something) to magnetize the slack-jawed pigs with whom they reproduced.

Damn, thought Colin. Sometimes his job was just too easy. It was fun to do what he was good at.

When Colin paged to the shot of Catherine Ankrum holding the garden hose, he just had to jack off. He shot semen across Catherine's four-color face the way he planned on doing it in real life, soon. She kept on smiling. Practice, practice, practice.

No way this bitch could be so clean, he thought. He wanted to ram into her and force her to tell the truth about what a slut she really was. She'd be licking her own shit off the crown of his dick in no time. Beautiful or not, famous or not, they all looked more or less the same with a cock in their mouths.

Colin napped, showered with antibacterial soap, and showed up in loose, comfy clothing at the appointed time. Ding-dong.

The bedchamber was the color of pale fire.

The bed was mahogany, draped in satin—not silk, as Colin had anticipated. He had nodded once on silk sheets and awakened with his cock-head swollen up like a party favor; something to do with static electricity. He hated silk. It was a cliché. Cotton was washable. Satin would pass.

Two tables with carafes. A vase of cut lilies. That was about it; the room was not tarted up. No mirrors, no rack of whips, no kitsch.

The camera lenses were innocuous, but their sweep covered every corner. He spotted them at about the fifteen-minute mark by his estimate, because he had not worn a watch. His brain was shrieking that it had been at least an hour before his date finally showed.

Catherine Ankrum entered wearing workout clothes and offered Colin a broken little smile. She smelled like cocoanut oil and her skittish manner kicked Colin's autopilot into overdrive; from now on he could steer.

"It's a little weird," he offered her confidentially. The return spark of fake hope in her eyes was something he never tired of seeing from women who had gotten themselves in too deep.

"My year has kind of sucked," she said, not going into the

details of a big heroin tab and a celebrity too slow in materializing. So much for the prefab bio.

"Doesn't matter." He took her hand, as if he planned to be kind to her.

She had eyes the color of decaf coffee—they looked strong but wouldn't keep you up. Not contact lenses; that was a point in her favor. Her face had been rebuilt, to lose the peasant nose, and plucked to pattern a genetically tragic hirsuteness. Her teeth had been straightened enough to leave the inside of her mouth ribbed with scar tissue. Stripped and lubricated, Colin found little to distinguish her. He hated implants, but decided to overlook hers since they weren't as grotesque as they might have been and the shiny slug-skids of surgery were well concealed. His big dick was bona fide, and the last place he wanted to put it was between two nerve-dead silicone sacs. She had undergone laser tightening and a slight labial tuck, leaving her with what Colin thought of as a too-symmetrical "stripper pussy," but the job was expensively good, and he wouldn't have his nose in it for long. Maybe that was the hole into which her bank had vanished.

Once he had helped her come—she wasn't faking because he could feel the difference—she admitted breathlessly that she had been watching him on the closed-circuit monitors before coming into the room. Just watching him walk around, looking for the cameras.

"Did that flip her switch, ole Miss Valentina?" said Colin.

"She was watching, too," said Catherine, as though they weren't wired for sound in this place of intimacy.

"The voyeur thing. She likes to watch."

Colin nearly bolted upright. *She likes to watch, all right—the way you watched* her, *in all those black-and-white antiques of motion picture history.* He squeezed his eyes shut. No way he was going to lose control, here; no way *she* was going to force him to lose control.

He took it out on Catherine after slapping himself erect. He could feel his knob bruising her uterus. Resolve clunked shut in his gut like the bolt of a lock, and when he finally pulled out and creamed her face, she was crying.

"Godammit, I'm *bleeding,* you *fucker!*"

Fucker's right, thought Colin. It's what I do for a living.

The amount of Valentina's check brought Colin back for more. Her smile was wry, bemused. "Everything satisfactory? No fallout?"

"What's next?"

"Not so fast. Savor each moment. Don't let them rush past untasted."

"What do you mean?"

"Like that bit where you confided in her, and turned her on just enough to trust you to mount her one more time, then hurting her when you did it."

Colin performed that little twitch of the head that announced he was guiltlessly at sea. Whatever.

"Come on, Colin, when you told her, *oh, Valentina likes to watch?* That united you both against me—the voyeur—and you immediately exploited that trust, and hurt her." Valentina's eyes held level and gray. "That's a tactic I'd expect from a chess player."

Colin smiled to cover the truth—he did not know what in hell Valentina was talking about. But her money spent excellently.

She snapped her fingers to bring him back. "You were asking what came next?"

Valentina had prepared a little sample reel for Colin, sort of a highlights tape of "adult" downloads from the Internet. The first clip featured a naked brunette executing ballistically improbable moves with a stallion, or vice versa. Typical gross-out stuff. The brunette had nice natural breasts, but Colin barely noticed them, and was surprised to find himself unaroused by the nudity. Bigger issues dominated.

"You might find this next one of interest," said Valentina of a clip in which a woman bent over to afford the camera a better angle, spread herself in tight close-up, and squeezed forth a full Coke can, as though giving birth. Over Colin's shoulder, Valentina said, "Letting a lens record this sort of thing is not the most dignified road to immortality, is it?"

"What, do I get a lecture now?"

"It was a rhetorical question." She lowered her eyes in a studied move that made her look bemused. "I apologize."

Somehow Colin did not feel empowered. This time, when he entered the bedchamber, he just sat on the bed. He'd done the tour last time. He felt the lenses, watching him.

He couldn't push Valentina's little Wild West video out of his mind. He kept circling back to the idea that it was not intended as outrageous . . .it was meant to overwhelm with inadequacy all who viewed it. Beyond the beery, frat-boy gross-out lurked an agenda that, in truth, debased the onscreen women last of all.

For the first time, Colin pondered whether women were repulsed by the taste of his own semen, then whether the women he'd like to fuck *might* be. He had tasted it himself—slippery, alkaline, not as "salty" as bad porn would have you believe. Perhaps his own was a special mix. Perhaps it would seem saltier if he were compelled to chug a tumbler of it. He thought about going down on women he'd known, on women he'd like to know. All that glaze and lube was just mucus, basically. You don't think about licking your girlfriend's nose when she has the flu.

Get real, he chided himself. Any chick who would humiliate herself, quote-unquote, like those in the video had certainly been solicited and paid, drugs or not. It was not some sniggering plot targeted on his own sexual fears; that required thought, and nobody actually *thought* about this shit—they just went ahead and did it.

"My name is Soliel." The voice whipped Colin's head around; he'd been caught with his alarms off.

The second thing that nailed him was how plain this one looked. No aerobics android, here. She had kept the nose Catherine Ankrum had erased. Her complexion was hit and miss; she was not so much unattractive as undistinguished. She came clad in the sort of junk women wear to hide their bodies when they feel ugly.

Soliel fondled his crotch, unzipped his pants, and did her best to suck him up hard. Colin recalled the high school joke about fat chicks; it took him forever to petrify. In his mind, he had to lapse purposefully back toward his reliable autopilot. Pretend he was on a set, fucking Cherry Canyon's honey hole (or vice versa); play the game where he strove to hump so long that the crew ran out of film, or, even better, videotape.

Soliel was due for the trick where Colin orgasmed, stayed inside, kept pumping, reengorged, and orgasmed again. Despite his performance she seemed a universe away, enwrapped in her own sensations. Her vagina was capacious and elastic, making sustained friction a problem.

Colin kept thinking about the damned video, and never managed that second erection.

He was able to locate nine of Valentina Sykes's films in one day, though it required four different video stores, none of them Blockbusters. His minimarathon had nothing to do with plot and everything to do with characterization. Valentina invariably portrayed strong-willed women who would destroy those around them rather than bend. Love was generally a bad idea that led to destruction. There remained only manipulations of greater or lesser finesse . . . and, sometimes, a victor, or at least a survivor, usually Valentina.

"I was an actress, Colin . . . what did you expect to see?"

It was easier to see her face, then, in her face, now. "I don't know; I'm not sure. I want to know what all this makes you feel, I guess."

"You don't know, you're not sure, you *guess.*" Valentina threw back enough straight Polish vodka to keep a tiki lamp going for an hour. "Did you masturbate or not?"

"In the end, yeah. Halfway through *The Stars in Her Eyes.*"

"Ah. The corset scene."

"It's the most naked you ever got in any of your pictures, when you stripped down to that lingerie."

"You're forgetting my bathing suit stuff."

"I haven't forgotten. The lingerie was more intimate."

"Made me look more available, you mean."

"I guess so."

"Don't *guess.*" She pursed her lips. He could see secrets stacked up in her eyes, inscribed like petroglyphs in a language he could not fathom. "You wanted to make love to me, the way I was, then." She did not wait for an answer. "Stupid question, really. Would it pique your interest a bit more to know that Soliel is my daughter?"

Colin swallowed hard, trying to make room in his throat for a response. The lump there decided to stay. He felt his heart speed up. He paled.

"Yes, Colin. Soliel—your previous 'date.' The one you were so . . . preoccupied with, or should I say during? I'd think that given the opportunity you'd be more than eager to make love to my daughter. The results weren't so tabloid-worthy, were they?"

"I didn't know," he choked out.

"But it shouldn't make any difference, should it? I *guess* sex may really be all in the mind, like they say." Her gaze critiqued him, seeking flaws when before it sufficed with approbation. "Still . . . I'd think that would be your dream encounter, to have sex with the daughter of the woman you fantasize about while masturbating. And you really couldn't get it up that second time."

"It happens."

"It doesn't happen to me."

"It won't happen again." *Not as long as I can distance myself from that damned horse video, Colin thought.* "Sometimes under the best conditions, with the sexiest woman in the world, the rhythm just gets bollixed."

"We'll see, won't we?"

Valentina rewarded him with a low-slung, sturdy vixen with genuine breasts, the type whose strong, saucy walk was both an announcement and a warning to those who would aspire to get between her legs. Her name was JodyRae and carnality was her main ingredient. She shamed the anorexic bimbos of men's mags and provided a full-body workout for Colin. All the time he pounded her, he was thinking of how much better he would perform if he ever got another shot at Soliel. Valentina, naturally, had anticipated this. The time for Soliel had passed, and JodyRae was just a warm-up for what was to follow.

Colin had been told the new girl's name was Bettina, and he found her already undressed and waiting for him the moment he entered the chamber. She did not say much of anything and only seemed dimly aware of what he was doing. Her body was flabby instead of detailed, pale in an unhealthy way, and her movements against him were clumsy and ineffectual, as though she was doped, or not accustomed to getting laid well. She smelled bad, a combination of body odor and starchy diet, plus a diapery pall that put Colin in mind of nurseries and baby drool.

This one was a bed-flop; no potential and no hope beyond a quick ram in the rack. What the hell was Valentina thinking?

Bettina grunted a few inarticulate words; Colin shellacked his expression and played strictly to the camera. Okay, she was obviously doped; it wasn't as if he'd never ridden that train himself.

He pushed off her and wiped down with the towel that was always there, waiting, on a small valet rack. Bettina was still making noise and when he actually paid attention he saw that she continued to murmur and thrust against air as though he were still inside her. Her arms looped around nothing above her; a ghost embrace.

That was when he finally realized: *She's mentally retarded.*

He could not get to the shower fast enough.

In his street duds, in the corridor, not twenty minutes later, he ran into Soliel. His brain was racing, trying to find some way to scour the previous hour out of every convolution.

"It's you," she said, looking at his crotch. They all did.

"Hey." Panic formed a fireball in Colin's head. He was trying to summon cheap charm and seductive small talk, to cultivate Valentina's daughter—for later—and all that would display was YOU FUCKED A SLOBBERING RETARD, UNH-UNH-UNH. His machine-gun nest of pheromones was dozing on duty.

"I have to kind of explain. About my mom."

"You don't have to explain anything. I just—"

She overrode him. "No, stop. You don't understand, even if you think you do. It might all seem very strange. But she does it for love."

He stood absorbing her, sensing his snap judgment was off. He could see Valentina in her daughter now, around the eyes, in the shape of the mouth, in the general body carriage. The prevailing makeup fashions of the fifties would have made Soliel's brows thicker and she probably would have bangs over her considerable expanse of forehead. She smelled pleasantly of night-blooming jasmine. When she said *she does it for love* she had reached out and touched Colin's hand, in entreaty, then withdrew it hastily, as though stung.

"What, even to the point of throwing her daughter into the mix, and watching her fuck?"

"That's not it. It's subject to my approval. I saw some of your movies and I said okay."

Colin abruptly remembered the capacity of Soliel's limousine-sized vagina. She had seen his dick in a few adult films and voted *yea*. She had volunteered to fuck him based on seeing his movies in the same way Colin was actualizing his vintage fantasies about Valentina Sykes. It scuffed his ego. He had treated Soliel like a charity fuck while she'd been going to the races.

"And you did it for your mom." He tried his best to sound wounded.

She touched his face. "Hey. You were wonderful. Really. I gotta go."

Somehow it didn't surprise Colin that his next "date" was a man. His name was Larry, and Colin forgot it as soon as he heard it. He'd done boy-on-boy scenes before, so it was no big deal. By the end of the month he had also fucked a bilateral amputee and a toothless Skids sterno-drinker who cackled and stank of piss.

He got a bonus when he actually made the wino come.

Hence, when he had to fuck a cadaver, he appreciated its cleanliness.

"I hate it," said Soliel. "She's gone overboard. It's become like a tug-of-war between you and her."

"She's not going to win," Colin said, mopping his groin with a damp towel. "I can fuck anything she throws at me, but I want you to be honest and tell me something."

Soliel's nipples were tumid from her latest climax. She teased them idly and the reverberations tingled her toes. She hefted Colin's cock. "The truth, you have to work for."

"Does Valentina want me to fuck her?"

Soliel shot him a glance. "Does that mean what you really want is to fuck my mom?" She began pumping. "Does that get you hard?"

"I wanted to fuck your mother when she was an image, an ideal. I toyed with the idea of fucking her when I met her, as a challenge. Now, after jumping through hoops for her, the answer is no. It must have been kind of the same for you, I mean, growing up with a manipulator."

"Yeah . . . what I'd expect to happen next is, now that you've rejected the notion of fucking her, she'd try to find a way to make you want to do it anyway, if that makes any sense."

"It makes too much sense."

Soliel had shown up on Colin's doorstep between his "dates" with Dayna, the amputee, and the cadaver (whose name Colin never did learn).

"I'm sorry I was rude the other day. Here." She'd handed Colin a little box of chocolates.

Colin was honestly moved, insofar as he could be. "Did your mom send you?"

"No. I need you to help . . . um, fill a void in my life." Her gaze came up steely and wanton. "And if you laugh, I'll break your teeth out of your head with a wrench."

Colin had not laughed, and pulled her into his arms instead. He spent private time wondering whether she was a spy, just as she doubted any and all of his motives. In a bizarre way, they were a good couple—mutual interests kept their relationship completely indoors.

Soliel loved sex with Colin. She whipped him up like a berserk rider, telling him that her size, her capacity, caused him to swell even larger inside her. Their sex became a runaway engine with the governor dumped, terminating in high-speed collision and the popcorn stutter of machine-gun multiple orgasms. It was worse than a letter to *Penthouse.*

Colin loved sex with Soliel. But then, Colin loved sex with anyone. It was his reason for being; he did what he was good at, and it was more than fun—it was why Valentina had hired him. The more he fucked Soliel, the more the old Valentina, the movie-fantasy Valentina, seemed to emerge from her daughter. Colin would never admit that his relationship with Soliel had the power to ground and stabilize him in a healing way, so he just stuck with the fantasy.

And when Colin was working, he fucked whatever flavor Valentina could conjure up from her kettle of pleasures and nightmares, until the day she actually drew him aside for a warning.

By now, Colin was used to being shocked, so Valentina's attempt to cushion him came as a complete surprise.

"Normally, I'd let you navigate on your own," she told him. "But if there is one cultural constant that cuts across every ideal of what is sexually attractive around the world, it is the absence of disease. You've done dirty-filthy-nasty, and it's not the same. I'm talking about you having sex with someone who is diseased."

"We talking AIDS here?"

"No. You are in no danger of contracting anything. I'm more concerned with the danger of you not being able to handle the idea of making love to a partner who is diseased, repellently so. I'm talking about sights you may not want to see, smells you definitely don't want to inhale, and textures that would make you sick to your stomach."

"I fucked a dead person for you, Valentina."

"That's clinical. Not the same."

"What about the chick with no limbs and the screaming wino lady?"

"This is different."

"No, it isn't. Are you offering me the opportunity to refuse?"

"I'd rather you didn't. We've come a long way and I have big plans for you."

"Then what's my incentive? I got a bonus for getting the wino lady's rocks off."

"You'll get a bonus for this."

"I want something new. I want you to give up something valuable. The money is nothing to you."

"You want my daughter, by now, I suspect."

"I already have your daughter." The sense of power over Valentina at last was giving Colin a hard-on. "I want you."

"Young man, haven't you given up your wet dream of screwing a woman old enough to be your—" She stopped. She had spieled off this script already.

"Not this particular old woman."

"You'd be disappointed."

"More disappointed than I was when I fucked a dead body?"

"You're going to insist, aren't you?"

Colin held fast, not giving an inch . . . so to speak.

"It seems I've outsmarted myself." Her crooked little smile resurged. She appeared to run scenarios in her head. "And what would I be giving up, exactly, that seems so valuable to you?"

"Power. You're going to have to relax your grip on things, just once."

"Why, Colin, are you going to make me come?"

"Yes or no."

Valentina released a long, slow breath of consideration. "You do this, today, and you can have what you want."

"Plus the money."

Valentina laughed. "Goes without saying, greedy boy." She chuckled. "You'll have to promise to be gentle."

They regarded each other, both knowing the market value of promises.

* * *

The chamber was darker than it ever had been before.

Colin was aware of walking down the corridor and turning right in the usual way, but in some way flirtatiously beyond the reach of his senses, this room felt different from the room in which all his previous tests had been conducted. There was no light, so much as luminescence. It was a mushroom-damp nocturnal environment, like a cavern of bats. The air was hothouse-thick and Colin's estimate put the chamber itself at body temperature.

It was a different room. Somehow Valentina had slid the facets of her spider's web puzzle-box around and caused him to take a familiar, by-rote route to a new destination.

Here the bed was canopied. Directly above it a bank of powerful full-spectrum UV tubes glowed, and as Colin approached—slowly—he picked out the vague rush of humidifiers, misting the atmosphere. Vents engirded the room at waist height. As Colin passed beneath the crimson glow of a heat lamp in the ceiling, he could make out a row of TV monitors above the vents, across from the bed. All dark. He felt the heat seek to penetrate the top of his skull; he shaded his eyes.

"Come on." It was Soliel, using the sort of tone with which one might coax a puppy. She revealed herself to be nearby the bed when she stepped into a pool of chromatic light. She was clothed.

"Okay," Colin ventured in anticipation of some weird punch line. "You care to give me a clue?"

Soliel withdrew a drape and the eyes of the bed's occupant rolled to register Colin. Its mass lolled, as though from internal tremors, and Colin could perceive its basic game form as humanoid—head, limbs, genitalia. In no respect did it violate the law of bilateral symmetry, not exactly, but the shifting nature of its gelatinous form made it seem shapeless. That maw, a hole punched in putty, could be a mouth; the upper appendages could pass for arms since the longer one had several fingers. It suffered from bedsores. Bilirubin-colored smudges mottled its surface like the spoor of leukemia. From what Colin could see of its pubis, he guessed it to be female.

Soliel passed by Colin like a wraith, kissing him lightly on the cheek. "I'll just leave you two alone."

"That's no goddamned answer."

She spun on him. "It's what you wanted."

"The more you talk, the less sense you make." He was getting angry, working up a good mad.

"That's Valentina's daughter, you idiot. That's Soliel. I'm just a hired gun. Like you." She stalked off and was enveloped by the dim haze that masked the limits of the chamber.

"Valentina!"

The monitors snowed briefly blue, then resolved into Valentina's image; her face, replicated in a row of screens.

Colin spoke to the screens. "You just violated my bullshit ceiling and I'm outta here as of now."

"No, you're not." The sound system was refined enough to make her transmitted voice sound intimately close. "You're going to stay here, Colin, and do what you do better than anyone."

Colin heard the door thunk shut with air lock finality. He was pretty sure he was not actually imprisoned, and wanted to know what Valentina thought she had, to keep him here.

"I'm sorry about the disease story; it is partially true. Technically."

"What about Soliel?"

"The woman you thought was Soliel is named Adela. She's been receiving regular injections, and it was necessary for you to make love to her in order to become immunized, yourself. The rest of the participants were to help you overcome your own fears and prejudices, so you could be effective here, with the real Soliel."

Colin's arms folded tightly, defensively. He didn't know where to look for the cameras, so he addressed the screens and tried not to look at the fleshy plasmodium awaiting him in bed.

"No," he said. "I don't think so."

"Then you haven't thought enough. There's nothing here that you haven't dealt with already. You can't claim to be repulsed and expect me to believe you."

"What if I have a headache?"

"What if I tell you that the mentally impaired young lady you mounted so manfully kept on making those grunts and thrusting motions until she died? Now that must've been a *headache.* What if I tell you the coroner could only identify JodyRae's remains by her dental records and a crookedly healed fibula she broke when she was nine, and—what do you know—you were the last person to see her before parts of her got, well, metabolized?"

"Excuse me?"

"You know—digested."

"*Eaten?*"

"Not exactly in the sense of chewed up and swallowed, but essentially, they provided nourishment." She lowered her voice into a tone Colin recalled from the movies, whenever her character got dead honest. "I love my daughter, Colin. More than anything. You saw me only as a manipulative old crone, a puppet mistress. That's what I was in a lot of movies made a long time ago, and you reinforced your biases by watching those movies and passing judgment on me. I project a hard exterior, like armor, because I'm an actress, and on occasion I can act very well. But more than that, I really do love my daughter. That probably doesn't 'track' for you, real love, I mean."

"It doesn't mean I have to get intimate with the Blob, here, either."

"Oh, but it does. Remember Catherine Ankrum, the foldout

woman? She died. I have you on tape with her just before she died to feed my little girl. Sex with the dead is also still against the law in this state, and I believe you indulged in a bit of that, as well."

In that moment, Colin tracked. Valentina liked to watch, and she was probably pretty good at *recording,* too. Videotape, from multiple angles, of Colin with *all* his partners, these past weeks. All her victims; now all *his* victims. Not counting the corpse from the morgue, that was what? At least six murders whose names he could almost remember? He'd be painted as a sexually predatory serial killer, and nobody would be interested in the innocence of a porn actor.

Soliel waited. She had been waiting such a long time, for a man that was right for her . . . which meant that she had spent even more time fantasizing and mentally preparing. She would expect not to be disappointed.

"You don't possess many true intimacies," said Valentina. "But the ones you have are sufficient to damn you a hundred-fold. Skin, hair, prints, blood, semen, DNA . . ." She left unspoken the part about how the brand of wealth that underwrote Colin's services could also buy the best legal pit bulls available—to be fired at will toward Colin's credibility in a salvo of torpedoes with teeth.

He wanted, more than anything, to revert to the unreal version of Soliel, and the fantasy that they had formed a human bond. She had slipped his grasp and walked out of the room. That woman was really named Adela, and she hadn't been much to look at, but she'd left a pang in Colin's gut, and by now she was catching a train that would whisk her into the coal-mine blackness of a subway tunnel whose depths smelled metallic and alien, like the real Soliel. He had taken up Valentina's challenge to bypass the fate of adult film hopefuls all over the world—a world where young meat could erode to nothing in a handful of years. A world that included dippy dream relationships, like the one he had with the fake Soliel, only as a preamble to the usual fucking and sucking . . .

There was no flattery here, no seduction. His partner did not look like all the other chicks, and Colin began to fall out of love—with his image of himself, his staying power, his ability to take and have anyone.

He disrobed with Valentina's face surrounding him on a dozen screens. He had been servicing her all along, not that he minded. He fancied himself, above all, a pro.

Now he was a pro with obligations and entanglements. He needed to avoid being arrested, should his ego force him to walk out, or consumed, should his libido fail this new standard before him. He detested responsibilities, but could exploit them to kick-start his good old autopilot.

With a rising erection, Colin approached the bed and commenced his foreplay. It was no longer fun to do what he was good at.

Starfucker

Mick Garris

I was the bastard son of Art and Commerce. Hollywood chewed me up and swallowed me whole, and when it had digested me, evacuated me like watery excreta from its overloaded bowels.

You'll have to excuse the unlovely imagery; I have no reason to be bitter. Everything that happened was my own damned fault.

It wasn't just the studio system. The independent world is almost as dire; it's just a smaller list of talentless money changers who have to justify their existence. The only reason you don't get rewritten by a list of hacks is not because of some kind of integrity inherent in the scruffy independent system; it's because they'd rather not pay all those dogs to piddle on your papers.

Well, there's no movie police forcing you to lie down and spread 'em for Hollywood. You don't like it, go back to the night shift at Vidiots.

There are many reasons to love an industry unburdened by morality. Primary among them is forgiveness. A hit forgives us all our trespasses, in fact, *rewards* us for them. One *Titanic* and you're allowed to scream and rant and fire and pull guns and fuck anybody who'll prance to the crook of your finger. And they forget all about *Piranha II: The Spawning*.

I had my big shot, my X-wing fighter to Alderaan, my major studio break . . . and I bombed out big time. It wasn't big budget, but it was high profile. The trades were filled with the saga of the film school prodigy who jumped right out of the gate and into studio features, even without a load of music video shit on his résumé. And how that first-time Hollywood Helmer never even finished the movie. The studio wouldn't even Alan Smithee the damned thing; they just flushed their investment away . . . and I followed it down the drain.

I learned a big lesson, and I'm ready to share it with you, free of charge.

Never work with puppies, kids, or mutant babies.

My own mutant kept me underground, feeding off my bodily fluids like Bernie Brillstein before meeting its untimely end as In-Sink-Erator chum for the Studio City sewer gators. As Asta's grue spattered the rusted porcelain of my kitchen sink, so did I. But I got over it. I even began to bathe again.

And work.

Well, when I say work, you won't find it on my résumé.

I wrote and wrote and wrote some more. And when I finished, I wrote some more. But the padlock had rusted shut. Nobody wanted to buy the stories I had to tell. Fair enough. Again, nobody's forcing me here. I serve of my own accord. So I wrote and wrote and wrote some more.

But I never sold any of it. And I can't blame anyone but myself. I thought that my experience had deepened me, and that my writing had matured, and reflected new reaches of insight into the human psyche. In truth, I was just jacking off.

But between then and now, I *did* shoot another feature-length film, though I haven't told my new best friends at CAA. And it made a fortune, though not for me. I say film, but it was shot on MiniDV video, for a Valley company called Vivid. The

San Fernando Valley is the red-rimmed sphincter of "adult entertainment," and for a shining moment—though I hadn't sported an erection in close to two years—I was its king. If you've spent way too many nights alone with your VCR and your left hand, you may be intimate with my timeless classic, *Gulp!* Yes, the exclamation mark is part of the title, your guarantee of artistic merit.

The two-day shoot had only one real disaster, though "disaster" is a subjective term. Patty Petty had just been implanted eight days before the shoot with massive bags of mammarian come-hither, topping her slender frame with enormous globes that stretched her fine alabaster skin so tight that, during a particularly energetic (and award-winning) coupling that involved five men, two women, and one excessively randy orangutan, her breasts just split right open, dropping the silicone bags to the floor like unwanted Gerber's from a baby's mouth.

It was beautifully lit, and the camera was in the perfect position to see it all. It may be my most memorable scene.

With an investment of eight thousand dollars—and one thousand of those crispy green boys were all *mine!*—*Gulp!* has grossed close to eight million dollars. Thank God for insurance. It swept the Adult Film Awards (Best Feature shot on Video, Best External Orgasm, Most Orifices Filled, and a host of others) and almost made me wish I'd used my own name on the damned thing. Almost.

Gulp Two! was a certainty. But I left that to other hands. Been there, porked that.

It's funny, if not really all that amusing, how one thing leads to another in this berg. In the afterglow of *Gulp!*'s transcendental performance, Patty was cast as a Wise-Beyond-Her-Years Stripper, a featured role that required Tasteful Nudity in an otherwise unmemorable Artistic Endeavor known as the Untitled Independent Feature. The *Sterling Stripper Story* crashed and burned before the first week was in the can, but pretty, petty

Patty introduced me to its producer, who had actually seen and enjoyed *Words Without Voices,* and he hired me to write his magnum opus . . . for the princely sum of two thousand American dollars. That was exactly double my *Gulp!* fee, so I wrote my little telltale heart out. It was a grim, violent Urban Drama, spattered with Red Humor and brotherly love. Well, our Masterwork of Renegade American Cinema stepped into mucky post-Columbine legal entanglements that kept it from even being midwifed on video.

But two years after it was collecting dust on the Payment Due shelf at the lab, Mr. Producer highjacked his finest hour (and forty minutes) and managed to book it illegally into the Slamdunk Festival. For the uninitiated, Slamdunk is the scruffy alternative to Sundance and Slamdance, where loft-living men in black get their tawdry little celluloid stories that no legitimate human will have anything to do with projected onto the big screen once before being consigned to a Kmart video transfer with felt marker labels that sit with pride on the apple crate next to the dying Korean TVCR and the Tarantino collection.

Luckily, Sundance stank on ice that January. People had grown tired of the sensitive as well as the insensitive. Cinematographic ennui blanketed Park City with eleven inches of dull snow. And, with a bit of help from unnamed sources, word began to creep out about the lesbian nipple-tonguing scene in our masterwork. It is said in the bible of American independent cinema that if you blanket raw eros in artful light and gorgeous surroundings, they will come. Give them guilt-free art-house erotica, wanking material for the intelligentsia, and the kilos to the kingdom are yours.

We played to a full house, breaking the legal logjam, and leading to an eleven-week run at the Nuart. It's still running midnights at the Angelika Center, even though it's been on video for months. Sure, most of the attention went to the snotty little auteur in the backward cap and the baggy Hilfigers, but you know, somebody writes this shit. And this time, that some-body was me, and that shit was *mine*.

So now I'm working again.

I mean, I'm not Kevin Williamson, but I'm doctoring a cou-ple of Gramercy scripts at ten grand a week, sold a spec to Fox Searchlight for the low six figures, and made an overall with Bob and Harvey over at Miramax that includes directing my third script for them. If and when.

But I've been through this before, and if you can't learn from experience, you are less than human, and consigned to a life as detritus. You exist to fail and provide an example to those who *can* learn from your mistakes.

So . . . no Porsche and big house for me. I'm driving a TT, with a condo at the Marina City Club. Leave the pretensions to the backward-cap crowd. I'm even letting my hair grow out brown.

There's even been a rebound in the social world. Invitations to screenings and parties are ubiquitous, and I don't even bother to RSVP. I haven't paid for a meal since Slamdunk. And that was a year and a half ago.

I wasn't even going to bother with the American Cinemath-eque opening party, except that I'd never seen DeMille's silent *Ten Commandments* before. Hell, I'd never seen *any* silent film before . . . or any DeMille, either, for that matter. But I'd heard about the grand old Egyptian Theatre, and there was a live or-chestra, and my tickets were free, but they'd have cost *you* a hun-dred bucks apiece . . . *if* you could get them. I was at a meeting at Paramount in the neighborhood anyway, and it was better than fighting traffic to the Marina. Well, the Cinematheque completely ruined Hollywood's first and greatest movie palace, cramming a hideously ugly high-tech architectural disaster into its beautiful shell, and I slept through the dusty old harridan of a movie.

But the party afterward made the evening more than worth-while.

Oh, it was littered with the usual suits and poseurs and perfect specimens at both ends of the Hollywood rectum spectrum. There were the witty and famous, the witless and gorgeous, the rich and the stitched, the sparkled and the spackled, the cream and its curdle. Milling about the cramped, crimson lobby were Golden Age Movie Star look-alikes serving drinks and the latest trendy biblical edibles from Along Came Mary. It was mildly clever. They did, however, manage to find some pretty good doubles: a Gable and a Lombard, a magnificent Monroe, a mammarian Mansfield. There was a remarkably unhaltered Harlow sheened in a *Platinum Blonde* satin gown that chilled and hugged her alabaster breasts with static electricity that made her nipples point shamelessly all the way to heaven.

It was almost enough to make me give a shit about Old Hollywood. It was fully enough to feel my first post-Asta stirrings Down There.

The tight marcel of her white-hot hair, the anachronistic, unathletic voluptuousness of her unfettered hips, the sea-bottom near translucence of her milky—no, *creamy*—skin enraptured me in unexpected ways. Everything old was new again. My fascination did not go unnoticed. A publicist for the Cinematheque, ever alert to the needs of Her People, smiled at my obvious rapture, sidled up to me, and gripped my elbow with her manicured claw, sipping champagne from a plastic flute from the other. Her lipstick smeared the rim a muddy, dried-blood color.

"Pretty, isn't she?"

Pretty. Meg Ryan is pretty. A nice day is pretty. A fucking *nose* is pretty. Harlow II was something way beyond that. I don't know that they've even got a word yet for what she was. Really, it's been a couple of years since I last gave a shit about sex. I mean, it was ruined for me, I thought, for good. And Madame Publicité only bittered the batter. Though her high, domed forehead was stretched tight and shiny, her telltale hands were creepy and crepey. Her thinning hair was coarse and wiry, her collagen lips bloated like a flounder's, her eager eyes trapped in a look of constant surprise. She was the sexual antichrist.

But what the antichrist taketh away, Harlow II gave back a thousand-fold. Hallelujah, I am reborn.

The publicity monster stroked the inside of my arm with her talons and released a string of intimate words in my ear in a voice I know she felt was sultry, but to me was a gaseous nicotine croak.

"You can have her, you know," she exhaled, wilting the rented flowers around us. "Let me introduce you." And the Publicity Pimp, gripping me so tight I feared blood loss, led me to the Goddess.

Well, suddenly realizing the woman was a professional wilted me a bit . . . until we were face-to-face. It turned out I was the proverbial man who needed no introduction. She knew who I was, had seen the Masterwork during its Nuart run, even *bought* the video, though it still hasn't come out at sell-through. She even knew about *Words Without Voices*.

Had to be an actress. Damn it.

But who else works these Hollywood gigs? Professional servers? Beautiful People entirely uninterested in the performing arts? What the fuck did I expect? It was a disappointment, though it did nothing to fade her glory. She was magnificent, one of a kind. And the wattage from her smile could run a thirty-plex projection booth for a year and a half.

The Pimp winked and left us, with a smutty exit line that dangled huskily in the air of her wake: "If you need a third party, you know who to call." I'd rather lick clean Michael Jackson's star on the Walk of Fame.

When the tendrils of her reeking Giorgio finally receded and I could draw the semblance of a breath, I laughed uncomfortably. "Seen any good movies lately?"

Her smile never broke, even with her simple answer. "No."

I was falling hard. They haven't made a good film in years. All they make are Crybaby Movies, no real guts or glory. Tobe Hooper can't get a studio picture set up. Gus Van Sant reshot fucking *Psycho*. It's all crybaby shit or comedies that aren't funny or send-ups. There hadn't been a real movie in the nineties, and the new millennium seems just as bleak.

But she had an addendum: "Not since your picture at the Nuart." And then her smile went sideways with the extra-added attraction. She whispered, "Gulp." Not like a title, or anything. Just the word. Gulp. Without the exclamation point. Just to let me know that she knew. And still, she never lost her smile.

I could only stare at her in admiration. "Same to you, but more of it." It was a lame retort, I know, but I had to say *something*. And she laughed, a tinkling shower of delight that prickled the hair on the back of my neck. Gulp, indeed.

"If you weren't an actress, I'd ask you to marry me." Chicks dig that.

"If you weren't a director, I'd slap you for that." But I was, so she didn't. "I like directors . . . especially the young, talented ones."

"If I meet one I'll be sure to introduce you." The self-deprecating stuff always hooks them. And I wanted her hooked. Gaffed. Boned.

"Oh, we've already met."

Her wet, crimson lips glistened, and I watched them stick together and peel apart as the "m" made its way through her mouth in slow motion.

"Will you be at the after-party?" she asked. After-party? What after-party? Was that on my invitation?

"Will *you*?"

"I have to be."

"Then so do I. When and where?"

"It's a secret." And then she leaned close, offering a bud-tipped alabaster view, and shared her secret with me.

* * *

The rain was biblical, but the directions very specific. The little roadster and I headed up Laurel Canyon, past Joel Silver's Frank Lloyd Wright masterpiece on Hollywood Boulevard, turned left on Wonderland, and slid through an aquarium of eely estuaries and sobbing oaks. We groped through the rare midnight storm, ever upward, evading the cracks of lightning that drew closer as we drove higher. At the applause of a particularly splendiferous hand of electrical fingers in the sky, I turned to look down at the basin below and behind, just in time to see its voracious maw go dark.

It made little difference to my slithering drive. Here in the jungle of the Hollywood Hills, there were no streetlights. The moonlight was my guide. I was so close to my destination, I could not give up my quest, even if the party was called off when the lights went out.

So I continued, the heart of Indiana Jones beating within my chest.

At last I emerged at the crest of the mountain, and I saw Xanadu. Not the Olivia Newton-John bowl-filler, but the Orson Wells original, done southern California style. It was vast and pink and Spanish-tiled, probably built in the twenties when this acreage could be had for pocket change. And though the dozens of windows were dark, red-vested car chimps were jockeying the Benzes and Beemers into place. I parked the TT myself, and let the rain submerge me as I walked to the door.

Cool.

Security was tight, but I didn't need a ticket. The enormous Polynesian totem at the door let me right in without even a word passing between us. Either a fan or he'd been primed.

I walked inside this Old Hollywood mansion, and found myself submerged in darkness. I squinted through the twisting hallway, choking on the musk of history, and stepped into the spider's parlor. It opened up into a giant room filled with over-stuffed furnishings and the glow of pale candlelight. It was a step into another era, one you only see on the screen, and even then only in black-and-white. This place was an education in early cinema, the kind I flunked out in at film school: an education I did not want, but could not avoid. The whole house was dressed in the elegance of a Hollywood long gone, like an Ernst Lubitsch drawing room comedy, dressed by William Cameron Menzies. The ceilings were high and scalloped, the maroon velvet draperies belted into place by gold ropes. It all looked so wrong in color.

This was a Hollywood for which I had no nostalgia. It had grown long in the tooth on quaintness and manners and dust and censorship. It was far removed from real life: cornball artifice with heavy makeup and jerky special effects. It looked like Cary Grant should step in and offer me a drink.

Which is exactly what happened.

His black hair oiled into a perfect, shining part, a pearly grin that rounded the dimpled chin into an undersized apple, he poured me champagne and wished me well before disappearing into the candlelit gloom.

As my pupils adjusted to the light, I realized that I stood in a room filled with perfect specimens of an age gone by. Elegant in their evening clothes, many of them had been at the Cinematheque gala. But none of the icons from the fifties or beyond were here. These replicants were strictly of prewar vintage. Most of these had *not* served at the Egyptian; they were *special:* the very most beautiful recreations of Hollywood's so-called Golden Era. My not really being a student of celluloid history, there were a lot of look-alikes I didn't recognize at the time. You know, if a movie was made before the birth of Michael Bay, I wasn't interested. But some of them you just couldn't avoid, so great was their status as pop culture icons.

Even the new generation of filmmakers that comes after me

would have recognized the young John Wayne, that woman with the big monkey in *King Kong,* Kate Hepburn, Jimmy Cagney, Jimmy Stewart, Lana Turner in a bright red sweater, that woman who always had her blond hair hanging over one eye, that *Thin Man* guy with the moustache, the old lady from *Big Valley,* who was a lot better looking young, but still no babe. Except for Lana's show-off sweater, all of them were in the most elegant evening clothes of the era: white tie and tails, satin gowns, real classy stuff.

But what really looked out of place, even more than seeing these facsimiles in full, living color, was watching what they were *doing.* The place was fetid with body heat. Those elegant clothes slid off of bare shoulders and dropped into elegant little pools of silk at the feet of the guests being serviced. I mean, it wasn't like everybody was whanging and banging in the middle of the room or anything; it was a little subtler than that.

But the Hollywood Hills were alive with coupling. Each massive easy chair, divan, or settee was occupied by at least one gorgeous specimen treating the guests to a taste of Old Hollywood. A hand cupped a puddle of breast here; a flesh probe reached between tight buttocks there. Lips met teats and groins lubricated to the gentle strains of the string section in the other room. This glamorous repast of bodies on bodies was still elegant, passionate yet ethereal. It was my first appreciation of Hollywood past.

I felt out of place, like a child, apart from the party, a guest but not a participant . . . until tapered porcelain fingers rested on my shoulders from behind. I turned, and joined the celebration. Harlow II touched her scarlet lips to my cheek and gently slid her fingers between mine. "I was waiting for you."

Jesus!

The words eased over me on her gentle breath, and every body hair prickled to attention. In the candlelight, she was even more luminous, practically digitally enhanced. Her fingers wrapped around mine, and it was as if we had melted together at the hand.

"Nice party," I managed, but my voice cracked the "nice" into two syllables. I couldn't imagine a modern woman as beautiful as my Jean . . . and I told her so.

"You should see me on a weekday."

I shuddered. The veil of imagination lifted for a moment, and for just a slice of that moment I could see past the platinum hair and the period lipstick, and saw her as just another beautiful actress in LA. Everything suddenly darkened in a crash of artifice, and my pulse dropped. The arousal waned, and I struggled to get it back, but without success. Jean was a working girl, another gorgeous face in the Academy Players Directory, with a wanna-be résumé and an attraction to randy directors. I went limp.

She noticed.

"What's the matter?"

"Nothing. I just imagined you without the wig, having lunch with your agent at the Ivy and checking your pages every hour on your cell phone. In the real world."

She looked at me, figuring me out. "This is my real world. Here. Now. With you. This is no wig; go ahead, feel it."

I did. I ran my fingers through the curling-iron waves, and she closed her eyes, enjoying the journey. "Pull on it." I gave it a little tug, and her lips parted, releasing that intoxicating breath. It was not a wig.

"I don't have an agent, I eat lunch at Musso and Frank's every day, and I hate cell phones. In fact, that's how I tell good people from evil people. If you talk on a cell phone in a restaurant, you're evil. Period. No way around it, no second chance. One strike and you're out. Cell phones in restaurants or talking in a movie theater: the true signs of human slime." I hoped nobody would choose this moment to reach out and touch me via the PacBell digital in my coat pocket. "This is me, the real me, the ever me. Just a little less dressy on weekdays. So mind your manners, or you'll have to be spanked."

Oh, please, not that. I apologized, and she forgave me.

"What would you like?"

"Are you kidding?" Uncharacteristically, her face flushed and she looked shyly down under my hungry gaze.

"You want something to drink?"

"Cary Grant gave me champagne, which I don't drink. I'll take a Coke, if you've got it. But I just want to be with you."

She smiled at me, all girlish and genuine. "That's so sweet." And she led me by the hand. We walked through dim caverns of candlelight, each containing bodies in rhythmic heat. I was not startled to see Cary lying beneath an energetically hyperventilating Madame Publicist, her eyes rolled back in her head in ecstasy, her nails gouging red rivers down Cary's chest. I tried to sneak past, but her eyes found me, and she gave me a yellow wink. Her words reached me on a wave of dragon breath: "Have a nice time. . . ." And then she came. Loudly.

Ugh.

Other couplings were more visually appealing. There were fantasies fulfilled throughout the house, animus cloaked in an historic glamour. Dead movie stars brought back to life by the vigor of our desire. I can't tell you how exciting these violations of the Hays Code were to watch.

Laid out in the elegance of the location, the perfect grooming and formal wear intensified the heat to an amazing degree. The power may have been off, but the house was filled with electricity. I had always seen that Old Hollywood shit as dull and historic and musty and grampy. But now it was making me sprout wood.

I'm a director, so I observe. I felt no guilt staring at the couplings as Jean led me through them. It was a symphony of flesh, and each of the players was first chair. And I was being led to the podium to conduct a little ditty of my own.

* * *

I couldn't believe that the dark room she eased me into was anchored by a heart-shaped bed. That image would have worn a beard even in one of those old thirties movies. But it did, and the bed was made up in pink satin, as if art-directed to set off Harlow II's peach gown. The high-ceilinged room was lit only by a shaft of blue moonlight through a curtain of rain. The chill of the moonlight was tempered by the heat of our bodies. When she slid lightly onto the corner of the bed, tiny arcs of static electricity crackled between her and the sheet. As she sat in the shaft, highlighted by the moon, I could only gasp. She lifted her arms to me, and I dropped down next to her. I knew this had to go slow. It had to be drawn out. This might only happen once.

She stroked my face with her delicate fingertips, a Mona Lisa grin tugging at her scarlet lips. Those lips moved slowly in, and I wanted them to just devour me: wrap around my head and work their way down to my toes until I was dinner. Instead, they eased against my cheek, pausing there before peeling wetly away and leaving their crimson imprint. She grinned at the lipstick she'd left on my face, and lunged in to lick it off in a swift wipe of her tongue. Then she laughed.

I put my hands up and gently held her face in them, as if it might shatter. Her skin was as smooth and white as an egg. She let me draw her face close to mine, and finally we kissed. No suction, no open mouths, just our lips touching each other, gently at first, breathing each other's breath. I kissed her upper lip, her lower lip, then tilted my head to kiss them both at a vertical angle. Then I got hungry. I started to pull her lower lip into my mouth, nursing on it. Soon, the tiny pink tip of her tongue ventured into my mouth, tracing my teeth and gums. There was the faintest taste of chocolate on her tongue, and I savored it. I wrapped my mouth around her tongue, and she slid it deeper inside, soon moving it to a samba rhythm. Then she took my tongue and nursed on it. I'm sure my eyes rolled back in my head in idiot abandon.

When finally we broke for air, we just looked unbelievingly into each other's eyes and breathed. And then we both just broke into laughter with the delight of it all. She nestled into the base of my neck, kissing it wet and warm, and I carefully lowered the satin strap that held in Nirvana. But I wasn't about to go right for the good stuff. I wouldn't be the pig with the hands that only wanted to grasp the tits and the clutch. For the first time in my life, I pleasured in the getting there. I felt the rich gloss of her neck and shoulders, stroked the clean, perfect whiteness of her deliriously long back. I kissed down her neck, tasted her wrists, even lifted her arm to cradle my head under it and kiss her pit. I tasted the slightest hint of salt and loved it. There wasn't even a trace of stubble.

And she, too, was happy to take her time with me. Her lips brushed lightly over my neck as she unbuttoned my shirt. I could feel the heat of her breath as she nuzzled my chest, her teeth lightly tugging on the hair around my nipples. She sucked easily on mine as I wanted hers. But I'd get there soon enough.

My hands went all exploratory, gently excavating the secrets of her body. I eased the satin down off of her breasts, and there were little sparkles of static electricity introducing them in a fanfare of tiny fireworks. Her happy little breasts were as white as the rest of her body, not surgically enhanced, and capped with tiny pink roses that almost disappeared in the moonlight. I first felt their heft with a light stroke of the underside with the back of my hand. I slowly closed in, palming them, holding them, clutching them. I nuzzled them, but that was it. Soon I had drawn them hungrily into my mouth, and I wanted to feed off of her: milk, blood, anything. I just wanted to swallow her fluids.

At that point, it wasn't long before I was atop her, the globes of her ass clutched tightly in my hands. Her legs scissored me tightly as she chewed voraciously on my earlobe. And as her body was wracked in orgasm, I was pumping two years of dormant seed endlessly into her. I thought it would never stop . . . but finally it did.

When the new sun peered into the bedroom window, the old movie was over. Jean was gliding into jeans and a T-shirt, and brushing her hair out of her eyes. She wasn't Jean anymore. I bet she lived in the Valley. I heard the leaden thump-thump of techno-disco booming through the old house, and a ripple of nausea curdled me. It took me a while to come to. The 2000s had fully replaced the 1930s. And I didn't like it.

I watched the muscles of her chest heave as she brushed her platinum and tried to figure out what came next. "Um . . . what do I owe you?"

"Don't worry about it. Last night was all taken care of."

Nice party.

I couldn't take my eyes off of her, and she winked at me in the mirror.

"When can I see you again?"

She turned to me. "Any time you've got fifteen hundred bucks. Or a part you might think I'm right for. I'm a very versatile actress."

I tried to smile back, but I'm sure she saw my face crash. Jean was gone. This stranger gave me a mock pout. "Aw, baby misses Jean Harlow, doesn't he? I can be Jean any time you can afford it." And she handed me a business card with her pager number on it. She kissed me hard on the lips and toodled.

What a crash. I don't know why I felt so devastated, so abandoned, so cheated. But here I was, hollow and deflated, still sticky from last night, inside and out. All I had left was the drive home.

Home.

I stared out at the sewage bobbing along the beach from my

tenth-floor condo. I hated the present. A second-stage smog alert hung heavy over the effluent, and the traffic on the boulevard below was blocked like a bowel. I had the Criterion *Armageddon* on the DVD player, enveloping me in full Dolby Digital surround, but even that couldn't bring me out of it. Normally its twenty-cuts-a-minute exhilarated me; today it merely enervated me. It just felt like a bunch of frantic, noisy crap, a cinematic nagging mother-in-law, screeching in my ear. I missed the past . . . and I'd never even been there.

So I decided to visit.

I made a sojourn to the dreaded San Fernando Valley to Dave's Video, a beacon in the midnight of Ventura Boulevard. I loaded up on every black-and-white DVD made before the Great War and charged it to my Gramercy account. Research, you know. Let them pay for my education in the classics.

I lugged the tonnage of my cinema booty back to the marina, and vegetated in front of the new HD screen from the Good Guys. Tendrils of beard sprouted as I reached back into the ghosts of the past. First, I made my way through every Jean Harlow film I could find, from *Hell's Angels* through *Saratoga*. She'd made a couple dozen pictures in the course of a half-dozen years, then up and died. But Jesus, what a legacy she left! Through Harlow, I discovered Howard Hawks, William Wellman, and Victor Fleming. The movies spoke to me in an eloquence I'd never known before. They just plain *spoke!* The words sparkled, the scenes played out without cuts, the camera observed, rather than led the characters! What a revelation!

I worked my way through the Harlow collection, hungering for her crumpled little expression, lusting after her pale, everbraless form. *Dinner at Eight* led me to George Cukor; Cukor led me to Ernst Lubitsch, who led me to Preston Sturges, who led me to John Sturges, who led to me John Ford, on to Hitchcock and Huston, David Lean and Frank Capra, Tod Browning and James Whale. And through the filmmakers I met some new dead friends: Jimmy Stewart, Robert Donat, Gene Tierney, Donna Reed, Ava Gardner, Rita Hayworth, Jean Simmons, Glenn Ford, Ann Savage, Veronica Lake, Boris Karloff, Fay Wray.

Who knew these creaky old grinders would be so filled with wit and beauty and humor and tension and revelation? Who knew that a film could be more than a barrage of flash-cut imagery, digital animation, and DTS explosions?

Maybe you did, but I didn't.

I know, I'm sounding like some old fart film instructor who can't let go of a past that's practically been buried alive, but it's true. I don't mean to preach here—I really don't—but I was born again. I guess I'd only seen the old shit. I didn't find the jewels. That would be like judging today's movies by the latest Adam Sandler.

The best of the old stuff was elegant and smart and breezy and entertaining and, well, *engaging*. And the worst of it was ... well, the worst of it was like most of the movies today. Bankrupt and boring.

I got it.

Bleary-eyed and exhausted but also wonderfully recharged after a dozen weeks of nonstop watching, I turned off the set. I'd forgotten the world was in color, and it startled me. The cleaning lady had vacuumed around me for the last couple of months, and thrown out all the food delivery cartons, but the place was still a litter of videos and detritus. As I stood, my head reeled. My eyes had stared at a fixed focus for so long that they found it difficult to hone in on anything else. My hair was a couple of inches longer, and I had the semblance of a Fu Manchu beard tickling my chin.

I slid the glass door to the balcony open and stepped out onto the cusp of the real world, and let it breathe on me. It was noisy and argumentative and its breath stank. I liked the movies better. Reality bathed me in ugliness, and I shivered. It reeled around me and my mind drifted away to beauty.

I remembered what brought this on in the first place. I opened up my wallet, and pulled out her card. It didn't have a name on it, just a number. I dialed it, got the system's nervous beep-beep-beep, punched in my number, and waited. This time, as I looked out into the vast Pacific, I couldn't discern the turds floating out there. Maybe they cleaned them out again; maybe they were just hiding. But the sea was as blue as the veins on Cher's forehead. If only the sky matched. Instead, it was congealing into a disgusting mauve solidity.

Her call booted me out of my coastal reverie. She knew who it was from just my "hello." She was good. I needed to see her. I wanted to share what I had found with her, and needed to siphon some of it off of her, so I invited her over. She came.

By the time she called up from the lobby, I was showered and shaved and reborn. My eyes could focus near and far again, and my breath was kissing sweet. My expectant erection tugged me like a divining rod to the door at the sound of her gentle rap. Oh, my lovely embodiment of the past, my alabaster testimony to all that once was beautiful and elegant and witty and desirable. My link to another, better world, the only world that mattered, a world without corruption or darkness or despair.

My Jean.

I pulled the door open . . . and wanted to cry.

This was not my Jean. This was that girl in the jeans and the T-shirt and the Reeboks and the backward Nike cap, fresh from the gym. This was all the girls I'd read and dated and sampled and discarded and been discarded by. This was now, and I wanted—*needed*—then.

She saw it and knew. She lifted a shopping bag from Trader Joe's and pulled out a bottle of wine. "I brought wine." I tried not to look so let down, and she dug deeper in the bag. "And Jean."

She held up the peach satin gown with a twinkling little smile that did its best to win me over. "Which way to the bathroom?"

Unable to speak, I merely pointed, and she scurried through

the condo and locked herself in. No matter what she looked like when she emerged, I had seen behind the facade. I knew it was fake now, and that it wasn't going to work. It was so perfect that night at the Cinematheque, until the fateful morning after. I wouldn't see Jean anymore, merely the actor playing her. It wasn't the same thing.

Still, when she emerged, the gown clinging to her like hot breath, she was stunning. The lips were sanguine, the hips unfettered, the breasts at full attention. But now, having experienced the real Jean Harlow in every one of her films—even the one with Laurel and Hardy—I realized she didn't really look all that much like Harlow. Beautiful, desirable, yes. Harlow, no.

"Forget about that girl at the door," she told me. "I sent her away. I want you all to myself." She gave me a sharp little bite on the lip. I tasted my own blood.

She stepped into the middle of the living room and appraised the place, knowing I would appraise her in the light of the picture windows. The room basically consisted of open space, the giant TV system, and a view of the murky marina. And now, her. She startled me with a sudden squeal of delight. "Look!" she said as she knelt at the pile of silver discs littering the floor. "You've got all my movies! Let's watch one!" She picked up a copy of *Red Dust* and held it out to me in front of the stack of electronic hardware. Then, in a baby-doll voice: "How do you work this thing?"

I popped the disc into the machine and fired up the monitor, filling it with the true Harlow and Clark Gable.

"Do you have any popcorn, Clark?" she asked me. I had to disappoint her, but she was good-natured about it all and pulled me into a pile of pillows with her. It was a strange experience looking from the screen to the siren curled in my lap. She mouthed all the dialogue that Harlow spoke as the sun outside sank into the marina.

As the movie continued, she slid up against me like a cat, and the contact was all warm and comfy and even arousing . . . but that's not what I wanted. I wanted the woman on the screen. The Jean in my lap started to purr, her engine ignited and accelerating. She pushed me back into the pillows and climbed atop me; I drowned in her body.

Her skin as smooth as the discarded satin gown, she flowed against me like butter on a frying pan, melting on me. Her talents spread throughout her body, but mine resisted. I tried closing my eyes, but could not keep the girl at the door out of my home. She drew me into her and we coupled ferociously, but it was nothing like that night. And I know it wasn't her fault, but I couldn't help but focus on the tiny red pimple sprouting on her chin. The *real* Harlow would never be so blemished. We united wetly and energetically, and our mutual release finally jettisoned enough unspilled juice to cramp my sphincter. But I was not satisfied, and she knew it.

"You know, I try my best to be her for you, but I can't really *be* her."

I couldn't say anything. I was spent and sweating, and just couldn't come up with an answer. I felt like the king of movie geeks, pining for a movie star who died before my parents were even conceived. What a fucking goober.

She just watched me, her mind working, and I felt like a twelve-year-old. My heart had been broken by an image on television. Her gaze just embarrassed me. Mama, make it stop. She just kept looking at me, judging me, shrinking me with her eyes. Meanwhile, the movie had come to an end.

Without saying anything, she walked across the room, still spectacularly naked, and picked up the phone. Her eyes still pinning me to the floor like a butterfly specimen, she started dialing and walked into the kitchen. I heard her dulcet, offscreen voice, but not the words. I heard her sign off before she reentered the room and cradled the phone, shameless in her sheath of flawless ivory flesh. She gently took me by the hand and took me to the glass doors overlooking the water. She stared out for long silent minutes before speaking.

"How much would you pay to spend the night with Harlow?"

I figured it was time to pay up. I guess fifteen hundred wasn't a lot to pay to discover what a retard I was.

"I'll get your money."

I went to the desk and brought her the cash.

"I didn't mean me," she said as she took the bills and folded them into her dainty Bakelite purse. "I meant Harlow."

"I think you're as close as I'm ever going to get."

That made her laugh. "I'm not."

I was sick of her laughing at me. *Think again about me casting you in anything,* I thought.

"I mean Harlow, Jean Harlow, exactly who we were watching on the screen."

"What are you talking about?" I didn't want to play this game.

"What would you pay for a night of connubial bliss with Jean Harlow?"

"The real Jean Harlow? If it were possible?"

"If it were possible."

"I don't know. I can't go that far into the abstract."

"Come on, think about it. If you could have one night with her, how much would it be worth to you?"

I thought about it. "Fifteen hundred?" I thought it would compliment her.

"Shit, you can get *me* for fifteen hundred. Come on, for real. An entire night with Jean Harlow, exactly as you've seen her in the movies. How much?"

"I don't know . . . ten thousand dollars?"

"Cheapskate."

"Twenty."

"Jesus."

I gave up. "Then let's stop doing this. I couldn't fuck Jean Harlow for all the money in the world, so let's just stop this. She's been rotting since 1937."

She just smiled sweetly and shook her marcelled little head. *"I don't think so. . . ."*

Where the fuck was this going? "Well, if she's a hundred years old and living in Argentina or something, I don't think I want a piece of her."

That fucking smile again.

"Would you pay a hundred grand to spend the night with the Jean Harlow of your dreams? The 1937 Jean Harlow? If you could. For real."

Just for the hell of it, I thought about it. Would I? The decision was a bit more difficult in the wake of the powerful orgasm I'd just experienced minutes ago. But with the Gramercy and Miramax deals set in hard copies, I had some disposable income. Is that how I'd dispose of it? A hundred grand? Hell, I could spec out a script in a month for double that. So that's like two weeks' pay. Of course, you can't crank out a dozen scripts a year, but Jesus, even if it's a couple months' pay . . . would it be worth it? I didn't have a wife or kids or anything: just me and my TT. I'd pay a hundred thousand dollars to sleep with Harlow.

If it were possible.

So I said yeah.

And she said really? And I said yeah, I think I would. And she said that was interesting and slid into her jeans and that fucking T-shirt again, kissed me good-bye, and fluttered away.

It was another week before she called me back. I was immersed in *Saratoga* when the machine picked up. I never answer the phone, especially not when I'm viewing, and *especially* not when it's Jean onscreen. But it was her voice: "Are you there? It's Jean."

The voice, I had to admit, was perfect. I picked up.

"Hi."

She giggled, sounding like New York in the thirties. "Go to the bank," she whispered.

"What for?"

"It's time."

"Time for what?"

"You know. Hundred-thousand-dollar time. Cash or traveler's checks."

Well, you and I both know what that meant. But what it meant was impossible. I didn't know how to respond to her, and just sat there with that porcelain face basting my brain, probably breathing funny.

"Are you still there?"

"I'm here."

"Can you get to the bank today? And meet me at Union Station tonight at eleven?"

I didn't understand. "I don't understand," I told her.

"Like heck you don't." And then, with another tinkling little titter, she hung up, as the real Jean smiled at me from my sixty-two-inch Pioneer, enhanced for sixteen-by-nine.

I'd spent a couple of nights sharing skin with this phenomenal creature, reaching a Nirvana Kurt Cobain never dreamed of, but what did I really know about her? That she could set me to palpitating was a given . . . but what kind of idiot would go to the bank, pull out a hundred grand, and meet this angel in the middle of the night at a train station in the cesspool of downtown Los Angeles? Surely this was a setup; obviously this, well, I'll say it, this *prostitute* had found a malleable mark, a sucker just dying to toss off his ill-gotten gains. She and her pierced and tattooed cohorts would beat me up and take my cash. *You* would never have gone for a crack-brained scenario like this one, and I would never have dared writing such a silly plotline. If I'd turned it in to Sid Fields, I'd have flunked Screenwriting 101.

But, you know, I did have a hundred grand. It was pretty much all I had at the moment, but, you know, I had more coming in. And I was unburdened by investments. What was the worst that could happen to me? Other than having my money stolen and my throat slashed, what did I have to lose? My soul? Yeah . . . *that's* worth a lot.

Was it really that preposterous to think that I might be able to have . . . *Jean?*

Well, the answer was obvious, but I sped down to Washington Mutual anyway.

Still grand but aging and missing a few teeth, Union Station reached coldly into the scuffed, blue-brown night sky. Mine was the only car in the desolate lot, and I parked as far as I could from the three creased, ruddy faces sharing hits off a bottle of violet rotgut. The sound of their retching was a perfect contemporary counterpoint to the timeless architectural elegance that reached out to embrace me. I was, as usual, anally punctual. Eleven distant chimes hung sweating in the muggy night air.

As I stepped into the empty vastness of the old dowager, it was like stepping into an evacuated Capra epic. I could imagine the postwar homecomings, the reunited sweethearts spotting one another through the teeming masses of humanity, the brassband send-offs to the senator's last hurrah. But the monochrome crowd evaporated, and the cracked leather seats and the gang-gouged woodwork brought me back home. It was an empty art deco barn strangling on its memories. I would be one of them.

Then, the tip-tap tip-tap of high heels echoed around me, and I turned just as an unmistakable silhouette rounded the corner. She stepped into a shaft of light, and its reflection off of her platinum hair ignited the room in yellow fire. She stood there, letting the spotlight caress her perfection.

"Hi."

"Hi back."

I walked to her, my heart suddenly racing in anticipation, the cash in a shoulder bag, suddenly weighing a hundred pounds. What the fuck was I doing here?

"What the fuck am I doing here?" I asked her.

"Dreaming. Give me your keys."

"Where are we going?"

"Heaven."

I followed her out of the cavernous, empty building and back to my car, unable to pull my eyes from the lift and ripple of the perfect globes of her rear as she walked.

The thick summer night laid on us like an oil change, even with the top down. She caromed through the dank darkness, the empty downtown Los Angeles streets choking on their past. Broadway was a desiccated corpse, the klieg lights of the grand Million Dollar, United Artists, and Los Angeles Theaters long extinguished. A handful of zombies lumbered like cancerous cells through her clogged artery. We were on our own Fantastic Voyage through Innerspace when Jean suddenly pulled off behind the old Times Mirror building, and guided us down a long, dark, seemingly endless alley.

That alley led to the decaying backside of a once-grand edifice, a cracked granite frown slowly settling into the sinking subway horizon. She pulled us into its gaping, festering maw, and kept driving like a drill into the ground. The corkscrew drive was seemingly hellbound as it dug us deeper into a quake-phobe's sweatiest nightmare. But as we plunged down beneath the city, lit only by headlights and the dim, browning sconces that studded the concrete wall, the temperature grew much cooler.

In moments, my grinning little TT peered into a grand open lobby, its flawless white-veined black marble gleaming in the shine of its headlights. A giant stone *Thinker* sat contemplating us in the middle of the vast room as Jean killed the engine and tip-tapped across the gleaming mirror of marble floor to the center pair of sculptured brass doors. The elegance of the lobby was impressive, and of another world: overstuffed leather and cherry sofas and chairs, vast WPA murals of noble working people on the job, a heavy walnut reception desk the size of a Beverly Center screen. It had all of the chi-chi quiet snootery of a Beverly Hills face-tightening clinic.

Jean said "I'm here" to nobody and nothing in particular, and the giant, wizard doors opened up to Oz.

The hallway was of impressive length and faded grandeur, lit by the dull Cocteau glow of faux lantern sconces. It was a soft, warm, but dim light . . . and in it, Harlow II was even more ravishing. She led me down the length of the hallway, and as we reached its end, the dark wood double doors opened up to us, revealing the Man Behind the Curtain.

The man was tiny, certainly not over five feet, with a venerable, dried-apple countenance tightly sheltered with a thick, pomaded landing strip of artificially bootblacked hair. A ghost of cataract and eyelids that drooped like sagging breasts almost hid the sparkle of his rheumy gray eyes, and his osteoporosis curled him into a tiny question mark. He looked up at Jean, apparently unwilling to make eye contact with me until getting her approval.

"He's good," she told him, and the little lawn gnome finally looked up at me, manufacturing a smile that revealed perfectly straight white teeth that were way too big for his crepe-paper mouth. He reached out his right hand—which was missing the thumb—and I shook it. I don't know if you've ever shaken hands with a guy without a thumb, but it just doesn't feel right. His other hand was tucked out of sight in his pocket, and I wondered if the little gremlin was born without opposable thumbs at all.

After I shook his hand, he kept it reaching out at me. I thought he was stuck on pause or something until I realized that he was waiting for me to hand over the shoulder bag with the cash in it.

"Who are you?" I asked, and he looked back up at Jean, who turned to me with a smile.

"No names."

That made the little homunculus grin, and his smile, even in the dim light, was blinding. I handed over the bag to PeeWee, who zipped it open and started carefully counting the bills. This was going to take a while. Jean leaned in to stick a kiss on my cheek.

"Have a great night." And she turned back down that long, lonesome hallway.

"Wait." She turned back with an expectant look. "Can this guy even talk?"

That made the withered little manikin testy. I thought he was going to bite my kneecap. "Of course I can talk! Oh, shit, I've lost count!" And he started over. From one.

With a "Nighty-bye," Harlow II was down the hall and out the door, leaving me with my own private Dr. Loveless. I waited in the doorway while he counted it all out: one hundred thousand dollars in hundred-dollar bills.

Eventually satisfied that I wasn't a piker, Mr. Subspecies turned and led me down the newly revealed corridor. I had to move slowly to keep from overtaking his baby steps.

We took another turn and he reached up on tippytoes to flip a light switch, revealing a long, antiquated chamber that opened out onto several apartments. Each of them had a large picture window that looked into the central chamber, and each window was draped with ornate wine velvet curtains on the inside. Most of the curtains were closed, but not all of them. As I followed in my munchkin's eensy steps, I was able to see into a drape that lolled lazily open. Inside was an ornate bedroom, decorated as if by Menzies: heavy wood pieces, a high molded ceiling, and a vast silk-sheeted bed against the wall. The only light was cast by the dim chamber sconce, but even in the shadows I could see that the bed was unmade.

Just as we passed the window to the clip-clop of teeny feet echoing through the otherwise silent chamber, a face suddenly appeared like a spotlight in the opening of the curtains. I jumped, I admit it, startled by its abrupt appearance, and the golden halo that surrounded her familiar face in the struggling, limp light reflected off her bottle blondness. But most unnerving of all was how her eyes were locked on mine, just a foot or so away from me. This was most definitely not Jean.

The face was enormous, a round, fleshy visage under a marigold mane, exquisitely painted in white-hot Helena Rubinstein beauty. The eyes, though—they were huge and liquid pale, drilling right into my own. But the spark was out behind them; they were gorgeous but empty, lifeless, shining husks of eyes. I wasn't sure she could even see me through them.

But boy, could I see her.

Striking in her red satin wrapper, she was an uncaged housefire. That huge moon of a face rose over an alarmingly ample décolletage and a waspy little waist I could circle in two hands. This was a woman you could only see in color: the red of her lips, the electric gold of her hair, the flamingo pink of her tongue, and— even though bound behind the thin red wrapper—the evident, nursed-dark muddy brown howdies of her vast, reaching nipples.

The Little Man gripped my hand in his gnarly, four-fingered tug, trying to pull me down the hall, but I couldn't move, not now that I recognized her. This incendiary explosion of boobs and blondness had been immortalized most spectacularly by Frank Tashlin in *Will Success Spoil Rock Hunter?* but that's not how I recognized her.

No. The little relentlessly yiping dog at her feet was a clue, but what finally led me to put it all together were the tiny, nearly invisible telltale sutures that circled her neck.

I was eye-locked with Jayne Mansfield.

Obviously, some assembly had been required, since she was decapitated in a car wreck in 1967. But that was Jayne. The real deal. Alive. Breathing. Her impressive water wings heaving with each breath. I could barely even blink as I riveted into her glassy, vacant orbs. She didn't blink at all, not once. It was unsettling, at the very least. I'd only seen eyes like that once before, and I didn't want to remember it, but now she made me.

When I was five years old, my dad was teaching me how to ride a bike without training wheels for the first time. He'd just taken them off without even telling me, and I was roaring down the street, oblivious of my new mastery of two-wheeled travel, when he shouted out for me to look, that I was riding without training wheels. I looked down, saw that it was true, and panicked. The handlebars shimmied and I lost control. Dad came running to help me, just as an ancient, wheezing Impala roared around the corner on a tail of gray exhaust, and slammed him into the phone pole. I skinned my knee through my jeans as I fell off the bike and ran to see my father, who was shattered and pinned between the empty grin of the Impala's grille and the cracked phone pole tower of Pisa. Our eyes were cinched as his life beat away with his slowing heart, leaving the flesh husk and the glazed, sightless eyes reflecting my own. I could see, even then, when his life had left him, and his eyes gone blind.

And now Jayne gave me the same vacancy sign before pulling the curtain shut.

"Come on," the tugging little gnome croaked as I allowed him to pull me from the blockaded showroom. "She's not for you."

"Was that Jayne Mansfield?" I asked him.

"No, it was Jane Pauley. What the fuck do you think?"

"You're a cranky old asshole, aren't you?"

"I'm actually very sweet once you get to know me."

I didn't believe him. But I followed him down the seemingly endless chamber anyway.

He stopped me at the very last room.

"You didn't bring flowers, did you," he said in a judgmental sneer. "She likes flowers."

"Nobody told me."

"It's breeding, common decency to bring a woman flowers. Now . . . you know the rules."

I looked at him. How should I know the rules? "Not really."

"Just be gentle. Thoughtful. And no rough-housing."

And then he was off, no doubt back to his place behind the curtain. His walk took him forever.

I gently rapped on the ornate door and waited, my heart trying to climb up my throat. I kept waiting, the mystery and marvel and anticipation shriveling my nerve as well as my manhood. I felt like a turtle pulled back in its shell. When it became evident that no one was coming to answer my knock, I reached out and gripped the doorknob. It was greasy with palm sweat, but wasn't locked. It opened, and I entered in quiet, tiny steps.

The room was hushed and dark, but so were my desires, I guess. But the dim light from the candle guttering on the nightstand couldn't extinguish the glow that Jean Harlow—the real Jean Harlow, alive and in full living breathing color—cast. She sat on the edge of the peach satin bed, draped in shadow and a fine silk chemise. She turned to face me, but the curtain of shadow blacked out her features. I was frozen in place, my mouth gawping; I hadn't the strength to take a breath. The hairs at the nape of my neck curdled and a shimmer of gooseflesh traversed my body. Jean. Jean. Roses are red. And all of my guts have gone green.

After a big slice of eternity, I made the next move, taking a step toward her and the bed. Jean glided back a few inches on the satin quilt, lifting her face into the warm, gentle caress of the candlelight. It was at that moment that it became obvious that Harlow II looked nothing like my Jean, the real Jean. The *faux* Harlow had been sandblasted by modernity, corrupted by the modern age, while Jean—milky, creamy, elegant Jean—was above all that passage-of-time nonsense. I don't know how she was here sitting on this bed in this room with me after dying in 1937, but she was. This was no imposter. Somehow, she had been rescued from the ravages of death, had earned a station in eternity, and for a hundred thousand dollars I had bought a share of that station. A night with my forever Jean. A taste of eternity. Whatever science or magic made it possible, I was its slave.

And Jean's.

Unlocking the invisible shackles that bolted me to the floor, I moved to the bed and looked down at her longingly. She looked up into my eyes and gently patted the space on the bed next to her with her palm, once, silently inviting me to sit. Her eyes, though pure and startlingly blue, were ringed in black mascara, and as vacant and unblinking as Jayne's, though larger and more inviting. Her mouth was painted in a rose red so dark it was almost black, and shone in the pale candlelight. Her lips eased open, just a sticky little fraction of an inch, releasing the softest, curious sound from within. She was purring a constant, sensual little rumble, her own internal combustion engine.

"Jean?"

Without blinking or moving her eyes from me, she nodded. I sat next to her and took her pale ice cream hand in mine. The hand was cool and soft, limp, barely motivated, and I drew it to my face. I touched the back of her hand with my lips, I couldn't help it, and she let me. Her skin tasted like vanilla and fresh hand soap. She watched me kiss her hand through barren, staring eyes, and I laid my hand on her cheek and turned her face toward me. Her eyes turned sluggishly to mine, and we were face-to-face. Her purr was more distinct now, though no less sensuous. I could feel her breath stroke my face in cool even waves. Its scent was a bit pungent, but no more than it might be after a plate of penne arrabiatta. But it sure didn't smell like vanilla.

She neither resisted nor encouraged me, so I bent in and kissed her. She kissed me back, and my eyes closed in exultation. Her full, soft lips parted, and her chilly pink tongue sought mine. She sucked it into her mouth and began to nurse off of it, and there's no way I was going to stop her. I sneaked a peek as she milked my tongue, and her eyes were wide open, still unblinking, her mouth sucking mechanically, almost painfully, on my tongue.

I pulled away to look at her, and she looked back, gorgeous but empty. No resistance, no encouragement.

"What would you like?" I asked her. She just looked back at me. No words. Never any words. I knew the lights were out, but it didn't keep my libido from raging. My fear was that, presented with a dream, my physiognomy might recede and that junior might chicken out; but *au contraire, mon ami, au contraire.* The passive, alabaster icon on the bed with me ignited my hormones and overcame my stupefaction. The ample voluptuousness of one of Hollywood's greatest stars awaited me; the dream of a lifetime was at my fingertips, and if it wouldn't come to life to a symphony of Preston Sturges dialogue, if it would instead be my own personal silent epic, well, shit, so be it.

I reached out and gently lifted the strap of her chemise from her shoulder and let it drop, revealing the delicate sundae of her breast to me. Her eyes locked shamelessly on mine, and I reached over to cup it in my palm. As her feline engine accelerated, I bent down and took her breast in my mouth. It yielded, its cool marshmallow vanilla a creamy treat. The nipple stayed relaxed, unresponsive, never flexing to attention. Her arms curled about me and limply came to rest on my shoulders. I looked up from her breast and she watched me nursing on her with those clear blue unblinking eyes. It stopped me. I raised my face to hers, tried to see beyond the pupils, but was blocked by absence.

She moved in, eyes still wide open, and kissed my mouth.

The hum from within was soothing and welcoming. I let her kiss me, closed my eyes, and ran my fingers through the tight marcels of her platinum hair. Her hair felt like weaves of satin, glossy and slippery, and my fingers got lost in it. My thumb tangled in one of her waves, and I gently tugged it free.

Her breath caught in a gasp and I opened my eyes, afraid I hurt her. Her eyes were even wider now as I lifted my hand from her hair . . . pulling a patch of it away with my thumb! There was a clot of grayish reddish brownish skin at the base of the tangle of spun gold wrapped around my thumb, and she reached for it, unable to take it in her own sleeping fingers.

"Oh, God, I'm so sorry, I'm so sorry!" I tried to calm her, but she just kept quietly and unsuccessfully reaching for her curls. There was a dark brown square on her scalp where the patch had pulled free, and a few drops of a dark fluid that could only have been blood wept to the surface.

"Are you okay?" She didn't answer me, of course. She had given up trying to retrieve her hair and was suddenly reaching for my groin with curious, less-than-dexterous fingers. I couldn't help it; the boy had a mind of his own. As she fumbled to release me, I helped her with the zipper, quickly forgetting about our little experience with the hair. The same mouth that had locked so successfully to my tongue now found succor in the netherworld.

The suction was remarkable considering the fragility of her other movements. I had never felt anything like the cool, muscular, rhythmic suction her mouth incurred. I couldn't help but grip her hair in my hands as I approached a bucking, uncontrollable orgasm that jolted through my body, emptying me of weeks of celibacy.

I jerked violently in fulfillment, and her head bobbed off and back onto my convulsing tissue. It was irresistible impulse; I didn't mean to pull away the handfuls of flaxen hair and gray, preserved flesh. And when she screamed—the first vocalizing she'd released since I entered her room—I looked down to see that one of those fragile, ice-blue, vacuous eyes had been punctured, and wept a clear tide of thick tears.

Her inhuman screech echoed through the silence and in moments the little gnome was charging into the room in hunched-over horror. *"Jeeeeeaaaaaaaannnnnnn!"* he howled. It was the longest single-syllable word I'd ever heard. He yanked me away from her in an incredibly powerful four-fingered grip, and in a cloak of guilt I climbed back into my khakis.

The little professor tended Jean with incredible gentleness, his own eyes going glassy as he dabbed her leaking eye socket with his hanky. *"I said no rough-housing!"* he told me as he soothed her delicate body. "You'd better get out of here."

I agreed. As I made my way to the door, I heard his plaintive, melancholy words evaporate into the velvet night: "Daddy fix, baby. Daddy fix again."

My hundred-thousand-dollar half hour was over.

I've tried several times to return to the House of Harlow, but it is long gone, and without a trace. I've called and called Pseudo-Jean, but that number is no longer in service, and there is no new number. Now all I have to remember Jean by are her movies. I've seen them so often that I know them all by heart, but it isn't just the movies themselves that so entrance me. It's the time long past, the dream long remembered. And I had a piece of that before I put its eye out.

Where the Black
Stars Fall

Brian Hodge

He held her hand and prayed.

He used to pray a lot on first dates—or was tonight their second, or even a date at all?—but twenty-odd years later it was nowhere close to being the same prayer. Used to be, he would pray to get lucky, straightforward invocations fueled by a lustful and all-consuming need, that he'd found that rare girl who would whisper to him an early *yes* because waiting for the next weekend and *maybe* would've been torture.

But tonight it was almost as if nothing had ever changed, and so he held her hand and prayed. Older now, though, and patient in a way he could never have been while so young and eager, asking now for nothing more mercenary than not to trip in the darkness of the park and fall on his own face.

"So who ordered the blackout, I wonder?" she said. "This could *not* have been timed any better."

He had to agree. "This is probably the first time since I was a kid I'm actually glad the lights went out."

"What would you pretend when it happened?" she asked, as

if it were every woman's obligation to dig down to the boy who had lived before the man.

And so he held her hand and walked, trying to recall the past as honestly as he could while the grass whisked dew-damp and slick beneath their shoes, and the encircling tree lines loomed against the sky as solid as a canyon rim.

"My mom would break out the candles," he said. "Blankets, too, it if was winter." Time had come full circle: another outage, another blanket, although this one was from her closet, and carried beneath his arm. "I'd pretend we were pioneers. Sometimes I'd get my BB gun and watch out the windows, like it was my job to shoot cougars."

"That's a cute touch," she said. "How many'd you bring down?"

"Too many to count. But their heads lined the cabin walls."

She made a sound as if she could actually see them, snarling faces lunging out of knotty pine. "Wasn't it always like the biggest disappointment in the world whenever the power finally came back on?"

"The worst," he said, and remembered it all so clearly, because tonight felt the same way, with precious little difference between then and now. The lights were out and magic had reclaimed the night.

"There's one!" She dropped his hand long enough to jab at the western sky with her finger. "Did you see it?"

He confessed that he hadn't. She took his hand again, her own warm against the November chill, and told him there would be plenty of others.

"This tonight is supposed to be the best one in our lifetime, I heard on the news."

"When I was a kid," he said, "my dad used to tell me that shooting stars were angels throwing down their cigarettes."

She laughed. "That's such a dad thing to make up." As he

wondered if she wondered if she would ever have occasion to meet his father. "I didn't even know angels smoked."

"They must," he told her. "It was on the art of a couple old album covers I had, so it's got to be true."

They picked their way along with hesitant care, still half blind to this most total of nights, the park rebuffed by the now-deadened streetlights and lamps that lined the curving walkways. As parks went, it was a humble place, if peaceful enough to pass a lazy afternoon. By day, it had enough playground equipment to keep a dozen kids occupied, and enough open meadow for two pickup games of football, with enough running space left over for someone's Frisbee-catching dog.

Tonight, though, it seemed immense, its borders limitlessly far, swallowed by the waiting dark. He suddenly felt much farther from home than they really were, barely a two-block walk from the condos where they lived. He in one building and she in another—it was a wonder they'd ever met at all.

Could he even say he knew her? Not really, no more than you can say you know anyone you've seen mostly in passing for a couple of months. No more than you can know anyone with whom you'd sat down the week before for not one, not two, but three coffees. He'd known her just enough to fantasize and hope.

And when she'd first taken his hand a block earlier, he held it as though it were the answer to a prayer.

Deep into the park by now, they spread the blanket and settled. She uncapped the thermos bottle she'd been carrying and poured them each a round of fresh cider, slow-warmed with spices on her stove. He swirled the first sip in his mouth, picked out the flavors of cinnamon and cloves and the applesweet distillate of a summer's worth of sunshine. If he kissed her now, she would taste exactly like this.

Overhead, the sky stretched horizons-wide and came alive with flash fire.

Would she mind? She couldn't be as innocent as she looked. Twice married, twice divorced, on her own for the first time in fifteen years—she'd been quite candid about it midway through last week's coffees, admitting how enormously happy she was with this renewed status. Although, later, he had wondered if this declaration hadn't been just for show. The stats could've been his own, give a year and take one marriage, and from where he sat the solitude still felt miserable.

While overhead, the stars streaked and burned like magnesium flares.

They came two, three, four per minute, sometimes in groups that appeared almost synchronized. They came arcing in from their own regions of the sky and immolated themselves into brilliant wakes of cold fire. The moon gave them little competition, not much more than a slivered crescent and, if you looked closely, a hulking shadow set against the infinite depths.

You tried to hang on to them but couldn't, no matter how earnest the attempt. They eluded, living and dying during eye blinks, so you either saw them or you didn't. They came and went at the speed of thought, faster than words could warn. They winked in and out of the edges of vision, or blazed directly before you and still left you wanting more.

They were everything that love should've felt like—and did, once—and were every bit as fleeting.

When she nudged his arm, he was afraid she'd read his mind.

"It looks like your father was right," she joked instead, pointing through the gloom, ahead and to their left.

In the distance, somewhere between here and the unseen swing set, the orange glow of a cigarette made tiny firefly arcs—up, down, up again. Of the person who held it, dragged on it, he could see nothing.

He hadn't given much thought to it, but supposed it wasn't realistic to expect that they could have been alone out here. If the two of them—office workers, the both of them—were hardy enough to endure the chill, then anyone could do it. Meteor showers would always draw an audience.

"When did he finally tell you the truth?" she asked.

For a moment he didn't know what she was talking about. Then, "Who—my dad?"

"About angels and cigarettes and falling stars. Or *did* he, ever?"

"I think he just let me pick it up in the street."

"I forgot—that *was* the preferred method of parenting back then."

"At least it guaranteed a well-rounded education."

"I don't think I asked last week," she said, "but *are* you? A parent?"

He hesitated, had to. Hadn't wanted to get into this yet, maybe would've been just as happy never to get into it at all.

"Not . . . anymore," he said, and even though he'd tried not to let the words slip with too much gravity, out they came like leaden weights, and he could feel her stiffen beside him. Asking if she'd brought up something wrong, and of course it was wrong, it would *always* be wrong—in the right kind of world, no man would ever need to remind a woman that sometimes little girls drown on perfect spring days. In the right kind of world, no man would ever feel he had to absolve that woman of asking innocent questions that still cut like razors, or hate himself for having to. He'd promised himself once that when the time came to date again, he would never use that emptied little bed, in the house where he no longer lived, as a ploy for sympathy.

"I'm so sorry," she told him, and didn't turn away as so many others did, in embarrassment or awkwardness. Instead, beside him, she faced him and couldn't have been more direct about it, less than an arm's length away.

In the night, she could have been fifteen or forty. Her mouth looked full and dark and serious against the paler skin, and her hair fell no farther than her jaw line. Last week, over their cof-fees, he'd glimpsed the photo on her driver's license, the longer hair, and was reminded that women often seemed prone to doing this after a divorce, cutting their hair in the same atavistic way that men once did, in some cultures, to mourn the deaths of those closest to them. He'd wondered if he would ever see it long again, if he could be the one for whom she might regrow it.

"Did your daughter ever ask about . . . ?" And she aimed her finger skyward, where, as if on cue, a streak of light seared greenish white. Seeing, he would've bet, if she couldn't ferret out some like-father-like-son connection, if he'd taken the same quiet glee in lying to the gullible.

"No. I don't think she ever saw one. And I never thought to wake her up any of the times she might've. It was always so late." He smiled, or tried to, at this other home, that other life. "Once or twice I almost did. But I only ended up standing in the doorway. Watching her sleep. It's so hard to wake them in the middle of the night like that. You just want to leave them right where they are and hope that nothing ever changes."

She smoothed her hand along his knee. "You're messing with Nature then."

"Yeah, but then it's not like the cruel bitch doesn't do enough messing with us, is it?" He tried shrugging it off. "What about you? So far I don't think I've heard you mention anyone more dependent than a tankful of fish."

She shook her head. "There are so so so many ways that would've been so wrong." A single firm pat on his knee, as bold as the period at the end of a sentence. "Next topic."

In the silence that came between them then, he could hear a sigh breathed somewhere behind their blanket, a drawn-out sound of contentment or maybe some early stage of pleasure. More unseen neighbors in the outer dark, and now he made it a point to attune himself to these scattered presences, to gauge how alone the two of them really *weren't* out here tonight.

From somewhere off to the right, a soft low rumble of laughter.

Ahead, the footsteps of latecomers, more than two, maybe more than four, then the snap of what might've been another blanket being opened to spread upon the ground. He could hear them settle onto it with a great rustling of cloth and rearranging of limbs.

"There goes the neighborhood," she whispered.

"Or here it comes," he said, because even if he could see them, how many of his neighbors did he know—she too, for that matter?

Both of them were recent arrivals in a place where the greatest challenge was simply knowing who lived above your own ceiling, let alone in the next building over. You might see them coming or going, but very often it was at too great a distance to speak, even if you actually had something to say. You might wonder why one limped, or what oddly shaped item another could be carrying beneath her coat, but these weren't the things to ask of total strangers. See enough solitary lights burning in the middle of the night, enough indistinct forms silhouetted at a window, and there were times when you couldn't help but wonder if it was your having noticed them that caused them to turn so suddenly, then disappear.

It had seemed the perfect place to lose himself, then find himself again, because what was he if not one of them—furtive and indistinct? All it had taken was losing everything that had given him grounding, that had made him feel real.

"They're not really stars, you know," she said, her face turned skyward again.

"You sound disappointed about that."

"I still remember what a lie it felt like when I first learned. The terms you hear when you're a child . . . 'shooting star,' 'falling star' . . . you take them so literally. And then to find out they're not . . ."

For him, it had always been one of those things that were a little too far out of reach to completely grasp: that ancient pebbles and specks of dust could fall in from out of an airless vacuum and burn brighter than distant suns. But they did. Even if it was only a trick of perspective, even if they couldn't sustain it, for a moment or two they shone like stars.

"Who would've thought," she said, "that garbage could be so beautiful?"

She was correct in her labeling, of course. If this same debris now flaming overhead was instead strewn across the kitchen floor, you would only reach for the broom and dustpan. Just the same, it pained him a bit to hear it so degraded.

We are made of star stuff—how many times had he heard this over the years? The phrase had always inspired in him a feeling of connection . . . although look how far he was stranded from all those distant cousins. They could be ages-dead before their light ever reached him.

From the darkness behind the blanket, the sighs continued, then turned to something deeper, more frantic.

"Okay," she whispered to him. "That's really starting to get noticeable. Are they doing . . . what I think they are?"

There was no other conclusion to come to. Nothing else sounded quite like two people making love. . . .

"Do you, um, want to move?"

. . . unless it was four of them. Or more.

"Not unless you do." She appeared not to give it much thought. "I mean, you usually have to rent a video to hear a soundtrack like that."

But was she growing as aware of it as he was? The sounds were no longer coming solely from behind them, but were arising from the front and sides as well, all breath and groans and the urgent soft slaps of skin on skin.

As he watched, listened, the night seemed divided into distinct realms, with the celestial show a domed canopy above this meadow and its earthbound longings. As for who each partner was, and what they were doing out there upon their own cloaked patches of ground, imagination had to suffice . . .

. . . until a car rounded a street corner near the edge of the park and sent its dual beam of headlights sweeping across the grounds. He dared not blink, transfixed by the sights revealed, their silhouettes backlit for an instant before the searchlight arc swept on to reveal more, and then just as quickly, the light was gone and the images remained seared into his eyes as though he'd stared into the sun.

Had he really seen a man standing and clutching his partner to him upside down, her thighs clenched around his shoulders as she dangled along the length of his body?

Had he really seen a small group holding someone else aloft in a cradle of their arms while yet another thrust away between the outstretched legs?

Had he really seen a dozen or more pairs of upraised and parted knees?

He had. And could only guess what was going on beyond the reach of that brief light. The only thing that he couldn't understand was why here, why now—if they'd all come out with rutting on their minds already, or if something intrinsic to this particular night and sky had driven them to it.

When younger, he used to fantasize about orgies. And still did, he supposed, but as the years passed, his chances of ever taking part in one seemed less and less likely. This, tonight? It should've been arousing—even inviting—but instead he found something disturbing about it. The acts may have been all he'd imagined, but the circumstances were all wrong. For God's sake, the air was frosty enough to freeze your breath.

"I don't know what made me think of this," she said, then with an easy laugh interrupted herself. "Well, that's a lie, of course I do, it's going to be obvious." At least she didn't sound embarrassed. "When we were teenagers, my girlfriends and I would get together every Fourth of July to drink and watch the fireworks. You know those kind that blow up and then there are all these squiggly ones twisting across the sky? Every year we'd go into silly giggling fits because one of us couldn't resist pointing out that they looked like sperm. And as if that wasn't enough, then one of us would start talking about us out there getting pregnant from them raining down on us, and we'd absolutely shriek. But, you know? There was something about talking about it like that that would leave us feeling soooo horny."

Beside him, she sighed with nostalgia and with pleasure, as if it were every woman's obligation to dig down to the girl who still lived inside herself, in all her giddy abandon.

"I haven't thought of that in . . . too long."

There was no single moment when it was decided, just a spontaneous and mutual knowing: whatever was taking place here tonight, they were not immune to it. He had to have her, here and now, and she him—no discussion, no risk of misread cues. The absolute conviction of it removed any possibility of guilt. It felt to him as certain as if it were written in the stars.

Zippers were yanked and buttons undone, and as the night air hit his bared skin he understood how the rest could tolerate it—he felt hot enough for plumes of steam to have risen from his hide. When she pulled him down to her on the blanket, pale as moonlight within the nest of her peeled clothing, that first fevered press of their bodies seared him from navel to throat.

His hands went high, sliding past her breasts and throat to bury themselves in her hair, and hers went low, cupping him through his pants, kneading him as if to stop would mean to wither and die. He sought her mouth, found her tongue yearning to mate with his own.

It had never been quite this way before—until now, just something that he had always suspected he'd been missing out on. Like cold water thrown onto a fire, the interruptions and disturbances had seemed almost inevitable before: a girlfriend's change of heart, a wife's swing of mood, the cries of the infant daughter he was only now ready to surrender to the water and earth that had reclaimed her.

Now, finally, with this woman he barely knew, it felt like everything it was supposed to be: a torch blazing against the loneliest night, a denial shouted into the face of death.

And then she pushed him off her—the same thing happening again? But no, something in her laughter told him otherwise, that she'd only come up with even better ideas. She took him by the hand and straggled to her feet, and so did he, needing a moment to steady their knees beneath them; then he followed as she tugged him headlong through the dark.

They navigated less by sight than by instinct and by sound. Every several yards they came across the thrash and roll of another coupling, marked by moans emitted into the night; then these would fade to one side, then behind him, and once he thought surely his ears must have been playing tricks because some pair's impassioned guttural keening seemed to abruptly rise and fade *above* him. But her hand only tightened on his and he still had no idea where she was leading.

As around them the dark spoke in cries and whispers, he thought of ancient rites he'd heard about taking place in wilder, more pagan times, couples spending a springtime night under the stars and making love upon the bare earth to awaken it, to remind it of both its fertility and their continued reliance on it.

Yet this could be nothing of the sort. Tonight, as autumn decayed into winter, they were all as far from springtime as they could possibly get, and the stars did not twinkle with approval, but burned and fell.

When she stopped, eyes alight with glee, he couldn't see any reason why she would've brought him here, to the children's swing set—not until she tugged his flapping pants the rest of the way down and pushed him onto one of the swings.

As he wrapped his fists around the icy chains, she cast off the rest of the clothes she'd been trailing ever since they fled the blanket, then stood before him and she too grabbed the chains and hoisted herself off the ground. Her legs reached around him to lock behind his back as she lowered herself into his lap, and only when they were locked together there, too, did she release the chains and cling to his shoulders instead.

When he first pushed off the ground to get them started, she breathed a gasp into his mouth, then sucked it back so fiercely he thought she was after his soul, too, but by now he could see no difference between what was his and what was hers.

Back and forth in ever-greater arcs, he rode the swing and she rode him, and he scarcely felt the wind at his back. There was only her, the radiant heat of her, and the wet fire at her core. Momentum worked miracles, pulling her away along his shaft as the swing swooped back, then pushing him deeply into her again as they rushed forward and he could look past her shoulder to see only sky.

At the apex of each arc came a breathless moment when they hung weightless and suspended. In delirium, he shook her streaming hair from his eyes and thought he glimpsed shapes conjoined and set against the night above him—arms and legs entwined and rising into the sky, as though they belonged to those ascending cries he'd just heard—but before he could track them the swing plunged down and back, and he saw only ground again.

On the next ascent he could no longer find them, seeing only streaks of white light. Very little about this night could he begin to understand, at least until another burst of incandescence showered down and reminded him of what she'd said about fireworks that looked like sperm, and so he wondered if that wasn't somehow the key to the impossible.

We're being seeded, he thought, and breathed it in like spores and dust, and believed once more that he glimpsed bodies in the heavens. *But by what?*

She grew bolder by the moment, letting go of his shoulders and holding on only with her legs as she leaned away from him, head thrown back and arms flung wide as she soared, then curling herself to him once again, always just in time to keep from being brained against the ground.

And then her mouth was at his ear and she licked at the lobe, and he could feel her smile spread against the side of his throat.

"Do you trust me?" she asked.

He didn't know what to say, or if he even could. No answer seemed right. No answer seemed wrong.

"If you trust me . . . let go," she said. "You'll know when."

And it *was* madness, wasn't it? Of course it was. But since when had love and lust not been? Sometimes madness was all that could take the place of courage.

She was right—when the moment came he knew it. As the swing reached one last zenith, he let the chains slip from his aching hands and for an instant it was like being a boy again, bailing from the swing on a playground dare, except this time two of them were launched out and up, and a moment later he came inside her in extravagant spasms and imagined droplets leaking free to rain back to the earth.

He waited for gravity to reclaim them, but somehow its grip fell short, as he had hoped it might and as she must've sensed without doubt, a certainty without knowing how, in that mysterious way of women beneath the moon. She only clung to him gasping, laughing, and rode the crest of her own ecstatic wave as they were borne aloft, higher and higher still, trees beneath them and stars above, and the magic of rapture in between.

His fingers cupped her face and she shivered with everything there was to shiver against except the cold, as they tumbled upward like two bodies locked into eternal orbit.

It was everything that love should've felt like—and did, once—except now it felt as though it might last forever.

They were not alone up here, just as they hadn't been in the meadow below, but the company was fewer, and even farther-flung. Bodies both pale and dark were joined as pairs and triads and foursomes—neighbors, he supposed, the ones he'd never gotten to know, and out of a benevolence he hadn't felt in what felt like a very long time, he wished them well.

The first distant scream came from far overhead, and each one after sounded that much closer, hurtling toward them from out of the heights and depths above. He watched it plummet and held her tightly to him as it neared, roaring now with the rushing sound of flames and a discordant cry ripped from two throats, its pitch the only thing that still climbed. It passed so close he could feel the heat blast across his skin, a fireball alive and twisting with a fused and blackened tangle of arms and legs thrashing from its center, and in its wake the stink of scorching meat.

He could not watch what happened when it struck the earth below.

"Don't think it," she said after a moment, the only thing to come from her tonight that seemed to have required real effort. "No. *No.*"

And he knew, in that rare way of men beneath the moon, that while she may have talked a defiant game last week, she really must've been as lonely as he.

"No. It *won't* happen," she said. "We got a better start than any of them."

So he closed his eyes while on the rise, and prayed to never feel the fall.

About the Authors

JOHN EDWARD AMES

Ames is the author of fifty published novels in the horror, western, historical, and romance genres. His novel *The Unwritten Order* was a finalist for the Western Writers of America Golden Spur Award. Ames began his writing career as a journalist in the Marine Corps, including a stint in Asia as a stringer for *Stars and Stripes.*

P.D. CACEK

The winner of both a Bram Stoker Award and a World Fantasy Award, Cacek's short fiction has appeared in numerous magazines, e-zines, and anthologies, including *David Copperfield's Tales of the Impossible, Peter S. Beagle's The Immortal Unicorn, Blood Muse, Desire Burn, Return to the Twilight Zone, Whitley Streiber's Aliens,* and *999.* She has also written the novels *Night Prayers* and its sequel, *Night Players, Canyons,* and *Reflections Through Beveled Glass.* She is currently putting together a second collection of her short fiction.

MATTHEW CLEMENS

Clemens is the president of Robin Vincent Publishing, as well as the author of the best-selling true-crime book, *Dead Water: The Klindt Affair.* He has published numerous short stories, many coauthored by Max Allan Collins. In addition, he has served as Collins's researcher on *The History of Mystery* (along with George Hagenauer) and *CSI: Double Dealer.*

MAX ALLAN COLLINS

Collins has won a record ten Shamus nominations from the Private Eye Writers of America for his historical thrillers, winning twice for the Nathan Heller novels *True Detective* and *Stolen Away*. His latest "history mysteries" are *The Lusitania Murders* and the Heller entry, *Chicago Confidential*. As a comics writer he is best known for his fifteen-year stint with the *Dick Tracy* comic strip; as the cocreator (with Terry Beatty) of the long-running *Ms. Tree;* and (working with illustrator Richard Piers Rayner) the author of the graphic novel *Road to Perdition*, which has been made into a DreamWorks feature film starring Tom Hanks and Paul Newman. Collins directed and wrote the cult thrillers *Mommy* and its sequel *Mommy's Day*, and his latest feature, *Real Time: Siege at Lucas Street*. He is married to writer Barbara Collins.

DEBRA GRAY DeNOUX

She was the longtime associate publisher of Pulphouse Publishing. Her fiction has appeared in magazines and anthologies in the U.S., Great Britain, and Germany. Her erotic fiction has appeared in dozens of men's magazines. She is the editor of *Erotic New Orleans Anthology*.

O'NEIL DeNOUX

Former homicide detective and private eye, DeNoux is the author of six novels, one true-crime book, and over 150 published short stories. His recent collection, *LaStanza: New Orleans Police Stories*, received an "A" rating by *Entertainment Weekly*. He has stories upcoming in *Flesh & Blood "Dark Desires"*, *Ellery Queen's Mystery Magazine*, and *Fantastic Stories of the Imagination Magazine*.

CHRISTA FAUST

Faust is a writer, bondage enthusiast, and *Hot Blood* alumna living and writing in Los Angeles. Her fiction has appeared in anthologies such as *Love In Vein, Revelations,* and *Aftershocks.* Her first novel, *Control Freak,* was recently published, and she is currently working on a second. She also wrote and directed a bondage serial called *Dita in Distress,* a campy homage to the Republic cliffhangers of the thirties and forties. Her hobbies include collecting vintage high-heeled shoes and tying pretty girls to railroad tracks.

MICK GARRIS

Garris is the director of the top-rated TV mini-series *The Stand* and *The Shining,* as well as *Sleepwalkers, Quicksilver Highway, Psycho IV,* and others. He wrote and directed many episodes of *Amazing Stories* and other TV series. Garris's first book, *A Life in the Cinema: Stories and a Screenplay,* was published in 2001.

MICHAEL GARRETT

Garrett is an internationally published author and fiction editor. He's the cocreator and coeditor of the *Hot Blood* series, and author of a nonfiction book for beginning writers, *The Prose Professional: Your Career as a Fiction Writer.* A new edition of his sold-out novel *Keeper* is now available. He's a Writer's Digest School instructor and also teaches writing workshops for colleges and writers' groups. Serving as a "book doctor," he specializes in mystery, suspense horror, and romance manuscripts. His Web site is www.writing2sell.com.

JEFF GELB

Hot Blood coeditor Jeff Gelb attributes his latest story to a lifetime of overindulging in horror movies, especially (but not limited to) those of David Cronenberg, George Romero, Tobe Hooper, Dario Argento, Wes Craven, Sam Raimi, and John Carpenter.

SEPHERA GIRON

Giron is the author of *House of Pain, The Birds and the Bees, Eternal Sunset,* and *Eternal Nightmare,* and of the nonfiction book *House Magic: The Good Witch's Guide to Bringing Grace to Your Space* under the witch name Ariana. When Giron isn't writing, she is a professional tarot counselor, and runs the online company Two Stupid Witches.

BRIAN HODGE

Hodge has flung around almost as many words as there are stars in the sky. His most recent works are the collection *Lies & Ugliness* and the novel *Mad Dogs,* and probably lots more things that weren't even conceived of until long after this bio was penned.

NANCY HOLDER

Holder has sold around fifty novels and 200 short stories and articles. Many of her titles are tie-in works for *Buffy the Vampire Slayer, Angel,* and the new *Smallville* series. She is currently working on a series about two feuding witch dynasties entitled *Wicked* for Pocket Books. She lives in San Diego most of the time with her daughter, Belle, and their animal husbandry: creatures Dot, Marykate, Bekah, Zoe, David, Sasha, and two anonymous frogs, neither of which they have kissed.

THEA HUTCHESON

Hutcheson is a member of the Northern Colorado Writers Workshop. Her work has appeared in *Amatory Ink,* the 2001 and 2002 editions of *Best Lesbian Erotica,* and elsewhere.

BOB INGERSOLL

By day Ingersoll is an attorney in Cleveland. But in the "real world," he has been a freelance writer since 1975, when he sold his first comic book story. His credits include myriad comic book stories, the long-running "The Law Is A Ass" column for *Comic Buyer's Guide*, and *Captain America: Liberty's Torch* (with Tony Isabella).

GRAHAM MASTERTON

Masterton's horror career began in 1976 with *The Manitou* and has continued to the present day. He has published over thirty-five horror novels, including *Charnel House*, which was awarded a special Edgar by Mystery Writers of America, and *Mirror*, which was awarded a Silver Medal by *West Coast Review of Books*. His latest works include *Spirit, Trauma, The Chosen Child*, and *Jessica's Angel*. Masterton has written over a hundred novels altogether, and a large number of short stories, including three that were filmed for *The Hunger* TV series.

YVONNE NAVARRO

Navarro is an award-winning novelist who has published thirteen novels since 1984, a reference dictionary, and over seventy short stories. She's written in the horror, science fiction, mystery, and mainstream genres; her latest media-related book is *Buffy the Vampire Slayer: Tempted Champions*. She recently completed a supernatural thriller called *Mirror Me*, and is working on several other projects, including another novel, a short story collection, and a children's book collaboration. She maintains the Web site yvonnenavarro.com.

DAVID J. SCHOW

Schow's short stories have been regularly selected for over twenty-five volumes of "Year's Best" anthologies across two decades and have won the World Fantasy Award as well as the Dimension Award from *Twilight Zone* magazine. His novels include *The Kill Riff* and *The Shaft*. His short stories are collected in *Seeing Red, Lost Angels, Black Leather Required*, and *Crypt Orchids*. He is the author of *The Outer Limits Companion* and has written extensively for films and television. His latest books are *Eye* and *Wild Hairs*. His Web site is Black Leather Required: http://gothic.net/~chromo.

EDO VAN BELKOM

Bram Stoker and Aurora Award–winner Van Belkom is the author of more than 175 short stories, and author and editor of more than twenty books. His novels include *Lord Soth, Teeth,* and *Martyrs,* while short story collections include *Death Drives a Semi* and *Six-Inch Spikes.* He has written the how-to guides *Writing Horror* and *Writing Erotica.* His Web site is *www.van-belkom.com.*

STANLEY WIATER

Wiater, who is based in Massachusetts, is a two-time Bram Stoker Award–winning author and editor. His most recent works include *The Stephen King Universe,* coauthored with Christopher Golden and Hank Wagner, and *Dark Dreamers: Facing the Masters of Fear,* coauthored with photographer Beth Gwinn. He is currently the writer and host of the *Dark Dreams* TV series, which profiles authors, artists, and filmmakers who work on the dark side of the arts.